Scenes of Bohemian Life

Scenes of Bohemian Life

Henri Murger

MINT EDITIONS

Scenes of Bohemian Life was first published in 1888.

This edition published by Mint Editions 2021.

ISBN 9781513292311 | E-ISBN 9781513295169

Published by Mint Editions®

 MINT
EDITIONS

minteditionbooks.com

Publishing Director: Jennifer Newens
Design & Production: Rachel Lopez Metzger
Project Manager: Micaela Clark
Typesetting: Westchester Publishing Services

Table of Contents

PREFACE

The Bohemians of whom it is a question in this book have no connection with the Bohemians whom melodramatists have rendered synonymous with robbers and assassins. Neither are they recruited from among the dancing-bear leaders, sword swallowers, gilt watch-guard vendors, street lottery keepers and a thousand other vague and mysterious professionals whose main business is to have no business at all, and who are always ready to turn their hands to anything except good.

The class of Bohemians referred to in this book are not a race of today, they have existed in all climes and ages, and can claim an illustrious descent. In ancient Greece, to go no farther back in this genealogy, there existed a celebrated Bohemian, who lived from hand to mouth round the fertile country of Ionia, eating the bread of charity, and halting in the evening to tune beside some hospitable hearth the harmonious lyre that had sung the loves of Helen and the fall of Troy. Descending the steps of time modern Bohemia finds ancestors at every artistic and literary epoch. In the Middle Ages it perpetuates the Homeric tradition with its minstrels and ballad makers, the children of the gay science, all the melodious vagabonds of Touraine, all the errant songsters who, with the beggar's wallet and the trouvere's harp slung at their backs, traversed, singing as they went, the plains of the beautiful land where the eglantine of Clemence Isaure flourished.

At the transitional period between the days of chivalry and the dawn of the Renaissance, Bohemia continued to stroll along all the highways of the kingdom, and already to some extent about the streets of Paris. There is Master Pierre Gringoire, friend of the vagrants and foe to fasting. Lean and famished as a man whose very existence is one long Lent, he lounges about the town, his nose in the air like a pointer's, sniffing the odor from kitchen and cook shop. His eyes glittering with covetous gluttony cause the hams hung outside the pork butcher's to shrink by merely looking at them, whilst he jingles in imagination—alas! and not in his pockets—the ten crowns promised him by the echevins in payment of the pious and devout fare he has composed for the theater in the hall of the Palais de Justice. Beside the doleful and melancholy figure of the lover of Esmeralda, the chronicles of Bohemia can evoke a companion of less ascetic humor and more cheerful face—Master

François Villon, par excellence, is this latter, and one whose poetry, full of imagination, is no doubt on account of those presentiments which the ancients attributed to their fates, continually marked by a singular foreboding of the gallows, on which the said Villon one day nearly swung in a hempen collar for having looked too closely at the color of the king's crowns. This same Villon, who more than once outran the watch started in his pursuit, this noisy guest at the dens of the Rue Pierre Lescot, this spunger at the court of the Duke of Egypt, this Salvator Rosa of poesy, has strung together elegies the heartbreaking sentiment and truthful accents of which move the most pitiless and make them forget the ruffian, the vagabond and the debauchee, before this muse drowned in her own tears.

Besides, amongst all those whose but little known work has only been familiar to men for whom French literature does not begin the day when "Malherbe came," François Villon has had the honor of being the most pillaged, even by the big-wigs of modern Parnassus. They threw themselves upon the poor man's field and coined glory from his humble treasure. There are ballads scribbled under a penthouse at the street corner on a cold day by the Bohemian rhapsodist, stanzas improvised in the hovel in which the "belle qui fut haultmire" loosened her gilt girdle to all comers, which now-a-days metamorphosed into dainty gallantries scented with musk and amber, figure in the armorial bearing enriched album of some aristocratic Chloris.

But behold the grand century of the Renaissance opens, Michaelangelo ascends the scaffolds of the Sistine Chapel and watches with anxious air young Raphael mounting the steps of the Vatican with the cartoon of the Loggie under his arm. Benvenuto Cellini is meditating his Perseus, Ghiberti is carving the Baptistery doors at the same time that Donatello is rearing his marbles on the bridges of the Arno; and whilst the city of the Medici is staking masterpieces against that of Leo X and Julius II, Titian and Paul Veronese are rendering the home of Doges illustrious. Saint Mark's competes with Saint Peter's.

This fever of genius that had broken out suddenly in the Italian peninsula with epidemic violence spreads its glorious contagion throughout Europe. Art, the rival of God, strides on, the equal of kings. Charles V stoops to pick up Titian's brush, and Francis I dances attendance at the printing office where Etienne Dolet is perhaps correcting the proofs of "Pantagruel."

Amidst this resurrection of intelligence, Bohemia continued as in the past to seek, according to Balzac's expression, a bone and a kennel. Clement Marot, the familiar of the ante-chamber of the Louvre, became, even before she was a monarch's mistress, the favorite of that fair Diana, whose smile lit up three reigns. From the boudoir of Diane de Poitiers, the faithless muse of the poet passed to that of Marguerite de Valois, a dangerous favor that Marot paid for by imprisonment. Almost at the same epoch another Bohemian, whose childhood on the shores of Sorrento had been caressed by the kisses of an epic muse, Tasso, entered the court of the Duke of Ferrara as Marot had that of Francis I. But less fortunate than the lover of Diane and Marguerite, the author of "Jerusalem Delivered" paid with his reason and the loss of his genius the audacity of his love for a daughter of the house of Este.

The religious contests and political storms that marked the arrival of Medicis in France did not check the soaring flight of art. At the moment when a ball struck on the scaffold of the Fontaine des Innocents Jean Goujon who had found the Pagan chisel of Phidias, Ronsard discovered the lyre of Pindar and founded, aided by his pleiad, the great French lyric school. To this school succeeded the reaction of Malherbe and his fellows, who sought to drive from the French tongue all the exotic graces that their predecessors had tried to nationalize on Parnassus. It was a Bohemian, Mathurin Regnier, who was one of the last defenders of the bulwarks of poetry, assailed by the phalanx of rhetoricians and grammarians who declared Rabelais barbarous and Montaigne obscure. It was this same cynic, Mathurin Regnier, who, adding fresh knots to the satiric whip of Horace, exclaimed, in indignation at the manners of his day, "Honor is an old saint past praying to."

The roll call of Bohemia during the seventeenth century contains a portion of the names belonging to the literature of the reigns of Louis XIII and Louis XIV, it reckons members amongst the wits of the Hôtel Rambouillet, where it takes its share in the production of the "Guirlande de Julie," it has its entries into the Palais Cardinal, where it collaborates, in the tragedy of "Marianne," with the poet-minister who was the Robespierre of the monarchy. It bestrews the couch of Marion Delorme with madrigals, and woos Ninon de l'Enclos beneath the trees of the Place Royal; it breakfasts in the morning at the tavern of the Goinfres or the Epee Royale, and sups in the evening at the table of the Duc de Joyeuse; it fights duels under a street lamp for the sonnet of Urania against the sonnet of

Job. Bohemia makes love, war, and even diplomacy, and in its old days, weary of adventures, it turns the Old and New Testament into poetry, figures on the list of benefices, and well nourished with fat prebendaryships, seats itself on an episcopal throne, or a chair of the Academy, founded by one of its children.

It was in the transition period between the sixteenth and eighteenth centuries that appeared those two lofty geniuses, whom each of the nations amongst which they lived opposed to one another in their struggles of literary rivalry. Moliere and Shakespeare, those illustrious Bohemians, whose fate was too nearly akin.

The most celebrated names of the literature of the eighteenth century are also to be found in the archives of Bohemia, which, amongst the glorious ones of this epoch, can cite Jean Jacques Rousseau and d'Alembert, the foundling of the porch of Notre Dame, and amongst the obscure, Malfilâtre and Gilbert, two overrated reputations, for the inspiration of the one was but a faint reflection of the weak lyricism of Jean Baptiste Rousseau, and the inspiration of the other but the blending of proud impotence with a hatred which had not even the excuse of initiative and sincerity, since it was only the paid instrument of party rancour.

We close with this epoch this brief summary of Bohemia in different ages, a prolegomena besprinkled with illustrious names that we have purposely placed at the beginning of this work, to put the reader on his guard against any misapplication he might fall into on encountering the title of Bohemians; long bestowed upon classes from which those whose manners and language we have striven to depict hold it an honor to differ.

Today, as of old, every man who enters on an artistic career, without any other means of livelihood than his art itself, will be forced to walk in the paths of Bohemia. The greater number of our contemporaries who display the noblest blazonry of art have been Bohemians, and amidst their calm and prosperous glory they often recall, perhaps with regret, the time when, climbing the verdant slope of youth, they had no other fortune in the sunshine of their twenty years than courage, which is the virtue of the young, and hope, which is the wealth of the poor.

For the uneasy reader, for the timorous citizen, for all those for whom an "i" can never be too plainly dotted in definition, we repeat as an axiom: "Bohemia is a stage in artistic life; it is the preface to the Academy, the Hôtel Dieu, or the Morgue."

We will add that Bohemia only exists and is only possible in Paris.

We will begin with unknown Bohemians, the largest class. It is made up of the great family of poor artists, fatally condemned to the law of incognito, because they cannot or do not know how to obtain a scrap of publicity, to attest their existence in art, and by showing what they are already prove what they may some day become. They are the race of obstinate dreamers for whom art has remained a faith and not a profession; enthusiastic folk of strong convictions, whom the sight of a masterpiece is enough to throw into a fever, and whose loyal heart beats high in presence of all that is beautiful, without asking the name of the master and the school. This Bohemian is recruited from amongst those young fellows of whom it is said that they give great hopes, and from amongst those who realize the hopes given, but who, from carelessness, timidity, or ignorance of practical life, imagine that everything is done that can be when the work is completed, and wait for public admiration and fortune to break in on them by escalade and burglary. They live, so to say, on the outskirts of life, in isolation and inertia. Petrified in art, they accept to the very letter the symbolism of the academical dithyrambic, which places an aureola about the heads of poets, and, persuaded that they are gleaming in their obscurity, wait for others to come and seek them out. We used to know a small school composed of men of this type, so strange, that one finds it hard to believe in their existence; they styled themselves the disciples of art for art's sake. According to these simpletons, art for art's sake consisted of deifying one another, in abstaining from helping chance, who did not even know their address, and in waiting for pedestals to come of their own accord and place themselves under them.

It is, as one sees, the ridiculousness of stoicism. Well, then we again affirm, there exist in the heart of unknown Bohemia, similar beings whose poverty excites a sympathetic pity which common sense obliges you to go back on, for if you quietly remark to them that we live in the nineteenth century, that the five-franc piece is the empress of humanity, and that boots do not drop already blacked from heaven, they turn their backs on you and call you a tradesman.

For the rest, they are logical in their mad heroism, they utter neither cries nor complainings, and passively undergo the obscure and rigorous fate they make for themselves. They die for the most part, decimated by that disease to which science does not dare give its real name, want. If they would, however, many could escape from this fatal *denouement* which suddenly terminates their life at an age when ordinary life is only beginning. It would suffice for that for them to make a few concessions to the stern laws of necessity; for them to know how to duplicate their being, to have within themselves two natures, the poet ever dreaming on the lofty summits where the choir of inspired voices are warbling, and the man, worker-out of his life, able to knead his daily bread, but this duality which almost always exists among strongly tempered natures, of whom it is one of the distinctive characteristics, is not met with amongst the greater number of these young fellows, whom pride, a bastard pride, has rendered invulnerable to all the advice of reason. Thus they die young, leaving sometimes behind them a work which the world admires later on and which it would no doubt have applauded sooner if it had not remained invisible.

In artistic struggles it is almost the same as in war, the whole of the glory acquired falls to the leaders; the army shares as its reward the few lines in a dispatch. As to the soldiers struck down in battle, they are buried where they fall, and one epitaph serves for twenty thousand dead.

So, too, the crowd, which always has its eyes fixed on the rising sun, never lowers its glance towards that underground world where the obscure workers are struggling; their existence finishes unknown and without sometimes even having had the consolation of smiling at an accomplished task, they depart from this life, enwrapped in a shroud of indifference.

There exists in ignored Bohemia another fraction; it is composed of young fellows who have been deceived, or have deceived themselves. They mistake a fancy for a vocation, and impelled by a homicidal fatality, they die, some the victims of a perpetual fit of pride, others worshippers of a chimera.

The paths of art, so choked and so dangerous, are, despite encumberment and obstacles, day by day more crowded, and consequently Bohemians were never more numerous.

If one sought out all the causes that have led to this influx, one might perhaps come across the following.

Many young fellows have taken the declamations made on the subject of unfortunate poets and artists quite seriously. The names of Gilbert, Malfilâtre, Chatterton, and Moreau have been too often, too imprudently, and, above all, too uselessly uttered. The tomb of these unfortunates has been converted into a pulpit, from whence has been preached the martyrdom of art and poetry,

"Farewell mankind, ye stony-hearted host,
Flint-bosomed earth and sun with frozen ray,
From out amidst you, solitary ghost
I glide unseen away."

This despairing song of Victor Escousse, stifled by the pride which had been implanted in him by a factitious triumph, was for a time the "Marseillaise" of the volunteers of art who were bent on inscribing their names on the martyrology of mediocrity.

For these funereal apotheoses, these encomiastic requiems, having all the attraction of the abyss for weak minds and ambitious vanities, many of these yielding to this attraction have thought that fatality was the half of genius; many have dreamt of the hospital bed on which Gilbert died, hoping that they would become poets, as he did a quarter of an hour before dying, and believing that it was an obligatory stage in order to arrive at glory.

Too much blame cannot be attached to these immortal falsehoods, these deadly paradoxes, which turn aside from the path in which they might have succeeded so many people who come to a wretched ending in a career in which they incommode those to whom a true vocation only gives the right of entering on it.

It is these dangerous preachings, this useless posthumous exaltations, that have created the ridiculous race of the unappreciated, the whining poets whose muse has always red eyes and ill-combed locks, and all the mediocrities of impotence who, doomed to non-publication, call the muse a harsh stepmother, and art an executioner.

All truly powerful minds have their word to say, and, indeed, utter it sooner or later. Genius or talent are not unforeseen accidents in humanity; they have a cause of existence, and for that reason cannot always remain in obscurity, for, if the crowd does not come to seek them, they know how to reach it. Genius is the sun, everyone sees it. Talent is the diamond that may for a long time remain hidden in obscurity, but which is always perceived by some one. It is, therefore, wrong to be moved to pity over the lamentations and stock phrases of that class of intruders and inutilities entered upon an artistic career in which idleness, debauchery, and parasitism form the foundations of manners.

Axiom, "Unknown Bohemianism is not a path, it is a blind alley."

Indeed, this life is something that does not lead to anything. It is a stultified wretchedness, amidst which intelligence dies out like a lamp in a place without air, in which the heart grows petrified in a fierce misanthropy, and in which the best natures become the worst. If one has the misfortune to remain too long and to advance too far in this blind alley one can no longer get out, or one emerges by dangerous breaches and only to fall into an adjacent Bohemia, the manners of which belong to another jurisdiction than that of literary physiology.

We will also cite a singular variety of Bohemians who might be called amateurs. They are not the least curious. They find in Bohemian life an existence full of seductions, not to dine every day, to sleep in the open air on wet nights, and to dress in nankeen in the month of December seems to them the paradise of human felicity, and to enter it some abandon the family home, and others the study which leads to an assured result. They suddenly turn their backs upon an honorable future to seek the adventure of a hazardous career. But as the most robust cannot stand a mode of living that would render Hercules consumptive, they soon give up the game, and, hastening back to the paternal roast joint, marry their little cousins, set up as a notary in a town of thirty thousand inhabitants, and by their fireside of an evening have the satisfaction of relating their artistic misery with the magniloquence of a traveller narrating a tiger hunt. Others persist and put their self-esteem in it, but when once they have exhausted those resources of credit which a young fellow with well-to-do relatives can always find, they are more wretched than the real Bohemians, who, never having had any other resources, have at least those of intelligence. We knew one of these amateur Bohemians who, after having remained three years in Bohemia and quarrelled with his family, died one morning, and was taken to the common grave in a pauper's hearse. He had ten thousand francs a year.

It is needless to say that these Bohemians have nothing whatever in common with art, and that they are the most obscure amongst the least known of ignored Bohemia.

We now come to the real Bohemia, to that which forms, in part, the subject of this book. Those who compose it are really amongst those called by art, and have the chance of being also amongst its elect. This Bohemia, like the others, bristles with perils, two abysses flank it on either side—poverty and doubt. But between these two gulfs there is at least a road leading to a goal which the Bohemians can see with their eyes, pending the time when they shall touch it with their hand.

It is official Bohemia so-called because those who form part of it have publicly proved their existence, have signalised their presence in the world elsewhere than on a census list, have, to employ one of their own expressions, "their name in the bill," who are known in the literary and artistic market, and whose products, bearing their stamp, are current there, at moderate rates it is true.

To arrive at their goal, which is a settled one, all roads serve, and the Bohemians know how to profit by even the accidents of the route. Rain or dust, cloud or sunshine, nothing checks these bold adventurers, whose sins are backed by virtue. Their mind is kept ever on the alert by their ambition, which sounds a charge in front and urges them to the assault of the future; incessantly at war with necessity, their invention always marching with lighted match blows up the obstacle almost before it incommodes them. Their daily existence is a work of genius, a daily problem which they always succeed in solving by the aid of audacious mathematics. They would have forced Harpagon to lend them money, and have found truffles on the raft of the "Medusa." At need, too, they know how to practice abstinence with all the virtue of an anchorite, but if a slice of fortune falls into their hands you will see them at once mounted on the most ruinous fancies, loving the youngest and prettiest, drinking the oldest and best, and never finding sufficient windows to throw their money out of. Then, when their last crown is dead and buried, they begin to dine again at that table spread by chance, at which their place is always laid, and, preceded by a pack of tricks, go poaching on all the callings that have any connection with art, hunting from morn till night that wild beast called a five-franc piece.

The Bohemians know everything and go everywhere, according as they have patent leather pumps or burst boots. They are to be met one day leaning against the mantel-shelf in a fashionable drawing room, and the next seated in the arbor of some suburban dancing place. They cannot take ten steps on the Boulevard without meeting a friend, and thirty, no matter where, without encountering a creditor.

Bohemians speak amongst themselves a special language borrowed from the conversation of the studios, the jargon of behind the scenes, and the discussions of the editor's room. All the eclecticisms of style are met with in this unheard of idiom, in which apocalyptic phrases jostle cock and bull stories, in which the rusticity of a popular saying is wedded to extravagant periods from the same mold in which Cyrano de Bergerac cast his tirades; in which the paradox, that spoilt child of modern literature, treats reason as the pantaloon is treated in a pantomime; in which irony has the intensity of the strongest acids and the skill of those marksmen who can hit the bull's-eye blindfold; a slang intelligent, though unintelligible to those who have not its key, and the audacity of which surpasses that of the freest tongues. This Bohemian vocabulary is the hell of rhetoric and the paradise of neologism.

Such is in brief that Bohemian life, badly known to the puritans of society, decried by the puritans of art, insulted by all the timorous and jealous mediocrities who cannot find enough of outcries, lies, and calumnies to drown the voices and the names of those who arrive through the vestibule to renown by harnessing audacity to their talent.

A life of patience, of courage, in which one cannot fight unless clad in a strong armour of indifference impervious to the attacks of fools and the envious, in which one must not, if one would not stumble on the road, quit for a single moment that pride in oneself which serves as a leaning staff; a charming and a terrible life, which has conquerors and its martyrs, and on which one should not enter save in resigning oneself in advance to submit to the pitiless law *væ victis*.

H. M.

I

How The Bohemian Club Was Formed

One morning—it was the eighth of April—Alexander Schaunard, who cultivated the two liberal arts of painting and music, was rudely awakened by the peal of a neighbouring cock, which served him for an alarm.

"By Jove!" exclaimed Schaunard, "my feathered clock goes too fast: it cannot possibly be today yet!" So saying, he leaped precipitately out of a piece of furniture of his own ingenious contrivance, which, sustaining the part of bed by night, (sustaining it badly enough too,) did duty by day for all the rest of the furniture which was absent by reason of the severe cold for which the past winter had been noted.

To protect himself against the biting north-wind, Schaunard slipped on in haste a pink satin petticoat with spangled stars, which served him for dressing-gown. This gay garment had been left at the artist's lodging, one masked-ball night, by a *folie*, who was fool enough to let herself be entrapped by the deceitful promises of Schaunard when, disguised as a marquis, he rattled in his pocket a seducingly sonorous dozen of crowns—theatrical money punched out of a lead plate and borrowed of a property-man. Having thus made his home toilette, the artist proceeded to open his blind and window. A solar ray, like an arrow of light, flashed suddenly into the room, and compelled him to open his eyes that were still veiled by the mists of sleep. At the same moment the clock of a neighbouring church struck five.

"It is the Morn herself!" muttered Schaunard; "astonishing, but"—and he consulted an almanac nailed to the wall—"not the less a mistake. The results of science affirm that at this season of the year the sun ought not to rise till half-past five: it is only five o'clock, and there he is! A culpable excess of zeal! The luminary is wrong; I shall have to make a complaint to the longitude-office. However, I must begin to be a little anxious. Today is the day after yesterday, certainly; and since yesterday was the seventh, unless old Saturn goes backward, it must be the eighth of April today. And if I may believe this paper," continued Schaunard, going to read an official notice-to-quit posted on the wall, "today, therefore, at twelve precisely, I ought to have evacuated the premises, and paid into the hands of my landlord, Monsieur Bernard, the sum of seventy-five francs for three quarters' rent due, which he demands of me in very bad handwriting. I had hoped—as I always do—that Providence would take the responsibility of discharging this debt, but it seems it hasn't had time. Well, I have six hours before me yet. By making good use of them, perhaps—to work! to work!"

He was preparing to put on an overcoat, originally of a long-haired, woolly fabric, but now completely bald from age, when suddenly, as if bitten by a tarantula, he began to execute around the room a polka of his own composition, which at the public balls had often caused him to be honoured with the particular attention of the police.

"By Jove!" he exclaimed, "it is surprising how the morning air gives one ideas! It strikes me that I am on the scent of my air; Let's see." And, half-dressed as he was, Schaunard seated himself at his piano. After having waked the sleeping instrument by a terrific hurly-burly of notes, he began, talking to himself all the while, to hunt over the keys for the tune he had long been seeking.

"Do, sol, mi, do la, si, do re. Bah! it's as false as Judas, that re!" and he struck violently on the doubtful note. "We must represent adroitly the grief of a young person picking to pieces a white daisy over a blue lake. There's an idea that's not in its infancy! However, since it is fashion, and you couldn't find a music publisher who would dare to publish a ballad without a blue lake in it, we must go with the fashion. Do, sol, mi, do, la, si, do, re! That's not so bad; it gives a fair idea of a daisy, especially to people well up in botany. La, si, do, re. Confound that re! Now to make the blue lake intelligible. We should have something moist, azure, moonlight—for the moon comes in too; here it is; don't let's forget the swan. Fa, mi, la, sol," continued Schaunard, rattling over the keys. "Lastly, an adieu of the young girl, who determines to throw herself into the blue lake, to rejoin her beloved who is buried under the snow. The catastrophe is not very perspicuous, but decidedly interesting. We must have something tender, melancholy. It's coming, it's coming! Here are a dozen bars crying like Magdalens, enough to split one's heart—Brr, brr!" and Schaunard shivered in his spangled petticoat, "if it could only split one's wood! There's a beam in my alcove which bothers me a good deal when I have company at dinner. I should like to make a fire with it—la, la, re, mi—for I feel my inspiration coming to me through the medium of a cold in the head. So much the worse, but it can't be helped. Let us continue to drown our young girl;" and while his fingers assailed the trembling keys, Schaunard, with sparkling eyes and straining ears, gave chase to the melody which, like an impalpable sylph, hovered amid the sonorous mist which the vibrations of the instrument seemed to let loose in the room.

"Now let us see," he continued, "how my music will fit into my poet's words;" and he hummed, in voice the reverse of agreeable, this fragment of verse of the patent comic-opera sort:

> *"The fair and youthful maiden,*
> *As she flung her mantle by,*
> *Threw a glance with sorrow laden*
> *Up to the starry sky*
> *And in the azure waters*
> *Of the silver-waved lake."*

"How is that?" he exclaimed, in transports of just indignation; "the azure waters of a silver lake! I didn't see that. This poet is an idiot. I'll bet he never saw a lake, or silver either. A stupid ballad too, in every way; the length of the lines cramps the music. For the future I shall compose my verses myself; and without waiting, since I feel in the humour, I shall manufacture some couplets to adapt my melody to."

So saying, and taking his head between his hands, he assumed the grave attitude of a man who is having relations with the Muses. After a few minutes of this sacred intercourse, he had produced one of those strings of nonsense-verses which the libretti-makers call, not without reason, monsters, and which they improvise very readily as a ground-work for the composer's inspiration. Only Schaunard's were no nonsense-verses, but very good sense, expressing with sufficient clearness the inquietude awakened in his mind by the rude arrival of that date, the eighth of April.

Thus they ran:

> *"Eight and eight make sixteen just,*
> *Put down six and carry one:*
> *My poor soul would be at rest*
> *Could I only find some one,*
> *Some honest poor relation,*
> *Who'd eight hundred francs advance,*
> *To pay each obligation,*
> *Whenever I've a chance."*

Chorus

"And ere the clock on the last and fatal morning
Should sound mid-day,
To old Bernard, like a man who needs no warning,
To old Bernard, like a man who needs no warning,
To old Bernard, like a man who needs no warning,
My rent I'd pay!"

"The duece!" exclaimed Schaunard, reading over his composition, "one and some one—those rhymes are poor enough, but I have no time to make them richer. Now let us try how the notes will unite with the syllables." And in his peculiarly frightful nasal tone he recommenced the execution of his ballad. Satisfied with the result he had just obtained, Schaunard congratulated himself with an exultant grimace, which mounted over his nose like a circumflex accent whenever he had occasion to be pleased with himself. But this triumphant happiness was destined to have no long duration. Eleven o'clock resounded from the neighbouring steeple. Every stroke diffused itself through the room in mocking sounds which seemed to say to the unlucky Schaunard, "Are you ready?"

The artist bounded on his chair. "The time flies like a bird!" he exclaimed. "I have but three-quarters of an hour left to find my seventy-five francs and my new lodging. I shall never get them; that would be too much like magic. Let me see: I give myself five minutes to find out how to obtain them;" and burying his head between his knees, he descended into the depths of reflection.

The five minutes elapsed, and Schaunard raised his head without having found anything which resembled seventy-five francs.

"Decidedly, I have but one way of getting out of this, which is simply to go away. It is fine weather and my friend Monsieur Chance may be walking in the sun. He must give me hospitality till I have found the means of squaring off with Monsieur Bernard."

Having stuffed into the cellar-like pockets of his overcoat all the articles they would hold, Schaunard tied up some linen in a handkerchief, and took an affectionate farewell of his home. While crossing the court, he was suddenly stopped by the porter, who seemed to be on the watch for him.

"Hallo! Monsieur Schaunard," cried he, blocking up the artist's way, "don't you remember that this is the eighth of April?"

> *"Eight and eight make sixteen just,*
> *Put down six and carry one,"*

hummed Schaunard. "I don't remember anything else."

"You are a little behindhand then with your moving," said the porter; "it is half-past eleven, and the new tenant to whom your room has been let may come any minute. You must make haste."

"Let me pass, then," replied Schaunard; "I am going after a cart."

"No doubt, but before moving there is a little formality to be gone through. I have orders not to let you take away a hair unless you pay the three quarters due. Are you ready?"

"Why, of course," said Schaunard, making a step forward.

"Well come into my lodge then, and I will give you your receipt."

"I shall take it when I come back."

"But why not at once?" persisted the porter.

"I am going to a money changer's. I have no change."

"Ah, you are going to get change!" replied the other, not at all at his ease. "Then I will take care of that little parcel under your arm, which might be in your way."

"Monsieur Porter," exclaimed the artist, with a dignified air, "you mistrust me, perhaps! Do you think I am carrying away my furniture in a handkerchief?"

"Excuse me," answered the porter, dropping his tone a little, "but such are my orders. Monsieur Bernard has expressly charged me not to let you take away a hair before you have paid."

"But look, will you?" said Schaunard, opening his bundle, "these are not hairs, they are shirts, and I am taking them to my washerwoman, who lives next door to the money changer's twenty steps off."

"That alters the case," said the porter, after he had examined the contents of the bundle. "Would it be impolite, Monsieur Schaunard, to inquire your new address?"

"Rue de Rivoli!" replied the artist, and having once got outside the gate, he made off as fast as possible.

"Rue de Rivoli!" muttered the porter, scratching his nose, "it's very odd they should have let him lodgings in the Rue de Rivoli, and never come here to ask about him. Very odd, that. At any rate, he can't carry off his furniture without paying. If only the new tenant don't come moving in just as Monsieur Schaunard is moving out! That would make a nice mess! Well, sure enough," he exclaimed, suddenly putting his head out of his little window, "here he comes, the new tenant!"

In fact, a young man in a white hat, followed by a porter who did not seem over-burdened by the weight of his load, had just entered the court. "Is my room ready?" he demanded of the house-porter, who had stepped out to meet him.

"Not yet, sir, but it will be in a moment. The person who occupies it has gone after a cart for his things. Meanwhile, sir, you may put your furniture in the court."

"I am afraid it's going to rain," replied the young man, chewing a bouquet of violets which he held in his mouth, "My furniture might be spoiled. My friend," continued he, turning to the man who was behind him, with something on a trunk which the porter could not exactly make out, "put that down and go back to my old lodging to fetch the remaining valuables."

The man ranged along the wall several frames six or seven feet high, folded together, and apparently being capable of being extended.

"Look here," said the new-comer to his follower, half opening one of the screens and showing him a rent in the canvas, "what an accident! You have cracked my grand Venetian glass. Take more care on your second trip, especially with my library."

"What does he mean by his Venetian glass?" muttered the porter, walking up and down with an uneasy air before the frames ranged against the wall. "I don't see any glass. Some joke, no doubt. I only see a screen. We shall see, at any rate, what he will bring next trip."

"Is your tenant not going to make room for me soon?" inquired the young man, "it is half-past twelve, and I want to move in."

"He won't be much longer," answered the porter, "but there is no harm done yet, since your furniture has not come," added he, with a stress on the concluding words.

As the young man was about to reply, a dragoon entered the court.

"Is this Monsieur Bernard's?" he asked, drawing a letter from a huge leather portfolio which swung at his side.

"He lives here," replied the porter.

"Here is a letter for him," said the dragoon; "give me a receipt," and he handed to the porter a bulletin of despatches which the latter entered his lodge to sign.

"Excuse me for leaving you alone," said he to the young man who was stalking impatiently about the court, "but this is a letter from the Minister to my landlord, and I am going to take it up to him."

HENRI MURGER

Monsieur Bernard was just beginning to shave when the porter knocked at his door.

"What do you want, Durand?"

"Sir," replied the other, lifting his cap, "a soldier has just brought this for you. It comes from the Ministry." And he handed to Monsieur Bernard the letter, the envelope of which bore the stamp of the War Department.

"Heavens!" exclaimed Monsieur Bernard, in such agitation that he all but cut himself. "From the Minister of War! I am sure it is my nomination as Knight of the Legion of Honour, which I have long solicited. At last they have done justice to my good conduct. Here, Durand," said he, fumbling in his waistcoat-pocket, "here are five francs to drink to my health. Stay! I haven't my purse about me. Wait, and I will give you the money in a moment."

The porter was so overcome by this stunning fit of generosity, which was not at all in accordance with his landlord's ordinary habits, that he absolutely put on his cap again.

But Monsieur Bernard, who at any other time would have severely reprimanded this infraction of the laws of social hierarchy, appeared not to notice it. He put on his spectacles, broke the seal of the envelope with the respectful anxiety of a vizier receiving a sultan's firman, and began to read the dispatch. At the first line a frightful grimace ploughed his fat, monk-like cheeks with crimson furrows, and his little eyes flashed sparks that seemed ready to set fire to his bushy wig. In fact, all his features were so turned upside-down that you would have said his countenance had just suffered a shock of face-quake.

For these were the contents of the letter bearing the ministerial stamp, brought by a dragoon—orderly, and for which Durand had given the government a receipt:

Friend landlord

Politeness-who, according to ancient mythology, is the grandmother of good manners—compels me to inform you that I am under the cruel necessity of not conforming to the prevalent custom of paying rent—prevalent especially when the rent is due. Up to this morning I had cherished the hope of being able to celebrate this fair day by the payments of my three quarters. Vain chimera, bitter illusion! While I was slumbering on the pillow of confidence, ill-luck—what the

Greeks call *ananke*—was scattering my hopes. The returns on which I counted—times are so bad!-have failed, and of the considerable sums which I was to receive I have only realised three francs, which were lent me, and I will not insult you by the offer of them. Better days will come for our dear country and for me. Doubt it not, sir! When they come, I shall fly to inform you of their arrival, and to withdraw from your lodgings the precious objects which I leave there, putting them under your protection and that of the law, which hinders you from selling them before the expiration of a year, in case you should be disposed to try to do so with the object of obtaining the sum for which you stand credited in the ledger of my honesty. I commend to your special care my piano, and also the large frame containing sixty locks of hair whose different colours run through the whole gamut of capillary shades; the scissors of love have stolen them from the forehead of the Graces."

"Therefore, dear sir, and landlord, you may dispose of the roof under which I have dwelt. I grant you full authority, and have hereto set my hand and seal."

ALEXANDER SCHAUNARD

On finishing this letter, (which the artist had written at the desk of a friend who was a clerk in the War Office,) Monsieur Bernard indignantly crushed it in his hand, and as his glance fell on old Durand, who was waiting for the promised gratification, he roughly demanded what he was doing.

"Waiting, sir."

"For what?"

"For the present, on account of the good news," stammered the porter.

"Get out, you scoundrel! Do you presume to speak to me with your cap on?"

"But, sir—"

"Don't you answer me! Get out! No, stay there! We shall go up to the room of that scamp of an artist who has run off without paying."

"What! Monsieur Schaunard?" exclaimed the porter.

"Yes," cried the landlord with increasing fury, "and if he has carried away the smallest article, I send you off, straight off!"

"But it can't be," murmured the poor porter, "Monsieur Schaunard has not run away. He has gone to get change to pay you, and order a cart for his furniture."

"A cart for his furniture!" exclaimed the other, "run! I'm sure he has it here. He laid a trap to get you away from your lodge, fool that you are!"

"Fool that I am! Heaven help me!" cried the porter, all in a tremble before the thundering wrath of his superior, who hurried him down the stairs. When they arrived in the court the porter was hailed by the young man in the white hat.

"Come now! Am I not soon going to be in possession of my lodging? Is this the eighth of April? Did I hire a room here and pay you a deposit to bind the bargain? Yes or no?"

"Excuse me, sir," interposed the landlord, "I am at your service. Durand, I will talk to the gentleman myself. Run up there, that scamp Schaunard has come back to pack up. If you find him, shut him in, and then come down again and run for the police."

Old Durand vanished up the staircase.

"Excuse me, sir," continued the landlord, with a bow to the young man now left alone with him, "to whom have I the honour of speaking?"

"Your new tenant. I have hired a room in the sixth story of this house, and am beginning to be tired of waiting for my lodging to become vacant."

"I am very sorry indeed," replied Monsieur Bernard, "there has been a little difficulty with one of my tenants, the one whom you are to replace."

"Sir," cried old Durand from a window at the very top of the house, "Monsieur Schaunard is not here, but his room—stupid!—I mean he has carried nothing away, not a hair, sir!"

"Very well, come down," replied the landlord. "Have a little patience, I beg of you," he continued to the young man. "My porter will bring down to the cellar the furniture in the room of my defaulting tenant, and you may take possession in half an hour. Beside, your furniture has not come yet."

"But it has," answered the young man quietly.

Monsieur Bernard looked around, and saw only the large screens which had already mystified his porter.

"How is this?" he muttered. "I don't see anything."

"Behold!" replied the youth, unfolding the leaves of the frame, and displaying to the view of the astonished landlord a magnificent interior of a palace, with jasper columns, bas-reliefs, and paintings of old masters.

"But your furniture?" demanded Monsieur Bernard.

"Here it is," replied the young man, pointing to the splendid furniture *painted* in the palace, which he had bought at a sale of second-hand theatrical decorations.

"I hope you have some more serious furniture than this," said the landlord. "You know I must have security for my rent."

"The deuce! Is a palace not sufficient security for the rent of a garret?"

"No sir, I want real chairs and tables in solid mahogany."

"Alas! Neither gold nor mahogany makes us happy, as for the ancient poet well says. And I can't bear mahogany; it's too common a wood. Everybody has it."

"But surely sir, you must have some sort of furniture."

"No, it takes up too much room. You are stuck full of chairs, and have no place to sit down."

"But at any rate, you have a bed. What do you sleep on?"

"On a good conscience, sir."

"Excuse me, one more question," said the landlord, "What is your profession?"

At this very moment the young man's porter, returning on his second trip, entered the court. Among the articles with which his truck was loaded, an easel occupied a conspicuous position.

"Sir! Sir!!" shrieked old Durance, pointing out the easel to his landlord, "it's a painter!"

"I was sure he was an artist!" exclaimed the landlord in his turn, the hair of his wig standing up in affright, "a painter!! And you never inquired after this person," he continued to his porter, "you didn't know what he did!"

"He gave me five francs *arrest*," answered the poor fellow, "how could I suspect—"

"When you have finished," put in the stranger—

"Sir," replied Monsieur Bernard, mounting his spectacles with great decision, "since you have no furniture, you can't come in. The law authorizes me to refuse a tenant who brings no security."

"And my word, then?"

"Your word is not furniture, you must go somewhere else. Durance will give you back your earnest money."

"Oh dear!" exclaimed the porter, in consternation, "I've put it in the Savings' Bank."

"But consider sir," objected the young man. "I can't find another lodging in a moment! At least grant me hospitality for a day."

"Go to a hotel!" replied Monsieur Bernard. "By the way," added he, struck with a sudden idea, "if you like, I can let you a furnished room, the one you were to occupy, which has the furniture of my defaulting tenant in it. Only you know that when rooms are let this way, you pay in advance."

"Well," said the artist, finding he could do no better, "I should like to know what you are going to ask me for your hole."

"It is a very comfortable lodging, and the rent will be twenty-five francs a month, considering the circumstances, paid in advance."

"You have said that already, the expression does not deserve being repeated," said the young man, feeling in his pocket. "Have you change for five hundred francs?"

"I beg your pardon," quoth the astonished landlord.

"Five hundred, half a thousand; did you never see one before?" continued the artist, shaking the bank-note in the faces of the landlord and porter, who fairly lost their balance at the sight.

"You shall have it in a moment, sir," said the now respectful owner of the house, "there will only be twenty francs to take out, for Durand will return your deposit."

"He may keep it," replied the artist, "on condition of coming every morning to tell me the day of the week and month, the quarter of the moon, the weather it is going to be, and the form of government we are under."

Old Durand described an angle of ninety degrees forward.

"Yes, my good fellow, you shall serve me for almanac. Meanwhile, help my porter to bring the things in."

"I shall send you your receipt immediately," said the landlord, and that very night the painter Marcel was installed in the lodging of the fugitive Schaunard. During this time the aforesaid Schaunard was beating his roll-call, as he styled it, through the city.

Schaunard had carried the art of borrowing to the perfection of a science. Foreseeing the possible necessity of having to *spoil the foreigners*, he had learned how to ask for five francs in every language of the world. He had thoroughly studied all the stratagems which specie employs to escape those who are hunting for it, and knew, better than a pilot knows the hours of the tide, at what periods it was high or low water; that is to say, on what days his friends and acquaintances were accustomed to be in funds. Accordingly, there were houses where his appearance of a morning made people say, not "Here is Monsieur Schaunard," but "This is the first or the fifteenth." To facilitate, and at the same time equalize this species of tax which he was going to levy, when compelled by necessity, from those who were able to pay it to him, Schaunard had drawn up by districts and streets an alphabetical table containing the names of all his acquaintances. Opposite each name was inscribed the maximum of the sum which the party's finances authorized the artist to borrow of him, the time when he was flush, and his dinner hour, as well as his usual bill of fare. Beside this table, he kept a book, in perfect order, on which he entered the sums lent him, down to the smallest fraction; for he would never burden himself beyond a certain amount which was within the fortune of a country relative, whose heir-apparent he was. As soon as he owed one person twenty francs, he closed the account and paid him off, even if obliged to borrow for the purpose of those to whom he owed less. In this way he always kept up a certain credit which he called his floating debt, and as people knew that he was accustomed to repay as soon as his means permitted him, those who could accommodate him were very ready to do so.

But on the present occasion, from eleven in the morning, when he had started to try and collect the seventy-five francs requisite, up to six in the afternoon, he had only raised three francs, contributed by three letters (M., V., and R.) of his famous list. All the rest of the alphabet, having, like himself, their quarter to pay, had adjourned his claim indefinitely.

The clock of his stomach sounded the dinner-hour. He was then at the Maine barrier, where letter U lived. Schaunard mounted to letter U's room, where he had a knife and fork, when there were such articles on the premises.

"Where are you going, sir?" asked the porter, stopping him before he had completed his ascent.

"To Monsieur U," replied the artist.

"He's out."

"And madame?"

"Out too. They told me to say to a friend who was coming to see them this evening, that they were gone out to dine. In fact, if you are the gentleman they expected, this is the address they left." It was a scrap of paper on which his friend U. had written. "We are gone to dine with Schaunard, No.__, Rue de__. Come for us there."

"Well," said he, going away, "accident does make queer farces sometimes." Then remembering that there was a little tavern near by, where he had more than once procured a meal at a not unreasonable rate, he directed his steps to this establishment, situated in the adjoining road, and known among the lowest class of artistdom as "Mother Cadet's." It is a drinking-house which is also an eating-house, and its ordinary customers are carters of the Orleans railway, singing-ladies of Mont Parnasse, and juvenile "leads" from the Bobino theatre. During the warm season the students of the numerous painters' studios which border on the Luxembourg, the unappreciated and unedited men of the letters, the writers of leaders in mysterious newspapers, throng to dine at "Mother Cadet's," which is famous for its rabbit stew, its veritable sour-crout, and a miled white wine which smacks of flint.

Schaunard sat down in the grove; for so at "Mother Cadet's" they called the scattered foliage of two or three rickety trees whose sickly boughs had been trained into a sort of arbor.

"Hang the expense!" said Schaunard to himself, "I have to have a good blow-out, a regular Belthazzar's feast in private life," and without more ado, he ordered a bowl of soup, half a plate of sour-crout, and two half stews, having observed that you get more for two halves than one whole one.

This extensive order attracted the attention of a young person in white with a head-dress of orange flowers and ballshoes; a veil of *sham imitation* lace streamed down her shoulders, which she had no special reason to be proud of. She was a *prima donna* of the Mont Parnasse theatre, the greenroom of which opens into Mother Cadet's kitchen; she had come to take a meal between two acts of *Lucia*, and was at that moment finishing with a small cup of coffee her dinner, composed exclusively of an artichoke seasoned with oil and vinegar.

"Two stews! Duece take it!" said she, in an aside to the girl who acted as waiter at the establishment. "That young man feeds himself well. How much do I owe, Adele?"

"Artichoke four, coffee four, bread one, that makes nine sous."

"There they are," said the singer and off she went humming:

"This affection Heaven has given."

"Why she is giving us the la!" exclaimed a mysterious personage half hidden behind a rampart of old books, who was seated at the same table with Schaunard.

"Giving it!" replied the other, "keeping it, I should say. Just imagine!" he added, pointing to the vinegar on the plate from which Lucia had been eating her artichoke, "pickling that falsetto of hers!"

"It is a strong acid, to be sure," added the personage who had first spoken. "They make some at Orleans which has deservedly a great reputation."

Schaunard carefully examined this individual, who was thus fishing for a conversation with him. The fixed stare of his large blue eyes, which always seemed looking for something, gave his features the character of happy tranquility which is common among theological students. His face had a uniform tint of old ivory, except his cheeks, which had a coat, as it were of brickdust. His mouth seemed to have been sketched by a student in the rudiments of drawing, whose elbow had been jogged while he was tracing it. His lips, which pouted almost like a negro's, disclosed teeth not unlike a stag-hound's and his double-chin reposed itself upon a white cravat, one of whose points threatened the stars, while the other was ready to pierce the ground. A torrent of light hair escaped from under the enormous brim of his well-worn felt-hat. He wore a hazel-coloured overcoat with a large cape, worn thread-bare and rough as a grater; from its yawning pockets peeped bundles of manuscripts and pamphlets. The enjoyment of his sour-crout, which he devoured with numerous and audible marks of approbation, rendered him heedless of the scrutiny to which he was subjected, but did not prevent him from continuing to read an old book open before him, in which he made marginal notes from time to time with a pencil that he carried behind his ear.

"Hullo!" cried Schaunard suddenly, making his glass ring with his knife, "my stew!"

"Sir," said the girl, running up plate in hand, "there is none left, here is the last, and this gentleman has ordered it." Therewith she deposited the dish before the man with the books.

"The deuce!" cried Schaunard. There was such an air of melancholy disappointment in his exclamation, that the possessor of the books was moved to the soul by it. He broke down the pile of old works which formed a barrier between him and Schaunard, and putting the dish in the centre of the table, said, in his sweetest tones:

"Might I be so bold as to beg you, sir, to share this with me?"

"Sir," replied the artist, "I could not think of depriving you of it."

"Then will you deprive me of the pleasure of being agreeable to you?"

"If you insist, sir," and Schaunard held out his plate.

"Permit me not to give you the head," said the stranger.

"Really sir, I cannot allow you," Schaunard began, but on taking back his plate he perceived that the other had given him the very piece which he implied he would keep for himself.

"What is he playing off his politeness on me for?" he muttered to himself.

"If the head is the most noble part of man," said the stranger, "it is the least agreeable part of the rabbit. There are many persons who cannot bear it. I happen to like it very much, however."

"If so," said Schaunard, "I regret exceedingly that you robbed yourself for me."

"How? Excuse me," quoth he of the books, "I kept the head, as I had the honor of observing to you."

"Allow me," rejoined Schaunard, thrusting his plate under his nose, "what part do you call that?"

"Good heavens!" cried the stranger, "what do I see? Another head? It is a bicephalous rabbit!"

"Buy what?" said Schaunard.

"Cephalous—comes from the Greek. In fact, Baffon (who used to wear ruffles) cites some cases of this monstrosity. On the whole, I am not sorry to have eaten a phenomenon."

Thanks to this incident, the conversation was definitely established. Schaunard, not willing to be behindhand in courtesy, called for an extra quart of wine. The hero of the books called for a third. Schaunard treated to salad, the other to dessert. At eight o'clock there were six empty bottles on the table. As they talked, their natural frankness, assisted by their libations, had urged them to interchange biographies, and they knew each other as well as if they had always lived together. He of the books, after hearing the confidential disclosures of Schaunard, had informed him that his name was Gustave Colline; he was a philosopher by profession, and got his living by giving lessons in rhetoric, mathematics and several other *ics*.

What little money he picked up by his profession was spent in buying books. His hazel-coloured coat was known to all the stall keepers on the quay from the Pont de la Concorde to the Pont Saint Michel. What he did with these books, so numerous that no man's lifetime would have been long enough to read them, nobody knew, least of all, himself. But this hobby of his amounted to monomania: when he came home at night without bringing a musty quarto with him, he would repeat the saying of Titus, "I have lost a day." His enticing manners, his language, which was a mosaic of every possible style, and the fearful puns which embellished his conversation, completely won Schaunard, who demanded on the spot permission of Colline to add his name to those on the famous list already mentioned.

They left Mother Cadet's at nine o'clock at night, both fairly primed, and with the gait of men who have been engaged in close conversation with sundry bottles.

Colline offered to stand coffee, and Schaunard accepted on condition that he should be allowed to pay for the accompanying nips of liquor. They turned into a cafe in the Rue Saint Germain l'Auxerrois, and bearing on its sign the name of Momus, god of play and pleasure.

At the moment they entered a lively argument broke out between two of the frequenters of the place. One of them was a young fellow whose face was hidden by a dense thicket of beard of several distinct shades. By way of a balance to this wealth of hair on his chin, a precocious baldness had despoiled his forehead, which was as bare as a billiard ball. He vainly strove to conceal the nakedness of the land by brushing forward a tuft of hairs so scanty that they could almost be counted. He wore a black coat worn at the elbows, and revealing whenever he raised his arms too high a ventilator under the armpits. His trousers might have once been black, but his boots, which had never been new, seemed to have already gone round the world two or three times on the feet of the Wandering Jew.

Schaunard noticed that his new friend Colline and the young fellow with the big beard nodded to one another.

"You know the gentleman?" said he to the philosopher.

"Not exactly," replied the latter, "but I meet him sometimes at the National Library. I believe that he is a literary man."

"He wears the garb of one, at any rate," said Schaunard.

The individual with whom this young fellow was arguing was a man of forty, foredoomed, by a big head wedged between his shoulders without any break in the shape of a neck, to the thunderstroke of apoplexy. Idiocy was written in capital letters on his low forehead, surmounted by a little black skull-cap. His name was Monsieur Mouton, and he was a clerk at the town hall of the 4th Arrondissement, where he acted as registrar of deaths.

"Monsieur Rodolphe," exclaimed he, in the squeaky tones of a eunuch, shaking the young fellow by a button of his coat which he had laid hold of. "Do you want to know my opinion? Well, all your newspapers are of no use whatsoever. Come now, let us put a supposititious case. I am the father of a family, am I not? Good. I go to the cafe for a game at dominoes? Follow my argument now."

"Go on," said Rodolphe.

"Well," continued Daddy Mouton, punctuating each of his sentences by a blow with his fist which made the jugs and glasses on the table rattle again. "Well, I come across the papers. What do I see? One which says black when the other says white, and so on and so on. What is all that to me? I am the father of a family who goes to the cafe—"

"For a game at dominoes," said Rodolphe.

"Every evening," continued Monsieur Mouton. "Well, to put a case—you understand?"

"Exactly," observed Rodolphe.

"I read an article which is not according to my views. That puts me in a rage, and I fret my heart out, because you see, Monsieur Rodolphe, newspapers are all lies. Yes, lies," he screeched in his shrillest falsetto, "and the journalists are robbers."

"But, Monsieur Mouton—"

"Yes, brigands," continued the clerk. "They are the cause of all our misfortunes; they brought about the Revolution and its paper money, witness Murat."

"Excuse me," said Rodolphe, "you mean Marat."

"No, no," resumed Monsieur Mouton, "Murat, for I saw his funeral when I was quite a child—"

"But I assure you—"

"They even brought you a piece at the Circus about him, so there."

"Exactly," said Rodolphe, "that was Murat."

"Well what else have I been saying for an hour past?" exclaimed the obstinate Mouton. "Murat, who used to work in a cellar, eh? Well, to put a case. Were not the Bourbons right to guillotine him, since he had played the traitor?"

"Guillotine who? Play the traitor to whom?" cried Rodolphe, button-holing Monsieur Mouton in turn.

"Why Marat."

"No, no, Monsieur Mouton. Murat, let us understand one another, hang it all!"

"Precisely, Marat, a scoundrel. He betrayed the Emperor in 1815. That is why I say all the papers are alike," continued Monsieur Mouton, returning to the original theme of what he called an explanation. "Do you know what I should like, Monsieur Rodolphe? Well, to put a case. I should like a good paper. Ah! not too large and not stuffed with phrases."

"You are exacting," interrupted Rodolphe, "a newspaper without phrases."

"Yes, certainly. Follow my idea?"

"I am trying to."

"A paper which should simply give the state of the King's health and of the crops. For after all, what is the use of all your papers that no one can understand? To put a case. I am at the town hall, am I not? I keep my books; very good. Well, it is just as if someone came to me and said, 'Monsieur Mouton, you enter the deaths—well, do this, do that.' What do you mean by this and that? Well, it is the same thing with newspapers," he wound up with.

"Evidently," said a neighbor who had understood.

And Monsieur Mouton having received the congratulations of some of the other frequenters of the cafe who shared his opinion, resumed his game at dominoes.

"I have taught him his place," said he, indicating Rodolphe, who had returned to the same table at which Schaunard and Colline were seated.

"What a blockhead!" said Rodolphe to the two young fellows.

"He has a fine head, with his eyelids like the hood of a cabriolet, and his eyes like glass marbles," said Schaunard, pulling out a wonderfully coloured pipe.

"By Jupiter, sir," said Rodolphe, "that is a very pretty pipe of yours."

"Oh! I have a much finer one I wear in society," replied Schaunard, carelessly, "pass me some tobacco, Colline."

"Hullo!" said the philosopher, "I have none left."

"Allow me to offer you some," observed Rodolphe, pulling a packet of tobacco out of his pocket and placing it on the table.

To this civility Colline thought it his duty to respond by an offer of glasses round.

Rodolphe accepted. The conversation turned on literature. Rodolphe, questioned as to the profession already revealed by his garb, confessed his relation with the Muses, and stood a second round of drinks. As the waiter was going off with the bottle Schaunard requested him to be good enough to forget it. He had heard the silvery tinkle of a couple of five-franc pieces in one of Colline's pockets. Rodolphe had soon reached the same level of expansiveness as the two friends, and poured out his confidences in turn.

They would no doubt have passed the night at the cafe if they had not been requested to leave. They had not gone ten steps, which had taken them a quarter of an hour to accomplish, before they were surprised by a violent downpour. Colline and Rodolphe lived at opposite ends of Paris, one on the Ile Saint Louis, and the other at Montmartre.

Schaunard, who had wholly forgotten that he was without a residence, offered them hospitality.

"Come to my place," said he, "I live close by, we will pass the night in discussing literature and art."

"You shall play and Rodolphe will recite some of his verses to us," said Colline.

"Right you are," said Schaunard, "life is short, and we must enjoy ourselves whilst we can."

Arriving at the house, which Schaunard had some difficulty in recognizing, he sat down for a moment on a corner-post waiting for Rodolphe and Colline, who had gone into a wine-shop that was still open to obtain the primary element of a supper. When they came back, Schaunard rapped several times at the door, for he vaguely recollected that the porter had a habit of keeping him waiting. The door at length opened, and old Durand, half aroused from his first sleep, and no longer recalling that Schaunard had ceased to be his tenant, did not disturb himself when the latter called out his name to him.

When they had all three gained the top of the stairs, the ascent of which had been as lengthy as it was difficult, Schaunard, who was the foremost, uttered a cry of astonishment at finding the key in the keyhole of his door.

"What is the matter?" asked Rodolphe.

"I cannot make it out," muttered the other. "I find the key in the door, though I took it away with me this morning. Ah! we shall see. I put it in my pocket. Why, confound it, here it is still!" he exclaimed, displaying a key. "This is witchcraft."

"Phantasmagoria," said Colline.

"Fancy," added Rodolphe.

"But," resumed Schaunard, whose voice betrayed a commencement of alarm, "do you hear that?"

"What?"

"What?"

"My piano, which is playing of its own accord *do la mi re do, la si sol re*. Scoundrel of a re, it is still false."

"But it cannot be in your room," said Rodolphe, and he added in a whisper to Colline, against whom he was leaning heavily, "he is tight."

"So I think. In the first place, it is not a piano at all, it is a flute."

"But you are screwed too, my dear fellow," observed the poet to the philosopher, who had sat down on the landing, "it is a violin."

"A vio—, pooh! I say, Schaunard," hiccupped Colline, pulling his friend by the legs, "here is a joke, this gentleman makes out that it is a vio—"

"Hang it all," exclaimed Schaunard in the height of terror, "it is magic."

"Phantasma-goria," howled Colline, letting fall one of the bottles he held by his hand.

"Fancy," yelled Rodolphe in turn.

In the midst of this uproar the room door suddenly opened, and an individual holding a triple-branched candlestick in which pink candles were burning, appeared on the threshold.

"What do you want, gentlemen?" asked he, bowing courteously to the three friends.

"Good heavens, what am I about? I have made a mistake, this is not my room," said Schaunard.

"Sir," added Colline and Rodolphe, simultaneously, addressing the person who had opened the door, "be good enough to excuse our friend, he is as drunk as three fiddlers."

Suddenly a gleam of lucidity flashed through Schaunard's intoxication, he read on his door these words written in chalk:

"I have called three times for my New Year's gift—Phemie."

"But it is all right, it is all right, I am indeed at home," he exclaimed, "here is the visiting card Phemie left me on New Year's Day; it is really my door."

"Good heavens, sir," said Rodolphe, "I am truly bewildered."

"Believe me, sir," added Colline, "that for my part, I am an active partner in my friend's confusion."

The young fellow who had opened the door could not help laughing.

"If you come into my room for a moment," he replied, "no doubt your friend, as soon as he has looked around, will see his mistake."

"Willingly."

And the poet and philosopher each taking Schaunard by an arm, led him into the room, or rather the palace of Marcel, whom no doubt our readers have recognized.

Schaunard cast his eyes vaguely around him, murmuring, "It is astonishing how my dwelling is embellished!"

"Well, are you satisfied now?" asked Colline.

But Schaunard having noticed the piano had gone to it, and was playing scales.

"Here, you fellows, listen to this," said he, striking the notes, "this is something like, the animal has recognized his master, *si la sol, fa mi re.* Ah! wretched re, you are always the same. I told you it was my instrument."

"He insists on it," said Colline to Rodolphe.

"He insists on it," repeated Rodolphe to Marcel.

"And that," added Schaunard, pointing to the star-adorned petticoat that was lying on a chair, "it is not an adornment of mine, perhaps? Ah!"

And he looked Marcel straight in the face.

"And this," continued he, unfastening from the wall the notice to quit already spoken of.

And he began to read, "Therefore Monsieur Schaunard is hereby required to give up possession of the said premises, and to leave them in tenantable repair, before noon on the eighth day of April. As witness the present formal notice to quit, the cost of which is five francs." "Ha! ha! so I am not the Monsieur Schaunard to whom formal notice to quit is given at a cost of five francs? And these, again," he continued, recognizing his slippers on Marcel's feet, "are not those my papouches, the gift of a beloved hand? It is your turn, sir," said he to Marcel, "to explain your presence amongst my household goods."

"Gentlemen," replied Marcel, addressing himself more especially to Colline and Rodolphe, "this gentleman," and he pointed to Schaunard, "is at home, I admit."

"Ah!" exclaimed Schaunard, "that's lucky."

"But," continued Marcel, "I am at home too."

"But, sir," broke in Rodolphe, "if our friend recognizes—"

"Yes," said Colline, "if our friend—"

"And if on your side you recall that—," added Rodolphe, "how is it that—"

"Yes," replied his echo Colline, "how is it that—"

"Have the kindness to sit down, gentlemen," replied Marcel, "and I will explain the mystery to you."

"If we were to liquify the explanation?" risked Colline.

"Over a mouthful of something," added Rodolphe.

The four young fellows sat down to table and attacked a piece of cold veal which the wine-shop keeper had let them have.

Marcel then explained what had taken place in the morning between himself and the landlord when he had come to move in.

"Then," observed Rodolphe, "this gentleman is quite right, and we are in his place?"

"You are at home," said Marcel politely.

But it was a tremendous task to make Schaunard understand what had taken place. A comical incident served to further complicate the situation. Schaunard, when looking for something in a sideboard, found the change of the five hundred franc note that Marcel had handed to Monsieur Bernard that morning.

"Ah! I was quite sure," he exclaimed, "that Fortune would not desert me. I remember now that I went out this morning to run after her. On account of its being quarter-day she must have looked in during my absence. We crossed one another on the way, that it is. How right I was to leave the key in my drawer!"

"Delightful madness!" murmured Rodolphe, looking at Schaunard, who was building up the money in equal piles.

"A dream, a falsehood, such is life," added the philosopher.

Marcel laughed.

An hour later they had all four fallen asleep.

The next day they woke up at noon, and at first seemed very much surprised to find themselves together. Schaunard, Colline, and Rodolphe did not appear to recognize one another, and addressed one another as "sir." Marcel had to remind them that they had come together the evening before.

At that moment old Durand entered the room.

"Sir," said he to Marcel, "it is the month of April, eighteen hundred and forty, there is mud in the streets, and His Majesty Louis-Philippe is still King of France and Navarre. What!" exclaimed the porter on seeing his former tenant, "Monsieur Schaunard, how did you come here?"

"By the telegraph," replied Schaunard.

"Ah!" replied the porter, "you are still a joker—"

"Durand," said Marcel, "I do not like subordinates mingling in conversation with me, go to the nearest restaurant and have a breakfast for four sent up. Here is the bill of fare," he added, handing him a slip of paper on which he had written it. "Go."

"Gentlemen," continued Marcel, addressing the three young fellows, "you invited me to supper last night, allow me to offer you a breakfast this morning, not in my room, but in ours," he added, holding out his hand to Schaunard.

"Oh! no," said Schaunard sentimentally, "let us never leave one another."

"That's right, we are very comfortable here," added Colline.

"To leave you for a moment," continued Rodolphe. "Tomorrow the 'Scarf of Iris,' a fashion paper of which I am editor, appears, and I must go and correct my proofs; I will be back in an hour."

"The deuce!" said Colline, "that reminds me that I have a lesson to give to an Indian prince who has come to Paris to learn Arabic."

"Go tomorrow," said Marcel.

"Oh, no!" said the philosopher, "the prince is to pay me today. And then I must acknowledge to you that this auspicious day would be spoilt for me if I did not take a stroll amongst the bookstalls."

"But will you come back?" said Schaunard.

"With the swiftness of an arrow launched by a steady hand," replied the philosopher, who loved eccentric imagery.

And he went out with Rodolphe.

"In point of fact," said Schaunard when left alone with Marcel, "instead of lolling on the sybarite's pillow, suppose I was to go out to seek some gold to appease the cupidity of Monsieur Bernard?"

"Then," said Marcel uneasily, "you still mean to move?"

"Hang it," replied Schaunard, "I must, since I have received a formal notice to quit, at a cost of five francs."

"But," said Marcel, "if you move, shall you take your furniture with you?"

"I have that idea. I will not leave a hair, as Monsieur Bernard says."

"The deuce! That will be very awkward for me," said Marcel, "since I have hired your room furnished."

"There now, that's so," replied Schaunard. "Ah! bah," he added in a melancholy tone, "there is nothing to prove that I shall find my thousand francs today, tomorrow, or even later on."

"Stop a bit," exclaimed Marcel, "I have an idea."

"Unfold it."

"This is the state of things. Legally, this lodging is mine, since I have paid a month in advance."

"The lodging, yes, but as to the furniture, if I pay, I can legally take it away, and if it were possible I would even take it away illegally."

"So that," continued Marcel, "you have furniture and no lodging, and I have lodging and no furniture."

"That is the position," observed Schaunard.

"This lodging suits me," said Marcel.

"And for my part is has never suited me better," said Schaunard.

"Well then, we can settle this business," resumed Marcel, "stay with me, I will apply house-room, and you shall supply the furniture."

"And the rent?" said Schaunard.

"Since I have some money just now I will pay it, it will be your turn next time. Think about it."

"I never think about anything, above all accepting a suggestion which suits me. Carried unanimously, in point of fact, Painting and Music are sisters."

"Sisters-in-law," observed Marcel.

At that moment Colline and Rodolphe, who had met one another, came in.

Marcel and Schaunard informed them of their partnership.

"Gentlemen," said Rodolphe, tapping his waistcoat pocket, "I am ready to stand dinner all round."

"That is just what I was going to have the honour of proposing," said Colline, taking out a gold coin which he stuck in his eye like a glass. "My prince gave me this to buy an Arabic grammar, which I have just paid six sous ready cash for."

"I," said Rodolphe, "have got the cashier of the 'Scarf of Iris' to advance me thirty francs under the pretext that I wanted it to get vaccinated."

"It is general pay-day then?" said Schaunard, "there is only myself unable to stand anything. It is humiliating."

"Meanwhile," said Rodolphe, "I maintain my offer of a dinner."

"So do I," said Colline.

"Very well," said Rodolphe, "we will toss up which shall settle the bill."

"No," said Schaunard, "I have something far better than that to offer you as a way of getting over the difficulty."

"Let us have it."

"Rodolphe shall pay for dinner, and Colline shall stand supper."

"That is what I call Solomonic jurisprudence," exclaimed the philosopher.

"It is worse than Camacho's wedding," added Marcel.

The dinner took place at a Provencal restaurant in the Rue Dauphine, celebrated for its literary waiters and its "Ayoli." As it was necessary to leave room for the supper, they ate and drank in moderation. The acquaintance, begun the evening before between Colline and Schaunard and later on with Marcel, became more intimate; each of the young fellows hoisted the flag of his artistic opinions, and all four recognized that they had like courage and similar hopes. Talking and arguing they perceived that their sympathies were akin, that they had all the same knack in that chaff which amuses without hurting, and that the virtues of youth had not left a vacant spot in their heart, easily stirred by the sight of the narration of anything noble. All four starting from the same mark to reach the same goal, they thought that there was something more than chance in their meeting, and that it might after all be Providence who thus joined their hands and whispered in their ears the evangelic motto, which should be the sole charter of humanity, "Love one another."

At the end of the repast, which closed in somewhat grave mood, Rodolphe rose to propose a toast to the future, and Colline replied in a short speech that was not taken from any book, had no pretension to style, and was merely couched in the good old dialect of simplicity, making that which is so badly delivered so well understood.

"What a donkey this philosopher is!" murmured Schaunard, whose face was buried in his glass, "here is he obliging me to put water in my wine."

After dinner they went to take coffee at the Cafe Momus, where they had already spent the preceding evening. It was from that day that the establishment in question became uninhabitable by its other frequenters.

After coffee and nips of liqueurs the Bohemian clan, definitely founded, returned to Marcel's lodging, which took the name of Schaunard's Elysium. Whilst Colline went to order the supper he had promised, the others bought squibs, crackers and other pyrotechnic materials, and before sitting down to table they let off from the windows a magnificent display of fireworks which turned the whole house topsy-turvey, and during which the four friends shouted at the top of their voices—

"Let us celebrate this happy day."

The next morning they again found themselves all four together but without seeming astonished this time. Before each going about his business they went together and breakfasted frugally at the Cafe Momus, where they made an appointment for the evening and where for a long time they were seen to return daily.

Such are the chief personages who will reappear in the episodes of which this volume is made up, a volume which is not a romance and has no other pretension than that set forth on its title-page, for the "Bohemians of the Latin Quarter" is only a series of social studies, the heroes of which belong to a class badly judged till now, whose greatest crime is lack of order, and who can even plead in excuse that this very lack of order is a necessity of the life they lead.

II

A Good Angel

S chaunard and Marcel, who had been grinding away valiantly a whole morning, suddenly struck work.

"Thunder and lightning! I'm hungry!" cried Schaunard. And he added carelessly, "Do we breakfast today?"

Marcel appeared much astonished at this very inopportune question.

"How long has it been the fashion to breakfast two days running?" he asked. "And yesterday was Thursday." He finished his reply by tracing with his mahl-stick the ecclesiastic ordinance:

> *"On Friday eat no meat,*
> *Nor aught resembling it."*

Schaunard, finding no answer, returned to his picture, which represented a plain inhabited by a red tree and a blue tree shaking branches; an evident allusion to the sweets of friendship, which had a very philosophical effect.

At this moment the porter knocked; he had brought a letter for Marcel.

"Three sous," said he.

"You are sure?" replied the artist. "Very well, you can owe it to us."

He shut the door in the man's face, and opened the letter. At the first line, he began to vault around the room like a rope-dancer and thundered out, at the top of his voice, this romantic ditty, which indicated with him the highest pitch of ecstasy:

> *"There were four juveniles in our street;*
> *They fell so sick they could not eat;*
> *They carried them to the hospital!—*
> *Tal! Tal! Tal! Tal!"*

"Oh yes!" said Schaunard, taking him up:

> *"They put all four into one big bed,*
> *Two at the feet and two at the head."*

"Think I don't know it?" Marcel continued:

> *"There came a sister of Charity—*
> *Ty! Ty! tee! tee!"*

"If you don't stop," said Schaunard, who suspected signs of mental alienation, "I'll play the allegro of my symphony on 'The Influence of Blue in the Arts.'" So saying, he approached the piano.

This menace had the effect of a drop of cold water in a boiling fluid. Marcel grew calm as if by magic. "Look there!" said he, passing the letter to his friend. It was an invitation to dine with a deputy, an enlightened patron of the arts in general and Marcel in particular, since the latter had taken the portrait of his country-house.

"For today," sighed Schaunard. "Unluckily the ticket is not good for two. But stay! Now I think of it, your deputy is of the government party; you cannot, you must not accept. Your principles will not permit you to partake of the bread which has been watered by the tears of the people."

"Bah!" replied Marcel, "my deputy is a moderate radical; he voted against the government the other day. Besides, he is going to get me an order, and he has promised to introduce me in society. Moreover, this may be Friday as much as it likes; I am famished as Ugolino, and I mean to dine today. There now!"

"There are other difficulties," continued Schaunard, who could not help being a little jealous of the good fortune that had fallen to his friend's lot. "You can't dine out in a red flannel shirt and slippers."

"I shall borrow clothes of Rodolphe or Colline."

"Infatuated youth! Do you forget that this is the twentieth, and at this time of the month their wardrobe is up to the very top of the spout?"

"Between now and five o'clock this evening I shall find a dress-coat."

"I took three weeks to get one when I went to my cousin's wedding and that was in January."

"Well, then, I shall go as I am," said Marcel, with a theatrical stride. "It shall certainly never be said that a miserable question of etiquette hindered me from making my first step in society."

"Without boots," suggested his friend.

Marcel rushed out in a state of agitation impossible to describe. At the end of two hours he returned, loaded with a false collar.

"Hardly worth while to run so far for that," said Schaunard. "There was paper enough to make a dozen."

"But," cried Marcel, tearing his hair, "we must have some things—confound it!" And he commenced a thorough investigation of every corner of the two rooms. After an hour's search, he realized a costume thus composed:

A pair of plaid trousers, a gray hat, a red cravat, a blue waistcoat, two boots, one black glove, and one glove that had been white.

"That will make two black gloves on a pinch," said Schaunard. "You are going to look like the solar spectrum in that dress. To be sure, a colourist such as you are—"

Marcel was trying the boots. Alas! They are both for the same foot! The artist, in despair, perceived an old boot in a corner which had served as the receptacle of their empty bladders. He seized upon it.

"From Garrick to Syllable," said his jesting comrade, "one square-toed and the other round."

"I am going to varnish them and it won't show."

"A good idea! Now you only want the dress-coat."

"Oh!" cried Marcel, biting his fists:

"To have one would I give ten years of life,
And this right hand, I tell thee."

They heard another knock at the door. Marcel opened it.

"Monsieur Schaunard?" inquired a stranger, halting on the threshold.

"At your service," replied the painter, inviting him in.

The stranger had one of those honest faces which typify the provincial.

"Sir," said he. "My cousin has often spoke to me of your talent for portrait painting, and being on the point of making a voyage to the colonies, whither I am deputed by the sugar refiners of the city of Nantes, I wish to leave my family something to remember me by. That is why I am come to see you."

"Holy Providence!" exclaimed Schaunard. "Marcel, a seat for Monsieur—"

"Blancheron," said the new-comer, "Blancheron of Nantes, delegate of the sugar interest, Ex-Mayor, Captain of the National Guard, and author of a pamphlet on the sugar question."

"I am highly honoured at having been chosen by you," said the artist, with a low reverence to the delegate of the refiners. "How do you wish to have your portrait taken?"

"In miniature," replied Blancheron, "like that," and he pointed to a portrait in oil, for the delegate was one of that class with whom everything smaller than the side of a house is miniature. Schaunard had the measure of his man immediately, especially when the other added that he wished to be painted with the best colours.

"I never use any other," said the artist. "How large do you wish it to be?"

"About so big," answered the other, pointing to a kit-cat. "How much will it be?"

"Sixty francs with the hands, fifty without."

"The deuce it will! My cousin talked of thirty francs."

"It depends on the season. Colours are much dearer at some times of the year than at others."

"Bless me! It's just like sugar!"

"Precisely."

"Fifty francs then be it."

"You are wrong there; for ten francs more you will have your hands, and I will put in them your pamphlet on the sugar question, which will have a very good effect."

"By Jove, you are right!"

"Thunder and lightning!" said Schaunard to himself, "if he goes on so, I shall burst, and hurt him with one of the pieces."

"Did you see?" whispered Marcel.

"What?"

"He has a black coat."

"I take. Let me manage."

"Well," quoth the delegate, "when do we begin? There is no time to lose, for I sail soon."

"I have to take a little trip myself the day after tomorrow; so, if you please, we will begin at once. One good sitting will help us along some way."

"But it will soon be night, and you can't paint by candle light."

"My room is arranged so that we can work at all hours in it. If you will take off your coat, and put yourself in position, we will commence."

"Take off my coat! What for?"

"You told me that you intend this portrait for your family."

"Certainly."

"Well, then, you ought to be represented in your at-home dress—in your dressing gown. It is the custom to be so."

"But I haven't any dressing gown here."

"But I have. The case is provided for," quoth Schaunard, presenting to his sitter a very ragged garment, so ornamented with paint-marks that the honest provincial hesitated about setting into it.

"A very odd dress," said he.

"And very valuable. A Turkish vizier gave it to Horace Vernet, and he gave it to me when he had done with it. I am a pupil of his."

"Are you a pupil of Vernet's?"

"I am proud to be," said the artist. "Wretch that I am!" he muttered to himself, "I deny my gods and masters!"

"You have reason to be proud, my young friend," replied the delegate donning the dressing-gown with the illustrious origin.

"Hang up Monsieur Blancheron's coat in the wardrobe," said Schaunard to his friend, with a significant wink.

"Ain't he too good?" whispered Marcel as he pounced on his prey, and nodded towards Blancheron. "If you could only keep a piece of him."

"I'll try; but do you dress yourself, and cut. Come back by ten; I will keep him till then. Above all, bring me something in your pocket."

"I'll bring you a pineapple," said Marcel as he evaporated.

He dressed himself hastily; the dress-coat fit him like a glove. Then he went out by the second door of the studio.

Schaunard set himself to work. When it was fairly night, Monsieur Blancheron heard the clock strike six, and remembered that he had not dined. He informed Schaunard of the fact.

"I am in the same position," said the other, "but to oblige you, I will go without today, though I had an invitation in the Faubourg St. Germain. But we can't break off now, it might spoil the resemblance." And he painted away harder than ever. "By the way," said he, suddenly, "we can dine without breaking off. There is a capital restaurant downstairs, which will send us up anything we like." And Schaunard awaited the effect of his trial of plurals.

"I accept your idea," said Blancheron, "an in return, I hope you will do me the honor of keeping me company at table."

Schaunard bowed. "Really," said he to himself, "this is a fine fellow—a very god-send. Will you order the dinner?" he asked his Amphitryon.

"You will oblige me by taking that trouble," replied the other, politely.

"So much the worse for you, my boy," said the painter as he pitched down the stairs, four steps at a time. Marching up to the counter, he wrote out a bill of fare that made the Vatel of the establishment turn pale.

"Claret! Who's to pay for it?"

"Probably not I," said Schaunard, "but an uncle of mine that you will find up there, a very good judge. So, do your best, and let us have dinner in half an hour, served on your porcelain."

At eight o'clock, Monsieur Blancheron felt the necessity of pouring into a friend's ear his idea on the sugar question, and accordingly recited his pamphlet to Schaunard, who accompanied him on the piano.

At ten, they danced the galop together.

At eleven, they swore never to separate, and to make wills in each other's favor.

At twelve, Marcel returned, and found them locked in a mutual embrace, and dissolved in tears. The floor was half an inch deep in fluid— either from that cause or the liquor that had been spilt. He stumbled against the table, and remarked the splendid relics of the sumptuous feast. He tried the bottles, they were utterly empty. He attempted to rouse Schaunard, but the later menaced him with speedy death, if he tore him from his friend Blancheron, of whom he was making a pillow.

"Ungrateful wretch!" said Marcel, taking out of his pocket a handful of nuts, "when I had brought him some dinner!"

III

LENTEN LOVES

One evening in Lent Rodolphe returned home early with the idea of working. But scarcely had he sat down at his table and dipped his pen in the ink than he was disturbed by a singular noise. Putting his ear to the treacherous partition that separated him from the next room, he listened, and plainly distinguished a dialogue broken by the sound of kisses and other amourous interruptions.

"The deuce," thought Rodolphe, glancing at his clock, "it is still early, and my neighbor is a Juliet who usually keeps her Romeo till long after the lark has sung. I cannot work tonight."

And taking his hat he went out. Handing in his key at the porter's lodge he found the porter's wife half clasped in the arms of a gallant. The poor woman was so flustered that it was five minutes before she could open the latch.

"In point of fact," though Rodolphe, "there are times when porters grow human again."

Passing through the door he found in its recess a sapper and a cook exchanging the luck-penny of love.

"Hang it," said Rodolphe, alluding to the warrior and his robust companion, "here are heretics who scarcely think that we are in Lent."

And he set out for the abode of one of his friends who lived in the neighborhood.

"If Marcel is at home," he said to himself, "we will pass the evening in abusing Colline. One must do something."

As he rapped vigorously, the door was partly opened, and a young man, simply clad in a shirt and an eye-glass, presented himself.

"I cannot receive you," said he to Rodolphe.

"Why not?" asked the latter.

"There," said Marcel, pointing to a feminine head that had just peeped out from behind a curtain, "there is my answer."

"It is not a pretty one," said Rodolphe, who had just had the door closed in his face. "Ah!" said he to himself when he got into the street, "what shall I do? Suppose I call on Colline, we could pass the time in abusing Marcel."

Passing along the Rue de l'Ouest, usually dark and unfrequented, Rodolphe made out a shade walking up and down in melancholy fashion, and muttering in rhyme.

"Ho, ho!" said Rodolphe, "who is this animated sonnet loitering here? What, Colline!"

"What Rodolphe! Where are you going?"

"To your place."

"You won't find me there."

"What are you doing here?"

"Waiting."

"What are you waiting for?"

"Ah!" said Colline in a tone of raillery, "what can one be waiting for when one is twenty, when there are stars in the sky and songs in the air?"

"Speak in prose."

"I am waiting for a girl."

"Good night," said Rodolphe, who went on his way continuing his monologue. "What," said he, "is it St. Cupid's Day and cannot I take a step without running up against people in love? It is scandalously immoral. What are the police about?"

As the gardens of the Luxembourg were still open, Rodolphe passed into them to shorten his road. Amidst the deserted paths he often saw flitting before him, as though disturbed by his footsteps, couples mysteriously interlaced, and seeking, as a poet has remarked, the two-fold luxury of silence and shade.

"This," said Rodolphe, "is an evening borrowed from a romance." And yet overcome, despite himself, by a languourous charm, he sat down on a seat and gazed sentimentally at the moon.

In a short time he was wholly under the spell of a feverish hallucination. It seemed to him that the gods and heroes in marble who peopled the garden were quitting their pedestals to make love to the goddesses and heroines, their neighbors, and he distinctly heard the great Hercules recite a madrigal to the Vedella, whose tunic appeared to him to have grown singularly short.

From the seat he occupied he saw the swan of the fountain making its way towards a nymph of the vicinity.

"Good," thought Rodolphe, who accepted all this mythology, "There is Jupiter going to keep an appointment with Leda; provided always that the park keeper does not surprise them."

Then he leaned his forehead on his hand and plunged further into the flowery thickets of sentiment. But at this sweet moment of his dream Rodolphe was suddenly awakened by a park keeper, who came up and tapped him on the shoulder.

"It is closing time, sir," said he.

"That is lucky," thought Rodolphe. "If I had stayed here another five minutes I should have had more sentiment in my breast than is to be found on the banks of the Rhine or in Alphonse Karr's romances."

And he hastened from the gardens humming a sentimental ballad that was for him the *Marseillaise* of love.

Half an hour later, goodness knows how, he was at the Prado, seated before a glass of punch and talking with a tall fellow celebrated on account of his nose, which had the singular privilege of being aquiline when seen sideways, and a snub when viewed in front. It was a nose that was not devoid of sharpness, and had a sufficiency of gallant adventures to be in such a case to give good advice and be useful to its friend.

"So," said Alexander Schaunard, the man with the nose, "you are in love."

"Yes, my dear fellow, it seized on me, just now, suddenly, like a bad toothache in the heart."

"Pass me the tobacco," said Alexander.

"Fancy," continued Rodolphe, "for the last two hours I have met nothing but lovers, men and women in couples. I had the notion of going into the Luxembourg Gardens, where I saw all manner of phantasmagorias, that stirred my heart extraordinarily. Ellegies are bursting from me, I bleat and I coo; I am undergoing a metamorphosis, and am half lamb half turtle dove. Look at me a bit, I must have wool and feathers."

"What have you been drinking?" said Alexander impatiently, "you are chaffing me."

"I assure you that I am quite cool," replied Rodolphe. "That is to say, no. But I will announce to you that I must embrace something. You see, Alexander, it is not good for man to live alone, in short, you must help me to find a companion. We will stroll through the ballroom, and the first girl I point out to you, you must go and tell her that I love her."

"Why don't you go and tell her yourself?" replied Alexander in his magnificent nasal bass.

"Eh? my dear fellow," said Rodolphe. "I can assure you that I have quite forgot how one sets about saying that sort of thing. In all my love stories it has been my friends who have written the preface, and sometimes even the *denouement*; I never know how to begin."

"It is enough to know how to end," said Alexander, "but I understand you. I knew a girl who loved the oboe, perhaps you would suit her."

"Ah!" said Rodolphe. "I should like her to have white gloves and blue eyes."

"The deuce, blue eyes, I won't say no—but gloves—you know that we can't have everything at once. However, let us go into the aristocratic regions."

"There," said Rodolphe, as they entered the saloon favored by the fashionables of the place, "there is one who seems nice and quiet," and he pointed out a young girl fairly well dressed who was seated in a corner.

"Very good," replied Alexander, "keep a little in the background, I am going to launch the fire-ship of passion for you. When it is necessary to put in an appearance I will call you."

For ten minutes Alexander conversed with the girl, who from time to time broke out in a joyous burst of laughter, and ended by casting towards Rodolphe a smiling glance which said plainly enough, "Come, your advocate has won the cause."

"Come," said Alexander, "the victory is ours, the little one is no doubt far from cruel, but put on an air of simplicity to begin with."

"You have no need to recommend me to do that."

"Then give me some tobacco," said Alexander, "and go and sit down beside her."

"Good heavens," said the young girl when Rodolphe had taken his place by her side, "how funny you friend is, his voice is like a trumpet."

"That is because he is a musician."

Two hours later Rodolphe and his companion halted in front of a house in the Rue St. Denis.

"It is here that I live," said the girl.

"Well, my dear Louise, when and where shall I see you again?"

"At your place at eight o'clock tomorrow evening."

"For sure?"

"Here is my pledge," replied Louise, holding up her rosy cheek to Rodolphe's, who eagerly tasted this ripe fruit of youth and health.

Rodolphe went home perfectly intoxicated.

"Ah!" said he, striding up and down his room, "it can't go off like that, I must write some verses."

The next morning his porter found in his room some thirty sheets of paper, at the top of which stretched in solitary majesty of line—

"Ah; love, oh! love, fair prince of youth."

That morning, contrary to his habits, Rodolphe had risen very early, and although he had slept very little, he got up at once.

"Ah!" he exclaimed, "today is the great day. But then twelve hours to wait. How shall I fill up these twelve eternities?"

And as his glance fell on his desk he seemed to see his pen wriggle as though intending to say to him "Work."

"Ah! yes, work indeed! A fig for prose. I won't stop here, it reeks of ink."

He went off and settled himself in a cafe where he was sure not to meet any friends.

"They would see that I am in love," he thought, "and shape my ideal for me in advance."

After a very brief repast he was off to the railway station, and got into a train. Half an hour later he was in the woods of Ville d'Avray.

Rodolphe strolled about all day, let loose amongst rejuvenated nature, and only returned to Paris at nightfall.

After having put the temple which was to receive his idol in nature, Rodolphe arrayed himself for the occasion, greatly regretting not being able to dress in white.

From seven to eight o'clock he was a prey to the sharp fever of expectation. A slow torture, that recalled to him the old days and the old loves which had sweetened them. Then, according to habit, he already began to dream of an exalted passion, a love affair in ten volumes, a genuine lyric with moonlight, setting suns, meetings beneath the willows, jealousies, sighs and all the rest. He was like this every time chance brought a woman to his door, and not one had left him without bearing away any aureola about her head and a necklace of tears about her neck.

"They would prefer new boots or a bonnet," his friend remarked to him.

But Rodolphe persisted, and up to this time the numerous blunders he had made had not sufficed to cure him. He was always awaiting a woman who would consent to pose as an idol, an angel in a velvet gown, to whom he could at his leisure address sonnets written on willow leaves.

At length Rodolphe heard the "holy hour" strike, and as the last stroke sounded he fancied he saw the Cupid and Psyche surmounting his clock entwine their alabaster arms about one another. At the same moment two timid taps were given at the door.

Rodolphe went and opened it. It was Louise.

"You see I have kept my word," said she.

Rodolphe drew the curtain and lit a fresh candle.

During this operation the girl had removed her bonnet and shawl, which she went and placed on the bed. The dazzling whiteness of the sheets caused her to smile, and almost to blush.

Louise was rather pleasing than pretty; her fresh colored face presented an attractive blending of simplicity and archness. It was something like an outline of Greuze touched up by Gavarni. All her youthful attractions were cleverly set off by a toilette which, although very simple, attested in her that innate science of coquetry which all women possess from their first swaddling clothes to their bridal robe. Louise appeared besides to have made an especial study of the theory of attitudes, and assumed before Rodolphe, who examined her with the artistic eye, a number of seductive poses. Her neatly shod feet were of satisfactory smallness, even for a romantic lover smitten by Andalusian or Chinese miniatures. As to her hands, their softness attested idleness. In fact, for six months past she had no longer any reason to fear needle pricks. In short, Louise was one of those fickle birds of passage who from fancy, and often from necessity, make for a day, or rather a night, their nest in the garrets of the students' quarter, and remain there willingly for a few days, if one knows how to retain them by a whim or by some ribbons.

After having chatted for an hour with Louise, Rodolphe showed her, as an example, the group of Cupid and Psyche.

"Isn't it Paul and Virginia?"

"Yes," replied Rodolphe, who did not want to vex her at the outset by contradicting her.

"They are very well done," said Louise.

"Alas!" thought Rodolphe, gazing at her, "the poor child is not up to much as regards literature. I am sure that her only orthography is that of the heart. I must buy her a dictionary."

However, as Louise complained of her boots incommoding her, he obligingly helped her to unlace them.

All at once the light went out.

"Hallo!" exclaimed Rodolphe, "who has blown the candle out?"

A joyful burst of laughter replied to him.

A few days later Rodolphe met one of his friends in the street.

"What are you up to?" said the latter. "One no longer sees anything of you."

"I am studying the poetry of intimacy," replied Rodolphe.

The poor fellow spoke the truth. He sought from Louise more than the poor girl could give him. An oaten pipe, she had not the strains of a lyre. She spoke to, so to say, the jargon of love, and Rodolphe insisted upon speaking the classic language. Thus they scarcely understood each other.

A week later, at the same ball at which she had found Rodolphe, Louise met a fair young fellow, who danced with her several times, and at the close of the entertainment took her home with him.

He was a second year's student. He spoke the prose of pleasure very fluently, and had good eyes and a well-lined pocket.

Louise asked him for ink and paper, and wrote to Rodolphe a letter couched as follows:—

"Do not rekkon on me at all. I sende you a kiss for the last time.

Good bye
Louise

As Rodolphe was reading this letter on reaching home in the evening, his light suddenly went out.

"Hallo!" said he, reflectively, "it is the candle I first lit on the evening that Louise came—it was bound to finish with our union. If I had known I would have chosen a longer one," he added, in a tone of half annoyance, half of regret, and he placed his mistress' note in a drawer, which he sometimes styled the catacomb of his loves.

One day, being at Marcel's, Rodolphe picked up from the ground to light his pipe with, a scrap of paper on which he recognized his handwriting and the orthography of Louise.

"I have," said he to his friend, "an autograph of the same person, only there are two mistakes the less than in yours. Does not that prove that she loved me better than you?"

"That proves that you are a simpleton," replied Marcel. "White arms and shoulders have no need of grammar."

IV

ALI RODOLPHE; OR, THE TURK PERFORCE

Ostracized by an inhospitable proprietor, Rodolphe had for some time been leading a life compared with which the existence of a cloud is rather stationary. He practiced assiduously the arts of going to bed without supper, and supping without going to bed. He often dined with Duke Humphrey, and generally slept at the sign of a clear sky. Still, amid all these crosses and troubles, two things never forsook him; his good humor and the manuscript of "The Avenger," a drama which had gone the rounds of all the theaters in Paris.

One day Rodolphe, who had been jugged for some slight choreographic extravagances, stumbled upon an uncle of his, one Monetti, a stove maker and smokey chimney doctor, and sargeant of the National Guard, whom he had not seen for an age. Touched by his nephew's misfortunes, Uncle Monetti promised to ameliorate his position. We shall see how, if the reader is not afraid of mounting six stories.

Take note of the banister, then, and follow. Up we go! Whew! One hundred and twenty-five steps! Here we are at last. One more step, and we are in the room; one more yet, and we should be out of it again. It's little, but high up, with the advantages of good air and a fine prospect.

The furniture is composed of two French stoves, several German ditto, some ovens on the economic plan, (especially if you never make fire in them,) a dozen stove pipes, some red clay, some sheet iron, and a whole host of heating apparatus. We may mention, to complete the inventory, a hammock suspended from two nails inserted in the wall, a three-legged garden chair, a candlestick adorned with its *bobeche*, and some other similar objects of elegant art. As to the second room—that is to say, the balcony—two dwarf cypresses, in pots, make a park of it for fine weather.

At the moment of our entry, the occupant of the premises, a young man, dressed like a Turk of the Comic Opera, is finishing a repast, in which he shamelessly violates the law of the Prophet. Witness a bone that was once a ham, and a bottle that has been full of wine. His meal over, the young Turk stretches himself on the floor in true Eastern style, and begins carelessly to smoke a *narghile*. While abandoning himself to this Asiatic luxury, he passes his hand from time to time over the back of a magnificent Newfoundland dog, who would doubtless respond to its caresses where he not also in terra cotta, to match the rest of the furniture.

Suddenly a noise was heard in the entry, and the door opened, admitting a person who, without saying a word, marched straight to one of the stoves, which served the purpose of a secretary, opened the stove-door, and drew out a bundle of papers.

"Hallo!" cried the new-comer, after examining the manuscript attentively, "the chapter on ventilators not finished yet!"

"Allow me to observe, uncle," replied the Turk, "the chapter on ventilators is one of the most interesting in your book, and requires to be studied with care. I am studying it."

"But you miserable fellow, you are always saying that same thing. And the chapter on stoves—where are you in that?"

"The stoves are going on well, but, by the way, uncle, if you could give me a little wood, it wouldn't hurt me. It is a little Siberia here. I am so cold, that I make a thermometer go down below zero by just looking at it."

"What! you've used up one faggot already?"

"Allow me to remark again, uncle, there are different kinds of faggots, and yours was the very smallest kind."

"I'll send you an economic log—that keeps the heat."

"Exactly, and doesn't give any."

"Well," said the uncle as he went off, "you shall have a little faggot, and I must have my chapter on stoves for tomorrow."

"When I have fire, that will inspire me," answered the Turk as he heard himself locked in.

Were we making a tragedy, this would be the time to bring in a confidant. Noureddin or Osman he should be called, and he should advance towards our hero with an air at the same time discreet and patronizing, to console him for his reverses, by means of these three verses:

> *'What saddening grief, my Lord, assails you now?*
> *Why sits this pallor on your noble brow?*
> *Does Allah lend your plans no helping hand?*
> *Or cruel Ali, with severe command,*
> *Remove to other shores the beauteous dame,*
> *Who charmed your eyes and set your heart on flame!'*

But we are not making a tragedy, so we must do without our confidant, though he would be very convenient.

Our hero is not what he appears to be. The turban does not make the Turk. This young man is our friend Rodolphe, entertained by his uncle, for whom he is drawing up a manual of "The Perfect Chimney Constructor." In fact, Monsieur Monetti, an enthusiast for his art, had consecrated his days to this science of chimneys. One day he formed the idea of drawing up, for the benefit of posterity, a theoretic code of the principles of that art, in the practice of which he so excelled, and he had chosen his nephew, as we have seen, to frame the substance of his ideas in an intelligible form. Rodolphe was found in board, lodging, and other contingencies, and at the completion of the manual was to receive a recompense of three hundred francs.

In the beginning, to encourage his nephew, Monetti had generously made him an advance of fifty francs. But Rodolphe, who had not seen so much silver together for nearly a year, half crazy, in company with his money, stayed out three days, and on the fourth came home alone! Thereupon the uncle, who was in haste to have his "Manual" finished inasmuch as he hoped to get a patent for it, dreading some new diversion on his nephew's part, determined to make him work by preventing him from going out. To this end he carried off his garments, and left him instead the disguise under which we have seen him. Nevertheless, the famous "Manual" continued to make very slow progress, for Rodolphe had no genius whatever for this kind of literature. The uncle avenged himself for this lazy indifference on the great subject of chimneys by making his nephew undergo a host of annoyances. Sometimes he cut short his commons, and frequently stopped the supply of tobacco.

One Sunday, after having sweated blood and ink upon the great chapter of ventilators, Rodolphe broke the pen, which was burning his fingers, and went out to walk—in his "park." As if on purpose to plague him, and excite his envy the more, he could not cast a single look about him without perceiving the figure of a smoker on every window.

On the gilt balcony of a new house opposite, an exquisite in his dressing gown was biting off the end of an aristocratic "Pantellas" cigar. A story above, an artist was sending before him an odorous cloud of Turkish tobacco from his amber-mouthed pipe. At the window of a *brasserie*, a fat German was crowning a foaming tankard, and emitting, with the regularity of a machine, the dense puffs that escaped from his meershaum. On the other side, a group of workmen were singing as they passed on their way to the barriers, their "throat-scorchers" between their teeth. Finally, all the other pedestrians visible in the street were smoking.

"Woe is me!" sighed Rodolphe, "except myself and my uncle's chimneys, all creation is smoking at this hour!" And he rested his forehead on the bar of the balcony, and thought how dreary life was.

Suddenly, a burst of long and musical laughter parted under his feet. Rodolphe bent forward a little, to discover the source of this volley of gaiety, and perceived that he had been perceived by the tenant of the story beneath him, Mademoiselle Sidonia, of the Luxembourg Theater. The young lady advanced to the front of her balcony, rolling between her fingers, with the dexterity of a Spaniard, a paper-full of light-colored tobacco, which she took from a bag of embroidered velvet.

"What a sweet cigar girl it is!" murmured Rodolphe, in an ecstacy of contemplation.

"Who is this Ali Baba?" thought Mademoiselle Sidonia on her part. And she meditated on a pretext for engaging in conversation with Rodolphe, who was himself trying to do the very same.

"Bless me!" cried the lady, as if talking to herself, "what a bore! I've no matches!"

"Allow me to offer you some, mademoiselle," said Rodolphe, letting fall on the balcony two or three lucifers rolled up in paper.

"A thousand thanks," replied Sidonia, lighting her cigarette.

"Pray, mademoiselle," continued Rodolphe, "in exchange for the trifling service which my good angel has permitted me to render you, may I ask you to do me a favor?"

"Asking already," thought the actress, as she regarded Rodolphe with more attention. "They say these Turks are fickle, but very agreeable. Speak sir," she continued, raising her head towards the young man, "what do you wish?"

"The charity of a little tobacco, mademoiselle, only one pipe. I have not smoked for two whole days."

"Most willingly, but how? Will you take the trouble to come downstairs?"

"Alas! I can't! I am shut up here, but am still free to employ a very simple means." He fastened his pipe to a string, and let it glide down to her balcony, where Sidonia filled it profusely herself. Rodolphe then proceeded, with much ease and deliberation, to remount his pipe, which arrived without accident. "Ah, mademoiselle!" he exclaimed, "how much better this pipe would have seemed, if I could have lighted it at your eyes!"

It was at least the hundredth edition of this amiable pleasantry, but Sidonia found it superb for all that, and thought herself bound to reply, "You flatter me."

"I assure you, mademoiselle, in right-down earnest, I think you handsomer than all the Three Graces together."

"Decidedly, Ali Baba is very polite," thought Sidonia. "Are you really a Turk?" she asked Rodolphe.

"Not by profession," he replied, "but by necessity. I am a dramatic author."

"I am an artist," she replied, then added, "My dear sir and neighbor, will you do me the honor to dine and spend the evening with me?"

"Alas!" answered Rodolphe, "though your invitation is like opening heaven to me, it is impossible to accept it. As I had the honor to tell you, I am shut up here by my uncle, Monsieur Monetti, stove-maker and chimney doctor, whose secretary I am now."

"You shall dine with me for all that," replied Sidonia. "Listen, I shall re-enter my room, and tap on the ceiling. Look where I strike and you will find the traces of a trap which used to be there, and has since been fastened up. Find the means of removing the piece of wood which closes the hole, and then, although we are each in our own room, we shall be as good as together."

Rodolphe went to work at once. In five minutes a communication was established between the two rooms.

"It is a very little hole," said he, "but there will always be room enough to pass you my heart."

"Now," said Sidonia, "we will go to dinner. Set your table, and I will pass you the dishes."

Rodolphe let down his turban by a string, and brought it back laden with eatables, then the poet and the actress proceeded to dine—on their respective floors. Rodolphe devoured the pie with his teeth, and Sidonia with his eyes.

"Thanks to you, mademoiselle," he said, when their repast was finished, "my stomach is satisfied. Can you not also satisfy the void of my heart, which has been so long empty?"

"Poor fellow!" said Sidonia, and climbing on a piece of furniture, she lifted up her hand to Rodolphe's lips, who gloved it with kisses.

"What a pity," he exclaimed, "you can't do as St. Denis, who had the privilege of carrying his head in his hands!"

To the dinner succeeded a sentimental literary conversation. Rodolphe spoke of "The Avenger," and Sidonia asked him to read it. Leaning over the hole, he began declaiming his drama to the actress, who, to hear better, had put her arm chair on the top of a chest of drawers. She pronounced "The Avenger" a masterpiece, and having some influence at the theater, promised Rodolphe to get his piece received.

But at the most interesting moment a step was heard in the entry, about as light as that of the Commander's ghost in "Don Juan." It was Uncle Monetti. Rodolphe had only just time to shut the trap.

"Here," said Monetti to his nephew, "this letter has been running after you for a month."

"Uncle! Uncle!" cried Rodolphe, "I am rich at last! This letter informs me that I have gained a prize of three hundred francs, given by an academy of floral games. Quick! my coat and my things! Let me go to gather my laurels. They await me at the Capitol!"

"And my chapter on ventilators?" said Monetti, coldly.

"I like that! Give me my things, I tell you; I can't go out so!"

"You shall go out when my 'Manual' is finished," quoth the uncle, shutting up his nephew under lock and key.

Rodolphe, when left alone, did not hesitate on the course to take. He transformed his quilt into a knotted rope, which he fastened firmly to his own balcony, and in spite of the risk, descended by this extempore ladder upon Mademoiselle Sidonia's.

"Who is there?" she cried, on hearing Rodolphe knock at her window.

"Hush!" he replied, "open!"

"What do you want? Who are you?"

"Can you ask? I am the author of 'The Avenger,' come to look for my heart, which I dropped through the trap into your room."

"Rash youth!" said the actress, "you might have killed yourself!"

"Listen, Sidonia," continued Rodolphe, showing her the letter he just received. "You see, wealth and glory smile on me, let love do the same!"

THE FOLLOWING MORNING, BY MEANS of a masculine disguise, which Sidonia procured for him, Rodolphe was enabled to escape from his uncle's lodging. He ran to the secretary of the academy of floral games, to receive a crown of gold sweetbrier, worth three hundred francs, which lived

> "—as live roses the fairest—
> The space of a day."

A month after, Monsieur Monetti was invited by his nephew to assist at the first representation of "The Avenger." Thanks to the talent of Mademoiselle Sidonia, the piece had a run of seventeen nights, and brought in forty francs to its author.

Some time later—it was in the warm season—Rodolphe lodged in the Avenue St. Cloud, third tree as you go out of the Bois de Boulogne, on the fifth branch.

V

The Carlovingian Coin

Towards the end of December the messengers of Bidault's agency were entrusted with the distribution of about a hundred copies of a letter of invitation, of which we certify that the following to be a true and genuine copy:—

M.M. Rodolphe and Marcel request the honor of your company on Saturday next, Christmas Eve. Fun!
P.S. Life is short!

Program of the Entertainment

Part I

7 o'clock—Opening of the saloons. Brisk and witty conversation.
8.—Appearance of the talented authors of "The Mountain in Labor," comedy refused at the Odeon Theater.
8:30.—M. Alexander Schaunard, the eminent virtuoso, will play his imitative symphony, "The Influence of Blue in Art," on the piano.
9.—First reading of the essay on the "Abolition of the penalty of tragedy."
9:30.—Philosophical and metaphysical argument between M. Colline, hyperphysical philosopher, and M. Schaunard. To avoid any collision between the two antagonists, they will both be securely fastened.
10.—M. Tristan, master of literature, will narrate his early loves, accompanied on the piano by M. Alexander Schaunard.
10:30.—Second reading of the essay on the "Abolition of the penalty of tragedy."
11.—Narration of a cassowary hunt by a foreign prince.

Part II

Midnight.—M. Marcel, historical painter, will execute with his eyes bandaged an impromptu sketch in chalk of the meeting of Voltaire and Napolean in the Elyssian Fields. M. Rodolphe will also improvise a parallel between the author of Zaire, and the victor of Austerlitz.

12:30.—M. Gustave Colline, in a decent undress, will give an imitation of the athletic games of the 4th Olympiad.

1.—Third reading of the essay on the "Abolition of the penalty of tragedy," and subscription on behalf of tragic authors who will one day find themselves out of employment.

2.—Commencement of games and organization of quadrilles to last until morning.

6.—Sunrise and final chorus.

During the whole of entertainment ventilators will be in action.

N.B. Anyone attempting to read or recite poetry will be summarily ejected and handed over to the police. The guests are equally requested not to help themselves to the candle ends.

Two days later, copies of this invitation were circulating among the lower depths of art and literature, and created a profound sensation.

There were, however, amongst the invited guests, some who cast doubt upon the splendor of the promises made by the two friends.

"I am very skeptical about it," said one of them. "I have sometimes gone to Rodolphe's Thursdays in the Rue de la Tour d'Auvergne, when one could only sit on anything morally, and where all one had to drink was a little filtered water in eclectic pottery."

"This time," said another, "it is really serious. Marcel has shown me the program of the fete, and the effect will be magical."

"Will there be any ladies?"

"Yes. Phemie Teinturiere has asked to be queen of the fete and Schaunard is to bring some ladies of position."

This is in brief the origin of this fete which caused such stupefaction in the Bohemian world across the water. For about a year past, Marcel and Rodolphe had announced this sumptuous gala which was always to take place "next Saturday," but painful circumstances had obliged their promise to extend over fifty-two weeks, so that they had come to pass of not being able to take a step without encountering some ironical remark from one of their friends, amongst whom there were some indiscreet enough to put forward energetic demand for its fulfillment. The matter beginning to assume the character of a plague, the two friends resolved to put an end to it by liquidating the undertaking into which they had entered. It was thus that they sent out the invitation given above.

"Now," said Rodolphe, "there is no drawing back. We have burnt our ships, and we have before us just a week to find the hundred francs that are indispensable to do the thing properly."

"Since we must have them, we shall," replied Marcel.

And with the insolent confidence which they had in luck, the two friends went to sleep, convinced that their hundred francs were already on the way, the way of impossibility.

However, as on the day before that appointed for the party, nothing as of yet had turned up, Rodolphe thought perhaps, be safer to give luck a helping hand, unless he were to be discredited forever, when the time came to light up. To facilitate matters the two friends progressively modified the sumptuosity of the program they had imposed upon themselves.

And proceeding from modification to modification, after having seriously reduced the item "cakes," and carefully revised and pruned down the item "liquors," the total cost was reduced to fifteen francs.

The problem was simplified, but not yet solved.

"Come, come," said Rodolphe, "we must now have recourse to strong measures, we cannot cry off this time."

"No, that is impossible," replied Marcel.

"How long is it since I have heard the story of the Battle of Studzianka?"

"About two months."

"Two months, good, that is a decent interval; my uncle will have no ground for grumbling. I will go tomorrow and hear his account of that engagement, that will be five francs for certain."

"I," said Marcel, "will go and sell a deserted manor house to old Medicis. That will make another five francs. If I have time enough to put in three towers and a mill, it will perhaps run to ten francs, and our budget will be complete."

And the two friends fell asleep dreaming that the Princess Belgiojoso begged them to change their reception day, in order not to rob her of her customary guests.

Awake at dawn, Marcel took a canvas and rapidly set to work to build up a deserted manor house, an article which he was in the habit of supplying to a broker of the Place de Carrousel. On his side, Rodolphe went to pay a visit to his Uncle Monetti, who shone in the story of the Retreat from Moscow, and to whom Rodolphe accorded five or six times in course of the year, when matters were really serious, the satisfaction of narrating his campaigns, in return for a small loan which the veteran stove maker did not refuse too obstinately when due enthusiasm was displayed in listening to his narrations.

About two o'clock, Marcel with hanging head and a canvas under his arm, met on the Place de Carrousel Rodolphe, who was returning from his uncle's, and whose bearing also presaged ill news.

"Well," asked Marcel, "did you succeed?"

"No, my uncle has gone to Versailles. And you?"

"That beast of a Medicis does not want any more ruined manor houses. He wants me to do him a Bombardment of Tangiers."

"Our reputations are ruined forever if we do not give this party," murmured Rodolphe. "What will my friend, the influential critic, think if I make him put on a white tie and yellow kids for nothing."

And both went back to the studio, a prey to great uneasiness.

At that moment the clock of a neighbor struck four.

"We have only three hours before us," said Rodolphe despondingly.

"But," said Marcel, going up to his friend, "are you quite sure, certain sure, that we have no money left anywhere hereabout? Eh?"

"Neither here, nor elsewhere. Where do you suppose it could come from?"

"If we looked under the furniture, in the stuffing of the arm chairs? They say that the emigrant noblemen used to hide their treasures in the days of Robespierre. Who can tell? Perhaps our arm chair belonged to an emigrant nobleman, and besides, it is so hard that the idea has often occurred to me that it must be stuffed with metal. Will you dissect it?"

"This is mere comedy," replied Rodolphe, in a tone in which severity was mingled with indulgence.

Suddenly Marcel, who had gone on rummaging in every corner of the studio, uttered a loud cry of triumph.

"We are saved!" he exclaimed. "I was sure that there was money here. Behold!" and he showed Rodolphe a coin as large as a crown piece, and half eaten away by rust and verdigris.

It was a Carlovingian coin of some artistic value. The legend, happily intact, showed the date of Charlemagne's reign.

"That, that's worth thirty sous," said Rodolphe, with a contemptuous glance at his friend's find.

"Thirty sous well employed will go a great way," replied Marcel. "With twelve hundred men Bonaparte made ten thousand Austrians lay down their arms. Skill can replace numbers. I will go and swap the Carlovingian crown at Daddy Medicis'. Is there not anything else saleable here? Suppose I take the plaster cast of the tibia of Jaconowski, the Russian drum major."

"Take the tibia. But it is a nuisance, there will not be a single ornament left here."

During Marcel's absence, Rodolphe, his mind made up that that party should be given in any case, went in search of his friend Colline, the hyperphysical philosopher, who lived hard by.

"I have come," said he, "to ask you to do me a favor. As host I must positively have a black swallow-tail, and I have not got one; lend me yours."

"But," said Colline hesitating, "as a guest I shall want my black swallow-tail too."

"I will allow you to come in a frock coat."

"That won't do. You know very well I have never had a frock coat."

"Well, then, it can be settled in another way. If needs be, you need not come to my party, and can lend me your swallow-tail."

"That would be unpleasant. I am on the program, and must not be lacking."

"There are plenty of other things that will be lacking," said Rodolphe. "Lend me your black swallow-tail, and if you will come, come as you like; in your shirt sleeves, you will pass for a faithful servant."

"Oh no!" said Colline, blushing. "I will wear my great coat. But all the same, it is very unpleasant." And as he saw Rodolphe had already seized on the famous black swallow-tail, he called out to him, "Stop a bit. There are some odds and ends in the pockets."

Colline's swallow-tail deserves a word or two. In the first place it was of a decided blue, and it was from habit that Colline spoke of it as "my black swallow-tail." And as he was the only one of the band owning a dress coat, his friends were likewise in the habit of saying, when speaking of the philosopher's official garment, "Colline's black swallow-tail." In addition to this, this famous garment had a special cut, the oddest imaginable. The tails, very long, and attached to a very short waist, had two pockets, positive gulfs, in which Colline was accustomed to store some thirty of the volumes which he eternally carried about with him. This caused his friends to remark that during the time that the public libraries were closed, savants and literary men could go and refer to the skirts of Colline's swallow-tail—a library always open.

That day, extraordinary to relate, Colline's swallow-tail only contained a quarto volume of Bayle, a treatise on the hyperphysical faculties in three volumes, a volume of Condillac, two of Swedenborg and Pope's "Essay on Man." When he had cleared his bookcase-garment, he allowed Rodolphe to clothe himself in it.

"Hallo!" said the latter, "the left pocket still feels very heavy; you have left something in it."

"Ah!" exclaimed Colline, "that is so. I forgot to empty the foreign languages pocket."

And he took out from this two Arabic grammars, a Malay dictionary, and a stock breeder's manual in Chinese, his favorite reading.

When Rodolphe returned home he found Marcel playing pitch-and-toss with three five franc pieces. At first Rodolphe refused his friend's proferred hand—he thought some crime had been committed.

"Let us make haste, let us make haste," said Marcel, "we have the fifteen francs required. This is how it happened. I met an antiquary at Medicis'. When he saw the coin he was almost taken ill; it was the only one wanting in his cabinet. He had sent everywhere to get this vacancy filled up, and had lost all hope. Thus, when he had thoroughly examined my Carlovingian crown piece, he did not hesitate for a moment to offer me five francs for it. Medicis nudged me with his elbow; a look from him completed the business. He meant, 'share the profits of the sale, and I will bid against him.' We ran it up to thirty francs. I gave the Jew fifteen, and here are the rest. Now our guests may come; we are in a position to dazzle them. Hallo! You have got a swallow-tail!"

"Yes," said Rodolphe, "Colline's swallow-tail." And as he was feeling for his handkerchief, Rodolphe pulled out a small volume in a Tartar dialect, overlooked in the foreign literature pocket.

The two friends at once proceeded to make their preparations. The studio was set in order, a fire kindled in the stove, the stretcher of a picture, garnished with composite candles, suspended from the ceiling as a chandelier, and a writing table placed in the middle of the studio to serve as a rostrum for the orators. The solitary armchair, which was to be reserved for the influential critic, was placed in front of it, and upon a table were arranged all the books, romances, poems, pamphlets, &c., the authors of which were to honor the company with their presence.

In order to avoid any collision between members of the different schools of literature, the studio had been, moreover, divided into four compartments, at the entrance to each of which could be read, on four hurriedly manufactured placards, the inscriptions—"Poets," "Prose Writers," "Classic School," and "Romantic School."

The ladies were to occupy a space reserved in the middle of the studio.

"Humph! Chairs are lacking," said Rodolphe.

"Oh!" remarked Marcel, "there are several on the landing, fastened along the wall. Suppose we were to gather them."

"Certainly, let us gather them by all means," said Rodolphe, starting off to seize on the chairs, which belonged to some neighbor.

Six o'clock struck: the two friends went off to a hasty dinner, and returned to light up the saloons. They were themselves dazzled by the result. At seven o'clock Schaunard arrived, accompanied by three ladies, who had forgotten their diamonds and their bonnets. One of them wore a red shawl with black spots. Schaunard pointed out this lady particularly to Rodolphe.

"She is a woman accustomed to the best society," said he, "an Englishwoman whom the fall of the Stuarts has driven into exile, she lives in a modest way by giving lessons in English. Her father was Lord Chancellor under Cromwell, she told me, so we must be polite with her. Don't be too familiar."

Numerous footsteps were heard on the stairs. It was the guests arriving. They seemed astonished to see a fire burning in the stove.

Rodolphe's swallow-tail went to greet the ladies, and kissed their hands with a grace worthy of the Regency. When there was a score of persons present, Schaunard asked whether it was not time for a round of drinks.

"Presently," said Marcel. "We are waiting for the arrival of the influential critic to set fire to the punch."

At eight o'clock the whole of the guests had arrived, and the execution of the program commenced. Each item was alternated with a round of drink of some kind, no one ever knew what.

Towards ten o'clock the white waistcoat of the influential critic made its appearance. He only stayed an hour, and was very sober in the consumption of refreshments.

At midnight, as there was no more wood, and it was very cold, the guests who were seated drew lots as to who should cast his chair into the fire.

By one o'clock every one was standing.

Amiable gaiety did not cease to reign amongst the guests. There were no accidents to be regretted, with the exception of a rent in the foreign languages pocket of Colline's swallow-tail and a smack in the face given by Schaunard to the daughter of Cromwell's Lord Chancellor.

This memorable evening was for a week the staple subject of gossip in the district, and Phemie Teinturiere, who had been the queen of the fete, was accustomed to remark, when talking it over with her friends,—

"It was awfully fine. There were composite candles, my dear."

VI

MADEMOISELLE MUSETTE

Mademoiselle Musette was a pretty girl of twenty who shortly after her arrival in Paris had become what many pretty girls become when they have a neat figure, plenty of coquesttishness, a dash of ambition and hardly any education. After having for a long time shone as the star of the supper parties of the Latin Quarter, at which she used to sing in a voice, still very fresh if not very true, a number of country ditties, which earned her the nickname under which she has since been immortalized by one of our neatest rhymsters, Mademoiselle Musette suddenly left the Rue de la Harpe to go and dwell upon the Cytherean heights of the Breda district.

She speedily became one of the foremost of the aristocracy of pleasure and slowly made her way towards that celebrity which consists in being mentioned in the columns devoted to Parisian gossip, or lithographed at the printsellers.

However Mademoiselle Musette was an exception to the women amongst whom she lived. Of a nature instinctively elegant and poetical, like all women who are really such, she loved luxury and the many enjoyments which it procures; her coquetry warmly coveted all that was handsome and distinguished; a daughter of the people, she would not have been in any way out of her element amidst the most regal sumptuosity. But Mademoiselle Musette, who was young and pretty, had never consented to be the mistress of any man who was not like herself young and handsome. She had been known bravely to refuse the magnificient offers of an old man so rich that he was styled the Peru of the Chaussee d'Antin, and who had offered a golden ladder to the gratification of her fancies. Intelligent and witty, she had also a repugnance for fools and simpletons, whatever might be their age, their title and their name.

Musette, therefore, was an honest and pretty girl, who in love adopted half of Champfort's famous amphoris, "Love is the interchange of two caprices." Thus her connection had never been preceded by one of those shameful bargains which dishonor modern gallantry. As she herself said, Musette played fair and insisted that she should receive full change for her sincerity.

But if her fancies were lively and spontaneous, they were never durable enough to reach the height of a passion. And the excessive mobility of her caprices, the little care she took to look at the purse and the boots of those who wished to be considered amongst them, brought about a corresponding mobility in her existence which was a perpetual alternation of blue broughams and omnibuses, first floors and fifth stories, silken gowns and cotton frocks. Oh cleaning girl! Living poem of youth with ringing laugh and joyous song! Tender heart beating for one and all beneath your half-open bodice! Ah Mademoiselle Musette, sister of Bernette and Mimi Pinson, it would need the pen of Alfred de Musset to fitly narrate your careless and vagabond course amidst the flowery paths of youth; and he would certainly have celebrated you, if like me, he had heard you sing in your pretty false notes, this couplet from one of your favorite ditties:

> *"It was a day in Spring*
> *When love I strove to sing*
> *Unto a nut brown maid.*
> *O'er face as fair as dawn*
> *Cast a bewitching shade."*

The story we are about to tell is one of the most charming in the life of this charming adventuress who wore so many green gowns.

At a time when she was the mistress of a young Counsellor of State, who had gallantly placed in her hands the key of his ancestral coffers, Mademoiselle Musette was in the habit of receiving once a week in her pretty drawing room in the Rue de la Bruyere. These evenings resembled most Parisian evenings, with the difference that people amused themselves. When there was not enough room they sat on one another's knees, and it often happened that the same glass served for two. Rodolphe, who was a friend of Musette and never anything more than a friend, without either of them knowing why—Rodolphe asked leave to bring his friend, the painter Marcel.

"A young fellow of talent," he added, "for whom the future is embroidering his Academician's coat."

"Bring him," said Musette.

The evening they were to go together to Musette's Rodolphe called on Marcel to fetch him. The artist was at his toilet.

"What!" said Rodolphe, "you are going into society in a colored shirt?"

"Does that shock custom?" observed Marcel quietly.

"Shock custom, it stuns it."

"The deuce," said Marcel, looking at his shirt, which displayed a pattern of boars pursued by dogs, on a blue ground. "I have not another here. Oh! Bah! So much the worse, I will put on a collar, and as 'Methuselah' buttons to the neck no one will see the color of my lines."

"What!" said Rodolphe uneasy, "you are going to wear 'Methuselah'?"

"Alas!" replied Marcel, "I must, God wills it and my tailor too; besides it has a new set of buttons and I have just touched it up with ivory black."

"Methuselah" was merely Marcel's dress coat. He called it so because it was the oldest garment of his wardrobe. "Methuselah" was cut in the fashion of four years' before and was, besides of a hideous green, but Marcel declared that it looked black by candlelight.

In five minutes Marcel was dressed, he was attired in the most perfect bad taste, the get-up of an art student going into society.

M. Casimir Bonjour will never be so surprised the day he learns his election as a member of the Institute as were Rodolphe and Marcel on reaching Mademoiselle Musette's.

This is the reason for their astonishment: Mademoiselle Musette who for some time past had fallen out with her lover the Counsellor of State, had been abandoned by him at a very critical juncture. Legal proceedings having been taken by her creditors and her landlord, her furniture had been seized and carried down into the courtyard in order to be taken away and sold on the following day. Despite this incident Mademoiselle Musette had not for a moment the idea of giving her guests the slip and did not put off her party. She had the courtyard arranged as a drawing room, spread a carpet on the pavement, prepared everything as usual, dressed to receive company, and invited all the tenants to her little entertainment, towards which Heaven contributed its illumination.

This jest had immense success, never had Musette's evenings displayed such go and gaiety; they were still dancing and singing when the porters came to take away furniture and carpets and the company was obliged to withdraw.

Musette bowed her guests out, singing:

> *"They will laugh long and loud, tralala,*
> *At my Thursday night's crowd*
> *They will laugh long and loud, tralala."*

Marcel and Rodolphe alone remained with Musette, who ascended to her room where there was nothing left but the bed.

"Ah, but my adventure is no longer such a lively one after all," said Musette. "I shall have to take up my quarters out of doors."

"Oh madame!" said Marcel, "if I had the gifts of Plutus I should like to offer you a temple finer than that of Solomon, but—"

"You are not Plutus. All the same I thank you for your good intentions. Ah!" she added, glancing around the room, "I was getting bored here, and then the furniture was old. I had had it nearly six months. But that is not all, after the dance one should sup."

"Let us sup-pose," said Marcel, who had an itch of punning, above all in the morning, when he was terrible.

As Rodolphe had gained some money at the lansquenet played during the evening, he carried off Musette and Marcel to a restaurant which was just opening.

After breakfast, the three, who had no inclination for sleep, spoke of finishing the day in the country, and as they found themselves close to the railway station they got into the first train that started, which landed them at Saint Germain.

During the whole of the night of the party and all of the rest of the day Marcel, who was gunpowder which a single glance sufficed to kindle, had been violently smitten by Mademoiselle Musette and paid her "highly-colored court," as he put it to Rodolphe. He even went so far as to propose to the pretty girl to buy her furniture handsomer than the last with the result of the sale of his famous picture, "The Passage of the Red Sea." Hence the artist saw with pain the moment arrive when it became necessary to part from Musette, who whilst allowing him to kiss her hands, neck and sundry other accessories, gently repulsed him every time that he tried to violently burgle her heart.

On reaching Paris, Rodolphe left his friend with the girl, who asked the artist to see her to her door.

"Will you allow me to call on you?" asked Marcel, "I will paint your portrait."

"My dear fellow," replied she, "I cannot give you my address, since tomorrow I may no longer have one, but I will call and see you, and I will mend your coat, which has a hole so big that one could shoot the moon through it."

"I will await your coming like that of the messiah," said Marcel.

"Not quite so long," said Musette, laughing.

"What a charming girl," said Marcel to himself, as he slowly walked away. "She is the Goddess of Mirth. I will make two holes in my coat."

He had not gone twenty paces before he felt himself tapped on the shoulder. It was Mademoiselle Musette.

"My dear Monsieur Marcel," said she, "are you a true knight?"

"I am. 'Rubens and my lady,' that is my motto."

"Well then, hearken to my woes and pity take, most noble sir," returned Musette, who was slightly tinged with literature, although she murdered grammar in fine style, "the landlord has taken away the key of my room and it is eleven o'clock at night. Do you understand?"

"I understand," said Marcel, offering Musette his arm. He took her to his studio on the Quai aux Fleurs.

Musette was hardly able to keep awake, but she still had strength enough to say to Marcel, taking him by the hand, "You remember what you have promised?"

"Oh Musette! charming creature!" said the artist in a somewhat moved tone, "you are here beneath a hospitable roof, sleep in peace. Good night, I am off."

"Why so?" said Musette, her eyes half closed. "I am not afraid, I can assure you. In the first place, there are two rooms. I will sleep on your sofa."

"My sofa is too hard to sleep on, it is stuffed with carded pebbles. I will give you hospitality here, and ask it for myself from a friend who lives on the same landing. It will be more prudent," said he. "I usually keep my word, but I am twenty-two and you are eighteen, Musette,— and I am off. Good night."

The next morning at eight o'clock Marcel entered her room with a pot of flowers that he had gone and bought in the market. He found Musette, who had thrown herself fully dressed on the bed, and was still sleeping. At the noise made by him she woke, and held out her hand.

"What a good fellow," said she.

"Good fellow," repeated Marcel, "is not that a term of ridicule?"

"Oh!" exclaimed Musette, "why should you say that to me? It is not nice. Instead of saying spiteful things offer me that pretty pot of flowers."

"It is, indeed, for you that I have brought them up," said Marcel. "Take it, and in return for my hospitality sing me one of your songs, the echo of my garret may perhaps retain something of your voice, and I shall still hear you after you have departed."

"Oh! so you want to show me the door?" said Musette. "Listen, Marcel, I do not beat about the bush to say what my thoughts are. You like me and I like you. It is not love, but it is perhaps its seed. Well, I am not going away, I am going to stop here, and I shall stay here as long as the flowers you have just given me remain unfaded."

"Ah!" exclaimed Marcel, "they will fade in a couple of days. If I had known I would have bought immortelles."

For a fortnight Musette and Marcel lived together, and led, although often without money, the most charming life in the world. Musette felt for the artist an affection which had nothing in common with her preceding passions, and Marcel began to fear that he was seriously in love with his mistress. Ignorant that she herself was very much afraid of being equally smitten, he glanced every morning at the condition of the flowers, the death of which was to bring about the severance of their connection, and found it very difficult to account for their continued freshness. But he soon had a key to the mystery. One night, waking up, he no longer found Musette beside him. He rose, hastened into the next room, and perceived his mistress, who profited nightly by his slumbers to water the flowers and hinder them from perishing.

VII

THE BILLOWS OF PACTOLUS

It was the nineteenth of March, 184—. Should Rodolphe reach the age of Methuselah, he will never forget the date; for it was on that day, at three in the afternoon, that our friend issued from a banker's where he had just received five hundred francs in current and sounding specie.

The first use Rodolphe made of this slice of Peru which had fallen into his pocket was not to pay his debts, inasmuch as he had sworn to himself to practice economy and go to no extra expense. He had a fixed idea on this subject, and declared that before thinking of superfluities, one ought to provide for necessaries. Therefore it was that he paid none of his creditors, and bought a Turkish pipe which he had long coveted.

Armed with this purchase, he directed his steps towards the lodging of his friend Marcel, who had for some time given him shelter. As he entered Marcel's studio, Rodolphe's pockets rang like a village-steeple on a grand holiday. On hearing this unusual sound, Marcel supposed it was one of his neighbors, a great speculator, counting his profits on 'Change, and muttered, "There's that impertinent fellow next door beginning his music again! If this is to go on, I shall give notice to the landlord. It's impossible to work with such a noise. It tempts one to quit one's condition of poor artist and turn robber, forty times over."

So, never suspecting that it was his friend Rodolphe changed into a Croesus, Marcel again set to work on his "Passage of the Red Sea," which had been on his easel nearly three years.

Rodolphe, who had not yet spoken, meditating an experiment which he was about to make on his friend, said to himself, "We shall laugh in a minute. Won't it be fun?" and he let fall a five-franc piece on the floor.

Marcel raised his eyes and looked at Rodolphe, who was as grave as an article in the "Revue des deux Mondes." Then he picked up the piece of money with a well-satisfied air, and made a courteous salute to it; for, vagabond artist as he was, he understood the usages of society, and was very civil to strangers. Knowing, moreover, that Rodolphe had gone out to look for money, Marcel, seeing that his friend had succeeded in his operations, contented himself with admiring the result, without inquiring by what means it had been obtained. Accordingly, he went to work again without speaking, and finished drowning an Egyptian in the waves of the Red Sea. As he was terminating this homicide, Rodolphe let fall another piece, laughing in his sleeve at the face the painter was going to make.

At the sonorous sound of the metal, Marcel bounded up as if he had received an electric shock, and cried, "What! Number two!"

A third piece rolled on the floor, then another, then one more; finally a whole quadrille of five-franc pieces were dancing in the room.

Marcel began to show evident signs of mental alienation; and Rodolphe laughed like the pit of a Parisian theatre at the first representation of a very tragical tragedy. Suddenly, and without any warning, he plunged both hands into his pockets, and the money rushed out in a supernatural steeple-chase. It was an inundation of Pactolus; it was Jupiter entering Danae's chamber.

Marcel remained silent, motionless, with a fixed stare; his astonishment was gradually operating upon him a transformation similar to that which the untimely curiosity of Lott's wife brought upon her: by the time that Rodolphe had thrown his last hundred francs on the floor, the painter was petrified all down one side of his body.

Rodolphe laughed and laughed. Compared with his stormy mirth, the thunder of an orchestra of sax-horns would have been no more than the crying of a child at the breast.

Stunned, strangled, stupefied by his emotions, Marcel thought himself in a dream. To drive away the nightmare, he bit his finger till he brought blood, and almost made himself scream with pain. He then perceived that, though trampling upon money, he was perfectly awake. Like a personage in a tragedy, he exclaimed:

"Can I believe my eyes?" and then seizing Rodolphe's hand, he added, "Explain to me this mystery."

"Did I explain it 'twould be one no more."

"Come, now!"

"This gold is the fruit of the sweat of my brow," said Rodolphe, picking up the money and arranging it on the table. He then went a few steps and looked respectfully at the five hundred francs ranged in heaps, thinking to himself, "Now then, my dreams will be realized!"

"There cannot be much less than six thousand francs there," thought Marcel to himself, as he regarded the silver which trembled on the table. "I've an idea! I shall ask Rodolphe to buy my 'Passage of the Red Sea.'"

All at once Rodolphe put himself into a theatrical attitude, and, with great solemnity of voice and gesture, addressed the artist:

"Listen to me, Marcel: the fortune which has dazzled your eyes is not the product of vile maneuvers; I have not sold my pen; I am rich, but honest. This gold, bestowed by a generous hand, I have sworn to use in laboriously acquiring a serious position—such as a virtuous man should occupy. Labor is the most scared of duties—"

"And the horse, the noblest of animals," interrupted Marcel.

"Bah! where did you get that sermon? Been through a course of good sense, no doubt."

"Interrupt me not," replied Rodolphe, "and truce to your railleries. They will be blunted against the buckler of invulnerable resolution in which I am from this moment clad."

"That will do for prologue. Now the conclusion."

"This is my design. No longer embarrassed about the material wants of life, I am going seriously to work. First of all, I renounce my vagabond existence: I shall dress like other people, set up a black coat, and go to evening parties. If you are willing to follow in my footsteps, we will continue to live together but you must adopt my program. The strictest economy will preside over our life. By proper management we have before us three months' work without any preoccupation. But we must be economical."

"My dear fellow," said Marcel, "economy is a science only practicable for rich people. You and I, therefore, are ignorant of its first elements. However, by making an outlay of six francs we can have the works of Monsieur Jean-Baptiste Say, a very distinguished economist, who will perhaps teach us how to practice the art. Hallo! You have a Turkish pipe there!"

"Yes, I bought it for twenty-five francs."

"How is that! You talk of economy, and give twenty-five francs for a pipe!"

"And this is an economy. I used to break a two-sous pipe every day, and at the end of the year that came to a great deal more."

"True, I should never have thought of that."

They heard a neighboring clock strike six.

"Let us have dinner at once," said Rodolphe. "I mean to begin from tonight. Talking of dinner, it occurs to me that we lose much valuable time every day in cooking ours; now time is money, so we must economize it. From this day we will dine out."

"Yes," said Marcel, "there is a capital restaurant twenty steps off. It's rather dear, but not far to go, so we shall gain in time what we lose in money."

"We will go there today," said Rodolphe, "but tomorrow or next day we will adopt a still more economical plan. Instead of going to the restaurant, we will hire a cook."

"No, no," put in Marcel, "we will hire a servant to be cook and everything. Just see the immense advantages which will result from it. First of all, our rooms will be always in order; he will clean our boots, go on errands, wash my brushes; I will even try and give him a taste of the fine arts, and make him grind colors. In this way, we shall save at least six hours a day."

Five minutes after, the two friends were installed in one of the little rooms of the restaurant, and continuing their schemes of economy.

"We must get an intelligent lad," said Rodolphe, "if he has a sprinkling of spelling, I will teach him to write articles, and make an editor of him."

"That will be his resource for his old age," said Marcel, adding up the bill. "Well, this is dear, rather! Fifteen francs! We used both to dine for a franc and a half."

"Yes," replied Rodolphe, "but then we dined so badly that we were obliged to sup at night. So, on the whole, it is an economy."

"You always have the best of the argument," muttered the convinced artist. "Shall we work tonight?"

"No, indeed! I shall go to see my uncle. He is a good fellow, and will give me good advice when I tell him my new position. And you, Marcel?"

"I shall go to Medicis to ask him if he has any restorations of pictures to give me. By the way, give me five francs."

"For what?"

"To cross the Pont des Arts."

"Two sous to cross a bridge when you can go over another for nothing! That is a useless expense; and, though an inconsiderable one, is a violation of our rule."

"I am wrong, to be sure," said Marcel. "I will take a cab and go by the Pont Neuf."

So the two friends quitted each other in opposite directions, but somehow the different roads brought them to the same place, and they didn't go home till morning.

Two days after, Rodolphe and Marcel were completely metamorphosed. Dressed like two bridegrooms of the best society, they were so elegant, and neat, and shining, that they hardly recognized each other when they met in the street. Still their system of economy was in full blast, though it was not without much difficulty that their "organization of labor" had been realized. They had taken a servant; a big fellow thirty-four years old, of Swiss descent, and about as clever as an average donkey.

But Baptiste was not born to be a servant; he had a soul above his business; and if one of his masters gave him a parcel to carry, he blushed with indignation, and sent it by porter. However, he had some merits; for instance, he could hash hare well and his first profession having been that of distiller, he passed much of his time— or his masters', rather—in trying to invent a new kind of liniment; he also succeeded in the preparation of lamp-black. But where he was unrivalled was in smoking Marcel's cigars and lighting them with Rodolphe's manuscripts.

One day Marcel wanted to put Baptiste into costume, and make him sit for Pharaoh in his "Passage of the Red Sea." To this proposition Baptiste replied by a flat refusal, and demanded his wages.

"Very well," said Marcel, "I will settle with you tonight."

When Rodolphe returned, his friends declared that they must send away Baptiste. "He is of no use to us at all."

"No, indeed—only an ornament, and not much of that."

"Awfully stupid."

"And equally lazy."

"We must turn him off."

"Let us!"

"Still, he has some good points. He hashes hare very well."

"And the lamp-black! He is a very Raphael for that."

"Yes, but that's all he is good for. We lose time arguing with him."

"He keeps us from working."

"He is the cause of my 'Passage' not being finished in time for the Exhibition. He wouldn't sit for Pharaoh."

"Thanks to him, I couldn't finish my article in time. He wouldn't go to the public library and hunt up the notes I wanted."

"He is ruining us."

"Decidedly we can't keep him."

"Send him away then! But we must pay him."

"That we'll do. Give me the money, and I will settle accounts with him."

"Money! But it is not I who keeps the purse, but you."

"Not at all! It is you who are charged with the financial department."

"But I assure you," said Marcel, "I have no money."

"Can there be no more? It is impossible! We can't have spent five hundred francs in eight days, especially living with the most rigid economy as we have done, and confining ourselves to absolute necessaries: (absolute superfluities, he should have said). We must look over our accounts; and we shall find where the mistake is."

"Yes, but we shan't find where the money is. However, let us see the account-book, at any rate."

And this is the way they kept their accounts which had been begun under the auspices of Saint Economy:

"March 19. Received 500 francs. Paid, a Turkish pipe, 25 fr.; dinner, 15 fr.; sundries, 40 fr."

"What are those sundries?" asked Rodolphe of Marcel, who was reading.

"You know very well," replied the other, "that night when we didn't go home till morning. We saved fuel and candles by that."

"Well, afterwards?"

"March 20. Breakfast, 1 fr. 50 c.; tobacco, 20 c.; dinner, 2 fr.; an opera glass, 2 fr. 50 c.—that goes to your account. What did you want a glass for? You see perfectly well."

"You know I had to give an account of the Exhibition in the 'Scarf of Iris.' It is impossible to criticize paintings without a glass. The expense is quite legitimate. Well?—"

"A bamboo cane—"

"Ah, that goes to your account," said Rodolphe. "You didn't want a cane."

"That was all we spent the 20th," was Marcel's only answer. "The 21st we breakfasted out, dined out, and supped out."

"We ought not to have spent much that day."

"Not much, in fact—hardly thirty francs."

"But what for?"

"I don't know; it's marked sundries."

"Vague and treacherous heading!"

"21st. (The day that Baptiste came.) 5 francs to him on account of his wages. 50 centimes to the organ man.'"

"23rd. Nothing set down. 24th, ditto. Two good days!"

"*25th. Baptiste, on account, 3 fr.* It seems to me we give him money very often," said Marcel, by way of reflection.

"There will be less owing to him," said Rodolphe. "Go on!"

"*26th. Sundries, useful in an artistic point of view, 36 fr.*'"

"What did we buy that was useful? I don't recollect. What can it have been?"

"You don't remember! The day we went to the top of Notre Dame for a bird's-eye view of Paris."

"But it costs only eight sous to go up the tower."

"Yes, but then we went to dine at Saint Germain after we came down."

"Clear as mud!"

"27th. Nothing to set down."

"Good! There's economy for you."

"*28th. Baptiste, on account, 6 fr.*'"

"Now this time I am sure we owe Baptiste nothing more. Perhaps he is even in our debt. We must see."

"29th. Nothing set down, except the beginning of an article on 'Social Morals.'"

"30th. Ah! We had company at dinner—heavy expenses the 30th, 55 fr. 31st.—that's today—we have spent nothing yet. You see," continued Marcel, "the account has been kept very carefully, and the total does not reach five hundred francs."

"Then there ought to be money in the drawer."

"We can see," said Marcel, opening it.

"Anything there?"

"Yes, a spider."

> *"A spider in the morning*
> *Of sorrow is a warning,"* hummed Rodolphe.

"Where the deuce has all the money gone?" exclaimed Marcel, totally upset at the sight of the empty drawer.

"Very simple," replied Rodolphe. "Baptiste has had it all."

"Stop a minute!" cried Marcel, rummaging in the drawer, where he perceived a paper. "The bill for last quarter's rent!"

"How did it come there?"

"And paid, too," added Marcel. "You paid the landlord, then!"

"Me! Come now!" said Rodolphe.

"But what means—"

"But I assure you—"

"Oh, what can be this mystery?" sang the two in chorus to the final air of "The White Lady."

Baptiste, who loved music, came running in at once. Marcel showed him the paper.

"Ah, yes," said Baptiste carelessly, "I forgot to tell you. The landlord came this morning while you were out. I paid him, to save him the trouble of coming back."

"Where did you find the money?"

"I took it out of the open drawer. I thought, sir, you had left it open on purpose, and forgot to tell me to pay him, so I did just as if you had told me."

"Baptiste!" said Marcel, in a white heat, "you have gone beyond your orders. From this day you cease to form part of our household. Take off your livery!"

Baptiste took off the glazed leather cap which composed his livery, and handed it to Marcel.

"Very well," said the latter, "now you may go."

"And my wages?"

"Wages? You scamp! You have had fourteen francs in a little more than a week. What do you do with so much money? Do you keep a dancer?"

"A rope dancer?" suggested Rodolphe.

"Then I am to be left," said the unhappy domestic, "without a covering for my head!"

"Take your livery," said Marcel, moved in spite of himself, and he restored the cap to Baptiste.

"Yet it is that wretch who has wrecked our fortunes," said Rodolphe, seeing poor Baptiste go out. "Where shall we dine today?"

"We shall know tomorrow," replied Marcel.

VIII

The Cost Of a Five Franc Piece

One Saturday evening, at a time when he had not yet gone into housekeeping with Mademoiselle Mimi, who will shortly make her appearance, Rodolphe made the acquaintance at the table d'hote he frequented of a ladies' wardrobe keeper, named Mademoiselle Laure. Having learned that he was editor of "The Scarf of Iris" and of "The Beaver," two fashion papers, the milliner, in hope of getting her goods puffed, commenced a series of significant provocations. To these provocations Rodolphe replied by a pyrotechnical display of madrigals, sufficient to make Benserade, Voiture, and all other dealers in the fireworks of gallantry jealous; and at the end of the dinner, Mademoiselle Laure, having learned that he was a poet, gave him clearly to understand that she was not indisposed to accept him as her Petrarch. She even, without circumlocution, made an appointment with him for the next day.

"By Jove," said Rodolphe to himself, as he saw Mademoiselle Laure home, "this is certainly a very amiable young person. She seems to me to have a good grammar and a tolerably extensive wardrobe. I am quite disposed to make her happy."

On reaching the door of her house, Mademoiselle Laure relinquished Rodolphe's arm, thanking him for the trouble he had taken in accompanying her to such a remote locality.

"Oh! madame," replied Rodolphe, bowing to the ground, "I should like you to have lived at Moscow or the islands of the Sound, in order to have had the pleasure of being your escort the longer."

"That would be rather far," said Laure, affectedly.

"We could have gone by way of the Boulevards, madame," said Rodolphe. "Allow me to kiss you hand in the shape of your cheek," he added, kissing his companion on the lips before Laure could make any resistance.

"Oh sir!" she exclaimed, "you go too fast."

"It is to reach my destination sooner," said Rodolphe. "In love, the first stages should be ridden at a gallop."

"What a funny fellow," though the milliner, as she entered her dwelling.

"A pretty girl," said Rodolphe, as he walked away.

Returning home, he went to bed at once, and had the most delightful dreams. He saw himself at balls, theaters, and public promenades with Mademoiselle Laure on his arm, clad in dresses more magnificent than those of the girl with the ass's skin of the fairy tale.

The next morning at eleven o'clock, according to habit, Rodolphe got up. His first thought was for Mademoiselle Laure.

"She is a very well mannered woman," he murmured, "I feel sure that she was brought up at Saint Denis. I shall at length realize the happiness of having a mistress who is not pitted with the small-pox. Decidedly I will make sacrifices for her. I will go and draw my screw at 'The Scarf of Iris.' I will buy some gloves, and I will take Laure to dinner at a restaurant where table napkins are in use. My coat is not up to much," said he as he dressed himself, "but, bah! black is good wear."

And he went out to go to the office of "The Scarf of Iris."

Crossing the street he came across an omnibus, on the side of which was pasted a bill, with the words, "Display of Fountains at Versailles, today, Sunday."

A thunderbolt falling at Rodolphe's feet would not have produced a deeper impression upon him than the sight of this bill.

"Today, Sunday! I had forgotten it," he exclaimed. "I shall not be able to get any money. Today, Sunday!!! All the spare coin in Paris is on its way to Versailles."

However, impelled by one of those fabulous hopes to which a man always clings, Rodolphe hurried to the office of the paper, reckoning that some happy chance might have taken the cashier there.

Monsieur Boniface had, indeed, looked in for a moment, but had left at once.

"For Versailles," said the office messenger to Rodolphe.

"Come," said Rodolphe, "it is all over! . . . But let me see," he thought, "my appointment is for this evening. It is noon, so I have five hours to find five francs in—twenty sous an hour, like the horses in the Bois du Boulogne. Forward."

As he found himself in a neighborhood where the journalist, whom he styled the influential critic, resided, Rodolphe thought of having a try at him.

"I am sure to find him in," said he, as he ascended the stairs, "it is the day he writes his criticism—there is no fear of his being out. I will borrow five francs of him."

"Hallo! it's you, is it?" said the journalist, on seeing Rodolphe. "You come at the right moment. I have a slight service to ask of you."

"How lucky it falls out," thought the editor of "The Scarf of Iris."

"Were you at the Odeon Theater last night?"

"I am always at the Odeon."

"You have seen the new piece, then?"

"Who else would have seen it? I am the Odeon audience."

"That is true," said the critic, "you are one of the caryatides of the theater. It is even rumored that it is you who finds the money for its subvention. Well, that is what I want of you, a summary of the plot of the new piece."

"That is easy, I have the memory of a creditor."

"Whom is this piece by?" asked the critic of Rodolphe, whilst the latter was writing.

"A gentleman."

"It cannot be up to much."

"Well, it is not as strong as a Turk."

"Then it cannot be very robust. The Turks, you see, have usurped a reputation for strength. Besides, there are no longer any Turks except at masked balls and in the Champs-Elysees where they sell dates. One of my friends knows the East and he assures me that all the natives of it were born in the Rue Coquenard."

"That is smart," said Rodolphe.

"You think so?" observed the critic, "I will put it in my article."

"Here is my analysis of the piece, it is to the point," resumed Rodolphe.

"Yes, but it is short."

"By putting in dashes and developing your critical opinion it will fill some space."

"I have scarcely time, my dear fellow, and then my critical opinion will not fill enough space either."

"You can stick in an adjective at every third word."

"Cannot you tail on to your analysis a little, or rather a long criticism of the piece, eh?" asked the critic.

"Humph," said Rodolphe. "I have certainly some opinions upon tragedy, but I have printed them three times in 'The Beaver' and 'The Scarf of Iris.'"

"No matter, how many lines do your opinions fill?"

"Forty lines."

"The deuce, you have strong opinions. Well, lend me your forty lines."

"Good," thought Rodolphe, "if I turn out twenty francs' worth of copy for him he cannot refuse me five. I must warn you," said he to the critic, "that my opinions are not quite novel. They are rather worn at the elbows. Before printing them I yelled them in every cafe in Paris, there is not a waiter who does not know them by heart."

"What does that matter to me? You surely do not know me. Is there anything new in the world except virtue?"

"Here you are," said Rodolphe, as he finished.

"Thunder and tempests, there is still nearly a column wanting. How is this chasm to be filled?" exclaimed the critic. "Since you are here supply me with some paradoxes."

"I have not any about me," said Rodolphe, "though I can lend you some. Only they are not mine, I bought them for half a franc from one of my friends who was in distress. They have seen very little use as yet."

"Very good," said the critic.

"Ah!" said Rodolphe to himself, setting to write again. "I shall certainly ask him for ten francs, just now paradoxes are as dear as partridges." And he wrote some thirty lines containing nonsense about pianos, goldfish and Rhine wine, which was called toilet wine just as we speak of toilet vinegar.

"It is very good," said the critic. "Now do me the favor to add that the place where one meets more honest folk than anywhere else is the galleys."

"Why?"

"To fill a couple of lines. Good, now it is finished," said the influential critic, summoning his servant to take the article to the printers.

"And now," thought Rodolphe, "let us strike home." And he gravely proposed his request.

"Ah! my dear fellow," said the critic, "I have not a sou in the place. Lolette ruins me in pommade, and just now she stripped me of my last copper to go to Versailles and see the Nereids and the brazen monsters spout forth the floods."

"To Versailles. But it is an epidemic!" exclaimed Rodolphe.

"But why do you want money?"

"That is my story," replied Rodolphe, "I have at five this evening an appointment with a lady, a very well bred lady who never goes out save in an omnibus. I wish to unite my fortunes with hers for a few days, and it appears to me the right thing to enable her to take the pleasures of this life. For dinner, dances, &c., &c., I must have five francs, and if I do not find them French literature is dishonoured in my person."

"Why don't you borrow the sum of the lady herself?" exclaimed the critic.

"The first time of meeting, it is hardly possible. Only you can get me out of this fix."

"By all the mummies of Egypt I give you my word of honor that I have not enough to buy a sou pipe. However, I have some books that you can sell."

"Impossible today, Mother Mansut's, Lebigre's, and all the shops on the quays and in the Rue Saint Jacques are closed. What books are they? Volumes of poetry with a portrait of the author in spectacles? But such things never sell."

"Unless the author is criminally convicted," said the critic. "Wait a bit, here are some romances and some concert tickets. By setting about it skillfully you may, perhaps, make money of them."

"I would rather have something else, a pair of trowsers, for instance."

"Come," said the critic, "take this copy of Bossuet and this plaster cast of Monsieur Odilon Barrot. On my word of honor, it is the widow's mite."

"I see that you are doing your best," said Rodolphe. "I will take away these treasures, but if I get thirty sous out of them I shall regard it as the thirteenth labor of Hercules."

After having covered about four leagues Rodolphe, by the aid of an eloquence of which he had the secret on great occasions, succeeded in getting his washerwoman to lend him two francs on the volumes of poetry, the romances and the bust of Monsieur Barrot.

"Come," said he, as he recrossed the Seine, "here is the sauce, now I must find the dish itself. Suppose I go to my uncle."

Half an hour later he was at his Uncle Monetti's, who read upon his nephew's face what was the matter. Hence he put himself on guard and forestalled any request by a series of complaints, such as:

"Times are hard, bread is dear, debtors do not pay up, rents are terribly high, commerce decaying, &c., &c.," all the hypocritical litany of shopkeepers.

"Would you believe it," said the uncle, "that I have been forced to borrow money from my shopman to meet a bill?"

"You should have sent to me," said Rodolphe. "I would have lent it you, I received two hundred francs three days ago."

"Thanks, my lad," said the uncle, "but you have need of your fortune. Ah! whilst you are here, you might, you who write such a good hand, copy out some bills for me that I want to send out."

"My five francs are going to cost me dear," said Rodolphe to himself, setting about the task, which he condensed.

"My dear uncle," said he to Monetti, "I know how fond you are of music and I have brought you some concert tickets."

"You are very kind, my boy. Will you stay to dinner?"

"Thanks, uncle, but I am expected at dinner in the Faubourg Saint Germain, indeed, I am rather put out about it for I have not time to run home and get the money to buy gloves."

"You have no gloves, shall I lend you mine?" said his uncle.

"Thanks, we do not take the same size, only you would greatly oblige me by the loan of—"

"Twenty nine sous to buy a pair? Certainly, my boy, here you are. When one goes into society one should be well dressed. Better be envied than pitied, as your aunt used to say. Come, I see you are getting on in the world, so much the better. I would have given you more," he went on, "but it is all I have in the till. I should have to go upstairs and I cannot leave the shop, customers drop in every moment."

"You were saying that business was not flourishing?"

Uncle Monetti pretended not to hear, and said to his nephew who was pocketing the twenty nine sous:

"Do not be in a hurry about repayment."

"What a screw," said Rodolphe, bolting. "Ah!" he continued, "there are still thirty-one sous lacking. Where am I to find them? I know, let's be off to the crossroads of Providence."

This was the name bestowed by Rodolphe on the most central point in Paris, that is to say, the Palais Royal, a spot where it is almost impossible to remain ten minutes without meeting ten people of one's acquaintance, creditors above all. Rodolphe therefore went and stationed himself at the entrance to the Palais Royal. This time Providence was long in coming. At last Rodolphe caught sight of it. Providence had a white hat, a green coat, and a gold headed cane—a well dressed Providence.

It was a rich and obliging fellow, although a phalansterian.

"I am delighted to see you," said he to Rodolphe, "come and walk a little way with me; we can have a talk."

"So I am to have the infliction of the phalanstere," murmured

Rodolphe, suffering himself to be led away from the wearer of the white hat, who, indeed, phalanstered him to the utmost.

As they drew near the Pont des Arts Rodolphe said to his companion—

"I must leave you, not having sufficient to pay the toll."

"Nonsense," said the other, catching hold of Rodolphe and throwing two sous to the toll keeper.

"This is the right moment," thought the editor of "The Scarf of Iris," as they crossed the bridge. Arrived at the further end in front of the clock of the Institute, Rodolphe stopped short, pointed to the dial with a despairing gesture, and exclaimed:—

"Confound it all, a quarter to five! I am done for."

"What is the matter?" cried his astonished friend.

"The matter is," said Rodolphe, "that, thanks to your dragging me here in spite of myself, I have missed an appointment."

"An important one?"

"I should think so; money that I was to call for at five o'clock at— Batignolles. I shall never be able to get there. Hang it; what am I to do?"

"Why," said the phalansterian, "nothing is simpler; come home with me and I will lend you some."

"Impossible, you live at Montrouge, and I have business at six o'clock at the Chaussee d'Antin. Confound it."

"I have a trifle about me," said Providence, timidly, "but it is very little."

"If I had enough to take a cab I might get to Batignolles in time."

"Here is the contents of my purse, my dear fellow, thirty one sous."

"Give it to me at once, that I may bolt," said Rodolphe, who had just heard five o'clock strike, and who hastened off to keep his appointment.

"It has been hard to get," said he, counting out his money. "A hundred sous exactly. At last I am supplied, and Laure will see that she has to do with a man who knows how to do things properly. I won't take a centime home this evening. We must rehabilitate literature, and prove that its votaries only need money to be wealthy."

Rodolphe found Mademoiselle Laure at the trysting place.

"Good," said he, "for punctuality she is a feminine chronometer."

He spent the evening with her, and bravely melted down his five francs in the crucible of prodigality. Mademoiselle Laure was charmed with his manners, and was good enough only to notice that Rodolphe had not escorted her home at the moment when he was ushering her into his own room.

"I am committing a fault," said she. "Do not make me repent of it by the ingratitude which is characteristic of your sex."

"Madame," said Rodolphe, "I am known for my constancy. It is such that all my friends are astonished at my fidelity, and have nicknamed me the General Bertrand of Love."

IX

THE WHITE VIOLETS

About this time Rodolphe was very much in love with his cousin Angela, who couldn't bear him; and the thermometer was twelve degrees below freezing point.

Mademoiselle Angela was the daughter of Monsieur Monetti, the chimney doctor, of whom we have already had occasion to speak. She was eighteen years old, and had just come from Burgundy, where she lived five years with a relative who was to leave her all her property. This relative was an old lady who had never been young apparently—certainly never handsome, but had always been very ill-natured, although—or perhaps because—very superstitious. Angela, who at her departure was a charming child, and promised to be a charming girl, came back at the end of the five years a pretty enough young lady, but cold, dry, and uninteresting. Her secluded provincial life, and the narrow and bigoted education she had received, had filled her mind with vulgar prejudices, shrunk her imagination, and converted her heart into a sort of organ, limited to fulfilling its function of physical balance wheel. You might say that she had holy water in her veins instead of blood. She received her cousin with an icy reserve; and he lost his time whenever he attempted to touch the chord of her recollections—recollections of the time when they had sketched out that flirtation in the Paul-and-Virginia style which is traditional between cousins of different sexes. Still Rodolphe was very much in love with his cousin Angela, who couldn't bear him; and learning one day that the young lady was going shortly to the wedding ball of one of her friends, he made bold to promise Angela a bouquet of violets for the ball. And after asking permission of her father, Angela accepted her cousin's gallant offer—always on condition that the violets should be white.

Overjoyed at his cousin's amiability, Rodolphe danced and sang his way back to Mount St. Bernard, as he called his lodging—why will be seen presently. As he passed by a florist's in crossing the Palais Royal, he saw some white violets in the showcase, and was curious enough to ask their price. A presentable bouquet could not be had for less than ten francs; there were some that cost more.

"The deuce!" exclaimed Rodolphe, "ten francs! and only eight days to find this fortune! It will be a hard pull, but never mind, my cousin shall have her flowers."

This happened in the time of Rodolphe's literary genesis, as the transcendentalists would say. His only income at that period was an allowance of fifteen francs a month, made him by a friend, who, after living a long while in Paris as a poet, had, by the help of influential acquaintances, gained the mastership of a provincial school. Rodolphe, who was the child of prodigality, always spent his allowance in four days; and, not choosing to abandon his holy but not very profitable profession of elegiac poet, lived for the rest of the month on the rare droppings from the basket of Providence. This long Lent had no terrors for him; he passed through it gaily, thanks to his stoical temperament and to the imaginary treasures which he expended every day while waiting for the first of the month, that Easter which terminated his fast. He lived at this time at the very top of one of the loftiest houses in Paris. His room was shaped like a belvidere, and was a delicious habitation in summer, but from October to April a perfect little Kamschatka. The four cardinal winds which penetrated by the four windows,—there was one on each of the four sides—made fearful music in it throughout the cold seasons. Then in irony as it were, there was a huge fireplace, the immense chimney of which seemed a gate of honor reserved for Boreas and his retinue. On the first attack of cold, Rodolphe had recourse to an original system of warming; he cut up successively what little furniture he had, and at the end of a week his stock was considerably abridged; in fact, he had only a bed and two chairs left; it should be remarked that these items were insured against fire by their nature, being of iron. This manner of heating himself he called *moving up the chimney*.

It was January, and the thermometer, which indicated twelve degrees below freezing point on the Spectacle Quay, would have stood two or three lower if moved to the belvidere, which Rodolphe called indifferently Mount St. Bernard, Spitzenberg, and Siberia.

The night when he promised his cousin the white violets, he was seized with a great rage on returning home; the four cardinal winds, in playing puss-in-the-corner round his chamber, had broken a pane of glass—the third time in a fortnight. After exploding in a volley of frantic imprecations upon Eolus and all his family, and plugging up the breach with a friend's portrait, Rodolphe lay down, dressed as he was, between his two mattresses, and dreamed of white violets all night.

At the end of five days, Rodolphe had found nothing to help him toward realizing his dreams. He must have the bouquet the day after tomorrow. Meanwhile, the thermometer fell still lower, and the luckless poet was ready to despair as he thought the violets might have risen higher. Finally his good angel had pity on him, and came to his relief as follows.

One morning, Rodolphe went to take his chance of getting a breakfast from his friend Marcel the painter, and found him conversing with a woman in mourning. It was a widow who had just lost her husband, and who wanted to know how much it would cost to paint on the tomb which she had erected, a man's hand, with this inscription beneath:

"I Wait for Her to Whom My Faith was Plighted."

To get the work at a cheaper rate, she observed to the artist that when she was called to rejoin her husband, he would have another hand to paint—her hand with a bracelet on the wrist and the supplementary line beneath:

"At Length, Behold Us Thus Once More United."

"I shall put this clause in my will," she said, "and require that the task be intrusted to you."

"In that case, madame," replied the artist, "I will do it at the price you offer—but only in the hope of seeing your hand. Don't go and forget me in your will."

"I should like to have this as soon as possible," said the disconsolate one, "nevertheless, take your time to do it well and don't forget the scar on the thumb. I want a living hand."

"Don't be afraid, madame, it shall be a speaking one," said Marcel, as he bowed the widow out. But hardly had she crossed the threshold when she returned, saying, "I have one more thing to ask you, sir: I should like to have inscribed on my husband's tomb something in verse which would tell of his good conduct and his last words. Is that good style?"

"Very good style—they call that an epitaph—the very best style."

"You don't know anyone who would do that for me cheap? There is my neighbor Monsieur Guerin, the public writer, but he asks the clothes off my back."

Here Rodolphe looked at Marcel, who understood him at once.

"Madame," said the artist, pointing to Rodolphe, "a happy fortune has conducted hither the very person who can be of service to you in this mournful juncture. This gentleman is a renowned poet; you couldn't find a better one."

"I want something very melancholy," said the widow, "and the spelling all right."

"Madame," replied Marcel, "my friend spells like a book. He had all the prizes at school."

"Indeed!" said the widow, "my grand-nephew had just had a prize too; he is only seven years old."

"A very forward child, madame."

"But are you sure that the gentleman can make very melancholy verses?"

"No one better, madame, for he has undergone much sorrow in his life. The papers always find fault with his verses for being too melancholy."

"What!" cried the widow, "do they talk about him in the papers? He must know quite as much, then, as Monsieur Guerin, the public writer."

"And a great deal more. Apply to him, madame, and you will not repent of it."

After having explained to Rodolphe the sort of inscription in verse which she wished to place on her husband's tomb, the widow agreed to give Rodolphe ten francs if it suited her—only she must have it very soon. The poet promised she should have it the very next day.

"Oh good genius of Artemisia!" cried Rodolphe as the widow disappeared. "I promise you that you shall be suited—full allowance of melancholy lyrics, better got up than a duchess, orthography and all. Good old lady! May Heaven reward you with a life of a hundred and seven years—equal to that of a good brandy!"

"I object," said Marcel.

"That's true," said Rodolphe, "I forgot that you have her hand to paint, and that so long a life would make you lose money." And lifting his hands he gravely exclaimed, "Heaven, do not grant my prayer! Ah!" he continued, "I was in jolly good luck to come here."

"By the way," asked Marcel, "what did you want?"

"I recollect—and now especially that I have to pass the night in making these verses, I cannot do without what I came to ask you for, namely, first, some dinner; secondly, tobacco and a candle; thirdly, your polar-bear costume."

"To go to the masked ball?"

"No, indeed, but as you see me here, I am as much frozen up as the grand army in retreat from Russia. Certainly my green frock-coat and Scotch-plaid trowsers are very pretty, but much too summery; they would do to live under the equator; but for one who lodges near the pole, as I do, a white bear skin is more suitable; indeed I may say necessary."

"Take the fur!" said Marcel, "it's a good idea; warm as a dish of charcoal; you will be like a roll in an oven in it."

Rodolphe was already inside the animal's skin.

"Now," said he, "the thermometer is going to be really mad."

"Are you going out so?" said Marcel to his friend, after they had finished an ambiguous repast served in a penny dish.

"I just am," replied Rodolphe. "Do you think I care for public opinion? Besides, today is the beginning of carnival."

He went half over Paris with all the gravity of the beast whose skin he occupied. Only on passing before a thermometer in an optician's window he couldn't help taking a sight at it.

Having returned home not without causing great terror to his porter, Rodolphe lit his candle, carefully surrounding it with an extempore shade of paper to guard it against the malice of the winds, and set to work at once. But he was not long in perceiving that if his body was almost entirely protected from the cold, his hands were not; a terrible numbness seized his fingers which let the pen fall.

"The bravest man cannot struggle against the elements," said the poet, falling back helpless in his chair. "Caeser passed the Rubicon, but he could not have passed the Beresina."

All at once he uttered a cry of joy from the depths of his bear-skin breast, and jumped up so suddenly as to overturn some of his ink on its snowy fur. He had an idea!

Rodolphe drew from beneath his bed a considerable mass of papers, among which were a dozen huge manuscripts of his famous drama, "The Avenger." This drama, on which he had spent two years, had been made, unmade, and remade so often that all the copies together weighed fully fifteen pounds. He put the last version on one side, and dragged the others towards the fireplace.

"I was sure that with patience I should dispose of it somehow," he exclaimed. "What a pretty fagot! If I could have foreseen what would happen, I could have written a prologue, and then I should have more fuel tonight. But one can't foresee everything." He lit some leaves of the manuscript, in the flame of which he thawed his hands. In five minutes the first act of "The Avenger" was over, and Rodolphe had written three verses of his epitaph.

It would be impossible to describe the astonishment of the four winds when they felt fire in the chimney.

"It's an illusion," quoth Boreas, as he amused himself by brushing back the hair of Rodolphe's bear skin.

"Let's blow down the pipe," suggested another wind, "and make the chimney smoke." But just as they were about to plague the poor poet, the south wind perceived Monsieur Arago at a window of the Observatory threatening them with his finger; so they all made off, for fear of being put under arrest. Meanwhile the second act of "The Avenger" was going off with immense success, and Rodolphe had written ten lines. But he only achieved two during the third act.

"I always thought that third act too short," said Rodolphe, "luckily the next one will take longer; there are twenty three scenes in it, including the great one of the throne." As the last flourish of the throne scene went up the chimney in fiery flakes, Rodolphe had only three couplets more to write. "Now for the last act. This is all monologue. It may last five minutes." The catastrophe flashed and smouldered, and Rodolphe in a magnificent transport of poetry had enshrined in lyric stanzas the last words of the illustrious deceased. "There is enough left for a second representation," said he, pushing the remainder of the manuscript under his bed.

At eight o'clock next evening, Mademoiselle Angela entered the ballroom; in her hand was a splendid nosegay of white violets, and among them two budding roses, white also. During the whole night men and women were complimenting the young girl on her bouquet. Angela could not but feel a little grateful to her cousin who had procured this little triumph for her vanity; and perhaps she would have thought more of him but for the gallant persecutions of one of the bride's relatives who had danced several times with her. He was a fair-haired youth, with a magnificent moustache curled up at the ends, to hook innocent hearts. The bouquet had been pulled to pieces by everybody; only two white roses were left. The young man asked Angela for them;

she refused—only to forget them after the ball on a bench, whence the young fair-haired youth hastened to take them.

At that moment it was fourteen degrees below freezing point in Rodolphe's belvidere. He was leaning against his window looking out at the lights in the ballroom, where his cousin Angela, who didn't care for him, was dancing.

X

The Cape of Storms

In the opening month of each of the four seasons there are some terrible epochs, usually about the 1st and the 15th. Rodolphe, who could not witness the approach of one or the other of these two dates without alarm, nicknamed them the Cape of Storms. On these mornings it is not Aurora who opens the portals of the East, but creditors, landlords, bailiffs and their kidney. The day begins with a shower of bills and accounts and winds up with a hailstorm of protests. *Dies irae*.

Now one morning, it was the 15th of April, Rodolphe was peacefully slumbering—and dreaming that one of his uncles had just bequeathed him a whole province in Peru, the feminine inhabitants included.

Whilst he was wallowing in this imaginary Pacolus, the sound of a key turning in the lock interrupted the heir presumptive just at the most dazzling point of his golden dream.

Rodolphe sat up in bed, his eyes and mind yet heavy with slumber, and looked about him.

He vaguely perceived standing in the middle of his room a man who had just entered.

This early visitor bore a bag slung at his back and a large pocketbook in his hand. He wore a cocked hat and a bluish-grey swallow-tailed coat and seemed very much out of breath from ascending the five flights of stairs. His manners were very affable and his steps sounded as sonorously as that of a money-changer's counter on the march.

Rodolphe was alarmed for a moment, and at the sight of the cocked hat and the coat thought that he had a police officer before him.

But the sight of the tolerably well filled bag made him perceive his mistake.

"Ah! I have it," thought he, "it is something on account of my inheritance, this man comes from the West Indies. But in that case why is he not black?"

And making a sign to the man, he said, pointing to the bag, "I know all about it. Put it down there. Thanks."

The man was a messenger of the Bank of France. He replied to Rodolphe's request by holding before his eyes a small strip of paper covered with writing and figures in various colored inks.

"You want a receipt," said Rodolphe. "That is right. Pass me the pen and ink. There, on the table."

"No, I have come to take money," replied the messenger. "An acceptance for a hundred and fifty francs. It is the 15th of April."

"Ah!" observed Rodolphe, examining the acceptance. "Pay to the order of—Birmann. It is my tailor. Alas," he added, in melancholy tones casting his eyes alternately upon a frock coat thrown on the bed and upon the acceptance, "causes depart but effects return. What, it is the 15th of April? It is extraordinary, I have not yet had any strawberries this year."

The messenger, weary of delay, left the room, saying to Rodolphe, "You have till four o'clock to pay."

"There is no time like the present," replied Rodolphe. "The humbug," he added regretfully, following the cocked hat with his eyes, "he has taken away his bag."

Rodolphe drew the curtains of his bed and tried to retrace the path to his inheritance, but he made a mistake on the road and proudly entered into a dream in which the manager of the Theatre Francais came hat in hand to ask him for a drama for his theater, and in which he, aware of the customary practice, asked for an advance. But at the very moment when the manager appeared to be willing to comply the sleeper was again half awakened by the entry of a fresh personage, another creature of the 15th.

It was Monsieur Benoit, landlord of the lodging house in which Rodolphe was residing. Monsieur Benoit was at once the landlord, the bootmaker and the money lender of his lodgers. On this morning he exhaled a frightful odor of bad brandy and overdue rent. He carried an empty bag in his hand.

"The deuce," thought Rodolphe, "this is not the manager of the Theater Francais, he would have a white cravat and the bag would be full."

"Good morning, Monsieur Rodolphe," said Monsieur Benoit, approaching the bed.

"Monsieur Benoit! Good morning. What has given me the pleasure of this visit?"

"I have come to remind you that it is the 15th of April."

"Already! How time flies, it is extraordinary, I must see about buying a pair of summer trousers. The 15th of April. Good heavens! I should never have thought of it but for you, Monsieur Benoit. What gratitude I owe you for this!"

"You also owe me a hundred and sixty-two francs," replied Monsieur Benoit, "and it is time this little account was settled."

"I am not in any absolute hurry—do not put yourself out, Monsieur Benoit. I will give you time."

"But," said the landlord, "you have already put me off several times."

"In that case let us come to a settlement, Monsieur Benoit, let us come to a settlement, it is all the same to me today as tomorrow. Besides we are all mortal. Let us come to a settlement."

An amiable smile smoothed the landlord wrinkles and even his empty bag swelled with hope.

"What do I owe you?" asked Rodolphe.

"In the first place, we have three months' rent at twenty-five francs, that makes seventy-five francs."

"Errors excepted," said Rodolphe. "And then?"

"Then three pairs of boots at twenty francs."

"One moment, one moment, Monsieur Benoit, do not let us mix matters, this is no longer to do with the landlord but the bootmaker. I want a separate account. Accounts are a serious thing, we must not get muddled."

"Very good," said Monsieur Benoit, softened by the hope of at length writing "Paid" at the foot of his accounts. "Here is a special bill for the boots. Three pairs of boots at twenty francs, sixty francs."

Rodolphe cast a look of pity on a pair of worn out boots.

"Alas!" he thought, "they could not be worse if they had been worn by the Wandering Jew. Yet it was in running after Marie that they got so worn out. Go on, Monsieur Benoit."

"We were saying sixty francs," replied the latter. "Then money lent, twenty seven francs."

"Stop a bit, Monsieur Benoit. We agreed that each dog would have his kennel. It is as a friend that you lent me money. Therefore, if you please, let us quit the regions of bootmaking and enter those of confidence and friendship which require a separate account. How much does your friendship for me amount to?"

"Twenty seven francs."

"Twenty seven francs. You have purchased a friend cheaply, Monsieur

Benoit. In short, we were saying, seventy five, sixty, and twenty seven. That makes altogether—?"

"A hundred and sixty two francs," said Monsieur Benoit, presenting the three bills.

"A hundred and sixty two francs," observed Rodolphe, "it is extraordinary. What a fine thing arithmetic is. Well, Monsieur Benoit, now that the account is settled we can both rest easy, we know exactly how we stand. Next month I will ask you for a receipt, and as during this time the confidence and friendship you must entertain towards me can only increase, you can, in case it should become necessary, grant me a further delay. However, if the landlord and the bootmaker are inclined to be hasty, I would ask the friend to get them to listen to reason. It is extraordinary, Monsieur Benoit, but every time I think of your triple character as a landlord, a bootmaker, and a friend, I am tempted to believe in the Trinity."

Whilst listening to Rodolphe the landlord had turned at one and the same time red, green, white, and yellow, and at each fresh jest from his lodger that rainbow of anger grew deeper and deeper upon his face.

"Sir," said he, "I do not like to be made game of. I have waited long enough. I give you notice of quit, and unless you let me have some money this evening, I know what I shall have to do."

"Money! money! Am I asking you for money?" said Rodolphe. "Besides, if I had any, I should not give it to you. On a Friday, it would be unlucky."

Monsieur Benoit's wrath grew tempestuous, and if the furniture had not belonged to him he would no doubt have smashed some of it.

"You are forgetting your bag," cried Rodolphe after him. "What a business," murmured the young fellow, as he found himself alone. "I would rather tame lions. But," he continued, jumping out of bed and dressing hurriedly, "I cannot stay here. The invasion will continue. I must flee; I must even breakfast. Suppose I go and see Schaunard. I will ask him for some breakfast, and borrow a trifle. A hundred francs will be enough. Yes, I'm off to Schaunard's."

Going downstairs, Rodolphe met Monsieur Benoit, who had received further shocks from his other lodgers, as was attested by his empty bag.

"If any one asks for me, tell them I have gone into the country—to the Alps," said Rodolphe. "Or stay, tell them that I no longer live here."

"I shall tell the truth," murmured Monsieur Benoit, in a very significant tone.

Schaunard was living at Montmartre. It was necessary to go right through Paris. This peregrination was one most dangerous to Rodolphe.

"Today," said he, "the streets are paved with creditors."

However, he did not go along by the outer Boulevards, as he had felt inclined to. A fanciful hope, on the contrary, urged him to follow the perilous itinerary of central Paris. Rodolphe thought that on a day when millions were going about the thoroughfares in the money-cases of bank messengers, it might happen that a thousand franc note, abandoned on the roadside, might lie awaiting its Good Samaritan. Thus he walked slowly along with his eyes on the ground. But he only found two pins.

After a two hours' walk he got to Schaunard's.

"Ah, it's you," said the latter.

"Yes, I have come to ask you for some breakfast."

"Ah, my dear fellow, you come at the wrong time. My mistress has just arrived, and I have not seen her for a fortnight. If you had only called ten minutes earlier."

"Well, have you got a hundred francs to lend me?"

"What! you too!" exclaimed Schaunard, in the height of astonishment. "You have come to ask me for money! You, in the ranks of my enemies!"

"I will pay you back on Monday."

"Or at the Greek Calends. My dear fellow, you surely forget what day it is. I can do nothing for you. But there is no reason to despair; the day is not yet over. You may still meet with Providence, who never gets up before noon."

"Ah!" replied Rodolphe, "Providence has too much to do looking after little birds. I will go and see Marcel."

Marcel was then residing in the Rue de Breda. Rodolphe found him in a very downcast mood, contemplating his great picture that was to represent the passage of the Red Sea.

"What is the matter?" asked Rodolphe, as he entered. "You seem quite in the dumps."

"Alas!" replied the painter, in allegorical language, "for the last fortnight it has been Holy Week."

"Red herrings and black radishes. Good, I remember."

Indeed, Rodolphe's memory was still salt with the remembrance of a time when he had been reduced to the exclusive consumption of the fish in question.

"The deuce," said he, "that is serious. I came to borrow a hundred francs of you."

"A hundred francs," said Marcel. "You are always in the clouds. The idea of coming and asking me for that mythological amount at a period when one is always under the equator of necessity. You must have been taking hashish."

"Alas!" said Rodolphe, "I have not been taking anything at all."

And he left his friend on the banks of the Red Sea.

From noon to four o'clock Rodolphe successively steered for every house of his acquaintance. He went through the forty eight districts of Paris, and covered about eight leagues, but without any success. The influence of the 15th of April made itself feel with equal severity everywhere. However, dinner time was drawing near. But it scarcely appeared that dinner was likely to follow its example, and it seemed to Rodolphe that he was on the raft of the wrecked Medusa.

As he was crossing the Pont Neuf an idea all at once occurred to him.

"Oh! oh!" said he to himself, retracing his steps, "the 15th of April. But I have an invitation to dinner for today."

And fumbling in his pocket, he drew out a printed ticket, running as follows:

Barriere de la Villette,
Au Grand Vainqueur.
Dining Room to seat 300 people.

Anniversary Dinner
In Honor of the Birth Of

THE HUMANITARIAN MESSIAH

April 15, 184-

Admit One
N.B.—Only half a bottle of wine per head

"I do not share the opinions of the disciples of this Messiah," said Rodolphe to himself, "but I will willingly share their repast." And with the swiftness of a bird he covered the distance separating him from the Barriere de la Villette.

When he reached the halls of the Grand Vainqueur, the crowd was enormous. The dining room, seating three hundred, was thronged with five hundred people. A vast horizon of veal and carrots spread itself before the eyes of Rodolphe.

At length they began to serve the soup.

As the guests were carrying their spoons to their lips, five or six people in plain clothes, and several police officers in uniform, pushed into the room, with a commissary of police at their head.

"Gentlemen," said the commissary, "by order of the authorities, this dinner cannot take place. I call upon you to withdraw."

"Oh!" said Rodolphe, retiring with everyone else. "Oh! what a fatality has spoiled my dinner."

He sadly resumed the road to his dwelling, and reached it at about eleven at night.

Monsieur Benoit was awaiting him.

"Ah! it is you," said the landlord. "Have you thought of what I told you this morning? Have you brought me any money?"

"I am to receive some tonight. I will give you some of it tomorrow morning," replied Rodolphe, looking for his key and his candlestick in their accustomed place. He did not find them.

"Monsieur Rodolphe," said the landlord, "I am very sorry, but I have let your room, and I have no other vacant now—you must go somewhere else."

Rodolphe had a lofty soul, and a night in the open air did not alarm him. Besides, in the event of bad weather, he could sleep in a box at the Odeon Theater, as he had already done before. Only he claimed "his property" from Monsieur Benoit, the said property consisting of a bundle of papers.

"That is so," said the landlord. "I have no right to detain those things. They are in the bureau. Come up with me; if the person who has taken your room has not gone to bed, we can go in."

The room had been let during the day to a girl named Mimi, with whom Rodolphe had formerly begun a love duet. They recognized one another at once. Rodolphe began to whisper to Mimi and tenderly squeezed her hand.

"See how it rains," said he, calling attention to the noise of the storm that had just broken overhead.

"Sir," said she, pointing to Rodolphe, "this is the gentleman I was expecting this evening."

"Oh!" said Monsieur Benoit, grinning on the wrong end of his face.

Whilst Mademoiselle Mimi was hurriedly getting ready an improvised supper, midnight struck.

"Ah!" said Rodolphe to himself, "the 15th of April is over. I have at length weathered my Cape of Storms. My dear Mimi," said the young man, taking the pretty girl in his arms and kissing her on the back of the neck, "it would have been impossible for you to have allowed me to be turned out of doors. You have the bump of hospitality."

XI

A Bohemian Cafe

You shall hear how it came to pass that Carolus Barbemuche, platonist and literary man generally, became a member of the Bohemian Club, in the twenty-fourth year of his age.

At that time, Gustave Colline, the great philosopher, Marcel, the great painter, Schaunard, the great musician, and Rodolphe, the great poet (as they called one another), regularly frequented the Momus Cafe, where they were surnamed "the Four Musqueteers," because they were always seen together. In fact, they came together, went away together, played together, and sometimes didn't pay their shot together, with a unison worthy of the best orchestra.

They chose to meet in a room where forty people might have been accommodated, but they were usually there alone, inasmuch as they had rendered the place uninhabitable by its ordinary frequenters. The chance customer who risked himself in this den, became, from the moment of his entrance, the victim of the terrible four; and, in most cases, made his escape without finishing his newspaper and cup of coffee, seasoned as they were by unheard-of maxims on art, sentiment, and political economy. The conversation of the four comrades was of such a nature that the waiter who served them had become an idiot in the prime of his life.

At length things reached such a point that the landlord lost all patience and came up one night to make a formal statement of his griefs:

"Firstly. Monsieur Rodolphe comes early in the morning to breakfast, and carries off to his room all the papers of the establishment, going so far as to complain if he finds that they have been opened. Consequently, the other customers, cut off from the usual channels of public opinion and intelligence, remain until dinner in utter ignorance of political affairs. The Bosquet party hardly knows the names of the last cabinet."

"Monsieur Rodolphe has even obliged the cafe to subscribe to 'The Beaver,' of which he is chief editor. The master of the establishment at first refused; but as Monsieur Rodolphe and his party kept calling the waiter every half hour, and crying, 'The Beaver! bring us 'The Beaver'' some other customers, whose curiosity was excited by these obstinate demands, also asked for 'The Beaver.' So 'The Beaver' was subscribed to—a hatter's journal, which appeared every month, ornamented with a vignette and an article on 'The Philosophy of Hats and other things in general,' by Gustave Colline."

"Secondly. The aforesaid Monsieur Colline, and his friend Monsieur Rodolphe, repose themselves from their intellectual labors by playing backgammon from ten in the morning till midnight and as the establishment possess but one backgammon board, they monopolize that, to the detriment of the other amateurs of the game; and when asked for the board, they only answer, 'Some one is reading it, call tomorrow.' Thus the Bosquet party find themselves reduced to playing piquet, or talking about their old love affairs."

"Thirdly. Monsieur Marcel, forgetting that a cafe is a public place, brings thither his easel, box of colors, and, in short, all the instruments of his art. He even disregards the usages of society as far as to send for models of different sexes; which might shock the morals of the Bosquet party."

"Fourthly. Following the example of his friend, Monsieur Schaunard talks of bringing his piano to the cafe and he has not scrupled to get up a chorus on a motive from his symphony, 'The Influence of Blue in Art.' Monsieur Schaunard has gone farther: he has inserted in the lantern which serves the establishment for sign, a transparency with this inscription:

'COURSE OF MUSIC, VOCAL AND INSTRUMENTAL,
FOR BOTH SEXES,
GRATIS.
APPLY AT THE COUNTER.'

In consequence of this, the counter aforesaid is besieged every night by a number of badly dressed individuals, wanting to know where you go in."

"Moreover, Monsieur Schaunard gives meetings to a lady calling herself Mademoiselle Phemie, who always forgets to bring her bonnet. Wherefore, Monsieur Bosquet, Jr., has declared that he will never more put foot in an establishment where the laws of nature are thus outraged."

"Fifthly. Not content with being very poor customers, these gentlemen have tried to be still more economical. Under pretence of having caught the mocha of the establishment in improper intercourse with chicory, they have brought a lamp with spirits-of-wine, and make their own coffee, sweetening it with their own sugar; all of which is an insult to the establishment."

"Sixthly. Corrupted by the discourse of these gentlemen, the waiter Bergami (so called from his whiskers), forgetting his humble origin and defying all control, has dared to address to the mistress of the house a piece of poetry suggestive of the most improper sentiments; by the irregularity of its style, this letter is recognized as a direct emanation from the pernicious influence of Monsieur Rodolphe and his literature."

"Consequently, in spite of the regret which he feels, the proprietor of the establishment finds himself obliged to request the Colline party to choose some other place for their revolutionary meetings."

Gustave Colline, who was the Cicero of the set, took the floor and demonstrated to the landlord that his complaints were frivolous and unfounded; that they did him great honor in making his establishment a home of intellect; that their departure and that of their friends would be the ruin of his house, which their presence elevated to the rank of a literary and artistic club.

"But," objected the other, "you and those who come to see you call for so little."

"This temperance to which you object," replied Colline, "is an argument in favor of our morals. Moreover, it depends on yourself whether we spend more or not. You have only to open an account with us."

The landlord pretended not to hear this, and demanded some explanation of the incendiary letter addressed by Bergami to his wife. Rodolphe, accused of acting as secretary to the waiter, strenuously asserted his innocence—

"For," said he, "the lady's virtue was a sure barrier—"

The landlord would not repress a smile of pride. Finally, Colline entangled him completely in the folds of his insidious oratory, and everything was arranged, on the conditions that the party should cease making their own coffee, that the establishment should receive "The Beaver" gratis, that Phemie should come in a bonnet, that the backgammon board should be given up to the Bosquets every Sunday from twelve to two, and above all, that no one should ask for tick.

On this basis everything went well for some time.

It was Christmas Eve. The four friends came to the cafe accompanied by their friends of the other sex. There was Marcel's Musette, Rodolphe's new flame, Mimi, a lovely creature, with a voice like a pair of cymbals, and Schaunard's idol, Phemie Teinturiere. That night, Phemie, according to agreement, had her bonnet on. As to Madame Colline that should have been, no one ever saw her; she was always at home, occupied in punctuating her husband's manuscripts. After the coffee, which was on this great occasion escorted by a regiment of small glasses of brandy, they called for punch. The waiter was so little accustomed to the order, that they had to repeat it twice. Phemie, who had never been to such a place before, seemed in a state of ecstacy at drinking out of glasses with feet. Marcel was quarreling with Musette about a new bonnet which he had not given her. Mimi and Rodolphe, who were in their honeymoon, carried on a silent conversation, alternated with suspicious noises. As to Colline, he went about from one to the other, distributing among them all the polite and ornamental phrases which he had picked up in the "Muses' Almanac."

While this joyous company was thus abandoning itself to sport and laughter, a stranger at the bottom of the room, who occupied a table by himself, was observing with extraordinary attention the animated scene before him. For a fortnight or thereabout, he had come thus every night, being the only customer who could stand the terrible row which the club made. The boldest pleasantries had failed to move him; he would remain all the evening, smoking his pipe with mathematical regularity, his eyes fixed as if watching a treasure, and his ears open to all what was said around him. As to his other qualities, he seemed quiet and well off, for he possessed a watch with a gold chain; and one day, Marcel, meeting him at the bar, caught him in the act of changing a louis to pay his score. From that moment, the four friends designated him by the name of "The Capitalist."

Suddenly Schaunard, who had very good eyes, remarked that the glasses were empty.

"Yes," exclaimed Rodolphe, "and this is Christmas Eve! We are good Christians, and ought to have something extra."

"Yes, indeed," added Marcel, "let's call for something supernatural."

"Colline," continued Rodolphe, "ring a little for the waiter."

Colline rang like one possessed.

"What shall we have?" asked Marcel.

Colline made a low bow and pointed to the women.

"It is the business of these ladies to regulate the nature and order of our refreshment."

"I," said Musette, smacking her lips, "should not be afraid of Champagne."

"Are you crazy?" exclaimed Marcel. "Champagne! That isn't wine to begin with."

"So much the worse; I like it, it makes a noise."

"I," said Mimi, with a coaxing look at Rodolphe, "would like some Beaune, in a little basket."

"Have you lost your senses?" said Rodolphe.

"No, but I want to lose them," replied Mimi. The poet was thunderstruck.

"I," said Phemie, dancing herself on the elastic sofa, "would rather have parfait amour; it's good for the stomach."

Schaunard articulated, in a nasal tone, some words which made Phemie tremble on her spring foundation.

"Bah!" said Marcel, recovering himself the first. "Let us spend a hundred francs for this once!"

"Yes," said Rodolphe, "they complain of our not being good customers. Let's astonish them!"

"Ay," said Colline, "let us give ourselves up to the delights of a splendid banquet! Do we not owe passive obedience to these ladies? Love lies on devotion; wine is the essence of pleasure, pleasure the duty of youth; women are flowers and must be moistened. Moisten away! Waiter, waiter!" and Colline hung upon the bell rope with feverish excitement.

Swift as the wind, the waiter came. When he heard talk of Champagne, Burgundy, and various liqueurs, his physiognomy ran through a whole gamut of astonishment. But there was more to come.

"I have a hole in my inside," said Mimi. "I should like some ham."

"And I some sardines, and bread and butter," struck in Musette.

"And I, radishes," quoth Phemie, "and a little meat with them."

"We should have no objection," answered they.

"Waiter!" quoth Colline, gravely, "bring us all that is requisite for a good supper."

The waiter turned all the colors of the rainbow. He descended slowly to the bar, and informed his master of the extraordinary orders he had received.

The landlord took it for a joke; but on a new summons from the bell, he ascended himself and addressed Colline, for whom he had a certain respect. Colline explained to him that they wished to see Christmas in at his house, and that he would oblige them by serving what they had asked for. Momus made no answer, but backed out, twisting his napkin. For a quarter of an hour he held a consultation with his wife, who, thanks to her liberal education at the St. Denis Convent, fortunately had a weakness for arts and letters, and advised him to serve the supper.

"To be sure," said the landlord, "they may have money for once, by chance."

So he told the waiter to take up whatever they asked for, and then plunged into a game of piquet with an old customer. Fatal imprudence!

From ten to twelve the waiter did nothing but run up and downstairs. Every moment he was asked for something more. Musette would eat English fashion, and change her fork at every mouthful. Mimi drank all sorts of wine, in all sorts of glasses. Schaunard had a quenchless Sahara in his throat. Colline played a crossfire with his eyes, and while munching his napkin, as his habit was, kept pinching the leg of the table, which he took for Phemie's knee. Marcel and Rodolphe maintained the stirrups of self-possession, expecting the catastrophe, not without anxiety.

The stranger regarded the scene with grave curiosity; from time to time he opened his mouth as if for a smile; then you might have heard a noise like that of a window which creaks in shutting. It was the stranger laughing to himself.

At a quarter before twelve the bill was sent up. It amounted to the enormous sum of twenty five francs and three-quarters.

"Come," said Marcel, "we will draw lots for who shall go and diplomatize with our host. It is getting serious." They took a set of dominoes; the highest was to go.

Unluckily, the lot fell upon Schaunard, who was an excellent virtuoso, but a very bad ambassador. He arrived, too, at the bar just as the landlord had lost his third game. Momus was in a fearful bad humor, and, at Schaunard's first words, broke out into a violent rage. Schaunard was a good musician, but he had an indifferent temper, and he replied by a double discharge of slang. The dispute grew more and more bitter, till the landlord went upstairs, swearing that he would be paid, and that no one should stir until he was. Colline endeavored to interpose his pacifying oratory; but, on perceiving a napkin which Colline had made lint of, the host's anger redoubled; and to indemnify himself, he actually dared to lay profane hands on the philosopher's hazel overcoat and the ladies' shawls.

A volley of abuse was interchanged by the Bohemians and the irate landlord.

The women talked to one another of their dresses and their conquests.

At this point the stranger abandoned his impassible attitude; gradually he rose, made a step forward, then another, and walked as an ordinary man might do; he approached the landlord, took him aside, and spoke to him in a low tone. Rodolphe and Marcel followed him with their eyes. At length, the host went out, saying to the stranger:

"Certainly, I consent, Monsieur Barbemuche, certainly; arrange it with them yourself."

Monsieur Barbemuche returned to his table to take his hat; put it on, turned around to the right, and in three steps came close to Rodolphe and Marcel. He took off his hat, bowed to the men, waved a salute to the women, pulled out his handkerchief, blew his nose, and began in a feeble voice:

"Gentlemen, excuse the liberty I am about to take. For a long time, I have been burning with desire to make your acquaintance, but have never, till now, found a favorable opportunity. Will you allow me to seize the present one?"

"Certainly, certainly," said Colline. Rodolphe and Marcel bowed, and said nothing. The excessive delicacy of Schaunard came nigh spoiling everything.

"Excuse me, sir," said he briskly, "but you have not the honor of knowing us, and the usages of society forbid—would you be so good as to give me a pipeful of tobacco? In other respects I am of my friends' opinion."

"Gentlemen," continued Barbemuche. "I am a disciple of the fine arts, like yourselves. So far as I have been able to judge from what I have heard of your conversation, our tastes are the same. I have a most eager desire to be a friend of yours, and to be able to find you here every night. The landlord is a brute: but I said a word to him, and you are quite free to go. I trust you will not refuse me the opportunity of finding you here again, by accepting this slight service."

A blush of indignation mounted to Schaunard's face. "He is speculating on our condition," said he. "We cannot accept. He has paid our bill. I will play him at billiards for the twenty five francs and give him points."

Barbemuche accepted his proposition, and had the good sense to lose. This gained him the esteem of the party. They broke up with the understanding that they were to meet next day.

"Now," said Schaunard, "our dignity is saved. We owe him nothing."

"We can almost ask him for another supper," said Colline.

XII

A Bohemian "At Home"

The night when he paid out of his own purse for the supper consumed at the cafe, Barbemuche managed to make Colline accompany him. Since his first presence at the meetings of the four friends whom he had relieved from their embarrassing position, Carolus had especially remarked Gustave, and already felt an attractive sympathy for this Socrates whose Plato he was destined to become. It was for this reason he had chosen him to be his introducer. On the way, Barbemuche proposed that they should enter a cafe which was still open, and take something to drink. Not only did Colline refuse, but he doubled his speed in passing the cafe, and carefully pulled down his hyperphysic hat over his face.

"But why won't you come in?" politely asked the other.

"I have my reasons," replied Colline. "There is a barmaid in that establishment who is very much addicted to the exact sciences, and I could not help having a long discussion with her, to avoid which I never pass through this street at noon, or any other time of day. To tell you the truth," added he innocently, "I once lived with Marcel in this neighborhood."

"Still I should be very glad to offer you a glass of punch, and have a few minutes' talk with you. Is there no other place in the vicinity where you could step in without being hindered by any mathematical difficulties?" asked Barbemuche, who thought it a good opportunity for saying something very clever.

Colline mused an instant. "There is a little place here," he said, pointing to a wine shop, "where I stand on a better footing."

Barbemuche made a face, and seemed to hesitate. "Is it a respectable place?" he demanded.

His cold and reserved attitude, his limited conversation, his discreet smile, and especially his watch chain with charms on it, all led Colline to suppose that Barbemuche was a clerk in some embassy, and that he feared to compromise himself by going into some wine shop.

"There is no danger of anyone seeing us," said he. "All the diplomatic body is in bed by this time."

Barbemuche made up his mind to go in, though at the bottom of his heart he would have given a good deal for a false nose. For greater security, he insisted on having a private room, and took care to fasten a napkin before the glass door of it. These precautions taken, he appeared more at ease, and called for a bowl of punch. Excited a little by the generous beverage, Barbemuche became more communicative, and, after giving some autobiographical details, made bold to express the hope he had conceived of being personally admitted a member of the Bohemian Club, for the accomplishment of which ambitious design he solicited the aid of Colline.

Colline replied that, for his part, he was entirely at the service of Barbemuche, but, nevertheless, he could make no positive promise. "I assure you of my vote," said he. "But I cannot take it upon me to dispose of those of my comrades."

"But," asked Barbemuche, "for what reasons could they refuse to admit me among them?"

Colline put down the glass which he was just lifting to his mouth, and, in a very serious tone, addressed the rash Carolus, saying, "You cultivate the fine arts?"

"I labor humble in those noble fields of intelligence," replied the other, who felt bound to hang out the colors of his style.

Colline found the phrase well turned, and bowed in acknowledgment.

"You understand music?" he continued.

"I have played on the bass-viol."

"A very philosophical instrument. Then, if you understand music, you also understand that one cannot, without violation of the laws of harmony, introduce a fifth performer into a quartet; it would cease to be a quartet."

"Exactly, and become a quintet."

"A quintet, very well, now attend to me. You understand astronomy?"

"A little, I'm a bachelor of arts."

"There is a little song about that," said Colline. "'Dear bachelor, says Lisette'—I have forgotten the tune. Well then, you know that there are four cardinal points. Now suppose there were to turn up a fifth cardinal point, all the harmony of nature would be upset. What they call a cataclysm—you understand?"

"I am waiting for the conclusion," said Carolus, whose intelligence began to be a little shaky.

"The conclusion—yes, that is the end of the argument, as death is the end of life, and marriage of love. Well, my dear sir, I and my friends are accustomed to live together, and we fear to impair, by the introduction of another person, the harmony which reigns in our habits, opinions, tastes, and dispositions. To speak frankly, we are going to be, some day, the four cardinal points of contemporary art; accustomed to this idea, it would annoy us to see a fifth point."

"Nevertheless," suggested Carolus, "where you are four it is easy to be five."

"Yes, but then we cease to be four."

"The objection is a trivial one."

"There is nothing trivial in this world; little brooks make great rivers; little syllables make big verses; the very mountains are made of grains of sand—so says 'The Wisdom of Nations,' of which there is a copy on the quay—tell me, my dear sir, which is the furrow that you usually follow in the noble fields of intelligence?"

"The great philosophers and the classic authors are my models. I live upon their study. 'Telemachus' first inspired the consuming passion I feel."

"'Telemachus'—there are lots of him on the quay," said Colline. "You can find him there at any time. I have bought him for five sous—a second-hand copy—I would consent to part with it to oblige you. In other respects, it is a great work; very well got up, considering the age."

"Yes, sir," said Carolus. "I aspire to high philosophy and sound literature. According to my idea, art is a priesthood—"

"Yes, yes," said Colline. "There's a song about that too," and he began to hum. . .

"Art's a priesthood, art's a priesthood,"

to the air of the drinking song in "Robert the Devil."

"I say, then, that art being a solemn mission, writers ought, above all things—"

"Excuse me," said Colline, who heard one of the small hours striking, "but it's getting to be tomorrow morning very fast."

"It is late, in fact," said Carolus. "Let us go."

"Do you live far off?"

"Rue Royale St. Honore, No. 10."

HENRI MURGER

Colline had once had occasion to visit this house, and remembered that it was a splendid private mansion.

"I will mention you to my friends," said he to Carolus on parting, "and you may be sure that I shall use all my influence to make them favorably disposed to you. Ah, let me give you one piece of advice."

"Go on," said the other.

"Be very amiable and polite to Mademoiselles Mimi, Musette and Phemie; these ladies exercise an authority over my friends, and by managing to bring their mistresses' influence to bear upon them you will contrive far more easily to obtain what you require from Marcel, Schaunard and Rodolphe."

"I'll try," said Carolus.

Next day, Colline tumbled in upon the Bohemian association. It was the hour of breakfast, and for a wonder, breakfast had come with the hour. The three couples were at table, feasting on artichokes and pepper sauce.

"The deuce!" exclaimed the philosopher. "This can't last, or the world would come to an end. I arrive," he continued, "as the ambassador of the generous mortal whom we met last night."

"Can he be sending already to ask for his money again?" said Marcel.

"It has nothing to do with that," replied Colline. "This young man wishes to be one of us; to have stock in our society, and share the profits, of course."

The three men raised their heads and looked at one another.

"That's all," concluded Colline. "Now the question is open."

"What is the social position of your principal?" asked Rodolphe.

"He is no principal of mine," answered the other. "Last night he begged me to accompany him, and overflowed me with attentions and good liquor for a while. But I have retained my independence."

"Good," said Schaunard.

"Sketch us some leading features of his character," said Marcel.

"Grandeur of soul, austerity of manners, afraid to go into wine shops, bachelor of arts, candid as a transparency, plays on the bass-viol, is disposed to change a five franc piece occasionally."

"Good again!" said Schaunard.

"What are his hopes?"

"As I told you already, his ambition knows no bounds; he aspires to be 'hail-fellow-well-met' with us."

"That is to say," answered Marcel, "he wishes to speculate upon us, and to be seen riding in our carriages."

"What is his profession?" asked Rodolphe.

"Yes," said Marcel, "what does he play on?"

"Literature and mixed philosophy. He calls art a priesthood."

"A priesthood!" cried Rodolphe, in terror.

"So he says."

"And what is his road in literature?"

"He goes after 'Telemachus'."

"Very good," said Schaunard, eating the seed of his artichoke.

"Very good! You dummy!" broke our Marcel. "I advise you not to say that in the street."

Schaunard relieved his annoyance at this reproof by kicking Phemie under the table for taking some of his sauce.

"Once more," said Rodolphe. "What is his condition in the world? What does he live on, and where does he live? And what is his name?"

"His station is honorable. He is professor of everything in a rich family. His name is Carolus Barbemuche. He spends his income in luxurious living and dwells in the Rue Royale."

"Furnished lodging?"

"No, there is real furniture."

"I claim the floor," said Marcel. "To me it is evident that Colline has been corrupted. He has already sold his vote for so many drinks. Don't interrupt me! (Colline was rising to protest.) You shall have your turn. Colline, mercenary soul that he is, has presented to you this stranger under an aspect too favorable to be true. I told you before; I see through this person's designs. He wants to speculate on us. He says to himself, 'Here are some chaps making their way. I must get into their pockets. I shall arrive with them at the goal of fame.'"

"Bravo!" quoth Schaunard, "have you any more sauce there?"

"No," replied Rodolphe, "the edition is out of print."

"Looking at the question from another point of view," continued Marcel, "this insidious mortal whom Colline patronizes, perhaps aspires to our intimacy only from the most culpable motives. Gentlemen, we are not alone here!" continued the orator, with an eloquent look at the women. "And Colline's client, smuggling himself into our circle under the cloak of literature, may perchance be but a vile seducer. Reflect! For one, I vote against his reception."

"I demand the floor," said Rodolphe, "only for a correction. In his remarkable extemporary speech, Marcel has said that this Carolus, with the view of dishonoring us, wished to introduce himself under the cloak of literature."

"A Parliamentary figure."

"A very bad figure; literature has no cloak!"

"Having made a report, as chairman of committee," resumed Colline, rising, "I maintain the conclusions therein embodied. The jealousy which consumes him disturbs the reason of our friend Marcel; the great artist is beside himself."

"Order!" cried Marcel.

"So much so, that, able designer as he is, he has just introduced into his speech a figure the incorrectness of which has been ably pointed out by the talented orator who preceded me."

"Colline is an ass!" shouted Marcel, with a bang of his fist on the table that caused a lively sensation among the plates. "Colline knows nothing in an affair of sentiment; he is incompetent to judge of such matters; he has an old book in place of a heart."

Prolonged laughter from Schaunard. During the row, Colline kept gravely adjusting the folds of his white cravat as if to make way for the torrents of eloquence contained beneath them. When silence was reestablished, he thus continued:

"Gentlemen, I intend with one word to banish from your minds the chimerical apprehensions which the suspicions of Marcel may have engendered in them respecting Carolus."

"Oh, yes!" said Marcel ironically.

"It will be as easy as that," continued Colline, blowing the match with which he had lighted his pipe.

"Go on! Go on!" cried Schaunard, Rodolphe, and the women together.

"Gentlemen! Although I have been personally and violently attacked in this meeting, although I have been accused of selling for base liquors the influence which I possess; secure in a good conscience I shall not deign to reply to those assaults on my probity, my loyalty, my morality. (Sensation.) But there is one thing which I will have respected. (Here the orator, endeavoring to lay his hand on his heart, gave himself a rap in the stomach.) My well tried and well known prudence has been called in question. I have been accused of wishing to introduce among you a person whose intentions were hostile to your happiness—in matters of sentiment. This supposition is an insult to the virtue of these ladies—nay more, an insult to their good taste. Carolus Barbemuche is decidedly ugly." (Visible denial on the face of Phemie; noise under the table; it is Schaunard kicking her by way of correcting her compromising frankness.)

"But," proceeded Colline, "what will reduce to powder the contemptible argument with which my opponent has armed himself against Carolus by taking advantage of your terrors, is the fact that the said Carolus is a Platonist." (Sensation among the men; uproar among the women.)

This declaration of Colline's produced a reaction in favor of Carolus. The philosopher wished to improve the effect of his eloquent and adroit defense.

"Now then," he continued, "I do not see what well founded prejudices can exist against this young man, who, after all, has rendered us a service. As to myself, who am accused of acting thoughtlessly in wishing to introduce him among us, I consider this opinion an insult to my dignity. I have acted in the affair with the wisdom of the serpent; if a formal vote does not maintain me this character for prudence, I offer my resignation."

"Do you make it a cabinet question?" asked Marcel.

"I do."

The three consulted, and agreed by common consent to restore to the philosopher that high reputation for prudence which he claimed. Colline then gave the floor to Marcel, who, somewhat relieved of his prejudices, declared that he might perhaps favor the adoption of the report. But before the decisive and final vote which should open to Carolus the intimacy of the club, he put to the meeting this amendment:

"WHEREAS, the introduction of a new member into our society is a grave matter, and a stranger might bring with him some elements of discord through ignorance of the habits, tempers, and opinions of his comrades,

RESOLVED, that each member shall pass a say with the said Carolus, and investigate his manner of life, tastes, literary capacity, and wardrobe. The members shall afterward communicate their several impressions, and ballot on his admission accordingly. Moreover, before complete admission, the said Carolus shall undergo a noviciate of one month, during which time he shall not have the right to call us by our first names or take our arm in the street. On the day of reception, a splendid banquet shall be given at the expense of the new member, at a cost of not less than twelve francs."

This amendment was adopted by three votes against one. The same night Colline went to the cafe early on purpose to be the first to see Carolus. He had not long to wait for him. Barbemuche soon appeared, carrying in his hand three huge bouquets of roses.

"Hullo!" cried the astonished Colline. "What do you mean to do with that garden?"

"I remember what you told me yesterday. Your friends will doubtless come with their ladies, and it is on their account that I bring these flowers—very handsome ones."

"That they are; they must have cost fifteen sous, at least."

"In the month of December! If you said fifteen francs you would have come nearer."

"Heavens!" cried Colline, "three crowns for these simple gifts of flora! You must be related to the Cordilleras. Well my dear sir, that is fifteen francs which we must throw out of the window."

It was Barbemuche's turn to be astonished. Colline related the jealous suspicions with which Marcel had inspired his friends, and informed Carolus of the violent discussion which had taken place between them that morning on the subject of his admission.

"I protested," said Colline, "that your intentions were the purest, but there was strong opposition nevertheless. Beware of renewing these suspicions by much politeness to the ladies; and to begin, let us put these bouquets out of the way." He took the roses and hid them in a cupboard. "But this is not all," he resumed. "Before connecting themselves intimately with you, these gentlemen desire to make a private examination, each for himself, of your character, tastes, etc."

Then, lest Barbemuche might do something to shock his friends, Colline rapidly sketched a moral portrait of each of them. "Contrive to agree with them separately," added the philosopher, "and they will end by all liking you."

Carolus agreed to everything. The three friends soon arrived with their friends of the other sex. Rodolphe was polite to Carolus, Schaunard familiar with him, while Marcel remained cold. Carolus forced himself to be gay and amiable with the men and indifferent to the women. When they broke up for the night, he asked Rodolphe to dine with him the next day, and to come as early as noon. The poet accepted, saying to himself, "Good! I am to begin the inquiry, then."

Next morning at the hour appointed, he called on Carolus, who did indeed live in a very handsome private house, where he occupied a sufficiently comfortable room. But Rodolphe was surprised to find at that time of day the shutters closed, the curtains drawn, and two lighted candles on the table. He asked Barbemuche the reason.

"Study," replied the other, "is the child of mystery and silence."

They sat down and talked. At the end of an hour, Carolus, with infinite oratorial address, brought in a phrase which, despite its humble form, was neither more nor less than a summons made to Rodolphe to hear a little work, the fruit of Barbemuche's vigils.

The poet saw himself caught. Curious, however, to learn the color of the other's style, he bowed politely, assured him that he was enchanted, that Carolus did not wait for him to finish the sentence. He ran to bolt the door, and then took up a small memorandum book, the thinness of which brought a smile of satisfaction to the poet's face.

"Is that the manuscript of your work?" he asked.

"No," replied Carolus. "It is the catalog of my manuscripts and I am looking for the one which you will allow me to read you. Here it is: 'Don Lopez or Fatality No. 14.' It's on the third shelf," and he proceeded to open a small closet in which Rodolphe perceived, with terror, a great quantity of manuscripts. Carolus took out one of these, shut the closet, and seated himself in front of the poet.

Rodolphe cast a glance at one of the four piles of elephant paper of which the work was composed. "Come," said he to himself, "it's not in verse, but it's called 'Don Lopez.'"

Carolus began to read:

"On a cold winter night, two cavaliers, enveloped in large cloaks, and mounted on sluggish mules, were making their way side by side over one of the roads which traverse the frightful solitudes of the Sierra Morena."

"May the Lord have mercy on me!" exclaimed Rodolphe mentally.

Carolus continued to read his first chapter, written in the style above throughout. Rodolphe listened vaguely, and tried to devise some means of escape.

"There is the window, but it's fastened; and beside, we are in the fourth story. Ah, now I understand all these precautions."

"What do you think of my first chapter?" asked Carolus. "Do not spare any criticism, I beg of you."

Rodolphe thought he remembered having heard some scraps of philosophical declamation upon suicide, put forth by the hero of the romance, Don Lopez, to wit; so he replied at hazard:

"The grand figure of Don Lopez is conscientiously studied; it reminds me of 'Savoyard Vicar's Confession of Faith;' the description of Don Alvar's mule pleases me exceedingly; it is like a sketch of Gericault's. There are good lines in the landscape; as to the thoughts, they are seeds of Rousseau planted in the soil of Lesage. Only allow me to make one observation: you use too many stops, and you work the word henceforward too hard. It is a good word, and gives color, but should not be abused."

Carolus took up a second pile of paper, and repeated the title "Don Lopez or, Fatality."

"I knew a Don Lopez once," said Rodolphe. "He used to sell cigarettes and Bayonne chocolate. Perhaps he was a relative of your man. Go on."

At the conclusion of the second chapter, the poet interrupted his host:

"Don't you feel your throat a little dry?" he inquired.

"Not at all," replied Carolus. "We are coming to the history of Inesilla."

"I am very curious to hear it, nevertheless, if you are tired—"

"Chapter third!" enunciated Carolus in a voice that gave no signs of fatigue.

Rodolphe took a careful survey of Barbemuche and perceived that he had a short neck and a ruddy complexion. "I have one hope left," thought the poet on making this discovery. "He may have an attack of apoplexy."

"Will you be so good as to tell me what you think of the love scene?"

Carolus looked at Rodolphe to observe in his face what effect the dialogue produced upon him. The poet was bending forward on his chair, with his neck stretched out in the attitude of one who is listening for some distant sound.

"What's the matter with you?"

"Hist!" said Rodolphe, "don't you hear? I thought somebody cried fire! Suppose we go and see."

Carolus listened an instant but heard nothing.

"It must have been a ringing in my ears," said the other. "Go on, Don Alvar interests me exceedingly; he is a noble youth."

Carolus continued with all the music that he could put into his voice:

"Oh Inesilla! Whatever thou art, angel or demon; and whatever be thy country, my life is thine, and thee will follow, be it to heaven or hell!"

Someone knocked at the door.

"It's my porter," said Barbemuche, half opening the door.

It was indeed the porter with a letter. "What an unlucky chance!" cried Carolus, after he had perused it. "We must put off our reading until some other time. I have to go out immediately. If you please, we will execute this little commission together, as it is nothing private, and then we can come back to dinner."

"There," thought Rodolphe, "is a letter that has fallen from heaven. I recognize the seal of Providence."

When he rejoined the comrades that night, the poet was interrogated by Marcel and Schaunard.

"Did he treat you well?" they asked.

"Yes, but I paid dear for it."

"How? Did Carolus make you pay?" demanded Schaunard with rising choler.

"He read a novel at me, inside of which the people are named Don Lopez and Don Alvar; and the tenors call their mistresses 'angel,' or 'demon.'"

"How shocking!" cried the Bohemians, in chorus.

"But otherwise," said Colline, "literature apart, what is your opinion of him?"

"A very nice young man. You can judge for yourselves; Carolus means to treat us all in turn; he invites Schaunard to breakfast with him tomorrow. Only look out for the closet with the manuscripts in it."

Schaunard was punctual and went to work with the minuteness of an auctioneer taking an inventory, or a sheriff levying an execution. Accordingly he came back full of notes; he had studied Carolus chiefly in respect of movables and worldly goods.

"This Barbemuche," he said, on being asked his opinion, "is a lump of good qualities. He knows the names of all the wines that were ever invented, and made me eat more nice things than my aunt ever did on her birthday. He is on very good terms with the tailors in the Rue Vivienne, and the bootmakers of the Passage des Panoramas; and I have observed that he is nearly our size, so that, in case of need, we can lend him our clothes. His habits are less austere than Colline chose to represent them; he went wherever I pleased to take him, and gave me breakfast in two acts, the second of which went off in a tavern by the fish market where I am known for some Carnival orgies. Well, Carolus went in there as any ordinary mortal might, and that's all. Marcel goes tomorrow."

Carolus knew that Marcel was the one who had made the most objections to his reception. Accordingly, he treated him with particular attention, and especially won his heart by holding out the hope of procuring him some sitters in the family of his pupil. When it came to Marcel's turn to make his report, there were no traces of his original hostility to Carolus.

On the fourth day, Colline informed Barbemuche that he was admitted, but under conditions. "You have a number of vulgar habits," he said, "which must be reformed."

"I shall do my best to imitate you," said Carolus.

During the whole time of his noviciate the Platonic philosopher kept company with the Bohemians continually, and was thus enabled to study their habits more thoroughly, not without being very much astonished at times. One morning, Colline came to see him with a joyful face.

"My dear fellow," he said, "it's all over; you are now definitely one of us. It only remains to fix the day and the place of the grand entertainment; I have come to talk with you about it."

"That can be arranged with perfect ease," said Carolus. "The parents of my pupil are out of town; the young viscount, whose mentor I am, will lend us the apartments for an evening, only we must invite him to the party."

"That will be very nice," replied Colline. "We will open to him the vistas of literature; but do you think he will consent?"

"I am sure of it."

"Then it only remains to fix the day."

"We will settle that tonight at the cafe."

Carolus then went to find his pupil and announced to him that he had just been elected into a distinguished society of literary men and artists, and that he was going to give a dinner, followed by a little party, to celebrate his admission. He therefore proposed to him to make him one of the guests. "And since you cannot be out late," added Carolus, "and the entertainment may last some time, it will be for our convenience to have it here. Your servant François knows how to hold his tongue; your parents will know nothing of it; and you will have made acquaintance with some of the cleverest people in Paris, artists and authors."

"In print?" asked the youth.

"Certainly, one of them edits 'The Scarf of Iris,' which your mother takes in. They are very distinguished persons, almost celebrities, intimate friends of mine, and their wives are charming."

"Will there be some women?" asked Viscount Paul.

"Delightful ones," returned Carolus.

"Oh, dear master, I thank you. The entertainment shall certainly take place here. All the lustres shall be lit up, and I will have the wrappers taken off the furniture."

That night at the cafe, Barbemuche announced that the party would come off next Saturday. The Bohemians told their mistresses to think about their toilettes.

"Do not forget," said they, "that we are going into the real drawing rooms. Therefore, make ready; a rich but simple costume."

And from that day all the neighborhood was informed that Mademoiselles Phemie, Mimi, and Musette were going into society.

On the morning of the festivity, Colline, Schaunard, Marcel, and Rodolphe called, in a body, on Barbemuche, who looked astonished to see them so early.

"Has anything happened which will oblige us to put it off?" he asked with some anxiety.

"Yes—that is, no," said Colline. "This is how we are placed. Among ourselves we never stand on ceremony, but when we are to meet strangers, we wish to preserve a certain decorum."

"Well?" said the other.

"Well," continued Colline, "since we are to meet tonight, the young gentleman to whom we are indebted for the rooms, out of respect to him and to ourselves, we come simply to ask you if you cannot lend us some becoming toggery. It is almost impossible, you see, for us to enter this gorgeous roof in frock-coats and colored trousers."

"But," said Carolus, "I have not black clothes for all of you."

"We will make do with what you have," said Colline.

"Suit yourselves then," said Carolus, opening a well-furnished wardrobe.

"What an arsenal of elegancies!" said Marcel.

"Three hats!" exclaimed Schaunard, in ecstasy. "Can a man want three hats when he had but one head?"

"And the boots!" said Rodolphe, "only look!"

"What a number of boots!" howled Colline.

In a twinkling of an eye each had selected a complete equipment.

"Till this evening," said they, taking leave of Barbemuche. "The ladies intend to be most dazzling."

"But," said Barbemuche, casting a glance at the emptied wardrobe. "You have left me nothing. What am I to wear?"

"Ah, it's different with you," said Rodolphe. "You are the master of the house; you need not stand upon etiquette."

"But I have only my dressing gown and slippers, flannel waistcoat and trousers with stocking feet. You have taken everything."

"Never mind; we excuse you beforehand," replied the four.

A very good dinner was served at six. The company arrived, Marcel limping and out of humor. The young viscount rushed up to the ladies and led them to the best seats. Mimi was dressed with fanciful elegance; Musette got up with seductive taste; Phemie looked like a stained glass window, and hardly dared sit down.

The dinner lasted two hours and a half, and was delightfully lively. The young viscount, who sat next to Mimi, kept treading on her foot. Phemie took twice of every dish. Schaunard was in clover. Rodolphe improvised sonnets and broke glasses in marking the rhyme. Colline talked to Marcel, who remained sulky.

"What is the matter with you?" asked the philosopher.

"My feet are in torture; this Carolus has boots like a woman's."

"He must be given to understand that, for the future, some of his shoes are to be made a little larger. Be easy, I will see to it. But now to the drawing room, where the coffee and liquers await us."

The revelry recommenced with increased noise. Schaunard seated himself at the piano and executed, with immense spirit, his new symphony, "The Death of the Damsel." To this succeeded the characteristic piece of "The Creditor's March," which was twice encored, and two chords of the piano were broken.

Marcel was still morose, and replied to the complaints and expostulations of Carolus:

"My dear sir, we shall never be intimate friends, and for this reason: Physical differences are almost always the certain sign of a moral difference; on this point philosophy and medicine agree."

"Well?" said Carolus.

"Well," continued Marcel, showing his feet, "your boots, infinitely too small for me, indicate a radical difference of temper and character; in other respects, your little party has been charming."

At one in the morning the guests took leave, and zig-zagged homeward. Barbemuche felt very ill, and made incoherent harangues to his pupil, who, for his part, was dreaming of Mademoiselle Mimi's blue eyes.

XIII

The House Warming

This took place some time after the union of the poet Rodolphe and Mademoiselle Mimi. For a week the whole of the Bohemian brotherhood were grievously perturbed by the disappearance of Rodolphe, who had suddenly become invisible. They had sought for him in all his customary haunts, and had everywhere been met by the same reply—

"We have not seen him for a week."

Gustave Colline above all was very uneasy, and for the following reason. A few days previously he had handed to Rodolphe a highly philosophical article, which the latter was to insert in the columns of "The Beaver," the organ of the hat trade, of which he was editor. Had this philosophical article burst upon the gaze of astonished Europe? Such was the query put to himself by the astonished Colline, and this anxiety will be understood when it is explained that the philosopher had never yet had the honor of appearing in print, and that he was consumed by the desire of seeing what effect would be produced by his prose in pica. To procure himself this gratification he had already expended six francs in visiting all the reading rooms of Paris without being able to find "The Beaver" in any one of them. Not being able to stand it any longer, Colline swore to himself that he would not take a moment's rest until he had laid hands on the undiscoverable editor of this paper.

Aided by chances which it would take too long to tell in detail, the philosopher was able to keep his word. Within two days he learned Rodolphe's abiding place and called on him there at six in the morning.

Rodolphe was then residing in a lodging house in a deserted street situated in the Faubourg Saint Germain, and was perched on the fifth floor because there was not a sixth. When Colline came to his door there was no key in the lock outside. He knocked for ten minutes without obtaining any answer from within; the din he made at this early hour attracted the attention of even the porter, who came to ask him to be quiet.

"You see very well that the gentleman is asleep," said he.

"That is why I want to wake him up," replied Colline, knocking again.

"He does not want to answer then," replied the porter, placing before Rodolphe's door a pair of patent leather boots and a pair of lady's boots that he had just cleaned.

"Wait a bit though," observed Colline, examining the masculine and feminine foot gear. "New patent leathers! I must have made a mistake; it cannot be here."

"Yes, by the way," said the porter, "whom do you want?"

"A woman's boots!" continued Colline, speaking to himself, and thinking of his friends austere manners, "Yes, certainly I must have made a mistake. This is not Rodolphe's room."

"I beg your pardon, sir, it is."

"You must be making a mistake, my good man."

"What do you mean?"

"Decidedly you must be making a mistake," said Colline, pointing to the patent leather boots. "What are those?"

"Those are Monsieur Rodolphe's boots. What is there to be wondered at in that?"

"And these?" asked Colline, pointing to the lady's boots. "Are they Monsieur Rodolphe's too?"

"Those are his wife's," said the porter.

"His wife's!" exclaimed Colline in a tone of stupefaction. "Ah! The voluptuary, that is why he will not open the door."

"Well," said the porter, "he is free to do as he likes about that, sir. If you will leave me your name I will let him know you called."

"No," said Colline. "Now that I know where to find him I will call again."

And he at once went off to tell the important news to his friends.

Rodolphe's patent leathers were generally considered to be a fable due to Colline's wealth of imagination, and it was unanimously declared that his mistress was a paradox.

This paradox was, however, a truism, for that very evening Marcel received a letter collectively addressed to the whole of the set. It was as follows:—

"Monsieur and Madame Rodolphe, literati, beg you to favor them with your company at dinner tomorrow evening at five o'clock sharp."

"N.B.—There will be plates."

"Gentlemen," said Marcel, when communicating the letter to his comrades, "the news is confirmed, Rodolphe has really a mistress;

further he invites us to dinner, and the postscript promises crockery. I will not conceal from you that this last paragraph seems to me a lyrical exaggeration, but we shall see."

The following day at the hour named, Marcel, Gustave Colline, and Alexander Schaunard, keen set as on the last day of Lent, went to Rodolphe's, whom they found playing with a sandy haired cat, whilst a young woman was laying the table.

"Gentlemen," said Rodolphe, shaking his friends' hands and indicating the young lady, "allow me to introduce you to the mistress of the household."

"You are the household, are you not?" said Colline, who had a mania for this kind of joke.

"Mimi," replied Rodolphe, "I present my best friends; now go and get the soup ready."

"Oh madame," said Alexander Schaunard, hastening towards Mimi, "you are as fresh as a wild flower."

After having satisfied himself that there were really plates on the table, Schaunard asked what they were going to have to eat. He even carried his curiosity so far as to lift up the covers of the stewpans in which the dinner was cooking. The presence of a lobster produced a lively impression upon him.

As to Colline, he had drawn Rodolphe aside to ask about his philosophical article.

"My dear fellow, it is at the printer's. 'The Beaver' appears next Thursday."

We give up the task of depicting the philosopher's delight.

"Gentlemen," said Rodolphe to his friends. "I ask your pardon for leaving you so long without any news of me, but I was spending my honeymoon." And he narrated the story of his union with the charming creature who had brought him as a dowry her eighteen years and a half, two porcelain cups, and a sandy haired cat named Mimi, like herself.

"Come, gentlemen," said Rodolphe, "we are going to celebrate my house warming. I forewarn you, though, that we are about to have merely a family repast; truffles will be replaced by frank cordiality."

Indeed, that amiable goddess did not cease to reign amongst the guests, who found, however, that the so-called frugal repast did not lack a certain amplitude. Rodolphe, indeed, had spread himself out. Colline called attention to the fact that the plates were changed, and declared aloud that Mademoiselle Mimi was worthy of the azure scarf with which the empresses of the cooking stove were adorned, a phrase which was Greek to the young girl, and which Rodolphe translated by telling her "that she would make a capital Cordon Bleu."

The appearance on the scene of the lobster caused universal admiration. Under the pretext that he had studied natural history, Schaunard suggested that he should carve it. He even profited by this circumstance to break a knife and to take the largest helping for himself, which excited general indignation. But Schaunard had no self respect, above all in the matter of lobsters, and as there was still a portion left, he had the audacity to put it on one side, saying that he would do for a model for a still life piece he had on hand.

Indulgent friendship feigned to believe this fiction, but fruit of immoderate gluttony.

As to Colline he reserved his sympathies for the dessert, and was even obstinate enough to cruelly refuse the share of a tipsy cake against a ticket of admission to the orangery of Versailles offered to him by Schaunard.

At this point conversation began to get lively. To three bottles with red seals succeeded three bottles with green seals, in the midst of which shortly appeared one which by its neck topped with a silver helmet, was recognized as belonging to the Royal Champagne Regiment—a fantastic Champagne vintaged by Saint Ouen, and sold in Paris at two francs the bottle as bankrupt's stock, so the vendor asserted.

But it is not the district that makes the wine, and our Bohemians accepted as the authentic growth of Ai the liquor that was served out to them in the appropriate glasses, and despite the scant degree of vivacity shown by the cork in popping from its prison, went into ecstacies over the excellence of the vintage on seeing the quality of the froth. Schaunard summoned up all his remaining self-possession to make a mistake as regards glasses, and help himself to that of Colline, who kept gravely dipping his biscuit in the mustard pot as he explained to Mademoiselle Mimi the philosophical article that was to appear in "The Beaver." All at once he grew pale, and asked leave to go to the window and look at the sunset, although it was ten o'clock at night, and the sun had set long ago.

"It is a pity the Champagne is not iced," said Schaunard, again trying to substitute his empty glass for the full one of his neighbor, an attempt this time without success.

"Madame," observed Colline, who had ceased to take the fresh air, to Mimi, "Champagne is iced with ice. Ice is formed by the condensation of water, in Latin aqua. Water freezes at two degrees, and there are four seasons, spring, summer, autumn, and winter, which was the cause of the retreat from Moscow."

All at once Colline suddenly slapped Rodolphe on the shoulder, and in a thick voice that seemed to mash all the syllables together, said to him—

"Tomorrow is Thursday, is it not?"

"No," replied Rodolphe. "Tomorrow is Sunday."

"Thursday."

"No, I tell you. Tomorrow is Sunday."

"Sunday!" said Colline, wagging his head, "not a bit of it, it is Thursday."

And he fell asleep, making a mold for a cast of his face in the cream cheese that was before him in his plate.

"What is he harping about Thursday?" observed Marcel.

"Ah, I have it!" said Rodolphe, who began to understand the persistency of the philosopher, tormented by a fixed idea, "it is on account of his article in 'The Beaver.' Listen, he is dreaming of it aloud."

"Good," said Schaunard. "He shall not have any coffee, eh, madame?"

"By the way," said Rodolphe, "pour out the coffee, Mimi."

The latter was about to rise, when Colline, who had recovered a little self possession, caught her around the waist and whispered confidentially in her ear:

"Madame, the coffee plant is a native of Arabia, where it was discovered by a goat. Its use expanded to Europe. Voltaire used to drink seventy cups a day. I like mine without sugar, but very hot."

"Good heavens! What a learned man!" thought Mimi as she brought the coffee and pipes.

However time was getting on, midnight had long since struck, and Rodolphe sought to make his guests understand that it was time for them to withdraw. Marcel, who retained all his senses, got up to go.

But Schaunard perceived that there was still some brandy in a bottle, and declared that it could not be midnight so long as there was any left. As to Colline, he was sitting astride his chair and murmuring in a low voice:

"Monday, Tuesday, Wednesday, Thursday."

"Hang it all," said Rodolphe, greatly embarrassed, "I cannot give them quarters here tonight; formerly it was all very well, but now it is another thing," he added, looking at Mimi, whose softly kindling eyes seemed to appeal for solitude for their two selves. "What is to be done? Give me a bit of advice, Marcel. Invent a trick to get rid of them."

"No, I won't invent," replied Marcel, "but I will imitate. I remember a play in which a sharp servant manages to get rid of three rascals as drunk as Silenus who are at his master's."

"I recollect it," said Rodolphe, "it is in 'Kean.' Indeed, the situation is the same."

"Well," said Marcel, "we will see if the stage holds the glass up to human nature. Stop a bit, we will begin with Schaunard. Here, I say, Schaunard."

"Eh? What is it?" replied the latter, who seemed to be floating in the elysium of mild intoxication.

"There is nothing more to drink here, and we are all thirsty."

"Yes," said Schaunard, "bottles are so small."

"Well," continued Marcel, "Rodolphe has decided that we shall pass the night here, but we must go and get something before the shops are shut."

"My grocer lives at the corner of the street," said Rodolphe. "Do you mind going there, Schaunard? You can fetch two bottles of rum, to be put down to me."

"Oh! yes, certainly," said Schaunard, making a mistake in his greatcoat and taking that of Colline, who was tracing figures on the table cloth with his knife.

"One," said Marcel, when Schaunard had gone. "Now let us tackle Colline, that will be a harder job. Ah! an idea. Hi, hi, Colline," he continued, shaking the philosopher.

"What? what? what is it?"

"Schaunard has just gone, and has taken your hazel overcoat by mistake."

Colline glanced round again, and perceived indeed in the place of his garment, Schaunard's little plaid overcoat. A sudden idea flashed across his mind and filled him with uneasiness. Colline, according to his custom, had been book-hunting during the day, and had bought for fifteen sous a Finnish grammar and a little novel of Nisard's entitled "The Milkwoman's Funeral." These two acquisitions were accompanied by seven or eight volumes of philosophy that he had always about him as an arsenal whence to draw reasons in case of an argument. The idea of this library being in the hands of Schaunard threw him into a cold perspiration.

HENRI MURGER

"The wretch!" exclaimed Colline, "what did he take my greatcoat for?"

"It was by mistake."

"But my books. He may put them to some improper purpose."

"Do not be afraid, he will not read them," said Rodolphe.

"No, but I know him; he is capable of lighting his pipe with them."

"If you are uneasy you can catch him up," said Rodolphe. "He has only just this moment gone out, you will overtake him at the street door."

"Certainly I will overtake him," replied Colline, putting on his hat, the brim of which was so broad that tea for six people might have been served upon it.

"Two," said Marcel to Rodolphe, "now you are free. I am off, and I will tell the porter not to open the outer door if anyone knocks."

"Goodnight and thanks," said Rodolphe.

As he was showing his friend out Rodolphe heard on the staircase a prolonged mew, to which his carroty cat replied by another, whilst trying at the same time to slip out adroitly by the half-opened door.

"Poor Romeo!" said Rodolphe, "there is his Juliet calling him. Come, off with you," he added opening the door to the enamored beast, who made a single leap down the stairs into its lover's arms.

Left alone with his mistress, who standing before the glass was curling her hair in a charmingly provocative attitude, Rodolphe approached Mimi and passed his arms around her. Then, like a musician, who before commencing a piece, strikes a series of notes to assure himself of the capacity of the instrument, Rodolphe drew Mimi onto his knee, and printed on her shoulder a long and sonorous kiss, which imparted a sudden vibration to the frame of the youthful beauty.

The instrument was in tune.

XIV

MADEMOISELLE MIMI

Oh! my friend Rodolphe, what has happened to change you thus? Am I to believe the rumors that are current, and that this misfortune has broken down to such a degree your robust philosophy? How can I, the historian in ordinary of your Bohemian epic, so full of joyous bursts of laughter, narrate in a sufficiently melancholy tone the painful adventure which casts a veil over your constant gaiety, and suddenly checks the ringing flow of your paradoxes?

Oh! Rodolphe, my friend, I admit that the evil is serious, but there, really it is not worthwhile throwing oneself into the water about it. So I invite you to bury the past as soon as possible. Shun above all the solitude peopled with phantoms who would help to render your regrets eternal. Shun the silence where the echoes of recollection would still be full of your past joys and sorrows. Cast boldly to all the winds of forgetfulness the name you have so fondly cherished, and with it all that still remains to you of her who bore it. Curls pressed by lips mad with desire, a Venice flask in which there still lurks a remainder of perfume, which at this moment it would be more dangerous for you to breathe than all the poisons in the world. To the fire with the flowers, the flowers of gauze, silk and velvet, the white geraniums, the anemones empurpled by the blood of Adonis, the blue forget-me-nots and all those charming bouquets that she put together in the far off days of your brief happiness. Then I loved her too, your Mimi, and saw no danger in your loving her. But follow my advice—to the fire with the ribbons, the pretty pink, blue, and yellow ribbons which she wore round her neck to attract the eye; to the fire with the lace, the caps, the veils and all the coquettish trifles with which she bedecked herself to go love-making with Monsieur Cesar, Monsieur Jerome, Monsieur Charles, or any other gallant in the calendar, whilst you were awaiting her at your window, shivering from the wintry blast. To the fire, Rodolphe, and without pity, with all that belonged to her and could still speak to you of her; to the fire with the love letters. Ah! here is one of them, and your tears have bedewed it like a fountain. Oh! my unhappy friend!

"As you have not come in, I am going out to call on my aunt. I have taken what money there was for a cab."

Lucille

That evening, oh! Rodolphe, you had, do you not recollect, to go without your dinner, and you called on me and let off a volley of jests which fully attested your tranquillity of mind. For you believed Lucille was at her aunt's, and if I had not told you that she was with Monsieur Cesar or with an actor of the Montparnasse Theater, you would have cut my throat! To the fire, too, with this other note, which has all the laconic affection of the first.

"I am gone out to order some boots, you must find the money for me to go and fetch them tomorrow."

Ah! my friend, those boots have danced many quadrilles in which you did not figure as a partner. To the flames with all these remembrances and to the winds with their ashes.

But in the first place, oh Rodolphe! for the love of humanity and the reputation of "The Scarf of Iris" and "The Beaver," resume the reins of good taste that you have egotistically dropped during your sufferings, or else horrible things may happen for which you will be responsible. We may go back to leg-of-mutton sleeves and frilled trousers, and some fine day see hats come into fashion which would afflict the universe and call down the wrath of heaven.

And now the moment is come to relate the loves of our friend Rodolphe and Mimi. It was just as he was turned four and twenty that Rodolphe was suddenly smitten with the passion that had such an influence upon his life. At the time he met Mimi he was leading that broken and fantastic existence that we have tried to describe in the preceding chapters of this book. He was certainly one of the gayest endurers of poverty in the world of Bohemia. When in course of the day he had made a poor dinner and a smart remark, he walked more proudly in his black coat (pleading for help through every gaping seam) along the pavement that often promised to be his only resting place for the night, than an emperor in his purple robe. In the group amongst whom Rodolphe lived, they affected, after a fashion common enough amongst some young fellows, to treat love as a thing of luxury, a pretext for jesting. Gustave Colline, who had for a long time past been in intimate relations with a waistcoat maker, whom he was rendering deformed in mind and body by obliging her to sit day and night copying the manuscripts of his philosophical works, asserted that love was a kind of purgative, good to take at the beginning of each season in order to get rid of humors. Amidst all these false sceptics Rodolphe was the only one who dared to talk of love with some reverence, and when they had the misfortune to let him harp on this string, he would go on for an hour plaintively wurbling elegies on the happiness of being loved, the deep blue of the peaceful lake, the song of the breeze, the harmony of the stars, &c., &c. This mania had caused him to be nicknamed the harmonica by Schaunard. Marcel had also made on this subject a very neat remark when, alluding to the Teutonically sentimental tirades of Rodolphe and to his premature calvity, he called him the bald forget-me-not. The real truth was this. Rodolphe then seriously believed he had done with all things of youth and love; he insolently chanted a *De profundis* over his heart, which he thought dead when it was only silent, yet still ready to awake, still accessible to joy, and more susceptible than ever to all the sweet pangs that he no longer hoped for, and that were now driving him to despair. You would have it, Rodolphe, and we shall not pity you, for the disease from which you are suffering is one of those we long for most, above all when we know that we are cured of it forever.

Rodolphe then met Mimi, whom he had formerly known when she was the mistress of one of his friends; and he made her his own. There was at first a great outcry amongst Rodolphe's friends when they learned of this union, but as Mademoiselle Mimi was very taking, not at all prudish, and could stand tobacco smoke and literary conversations without a headache, they became accustomed to her and treated her as a comrade. Mimi was a charming girl, and especially adapted for both the plastic and poetical sympathies of Rodolphe. She was twenty two years of age, small, delicate, and arch. Her face seemed the first sketch of an aristocratic countenance, but her features, extremely fine in outline, and as it were, softly lit up by the light of her clear blue eyes, wore, at certain moments of weariness or ill-humor, an expression of almost savage brutality, in which a physiologist would perhaps have recognized the indication of profound egotism or great insensibility. But hers was usually a charming head, with a fresh and youthful smile and glances either tender or full of imperious coquetry. The blood of youth flowed warm and rapid in her veins, and imparted rosy tints to her transparent skin of camellia-like whiteness. This unhealthy beauty captivated Rodolphe, and he often during the night spent hours in covering with kisses the pale forehead of his slumbering mistress, whose humid and weary eyes shone half-closed beneath the curtain of her magnificent brown hair. But what contributed above all to make Rodolphe madly in love with Mademoiselle Mimi were her hands, which in spite of household cares, she managed to keep as white as those of the Goddess of Idleness. However, these hands so frail, so tiny, so soft to the lips; these child-like hands in which Rodolphe had placed his once more awakened heart; these white hands of Mademoiselle Mimi were soon to rend that heart with their rosy nails.

At the end of a month Rodolphe began to perceive that he was wedded to a thunderstorm, and that his mistress had one great fault. She was a "gadabout," as they say, and spent a great part of her time amongst the kept women of the neighborhood, whose acquaintance she had made. The result that Rodolphe had feared, when he perceived the relations contracted by his mistress, soon took place. The variable opulence of some of her new friends caused a forest of ambitious ideas to spring up in the mind of Mademoiselle Mimi, who up until then had only had modest tastes, and was content with the necessaries of life that Rodolphe did his best to procure for her. Mimi began to dream of silks, velvets, and lace. And, despite Rodolphe's prohibition, she continued to frequent these women, who were all of one mind in persuading her to break off with the Bohemian who could not even give her a hundred and fifty francs to buy a stuff dress.

"Pretty as you are," said her advisers, "you can easily secure a better position. You have only to look for it."

And Mademoiselle Mimi began to look. A witness of her frequent absences, clumsily accounted for, Rodolphe entered upon the painful track of suspicion. But as soon as he felt himself on the trail of some proof of infidelity, he eagerly drew a bandage over his eyes in order to see nothing. However, a strange, jealous, fantastic, quarrelsome love which the girl did not understand, because she then only felt for Rodolphe that lukewarm attachment resulting from habit. Besides, half of her heart had already been expended over her first love, and the other half was still full of the remembrance of her first lover.

Eight months passed by in this fashion, good and evil days alternating. During this period Rodolphe was a score of times on the point of separating from Mademoiselle Mimi, who had for him all the clumsy cruelties of the woman who does not love. Properly speaking, this life had become a hell for both. But Rodolphe had grown accustomed to these daily struggles, and dreaded nothing so much as a cessation of this state of things; for he felt that with it would cease forever the fever and agitations of youth that he had not felt for so long. And then, if everything must be told, there were hours in which Mademoiselle Mimi knew how to make Rodolphe forget all the suspicions that were tearing at his heart. There were moments when she caused him to bend like a child at her knee beneath the charm of her blue eyes—the poet to whom she had given back his lost poetry—the young man to whom she had restored his youth, and who, thanks to her, was once more beneath love's equator. Two or three times a month, amidst these stormy quarrels, Rodolphe and Mimi halted with one accord at the verdant oasis of a night of love, and for whole hours would give himself up to addressing her in that charming yet absurd language that passion improvises in its hour of delirium. Mimi listened calmly at first, rather astonished than moved, but, in the end, the enthusiastic eloquence of Rodolphe, by turns tender, lively, and melancholy, won on her by degrees. She felt the ice of indifference that numbed her heart melt at the contact of the love; she would throw herself on Rodolphe's breast, and tell him by kisses all that she was unable to tell him in words. And dawn surprised them thus enlaced together—eyes fixed on eyes, hands clasped in hands—whilst their moist and burning lips were still murmuring that immortal word "that for five thousand years has lingered nightly on lovers' lips."

But the next day the most futile pretext brought about a quarrel, and love alarmed fled again for some time.

In the end, however, Rodolphe perceived that if he did not take care the white hands of Mademoiselle Mimi would lead him to an abyss in which he would leave his future and his youth. For a moment stern reason spoke in him more strongly than love, and he convinced himself by strong arguments, backed up by proofs, that his mistress did not love him. He went so far as to say to himself, that the hours of love she granted him were nothing but a mere sensual caprice such as married women feel for their husbands when they long for a cashmere shawl or a new dress, or when their lover is away, in accordance with the proverb that half a loaf is better than no bread. In short, Rodolphe could forgive his mistress everything except not being loved. He therefore took a supreme resolution, and announced to Mademoiselle Mimi that she would have to look out for another lover. Mimi began to laugh and to utter bravados. In the end, seeing that Rodolphe was firm in his resolve, and greeted her with extreme calmness when she returned home after a day and a night spent out of the house, she began to grow a little uneasy in face of this firmness, to which she was not accustomed. She was then charming for two or three days. But her lover did not go back on what he had said, and contented himself with asking whether she had found anyone.

"I have not even looked," she replied.

However, she had looked, and even before Rodolphe had advised her to do so. In a fortnight she had made two essays. One of her friends had helped her, and had at first procured her the acquaintance of a very tender youth, who had unfolded before Mimi's eyes a horizon of Indian cashmeres and suites of furniture in rosewood. But in the opinion of Mimi herself this young schoolboy, who might be very good at algebra, was not very advanced in the art of love, and as she did not like undertaking education, she left her amorous novice on the lurch, with his cashmeres still browsing on the plains of Tibet, and his rosewood furniture still growing in the forests of the New World.

The schoolboy was soon replaced by a Breton gentleman, with whom Mimi was soon rapidly smitten, and she had no need to pray long before becoming his nominal countess.

Despite his mistress's protestations, Rodolphe had wind of some intrigue. He wanted to know exactly how matters stood, and one morning, after a night during which Mademoiselle Mimi had not returned, hastened to the place where he suspected her to be. There he was able to strike home at his heart with one of those proofs to which one must give credence in spite of oneself. He saw Mademoiselle Mimi, with two eyes encircled with an aureola of satisfied voluptuousness, leaving the residence in which she had acquired her title of nobility, on the arm of her new lord and master, who, to tell the truth, appeared far less proud of her new conquest than Paris after the rape of Helen.

On seeing her lover appear, Mademoiselle Mimi seemed somewhat surprised. She came up to him, and for five minutes they talked very quietly together. They then parted, each on their separate way. Their separation was agreed upon.

Rodolphe returned home, and spent the day in packing up all the things belonging to his mistress.

During the day that followed his divorce, he received the visit of several friends, and announced to them what had happened. Every one congratulated him on this event as on a piece of great good fortune.

"We will aid you, oh poet!" said one of those who had been the most frequent spectator of the annoyances Mademoiselle Mimi had made Rodolphe undergo, "we will help you to free your heart from the clutches of this evil creature. In a little while you will be cured, and quite ready to rove with another Mimi along the green lanes of Aulnay and Fontenay-aux-Roses."

Rodolphe swore that he had forever done with regrets and despair. He even let himself be led away to the Bal Mabille, when his dilapidated get-up did scant honor to "The Scarf of Iris," his editorship of which procured him free admission to this garden of elegance and pleasure. There Rodolphe met some fresh friends, with whom he began to drink. He related to them his woes an unheard of luxury of imaginative style, and for an hour was perfectly dazzling with liveliness and go. "Alas!" said the painter Marcel, as he listened to the flood of irony pouring from his friend's lips, "Rodolphe is too lively, far too lively."

"He is charming," replied a young woman to whom Rodolphe had just offered a bouquet, "and although he is very badly got up I would willingly compromise myself by dancing with him if he would invite me."

Two seconds later Rodolphe, who had overheard her, was at her feet, enveloping his invitation in a speech, scented with all the musk and benjamin of a gallantry at eighty degrees Richelieu. The lady was confounded by the language sparkling with dazzling adjectives and phrases modelled on those in vogue during the Regency, and the invitation was accepted.

Rodolphe was as ignorant of the elements of dancing as of the rule of three. But he was impelled by an extraordinary audacity. He did not hesitate, but improvised a dance unknown to all bygone choreography. It was a step the originality of which obtained an incredible success, and that has been celebrated under the title of "regrets and sighs." It was all very well for the three thousand jets of gas to blink at him, Rodolphe went on at it all the same, and continued to pour out a flood of novel madrigals to his partner.

"Well," said Marcel, "this is incredible. Rodolphe reminds me of a drunken man rolling amongst broken glass."

"At any rate he has got hold of a deuced fine woman," said another, seeing Rodolphe about to leave with his partner.

"Won't you say good night?" cried Marcel after him.

Rodolphe came back to the artist and held out his hand, it was cold and damp as a wet stone.

Rodolphe's companion was a strapping Normandy wench, whose native rusticity had promptly acquired an aristocratic tinge amidst the elegancies of Parisian luxury and an idle life. She was styled Madame Seraphine, and was for the time being mistress of an incarnate rheumatism in the shape of a peer of France, who gave her fifty louis a month, which she shared with a counter-jumper who gave her nothing but hard knocks. Rodolphe had pleased her, she hoped that he would not think of giving her anything, and took him off home with her.

"Lucille," said she to her waiting maid, "I am not at home to anyone." And passing into her bedroom, she came out ten minutes later, in a special costume. She found Rodolphe dumb and motionless, for since he had come in he had been plunged, despite himself, into a gloom full of silent sobs.

"Why you no longer look at me or speak to me!" said the astonished Seraphine.

"Come," said Rodolphe to himself, lifting his head. "Let us look at her, but only for the sake of art."

"And then what a sight met his eyes," as Raoul says in "The Huguenots."

Seraphine was admirable beautiful. Her splendid figure, cleverly set off by the cut of her solitary garment, showed itself provocatively through the half-transparent material. All the imperious fever of desire woke afresh in Rodolphe's veins. A warm mist mounted to his brain. He looked at Seraphine otherwise than from a purely aesthetic point of view and took the pretty girl's hands in his own. They were divine hands, and might have been wrought by the purest chisels of Grecian statuary. Rodolphe felt these admirable hands tremble in his own, and feeling less and less of an art critic, he drew towards him Seraphine, whose face was already tinged with that flush which is the aurora of voluptuousness.

"This creature is a true instrument of pleasure, a real Stradivarius of love, and one on which I would willingly play a tune," thought Rodolphe, as he heard the fair creature's heart beating a hurried charge in a very distinct fashion.

At that moment there was a violent ring at the door of the rooms.

"Lucile, Lucile," cried Seraphine to the waiting maid, "do not let anyone in, say I am not home yet."

At the name of Lucile uttered twice, Rodolphe rose.

"I do not wish to incommode you in any way, madame," said he. "Besides, I must take my leave, it is late and I live a long way off. Good evening."

"What! You are going?" exclaimed Seraphine, augmenting the fire of her glances. "Why, why should you go? I am free, you can stay."

"Impossible," replied Rodolphe, "I am expecting one of my relatives who is coming from Terra del Fuego this evening, and he would disinherit me if he did not find me waiting to receive him. Good evening, madame."

And he quitted the room hurriedly. The servant went to light him out. Rodolphe accidentally cast his eye on her. She was a delicate looking girl, with slow movements; her extremely pale face offered a charming contrast to her dark and naturally curling hair, whilst her blue eyes resembled two sickly stars.

"Oh phantom!" exclaimed Rodolphe, shrinking from one who bore the name and the face of his mistress. "Away, what would you with me?" And he rushed down the stairs.

"Why, madame," said the lady's maid, returning to her mistress's room. "The young fellow is mad."

"Say rather that he is a fool," claimed the exasperated Seraphine. "Oh!" she continued, "this will teach me to show kindness. If only that brute of a Leon had the sense to drop in now!"

Leon was the gentleman whose love carried a whip.

Rodolphe ran home without waiting to take breath. Going upstairs he found his carroty-haired cat giving vent to piteous mewings. For two nights already it has thus been vainly summoning its faithless love, an agora Manon Lescaut, who had started on a campaign of gallantry on the house-tops adjacent.

"Poor beast," said Rodolphe, "you have been deceived. Your Mimi has jilted you like mine has jilted me. Bah! Let us console ourselves. You see, my poor fellow, the hearts of women and she-cats are abysses that neither men nor toms will ever fathom."

When he entered his room, although it was fearfully hot, Rodolphe seemed to feel a cloak of ice about his shoulders. It was the chill of solitude, that terrible nocturnal solitude that nothing disturbs. He lit his candle and then perceived the ravaged room. The gaping drawers in the furniture showed empty, and from floor to ceiling sadness filled the little room that seemed to Rodolphe vaster than a desert. Stepping forward he struck his foot against the parcels containing the things belonging to Mademoiselle Mimi, and he felt an impulse of joy to find that she had not yet come to fetch them as she had told him in the morning she would do. Rodolphe felt that, despite all his struggles, the moment of reaction was at hand, and readily divined that a cruel night was to expiate all the bitter mirth that he had dispensed in the course of the evening. However, he hoped that his body, worn out with fatigue, would sink to sleep before the reawakening of the sorrows so long pent back in his heart.

As he approached the couch, and on drawing back the curtains saw the bed that had not been disturbed for two days, the pillows placed side by side, beneath one of which still peeped out the trimming of a woman's night cap, Rodolphe felt his heart gripped in the pitiless vice of that desolate grief that cannot burst forth. He fell at the foot of the bed, buried his face in his hands, and, after having cast a glance round the desolate room, exclaimed:

"Oh! Little Mimi, joy of my home, is it really true that you are gone, that I have driven you away, and that I shall never see you again, my God. Oh! Pretty brown curly head that has slept so long on this spot, will you never come back to sleep here again? Oh! Little white hands with the blue veins, little white hands to whom I had affianced my lips, have you too received my last kiss?"

And Rodolphe, in delirious intoxication, plunged his head amongst the pillows, still impregnated with the perfume of his love's hair. From the depth of the alcove he seemed to see emerge the ghosts of the sweet nights he had passed with his young mistress. He heard clear and sonorous, amidst the nocturnal silence, the open-hearted laugh of Mademoiselle Mimi, and he thought of the charming and contagious gaiety with which she had been able so many times to make him forget all the troubles and all the hardships of their hazardous existence.

Throughout the night he kept passing in review the eight months that he had just spent with this girl, who had never loved him perhaps, but whose tender lies had restored to Rodolphe's heart its youth and virility.

Dawn surprised him at the moment when, conquered by fatigue, he had just closed his eyes, red from the tears shed during the night. A doleful and terrible vigil, yet such a one as even the most sneering and sceptical amongst us may find in the depths of their past.

When his friends called on him in the morning they were alarmed at the sight of Rodolphe, whose face bore the traces of all the anguish that had awaited him during his vigil in the Gethsemane of love.

"Good!" said Marcel, "I was sure of it; it is his mirth of yesterday that has turned in his heart. Things must not go on like this."

And in concert with two or three comrades he began a series of privately indiscreet revelations respecting Mademoiselle Mimi, every word of which pierced like a thorn in Rodolphe's heart. His friends "proved" to him that all the time his mistress had tricked him like a simpleton at home and abroad, and that this fair creature, pale as the angel of phthisis, was a casket filled with evil sentiments and ferocious instincts.

One and another they thus took it in turns at the task they had set themselves, which was to bring Rodolphe to that point at which soured love turns to contempt; but this object was only half attained. The poet's despair turned to wrath. He threw himself in a rage upon the packages which he had done up the day before, and after having put on one side all the objects that his mistress had in her possession when she came to him, kept all those he had given her during their union, that is to say, by far the greater number, and, above all, the articles connected with the toilette to which Mademoiselle Mimi was attached by all the fibers of a coquetry that had of late become insatiable.

Mademoiselle Mimi called in course of the next day to take away her things. Rodolphe was at home and alone. It needed all his powers of self esteem to keep him from throwing himself upon his mistress's neck. He gave her a reception full of silent insult, and Mademoiselle Mimi replied by those cold and keen scoffs that drive the weakest and most timid to show their teeth. In face of the contempt with which his mistress flagellated him with insolent hardihood, Rodolphe's anger broke out fearfully and brutally. For a moment Mimi, white with terror, asked herself whether she would escape from his hands alive. At the cries she uttered some neighbors rushed in and dragged her out of Rodolphe's room.

Two days later a female friend of Mimi came to ask Rodolphe whether he would give up the things he had kept.

"No," he replied.

And he got his mistress's messenger to talk about her. She informed him that Mimi was in a very unfortunate condition, and that she would soon find herself without a lodging.

"And the lover of whom she is so fond?"

"Oh!" replied Amelie, the friend in question, "the young fellow has no intention of taking her for his mistress. He has been keeping another for a long time past, and he does not seem to trouble much about Mimi, who is living at my expense, which causes me a great deal of embarrassment."

"Let her do as she can," said Rodolphe. "She would have it,—it is no affair of mine."

And he began to sing madrigals to Mademoiselle Amelie, and persuaded her that she was the prettiest woman in the world.

Amelie informed Mimi of her interview with Rodolphe.

"What did he say? What is he doing? Did he speak to you about me?" asked Mimi.

"Not at all; you are already forgotten, my dear. Rodolphe has a fresh mistress, and he has bought her a superb outfit, for he has received a great deal of money, and is himself dressed like a prince. He is a very amiable fellow, and said a lot of nice things to me."

"I know what all that means," thought Mimi.

Every day Mademoiselle Amelie called to see Rodolphe on some pretext or other, and however much the latter tried he could not help speaking of Mimi to her.

"She is very lively," replied her friend, "and does not seem to trouble herself about her position. Besides she declares that she will come back to you whenever she chooses, without making any advances and merely for the sake of vexing your friends."

"Very good," said Rodolphe, "let her come and we shall see."

And he began to pay court to Amelie, who went off to tell everything to Mimi, and to assure her that Rodolphe was very much in love with herself.

"He kissed me again on the hand and the neck; see it is quite red," said she. "He wants to take me to a dance tomorrow."

"My dear friend," said Mimi, rather vexed, "I see what you are driving at, to make me believe that Rodolphe is in love with you and thinks no more about me. But you are wasting your time both for him and me."

The fact was that Rodolphe only showed himself amiable towards Amelie to get her to call on him the oftener, and to have the opportunity of speaking to her about his mistress. But with a Machiavelism that had perhaps its object, and whilst perceiving very well that Rodolphe still loved Mimi, and that the latter was not indisposed to rejoin him, Amelie strove, by ingeniously inventive reports, to fend off everything that might serve to draw the pair together again.

The day on which she was to go to the ball Amelie called in the morning to ask Rodolphe whether the engagement still held good.

"Yes," he replied, "I do not want to miss the opportunity of being the cavalier of the most beautiful woman of the day."

Amelie assumed the coquettish air that she had put on the occasion of her solitary appearance at a suburban theater as fourth chambermaid, and promised to be ready that evening.

"By the way," said Rodolphe, "tell Mademoiselle Mimi that if she will be guilty of an infidelity to her lover in my favor, and come and pass a night with me, I will give her up all her things."

Amelie executed Rodolphe's commission, and gave to his words quite another meaning than that which she had guessed they bore.

"Your Rodolphe is a rather base fellow," said she to Mimi. "His proposal is infamous. He wishes by this step to make you descend to the rank of the vilest creatures, and if you go to him not only will he not give you your things, but he will show you up as a jest to all his comrades. It is a plot arranged amongst them."

"I will not go," said Mimi, and as she saw Amelie engaged in preparing her toilette, she asked her whether she was going to the ball.

"Yes," replied the other.

"With Rodolphe?"

"Yes, he is to wait for me this evening twenty yards or so from here."

"I wish you joy," said Mimi, and seeing the hour of the appointment approach, she hurried off to Mademoiselle Amelie's lover, and informed him that the latter was engaged in a little scheme to deceive him with her own old lover.

The gentleman, jealous as a tiger and brutal to boot, called at once on Mademoiselle Amelie, and announced that he would like her to spend the evening in his company.

At eight o'clock Mimi flew to the spot at which Rodolphe was to meet Amelie. She saw her lover pacing up and down after the fashion of a man waiting for some one, and twice passed close to him without daring to address him. Rodolphe was very well dressed that evening, and the violent crises through which he had passed during the week had imparted great character on his face. Mimi was singularly moved. At length she made up her mind to speak to him. Rodolphe received her without anger, and asked how she was, after which he inquired as to the motive that had brought her to him, in mild voice, in which there was an effort to check a note of sadness.

"It is bad news that I come to bring you. Mademoiselle Amelie cannot come to the ball with you. Her lover is keeping her."

"I shall go to the ball alone, then."

Here Mademoiselle Mimi feigned to stumble, and leaned against Rodolphe's shoulder. He took her arm and proposed to escort her home.

"No," said Mimi. "I am living with Amelie, and as her lover is there I cannot go in until he has left."

"Listen to me, then," said the poet. "I made a proposal to you today through Mademoiselle Amelie. Did she transmit it to you?"

"Yes," said Mimi, "but in terms which, even after what has happened, I could not credit. No, Rodolphe, I could not believe that, despite all that you might have to reproach me with, you thought me so worthless as to accept such a bargain."

"You did not understand me, or the message has been badly conveyed to you. My offer holds good," said Rodolphe. "It is nine o'clock. You still have three hours for reflection. The door will be unlocked until midnight. Good night. Farewell, or—till we meet again."

"Farewell, then," said Mimi, in trembling tones.

And they separated. Rodolphe went home and threw himself, without undressing, upon his bed. At half past eleven, Mademoiselle Mimi entered his room.

"I have come to ask your hospitality," said she. "Amelie's lover has stayed with her, and I cannot get in."

They talked together until three in the morning—an explanatory conversation which grew gradually more familiar.

At four o'clock their candle went out. Rodolphe wanted to light another.

"No," said Mimi, "it is not worth the trouble. It is quite time to go to bed."

Five minutes later her pretty brown curly head had once more resumed its place on the pillow, and in a voice full of affection she invited Rodolphe's lips to feast on her little white hand with their blue veins, the pearly pallor of which vied with the whiteness of the sheets. Rodolphe did not light the candle.

In the morning Rodolphe got up first, and pointing out several packages to Mimi, said to her, very gently, "There is what belongs to you. You can take it away. I keep my word."

"Oh!" said Mimi. "I am very tired, you see, and I cannot carry all these heavy parcels away at once. I would rather call again."

And when she was dressed she only took a collar and a pair of cuffs.

"I will take away the rest by degrees," she added, smiling.

"Come," said Rodolphe, "take away all or take away none, and let there be an end of it."

"Let it, on the contrary, begin again, and, above all, let it last," said Mimi, kissing Rodolphe.

After breakfasting together they started off for a day in the country. Crossing the Luxembourg gardens Rodolphe met a great poet who had always received him with charming kindness. Out of respect for the conventionalities Rodolphe was about to pretend not to see him but the poet did not give him time, and passing by him greeted him with a friendly gesture and his companion with a smile.

"Who is that gentleman?" asked Mimi.

Rodolphe answered her by mentioning a name which made her blush with pleasure and pride.

"Oh!" said Rodolphe. "Our meeting with the poet who has sung of love so well is a good omen, and will bring luck to our reconciliation."

"I do love you," said Mimi, squeezing his hand, although they were in the midst of the crowd.

"Alas!" thought Rodolphe. "Which is better; to allow oneself always to be deceived through believing, or never to believe for fear of always being deceived?"

XV

Donec Gratus

We have told how the painter Marcel made the acquaintance of Mademoiselle Musette. United one morning by the ministry of caprice, the registrar of the district, they had fancied, as often happens, that their union did not extend to their hearts. But one evening when, after a violent quarrel, they resolved to leave one another on the spot, they perceived that their hands, which they had joined in a farewell clasp, would no longer quit one another. Almost in spite of themselves fancy had become love. Both, half laughingly, acknowledged it.

"This is very serious. What has happened to us?" said Marcel. "What the deuce have we been up to?"

"Oh!" replied Musette. "We must have been clumsy over it. We did not take enough precautions."

"What is the matter?" asked Rodolphe, who had become Marcel's neighbor, entering the room.

"The matter is," replied Marcel, "that this lady and myself have just made a pretty discovery. We are in love with one another. We must have been attacked by the complaint whilst asleep."

"Oh oh! I don't think that it was whilst you were asleep," observed Rodolphe. "But what proves that you are in love with one another? Possibly you exaggerate the danger."

"We cannot bear one another," said Marcel.

"And we cannot leave one another," added Musette.

"There, my children, your business is plain. Each has tried to play cunning, and both have lost. It is the story of Mimi and myself. We shall soon have run through two almanacs quarrelling day and night. It is by that system that marriages are rendered eternal. Wed a 'yes' to a 'no,' and you obtain the union of Philemon and Baucis. Your domestic interior will soon match mine, and if Schaunard and Phemie come and live in the house, as they have threatened, our trio of establishments will render it a very pleasant place of residence."

At that moment Gustave Colline came in. He was informed of the accident that had befallen Musette and Marcel.

"Well, philosopher," said the latter, "what do you think of this?"

Colline rubbed the hat that served him for a roof, and murmured, "I felt sure of it beforehand. Love is a game of chance. He who plays at bowls may expect rubbers. It is not good for man to live alone."

That evening, on returning home, Rodolphe said to Mimi—

"There is something new. Musette dotes on Marcel, and will not leave him."

"Poor girl!" replied Mimi. "She who has such a good appetite, too."

"And on his side, Marcel is hard and fast in love with Musette."

"Poor fellow!" said Mimi. "He who is so jealous."

"That is true," observed Rodolphe. "He and I are pupils of Othello."

Shortly afterwards the households of Rodolphe and Marcel were reinforced by the household of Schaunard, the musician, moving into the house with Phemie Teinturiere.

From that day all the other inhabitants slept upon a volcano, and at quarter day sent in a unanimous notice of their intention to move to the landlord.

Indeed, hardly a day passed without a storm breaking out in one of these households. Now it was Mimi and Rodolphe who, no longer having strength to speak, continued their conversation with the aid of such missiles as came under their hands. But more frequently it was Schaunard addressing a few observations to the melancholy Phemie with the end of a walking stick. As to Marcel and Musette, their arguments were carried on in private sittings; they took at least the precaution to close their doors and windows.

If by chance peace reigned in the three households, the other lodgers were not the less victims of this temporary concord. The indiscretion of partition walls allowed all the secrets of Bohemian family life to transpire, and initiated them, in spite of themselves, into all its mysteries. Thus more than one neighbor preferred the *casus belli* to the ratification of treaties of peace.

It was, in truth, a singular life that was led for six months. The most loyal fraternity was practiced without any fuss in this circle, in which everything was for all, and good or evil fortune shared.

There were in the month certain days of splendor, when no one would have gone out without gloves—days of enjoyment, when dinner lasted all day long. There were others when one would have almost gone to Court without boots; Lenten days, when, after going without breakfast in common, they failed to dine together, or managed by economic combination to furnish forth one of those repasts at which plates and knives were "resting," as Mademoiselle Mimi put it, in theatrical parlance.

But the wonderful thing is that this partnership, in which there were three young and pretty women, no shadow of discord was found amongst the men. They often yielded to the most futile fancies of their mistresses, but not one of them would have hesitated for a moment between the mistress and the friend.

Love is born above all from spontaneity—it is an improvisation. Friendship, on the contrary, is, so to say, built up. It is a sentiment that progresses with circumspection. It is the egoism of the mind, whilst love is the egoism of the heart.

The Bohemians had known one another for six years. This long period of time spent in a daily intimacy had, without altering the well-defined individuality of each, brought about between them a concord of ideas—a unity which they would not have found elsewhere. They had manners that were their own, a tongue amongst themselves to which strangers would not have been able to find the key. Those who did not know them very well called their freedom of manner cynicism. It was however, only frankness. With minds impatient of imposed control, they all hated what was false, and despised what was low. Accused of exaggerated vanity, they replied by proudly unfurling the program of their ambition, and, conscious of their worth, held no false estimate of themselves.

During the number of years that they had followed the same life together, though often placed in rivalry by the necessities of their profession, they had never let go one another's hands, and had passed without heeding them over personal questions of self-esteem whenever an attempt had been made to raise these between them in order to disunite them. Besides, they each esteemed one another at their right worth, and pride, which is the counter poison of envy, preserved them from all petty professional jealousy.

However, after six months of life in common, an epidemic of divorce suddenly seized on the various households.

Schaunard opened the ball. One day he perceived that Phemie Teinturiere had one knee better shaped than the other, and as his was an austere purism as regards plastics, he sent Phemie about her business, giving her as a souvenir the cane with which he had addressed such frequent remarks to her. Then he went back to live with a relative who offered him free quarters.

A fortnight later Mimi left Rodolphe to step into the carriage of the young Vicomte Paul, the ex-pupil of Carolus Barbemuche, who had promised her dresses to her heart's desire.

After Mimi it was Musette who went off, and returned with a grand flourish of trumpets amongst the aristocracy of the world of gallantry which she had left to follow Marcel.

This separation took place without quarrel, shock or premeditation. Born of a fancy that had become love, this union was broken off by another fancy.

One evening during the carnival, at the masked ball at the Opera, whither she had gone with Marcel, Mimi, Musette had for her *vis-a-vis* in a quadrille a young man who had formerly courted her. They recognized one another, and, whilst dancing exchanged a few words. Unintentionally, perhaps, whilst informing the young man of her present condition in life, she may have dropped a word of regret as to her past one. At any rate, at the end of the quadrille Musette made a mistake, and instead of giving her hand to Marcel, who was her partner, give it to her *vis-a-vis*, who led her off, and disappeared with her in the crowd.

Marcel looked for her, feeling somewhat uneasy. In an hour's time he found her on the young man's arm; she was coming out of the Cafe de l'Opera, humming a tune. On catching sight of Marcel, who had stationed himself in a corner with folded arms, she made him a sign of farewell, saying—"I shall be back."

"That is to say, 'Do not expect me,'" translated Marcel.

He was jealous but logical, and knew Musette, hence he did not wait for her, but went home with a full heart and an empty stomach. He looked into the cupboard to see whether there were not a few scraps to eat, and perceived a bit of stale bread as hard as granite and a skeleton-like red herring.

"I cannot fight against truffles," he thought. "At any rate, Musette will have some supper."

And after passing his handkerchief over his eyes under pretext of wiping his nose, he went to bed.

Two days later Musette woke up in a boudoir with rose-covered hangings. A blue brougham was at her door, and all the fairies of fashion had been summoned to lay their wonders at her feet. Musette was charming, and her youth seemed yet further rejuvenated in this elegant setting. Then she began her old life again, was present at every festivity, and re-conquered her celebrity. She was spoken of everywhere—in the lobbies of the Bourse, and even at the parliamentary refreshment bars. As to her new lover, Monsieur Alexis, he was a charming young fellow. He often complained to Musette of her being somewhat frivolous and inattentive when he spoke to her of his love. Then Musette would look at him laughingly, and say—

"What would you have, my dear fellow? I stayed six months with a man who fed me on salad and soup without butter, who dressed me in a cotton gown, and usually took me to the Odeon because he was not well off. As love costs nothing, and as I was wildly in love with this monster, we expended a great deal of it together. I have scarcely anything but its crumbs left. Pick them up, I do no hinder you. Besides, I have not deceived you about it; if ribbons were not so dear I should still be with my painter. As to my heart, since I have worn an eighty franc corset I do not hear it, and I am very much afraid that I have left it in one of Marcel's drawers."

The disappearance of the three Bohemian households was the occasion of a festival in the house they had inhabited. As a token of rejoicing the landlord gave a grand dinner, and the lodgers lit up their windows.

Rodolphe and Marcel went to live together. Each had taken a new idol whose name they were not exactly acquainted with. Sometimes it happened that one spoke of Musette and the other of Mimi, and then they had a whole evening of it. They recalled to one another their old life, the songs of Musette and the songs of Mimi, nights passed without sleep, idle mornings, and dinners only partaken of in dreams. One by one they hummed over in these recolletive ducts all the bygone hours, and they usually wound up by saying that after all they were still happy to find themselves together, their feet on the fender, stirring the December log, smoking their pipes, and having as a pretext for open conversation between them that which they whispered to themselves when alone—that they had dearly loved these beings who had vanished, bearing away with them a part of their youth, and that perhaps they loved them still.

One evening when passing along the Boulevard, Marcel perceived a few paces ahead of him a young lady who, in alighting from a cab, exposed the lower part of a white stocking of admirable shape. The very driver himself devoured with his eyes this charming gratification in excess of his fare.

"By Jove," said Marcel. "That is a neat leg, I should like to offer it my arm. Come, now, how shall I manage to accord it? Ha! I have it—it is a fairly novel plan. Excuse me, madame," continued he, approaching the fair unknown, whose face at the outset he could not at first get a full view of, "but you have not by chance found my handkerchief?"

"Yes, sir," replied the young lady, "here it is." And she placed in Marcel's hand a handkerchief she had been holding in her own.

The artist rolled into an abyss of astonishment.

But all at once a burst of laughter full in his face recalled him to himself. By this joyous outbreak he recognized his old love.

It was Mademoiselle Musette.

"Ah!" she exclaimed. "Monsieur Marcel in quest of gallant adventures. What do you think of this one, eh? It does not lack fun."

"I think it endurable," replied Marcel.

"Where are you going so late in this region?" asked Musette.

"I am going into that edifice," said the artist, pointing to a little theater where he was on the free list.

"For the sake of art?"

"No, for the sake of Laura."

"Who is Laura?" continued Musette, whose eyes shot forth notes of interrogation.

Marcel kept up the tone.

"She is a chimera whom I am pursuing, and who plays here."

And he pretended to pull out an imaginary shirt frill.

"You are very witty this evening," said Musette.

"And you very curious," observed Marcel.

"Do no speak so loud, everyone can hear us, and they will take us for two lovers quarrelling."

"It would not be the first time that that happened," said Marcel.

Musette read a challenge in this sentence, and quickly replied, "And it will not perhaps be the last, eh?"

Her words were plain, they whizzed past Marcel's ear like a bullet.

"Splendors of heaven," said he, looking up at the stars, "you are witness that it is not I who opened fire. Quick, my armor."

From that moment the firing began.

It was now only a question of finding some appropriate pretext to bring about an agreement between these two fancies that had just woke up again so lively.

As they walked along, Musette kept looking at Marcel, and Marcel kept looking at Musette. They did not speak, but their eyes, those plenipotentiaries of the heart, often met. After a quarter of an hour's diplomacy this congress of glances had tacitly settled the matter. There was nothing to be done save to ratify it.

The interrupted conversation was renewed.

"Candidly now," said Musette to Marcel, "where were you going just now?"

"I told you, to see Laura."

"Is she pretty?"

"Her mouth is a nest of smiles."

"Oh! I know all that sort of thing."

"But you yourself," said Marcel, "whence came you on the wings of this four-wheeler?"

"I came back from the railway station where I had been to see off Alexis, who is going on a visit to his family."

"What sort of man is Alexis?"

In turn Musette sketched a charming portrait of her present lover. Whilst walking along Marcel and Musette continued thus on the open Boulevard the comedy of reawakening love. With the same simplicity, in turn tender and jesting, they went verse by verse through that immortal ode in which Horace and Lydia extol with such grace the charms of their new loves, and end by adding a postscript to their old ones. As they reached the corner of the street a rather strong picket of soldiers suddenly issued from it.

Musette struck an attitude of alarm, and clutching hold of Marcel's arm said, "Ah! Good heavens! Look there, soldiers; there is going to be another revolution. Let us bolt off, I am awfully afraid. See me indoors."

"But where shall we go?" asked Marcel.

"To my place," said Musette. "You shall see how nice it is. I invite you to supper. We will talk politics."

"No," replied Marcel, who thought of Monsieur Alexis. "I will not go to your place, despite your offer of a supper. I do not like to drink my wine out of another's glass."

Musette was silent in face of this refusal. Then through the mist of her recollections she saw the poor home of the artist, for Marcel had not become a millionaire. She had an idea, and profiting by meeting another picket she manifested fresh alarm.

"They are going to fight," she exclaimed. "I shall never dare go home. Marcel, my dear fellow, take me to one of my lady friends, who must be living in your neighborhood."

As they were crossing the Pont Neuf Musette broke into a laugh.

"What is it?" asked Marcel.

"Nothing," replied Musette, "only I remember that my friend has moved. She is living at Batignolles."

On seeing Marcel and Musette arrive arm in arm Rodolphe was not astonished.

"It is always so," said he, "with these badly buried loves."

XVI

The Passage of the Red Sea

For five or six years Marcel had worked at the famous painting which (he said) represented the Passage of the Red Sea; and for five or six years, this masterpiece of color had been obstinately refused by the jury. In fact, by dint of going and returning so many times from the artist's study to the Exhibition, and from the Exhibition to the study, the picture knew the road to the Louvre well enough to have gone thither of itself, if it had been put on wheels. Marcel, who had repainted the canvas ten times over, from top to bottom, attributed to personal hostility on the part of the jury the ostracism which annually repulsed him from the large saloon; nevertheless he was not totally discouraged by the obstinate rejection which greeted him at every Exhibition. He was comfortably established in the persuasion that his picture was, on a somewhat smaller scale, the pendant required by "The Marriage of Cana," that gigantic masterpiece whose astonishing brilliancy the dust of three centuries has not been able to tarnish. Accordingly, every year at the epoch of the Exhibition, Marcel sent his great work to the jury of examiners; only, to deceive them, he would change some details of his picture, and the title of it, without disturbing the general composition.

Thus, it came before the jury once, under the name of "The Passage of the Rubicon," but Pharaoh, badly disguised under the mantle of Caeser, was recognized and rejected with all the honors due him. Next year, Marcel threw a coat of white over the foreground, to imitate snow, planted a fir tree in one corner, and dressing an Egyptian like a grenadier of the Imperial Guard, christened his picture, "The Passage of the Beresina."

But the jury had wiped its glasses that day, and were not to be duped by this new stratagem. It recognized the pertinacious picture by a thundering big pie-bald horse that was prancing on top of a wave of the Red Sea. The skin of this horse served Marcel for all his experiments in coloring; he used to call it, familiarly, his "synoptic table of fine tones," because it reproduced the most varied combinations of color, with the different plays of light and shade. Once again, however, the jury could not find black balls enough to refuse "The Passage of Beresina."

"Very well," said Marcel, "I thought so! Next year, I shall send it under the title of 'The Passage of the Panoramas.'"

"They're going to be jolly caught—caught!"

sang Schaunard to a new air of his own composition; a terrible air, like a gamut of thunder-claps, the accompaniment whereof was a terror to all pianos within hearing.

"How can they refuse it, without all the vermilion of my Red Sea mounting to their cheeks, and covering them with the blush of shame?" exclaimed the artist, as he gazed on his picture. "When I think that there is five hundred francs' worth of color there, and at least a million of genius, without counting my lovely youth, now as bald as my old hat! But they shan't get the better of me! Till my dying day, I will send them my picture. It shall be engraved on their memories."

"The surest way of ever having it engraved," said Colline, in a plaintive tone, and then added to himself, "very neat, that; I shall repeat it in society!"

Marcel continued his imprecations, which Schaunard continued to put to music.

"Ah they won't admit me! The government pays them, lodges them, and gives them decorations, on purpose to refuse me once a year; every first of March! I see their idea! I see it clearly! They want to make me burn my brushes. They hope that when my Red Sea is refused, I will throw myself out of the window of despair. But they little know the heart of man, if they think to take me thus. I will not wait for the opening of the Exhibition. From today, my work shall be a picture of Damocles, eternally suspended over their existence. I will send it once a week to each of them, at his home in the bosom of his family; in the very heart of his private life. It shall trouble their domestic joys; they shall find their roasts burnt, their wines sour, and their wives bitter! They will grow mad rapidly, and go to the Institute in strait-waistcoats. Ha! Ha! The thought consoles me."

Some days later, when Marcel had already forgotten his terrible plans of vengeance against his persecutors, he received a visit from Father Medicis. So the club called a Jew, named Salomon, who at that time was well known to all the vagabond of art and literature, and had continual transactions with them. Father Medicis traded in all sorts of trumpery. He sold complete sets of furniture from twelve francs up to five thousand; he bought everything, and knew how to dispose of it again, at a profit. Proudhon's bank of exchange was nothing in comparison with the system practiced by Medicis, who possessed the genius of traffic to a degree at which the ablest of his religion had never before arrived. His shop was a fairy region where you found anything you wished for. Every product of nature, every creation of art; whatever issued from the bowels of the earth or the head of man, was an object of commerce for him. His business included everything; literally everything that exists; he even trafficked in the ideal. He bought ideas to sell or speculate in them. Known to all literary men and all artists, intimate with the palette and familiar with the desk, he was the very Asmodeus of the arts. He would sell you cigars for a column of your newspaper, slippers for a sonnet, fresh fish for paradoxes; he would talk, for so much an hour, with the people who furnished fashionable gossip to the journals. He would procure you places for the debates in the Chambers, and invitations to parties. He lodged wandering artistlings by the day, week, or month, taking for pay, copies of the pictures in the Louvre. The green room had no mysteries for him. He would get your pieces into the theater, or yourself into the boudoir of an actress. He had a copy of the "Almanac of Twenty Five Thousand Addresses" in his head, and knew the names, residences, and secrets of all celebrities, even those who were not celebrated.

A few pages copied from his waste book, will give a better idea of the universality of his operations than the most copious explanation could.

"March 20, 184—."

"Sold to M. L——, antiquary, the compass which Archimedes used at the siege of Syracuse. 75 fr.

Bought of M. V——, journalist, the entire works, uncut, of M. X——, Member of the Academy. 10 fr.

Sold to the same, a criticism of the complete works of M. X——, of the Academy. 30 fr.

Bought of M. R——, literary man, a critical article on the complete works of M. Y——, of the Academy. 10 fr., plus half a cwt. of charcoal and 4 lbs. of coffee.

Sold to M. Y——, of the Academy, a laudatory review (twelve columns) of his complete works. 250 fr.

Sold to M. G——, a porcelain vase which had belonged to Madame Dubarry. 18 fr.

Bought of little D——, her hair. 15 fr.

Bought of M. B——, a lot of articles on Society, and the last three mistakes in spelling made by the Prefect of the Seine. 6 fr, plus a pair of Naples shoes.

Sold to Mdlle. O——, a flaxen head of hair. 120 fr.

Bought of M. M——, historical painter, a series of humorous designs. 25 fr.

Informed M. Ferdinand the time when Mme. la Baronne de T—— goes to mass, and let him for the day the little room in the Faubourg Montmartre: together 30 fr.

Bought of M. J——, artist, a portrait of M. Isidore as Apollo. 6 fr.

Sold to Mdlle R—— a pair of lobsters and six pair of gloves. 36 fr. Received 3 fr.

For the same, procured a credit of six months with Mme. Z——, dressmaker. (Price not settled.)

Procured for Mme. Z——, dressmaker, the custom of Mdlle. R——. Received for this three yards of velvet, and three yards of lace.

Bought of M. R——, literary man, a claim of 120 fr. against the—newspaper. 5 fr., plus 2 lbs. of tobacco.

Sold M. Ferdinand two love letters. 12 fr.

Sold M. Isidore his portrait as Apollo. 30 fr.

Bought of M. M——, a cwt. and a half of his work, entitled 'Submarine Revolutions.' 15 fr.

Lent Mme la Comtesse de G—— a service of Dresden china. 20 fr.

Bought of M. G——, journalist, fifty-two lines in his article of town talk. 100 fr., plus a set of chimney ornaments.

Sold to Messrs. O—— and Co., fifty-two lines in the town talk of the—. 300 fr., plus two sets of chimney ornaments.

Let to Mdlle. S. G—— a bed and a brougham for the day (nothing). See Mdlle. S. G——'s account in private ledger, folios 26 and 27.

Bought of M. Gustave C——a treatise on the flax and linen trade. 50 fr., and a rare edition of Josephus.

Sold Mdlle. S. G—— a complete set of new furniture. 5000 fr.

For the same, paid an apothecary's bill. 75 fr.

For the same, paid a milkman's bill. 3 fr. 85 c."

Those quotations show what an extensive range the operations of the Jew Medici covered. It may be added, that although some articles of his commerce were decidedly illicit, he had never got himself into any trouble.

The Jew comprehended, on his entrance, that he had come at a favorable time. In fact, the four friends were at that moment in council, under the auspices of a ferocious appetite, discussing the grave question of meat and drink. It was a Sunday at the end of the month—sinister day.

The arrival of Medicis was therefore hailed by a joyous chorus, for they knew that he was too saving of his time to spend it in visits of polite ceremony; his presence announced business.

"Good evening, gentlemen!" said the Jew. "How are you all?"

"Colline!" said Rodolphe, who was studying the horizontal line at full length on his bed. "Do the hospitable. Give our guest a chair; a guest is sacred. I salute Abraham in you," added he.

Colline took an arm chair about as soft as iron, and shoved it towards the Jew, saying:

"Suppose, for once, you were Cinna, (you *are* a great sinner, you know), and take this seat."

"Oh, oh, oh!" shouted the others, looking at the floor to see if it would not open and swallow up the philosopher. Meanwhile the Jew let himself fall into the arm chair, and was just going to cry out at its hardness, when he remembered that it was one which he himself had sold to Colline for a deputy's speech. As the Jew sat down, his pockets re-echoed with a silvery sound; melodious symphony, which threw the four friends into a reverie of delight.

"The accompaniment seems pretty," said Rodolphe aside to Marcel. "Now for the air!"

"Monsieur Marcel," said Medicis, "I have merely come to make your fortune; that is to say, I offer you a superb opportunity of making your entry into the artistic world. Art, you know, is a barren route, of which glory is the oasis."

"Father Medicis," cried Marcel, on the tenter-hooks of impatience, "in the name of your revered patron, St. Fifty-percent, be brief!"

"Here it is," continued Medicis, "a rich amateur, who is collecting a gallery destined to make the tour of Europe, has charged me to procure him a series of remarkable works. I come to offer you admission into this museum—in a word, to buy your 'Passage of the Red Sea.'"

"Money down?" asked Marcel.

"Specie," replied the Jew, making the orchestra pockets strike up.

"Do you accept this serious offer?" asked Colline.

"Of course I do!" shouted Rodolphe, "don't you see, you wretch, that he is talking of 'tin'? Is there nothing sacred for you, atheist that you are?"

Colline mounted on a table and assumed the attitude of Harpocrates, the God of Silence.

"Push on, Medicis!" said Marcel, exhibiting his picture. "I wish to leave you the honor of fixing the price of this work, which is above all price."

The Jew placed on the table a hundred and fifty francs in new coin.

"Well, what more?" said Marcel, "that's only the prologue."

"Monsieur Marcel," replied the Jew, "you know that my first offer is my last. I shall add nothing. Reflect, a hundred and fifty francs; that is a sum, it is!"

"A very small sum," said the artist. "There is that much worth of cobalt in my Pharaoh's robe. Make it a round sum, at any rate! Square it off; say two hundred!"

"I won't add a sou!" said Medicis. "But I stand dinner for the company, wine to any extent."

"Going, going, going!" shouted Colline, with three blows of his fist on the table, "no one speaks?—gone!"

"Well it's a bargain!" said Marcel.

"I will send for the picture tomorrow," said the Jew, "and now, gentlemen, to dinner!"

The four friends descended the staircase, singing the chorus of "The Huguenots"—"*A table! A table!*"

Medicis treated the Bohemians in a really magnificent way, and gave them their choice of a number of dishes, which until then were completely unknown to them. Henceforward hot lobster ceased to be a myth with Schaunard, who contracted a passion for it that bordered on delirium. The four friends departed from the gorgeous banquet as drunk as a vintage-day. Marcel's intoxication was near having the most deplorable consequences. In passing by his tailor's, at two in the morning, he absolutely wanted to wake up his creditor, and pay him the hundred and fifty francs on account. A ray of reason which flashed across the mind of Colline, stopped the artist on the border of this precipice.

A week after, Marcel discovered in what gallery his picture had been placed. While passing through the Faubourg St. Honore, he stopped in the midst of a group which seemed to regard with curiosity a sign that was being put up over a shop door. The sign was neither more nor less than Marcel's picture, which Medicis had sold to a grocer. Only "the Passage of the Red Sea" had undergone one more alteration, and been given one more new name. It had received the addition of a steamboat and was called "the Harbor of Marseilles." The curious bystanders were bestowing on it a flattering ovation. Marcel returned home in ecstacy at his triumph, muttering to himself, *Vox populi, vox Dei*.

XVII

The Toilette of the Graces

Mademoiselle Mimi, who was accustomed to sleep far into the day, woke up one morning at ten o'clock, and was greatly surprised not to find Rodolphe beside her, nor even in the room. The preceding night, before falling to sleep, she had, however, seen him at his desk, preparing to spend the night over a piece of literary work which had been ordered of him, and in the completion of which Mimi was especially interested. In fact, the poet had given his companion hopes that out of the fruit of his labors he would purchase a certain summer gown, that she had noticed one day at the "Deux Magots," a famous drapery establishment, to the window of which Mimi's coquetry used very frequently to pay its devotions. Hence, ever since the work in question had been begun, Mimi had been greatly interested in its progress. She would often come up to Rodolphe whilst he was writing, and leaning her head on his shoulder would say to him in serious tones—

"Well, is my dress getting on?"

"There is already enough for a sleeve, so be easy," replied Rodolphe.

One night having heard Rodolphe snap his fingers, which usually meant that he was satisfied with his work, Mimi suddenly sat up in bed and passing her head through the curtains said, "Is my dress finished?"

"There," replied Rodolphe, showing her four large sheets of paper, covered with closely written lines. "I have just finished the body."

"How nice," said Mimi. "Then there is only the skirt now left to do. How many pages like that are wanted for the skirt?"

"That depends; but as you are not tall, with ten pages of fifty lines each, and eight words to the line, we can get a decent skirt."

"I am not very tall, it is true," said Mimi seriously, "but it must not look as if we had skimped the stuff. Dresses are worn full, and I should like nice large folds so that it may rustle as I walk."

"Very good," replied Rodolphe, seriously. "I will squeeze another word in each line and we shall manage the rustling." Mimi fell asleep again quite satisfied.

As she had been guilty of the imprudence of speaking of the nice dress that Rodolphe was engaged in making for her to Mademoiselles

Musette and Phemie, these two young persons had not failed to inform Messieurs Marcel and Schaunard of their friend's generosity towards his mistress, and these confidences had been followed by unequivocal challenges to follow the example set by the poet.

"That is to say," added Mademoiselle Musette, pulling Marcel's moustache, "that if things go on like this a week longer I shall be obliged to borrow a pair of your trousers to go out in."

"I am owed eleven francs by a good house," replied Marcel. "If I get it in I will devote it to buying you a fashionable fig leaf."

"And I," said Phemie to Schaunard, "my gown is in ribbons."

Schaunard took three sous from his pocket and gave them to his mistress, saying, "Here is enough to buy a needle and thread with. Mend your gown, that will instruct and amuse you at the same time, *utile dulci*."

Nevertheless, in a council kept very secret, Marcel and Schaunard agreed with Rodolphe that each of them should endeavor to satisfy the justifiable coquetry of their mistresses.

"These poor girls," said Rodolphe, "a trifle suffices to adorn them, but then they must have this trifle. Latterly fine arts and literature have been flourishing; we are earning almost as much as street porters."

"It is true that I ought not to complain," broke in Marcel. "The fine arts are in a most healthy condition, one might believe oneself under the sway of Leo the Tenth."

"In point of fact," said Rodolphe. "Musette tells me that for the last week you have started off every morning and do not get home till about eight in the evening. Have you really got something to do?"

"My dear fellow, a superb job that Medicis got me. I am painting at the Ave Maria barracks. Eight grenadiers have ordered their portraits at six francs a head taken all round, likenesses guaranteed for a year, like a watch. I hope to get the whole regiment. I had the idea, on my own part, of decking out Musette when Medicis pays me, for it is with him I do business and not my models."

"As to me," observed Schaunard carelessly, "although it may not look like it, I have two hundred francs lying idle."

"The deuce, let us stir them up," said Rodolphe.

"In two or three days I count on drawing them," replied Schaunard. "I do not conceal from you that on doing so I intend to give a free rein to some of my passions. There is, above all, at the second hand clothes shop close by a nankeen jacket and a hunting horn, that have for a long time caught my eye. I shall certainly present myself with them."

"But," added Marcel and Rodolphe together, "where do you hope to draw this amount of capital from?"

"Hearken gentlemen," said Schaunard, putting on a serious air, and sitting down between his two friends, "we must not hide from one another that before becoming members of the Institute and ratepayers, we have still a great deal of rye bread to eat, and that daily bread is hard to get. On the other hand, we are not alone; as heaven has created us sensitive to love, each of us has chosen to share his lot."

"Which is little," interrupted Marcel.

"But," continued Schaunard, "whilst living with the strictest economy, it is difficult when one has nothing to put anything on one side, above all if one's appetite is always larger than one's plate."

"What are you driving at?" asked Rodolphe.

"This," resumed Schaunard, "that in our present situation we should all be wrong to play the haughty when a chance offers itself, even outside our art, of putting a figure in front of the cypher that constitutes our capital."

"Well!" said Marcel, "which of us can you reproach with playing the haughty. Great painter as I shall be some day, have I not consented to devote my brush to the pictorial reproduction of French soldiers, who pay me out of their scanty pocket money? It seems to me that I am not afraid to descend the ladder of my future greatness."

"And I," said Rodolphe, "do not you know that for the past fortnight I have been writing a medico-chirurgical epic for a celebrated dentist, who has hired my inspiration at fifteen sous the dozen lines, about half the price of oysters? However, I do not blush; rather than let my muse remain idle, I would willingly put a railway guide into verse. When one has a lyre it is meant to be made use of. And then Mimi has a burning thirst for boots."

"Then," said Schaunard, "you will not be offended with me when you know the source of that Pactolus, the overflowing of which I am awaiting."

The following is the history of Schaunard's two hundred francs:—

About a fortnight before he had gone into the shop of a music publisher who had promised to procure him amongst his customers' pupils for pianoforte lessons or pianofortes to tune.

"By Jove!" said the publisher, on seeing him enter the shop, "you are just in time. A gentleman has been here who wants a pianist; he is an Englishman, and will probably pay well. Are you really a good one?"

Schaunard reflected that a modest air might injure him in the publisher's estimation. Indeed, a modest musician, and especially a modest pianist, is a rare creation. Accordingly, he replied boldly:

"I am a first rate one; if I only had a lung gone, long hair and a black coat, I should be famous as the sun in the heavens; and instead of asking me eight hundred francs to engrave my composition 'The Death of the Damsel,' you would come on your knees to offer me three thousand for it on a silver plate."

The person whose address Schaunard took was an Englishman, named Birne. The musician was first received by a servant in blue, who handed him over to a servant in green, who passed him on to a servant in black, who introduced him into a drawing room, where he found himself face to face with a Briton coiled up in an attitude which made him resemble Hamlet mediating on human nothingness. Schaunard was about to explain the reason of his presence, when a sudden volley of shrill cries cut short his speech. These horrid and ear piercing sounds proceeded from a parrot hung out on the balcony of the story below.

"Oh! That beast, that beast!" exclaimed the Englishman, with a bound on his arm chair, "it will kill me."

Thereupon the bird began to repeat its vocabulary, much more extensive than that of ordinary Pollies; and Schaunard stood stupefied when he heard the animal, prompted by a female voice, reciting the speech of Theramenes with all the professional intonations.

This parrot was the favorite of an actress who was then a great favorite herself, and very much the rage—in her own boudoir. She was one of those women who, no one knows why, was quoted at fancy prices on the 'Change of dissipation, and whose names are inscribed on the bills of fare of young noblemen's suppers, where they form the living dessert. It gives a Christian standing now-a-days to be seen with one of these Pagans, who often have nothing of antiquity about them except their age. When they are handsome, there is no such great harm after all; the worst one risks is to sleep on straw in return for making them sleep on rosewood. But when their beauty is bought by the ounce at the perfumer's, and will not stand three drops of water on a rag; then their wit consists in a couplet of a farce, and their talent lies in the hand of the *claqueur*, it is hard indeed to understand how respectable men with good names, ordinary sense, and decent coats, can let themselves be carried away by a common place passion for these most mercenary creatures.

The actress in question was one of these belles of the day. She called herself Delores, and professed to be a Spaniard, although she was born in that Parisian Andalusia known as the Rue Coquenard. From there to the Rue de Provence is about ten minute's walk, but it had cost her seven years to make the transit. Her prosperity had begun with the decline of her personal charms. She had a horse the day when her first false tooth was inserted, and a pair the day of her second. Now she was living at a great rate, lodging in a palace, driving four horses on holidays, and giving balls to which all Paris came—the "all Paris" of these ladies—that is to say, that collection of lazy seekers after jokes and scandal; the "all Paris" that plays lansquenet; the sluggards of head and hand, who kill their own time and other people's; the writers who turn literary men to get some use out of the feather which nature placed on their backs; the bullies of the revel, the clipped and sweated gentlemen, the chevaliers of doubtful orders, all the vagabonds of kid-glove-dom, that come from God knows where, and go back tither again some day; all the marked and remarked notorieties; all those daughters of Eve who retail what they once sold wholesale; all that race of beings, corrupt from their cradle to their coffin, whom one sees on first nights at the theater, with Golconda on foreheads and Thibet on their shoulders, and for whom, notwithstanding, bloom the first violets of spring and the first passions of youth—all this world which the chronicles of gossip call "all Paris," was received by Delores who owned the parrot aforesaid.

This bird, celebrated for its oratorical talents among all the neighbors, had gradually become the terror of the nearest. Hung out on the balcony, it made a pulpit of its perch and spouted interminable harangues from morning to night. It had learned certain parliamentary topics from some political friends of the mistress, and was very strong on the sugar question. It knew all the actress's repertory by heart, and declaimed it well enough to have been her substitute, in case of indisposition. Moreover, as she was rather polyglot in her flirtations, and received visitors from all parts of the world, the parrot spoke all languages, and would sometimes let out a *lingua Franca* of oaths enough to shock the sailors to whom "Vert-Vert" owed his profitable education. The company of this bird, which might be instructive and amusing for ten minutes, became a positive torture when prolonged. The neighbors had often complained; the actress insolently disregarded their complaints. Two or three other tenants of the house, respectable fathers of families, indignant at the scandalous state of morals into which they were initiated by the indiscretions of the parrot, had given warning to the landlord. But the actress had got on his weak side; whoever might go, she stayed.

The Englishman whose sitting room Schaunard now entered, had suffered with patience for three months. One day he concealed his fury, which was ready to explode, under a full dress suit and sent in his card to Mademoiselle Dolores.

When she beheld him enter, arrayed almost as he would have been to present himself before Queen Victoria, she at first thought it must be Hoffmann, in his part of Lord Spleen; and wishing to be civil to a fellow artist, she offered him some breakfast.

The Englishman understood French. He had learned it in twenty five lessons from a Spanish refugee. Accordingly he replied:

"I accept your invitation on condition of our eating this disagreeable bird," and he pointed to the cage of the parrot, who, having smelled an Englishman, saluted him by whistling "God Save the King."

Dolores thought her neighbor was quizzing her, and was beginning to get angry, when Mr. Birne added:

"As I am very rich, I will buy the animal. Put your price on it."

Dolores answered that she valued the bird, and liked it, and would not wish to see it pass into the hands of another.

"Oh, it's not in my hands I want to put it," replied the Englishman, "But under my feet—so—," and he pointed to the heels of his boots.

Dolores shuddered with indignation and would probably have broken out, when she perceived on the Englishman's finger a ring, the diamond of which represented an income of twenty five hundred francs. The discovery was like a shower bath to her rage. She reflected that it might be imprudent to quarrel with a man who carried fifty thousand francs on his little finger.

"Well, sir," she said, "as poor Coco annoys you, I will put him in a back room, where you cannot hear him."

The Englishman made a gesture of satisfaction.

"However," added he, pointing once more to his boots, "I should have preferred—"

"Don't be afraid. Where I mean to put him it will be impossible for him to trouble milord."

"Oh! I am not a lord; only an esquire."

With that, Mr. Birne was retiring, after a very low bow, when Delores, who never neglected her interests, took up a small pocket from a work table and said:

"Tonight sir, is my benefit at the theater. I am to play in three pieces. Will you allow me to offer you some box tickets? The price has been but very slightly raised." And she put a dozen boxes into the Briton's hand.

"After showing myself so prompt to oblige him," thought she, "he cannot refuse, if he is a gentleman, and if he sees me play in my pink costume, who knows? He is very ugly, to be sure, and very sad looking, but he might furnish me the means of going to England without being sea sick."

The Englishman having taken the tickets, had their purport explained to him a second time. He then asked the price.

"The boxes are sixty francs each, and there are ten there, but no hurry," said added, seeing the Englishman take out his pocketbook. "I hope that as we are neighbors, this is not the last time I shall have the honor of a visit from you."

"I do not like to run up bills," replied Mr. Birne and drawing from the pocketbook a thousand franc note, he laid it on the table and slid the tickets into his pockets.

"I will give you change," said Dolores, opening a little drawer.

"Never mind," said the Englishman, "the rest will do for a drink," and he went off leaving Dolores thunder struck at his last words.

"For a drink!" she exclaimed. "What a clown! I will send him back his money."

But her neighbor's rudeness had only irritated the epidermis of her vanity; reflection calmed her. She thought that a thousand francs made a very nice "pile," after all, and that she had already put up with impertinences at a cheaper rate.

"Bah!" she said to herself. "It won't do to be so proud. No one was by, and this is my washerwoman's mouth. And this Englishman speaks so badly, perhaps he only means to pay me a compliment."

So she pocketed her bank note joyfully.

But that night after the theater she returned home furious. Mr. Birne had made no use of the tickets, and the ten boxes had remained vacant.

Thus on appearing on the stage, the unfortunate *beneficiaire* read on the countenances of her lady friends, the delight they felt at seeing the house so badly filled. She even heard an actress of her acquaintance say to another, as she pointed to the empty boxes, "Poor Dolores, she has only planted one stage box."

"True, the boxes are scarcely occupied," was the rejoinder.

"The stalls, too, are empty."

"Well, when they see her name on the bill, it acts on the house like an air pump."

"Hence, what an idea to put up the price of the seats!"

"A fine benefit. I will bet that the takings would not fill a money box or the foot of a stocking."

"Ah! There she is in her famous red velvet costume."

"She looks like a lobster."

"How much did you make out of your last benefit?" said another actress to her companion.

"The house was full, my dear, and it was a first night; chairs in the gangway were worth a louis. But I only got six francs; my milliner had all the rest. If I was not afraid of chilblains, I would go to Saint Petersburg."

"What, you are not yet thirty, and are already thinking of doing your Russia?"

"What would you have?" said the other, and she added, "and you, is your benefit soon coming on?"

"In a fortnight, I have already three thousand francs worth of tickets taken, without counting my young fellows from Saint Cyr."

"Hallo, the stalls are going out."

"It is because Dolores is singing."

In fact, Dolores, as red in the face as her costume, was warbling her verses with a vinegary voice. Just as she was getting though it with difficulty, two bouquets fell at her feet, thrown by two actresses, her dear friends, who advanced to the front of their box, exclaiming—

"Bravo, Dolores!"

The fury of the latter may be readily imagined. Thus, on returning home, although it was the middle of the night, she opened the window and woke up Coco, who woke up the honest Mr. Birne, who had dropped off to sleep on the faith of her promise.

From that day war was declared between the actress and the Englishman; a war to the knife, without truce or repose, the parties engaged in which recoiled before no expense or trouble. The parrot took finishing lessons in English and abused his neighbor all day in it, and in his shrillest falsetto. It was something awful. Dolores suffered from it herself, but she hoped that one day or other Mr. Birne would give warning. It was on that she had set her heart. The Englishman, on his part, began by establishing a school of drummers in his drawing room, but the police interfered. He then set up a pistol gallery; his servants riddled fifty cards a day. Again the commissary of police interposed, showing him an article in the municipal code, which forbids the usage of firearms indoors. Mr. Birne stopped firing, but a week after, Dolores found it was raining in her room. The landlord went to visit Mr. Birne, and found him taking saltwater baths in his drawing room. This room, which was very large, had been lined all round with sheets of metal, and had had all the doors fastened up. Into this extempore pond some hundred pails of water were poured, and a few tons of salt were added to them. It was a small edition of the sea. Nothing was lacking, not even fishes. Mr. Birne bathed there everyday, descending into it by an opening made in the upper panel of the center door. Before long an ancient and fish-like smell pervaded the neighborhood, and Dolores had half an inch of water in her bedroom.

The landlord grew furious and threatened Mr. Birne with an action for damages done to his property.

"Have I not a right," asked the Englishman, "to bathe in my rooms?"

"Not in that way, sir."

"Very well, if I have no right to, I won't," said the Briton, full of respect for the laws of the country in which he lived. "It's a pity; I enjoyed it very much."

That very night he had his ocean drained off. It was full time: there was already an oyster bed forming on the floor.

However, Mr. Birne had not given up the contest. He was only seeking some legal means of continuing his singular warfare, which was "nuts" to all the Paris loungers, for the adventure had been blazed about in the lobbies of the theaters and other public places. Dolores felt equally bound to come triumphant out of the contest. Not a few bets were made upon it.

It was then that Mr. Birne thought of the piano as an instrument of warfare. It was not so bad an idea, the most disagreeable of instruments being well capable of contending against the most disagreeable of birds. As soon as this lucky thought occurred to him, he hastened to put it into execution, hired a piano, and inquired for a pianist. The pianist, it will be remembered, was our friend Schaunard. The Englishman recounted to him his sufferings from the parrot, and what he had already done to come to terms with the actress.

"But milord," said Schaunard, "there is a sure way to rid yourself of this creature—parsley. The chemists are unanimous in declaring that this culinary plant is prussic acid to such birds. Chop up a little parsley, and shake it out of the window on Coco's cage, and the creature will die as certainly as if Pope Alexander VI had invited it to dinner."

"I thought of that myself," said the Englishman, "but the beast is taken good care of. The piano is surer."

Schaunard looked at the other without catching his meaning at once.

"See here," resumed the Englishman, "the actress and her animal always sleep till twelve. Follow my reasoning—"

"Go on. I am at the heels of it."

"I intend to disturb their sleep. The law of the country authorizes me to make music from morning to night. Do you understand?"

"But that will not be so disagreeable to her, if she hears me play the piano all day—for nothing, too. I am a first-rate hand, if I only had a lung gone—"

"Exactly, but I don't want you to make good music. You must only strike on your instrument thus," trying a scale, "and always the same thing without pity, only one scale. I understand medicine a little; that drives people mad. They will both go mad; that is what I look for. Come, Mr. Musician, to work at once. You shall be well paid."

"And so," said Schaunard, who had recounted the above details to his friends, "this is what I have been doing for the last fortnight. One scale continually from seven in the morning till dark. It is not exactly serious art. But then the Englishman pays me two hundred francs a month for my noise; it would be cutting one's throat to refuse such a windfall. I accepted, and in two or three days I take my first month's money."

It was after those mutual confidences that the three friends agreed amongst themselves to profit by the general accession of wealth to give their mistresses the spring outfit that the coquetry of each of them had been wishing for so long. It was further agreed that whoever pocketed his money first should wait for the others, so that the purchases should be made at the same time, and that Mademoiselle Mimi, Musette, and Phemie should enjoy the pleasure of casting their old skins, as Schaunard put it, together.

Well, two or three days after this council Rodolphe came in first; his dental poem had been paid for; it weighed in eighty francs. The next day Marcel drew from Medicis the price of eighteen corporal's likenesses, at six francs each.

Marcel and Rodolphe had all the difficulty in the world to hide their good fortune.

"It seems to me that I sweat gold," said the poet.

"It is the same with me," said Marcel. "If Schaunard delays much longer, it would be impossible for me to continue to play the part of the anonymous Croesus."

But the very next morning saw Schaunard arrive, splendidly attired in a bright yellow nankeen jacket.

"Good heavens!" exclaimed Phemie, dazzled on seeing her lover so elegantly got up, "where did you find that jacket?"

"I found it amongst my papers," replied the musician, making a sign to his two friends to follow him. "I have drawn the coin," said he, when they were alone. "Behold it," and he displayed a handful of gold.

"Well," exclaimed Marcel, "forward, let us sack the shops. How happy Musette will be."

"How pleased Mimi will be," added Rodolphe. "Come, are you coming Schaunard?"

"Allow me to reflect," replied the musician. "In decking out these ladies with the thousand caprices of fashion, we shall perhaps be guilty of a mistake. Think on it. Are you not afraid that when they resemble the engravings in 'The Scarf of Iris,' these splendors will exercise a deplorable influence upon their characters, and does it suit young fellows like us to behave towards women as if we were aged and wrinkled dotards? It is not that I hesitate about sacrificing fifteen or eighteen francs to dress Phemie; but I tremble. When she has a new bonnet she will not even recognize me, perhaps. She looks so well with only a flower in her hair. What do you think about it, philosopher?" broke off Schaunard, addressing Colline, who had come in within the last few minutes.

"Ingratitude is the offspring of kindness," observed the philosopher.

"On the other hand," continued Schaunard, "when your mistresses are well dressed, what sort of figure will you cut beside them in your dilapidated costumes? You will look like their waiting maids. I do not speak for myself," he broke off, drawing himself up in his nankeen jacket, "for thank heaven, I could go anywhere now."

However, despite the spirit of opposition shown by Schaunard, it was once more agreed that the next day all the shops of the neighborhood should be ransacked to the advantage of the ladies.

And, indeed, the next day, at the very moment that we have seen, at the beginning of this chapter, Mademoiselle Mimi wakes up very much astonished at Rodolphe's absence, the poet and his two friends were ascending the stairs, accompanied by a shopman from the Deux Magots and a milliner with specimens. Schaunard, who had bought the famous hunting horn, marched before them playing the overture to "The Caravan."

Musette and Phemie, summoned by Mimi, who was living on the lower floor, descended the stairs with the swiftness of avalanches on hearing the news that the bonnets and dresses had been brought for them. Seeing this poor wealth spread out before them, the three women went almost mad with joy. Mimi was seized with a fit of hysterical laughter, and skipped about like a kid, waving a barege scarf. Musette threw her arms around Marcel's neck, with a little green boot in each hand, which she smote together like cymbals. Phemie looked at Schaunard and sobbed. She could only say, "Oh Alexander, Alexander!"

"There is no danger of her refusing the presents of Artaxerxes," murmured Colline the philosopher.

After the first outbursts of joy were over, when the choices had been made and the bills settled, Rodolphe announced to the three girls that they would have to make arrangements to try on their new things the next morning.

"We will go into the country," said he.

"A fine thing to make a fuss of," exclaimed Musette. "It is not the first time that I have bought, cut out, sewn together, and worn a dress the same day. Besides, we have the night before us, too. We shall be ready, shall we not, ladies?"

"Oh yes! We shall be ready," exclaimed Mimi and Phemie together.

They at once set to work, and for sixteen hours did not lay aside scissors or needle.

The next day was the first of May. The Easter bells had rung in the resurrection of spring a few days before, and she had come eager and joyful. She came, as the German ballad says, light-hearted as the young lover who is going to plant a maypole before the window of his betrothed. She painted the sky blue, the trees green, and all things in bright colors. She aroused the torpid sun, who was sleeping in his bed of mists, his head resting on the snow leaden clouds that served him as a pillow, and cried to him, "Hi! Hi! My friend, time is up, and I am here; quick to work. Put on your fine dress of fresh rays without further delay, and show yourself at once on your balcony to announce my arrival."

Upon which the sun had indeed set out, and was marching along as proud and haughty as some great lord of the court. The swallows, returned from their Eastern pilgrimage, filled the air with their flight, the may whitened the bushes, the violets scented the woods, in which the birds were leaving their nests each with a roll of music under its wings. It was spring indeed, the true spring of poets and lovers, and not the spring of the almanac maker—an ugly spring with a red nose and frozen fingers, which still keeps poor folk shivering at the chimney corner when the last ashes of the last log have long since burnt out. The balmy breeze swept through the transparent atmosphere and scattered throughout the city the first scent of the surrounding country. The rays of the sun, bright and warm, tapped at the windows. To the invalid they cried, "open, we are health," and at the garret of the young girl bending towards her mirror, innocent first love of the most innocent, they said, "open darling, that we may light up your beauty. We are the messengers of fine weather. You can now put on your cotton frock and your straw hat, and lace your smart boots; the groves in which folk foot it are decked with bright new flowers, and the violins are tuning for the Sunday dance. Good morning, my dear!"

When the angelus rang out from the neighboring church, the three hard working coquettes, who had had scarcely time to sleep a few hours, were already before their looking glasses, giving their final glance at their new attire.

They were all three charming, dressed alike, and wearing on their faces the same glow of satisfaction imparted by the realization of a long cherished wish.

Musette was, above all, dazzlingly beautiful.

"I have never felt so happy," said she to Marcel. "It seems to me that God has put into this hour all the happiness of my life, and I am afraid that there will be no more left me. Ah bah! When there is no more left, there will still be some more. We have the receipt for making it," she added, gaily kissing him.

As to Phemie, one thing vexed her.

"I am very fond of green grass and the little birds," said she, "but in the country one never meets anyone, and there will be no one to see my pretty bonnet and my nice dress. Suppose we went into the country on the Boulevards?"

At eight in the morning the whole street was in commotion, due to the blasts from Schaunard's horn giving the signal to start. All the neighbors were at their windows to see the Bohemians go by. Colline, who was of the party, brought up the rear, carrying the ladies' parasols. An hour later the whole of the joyous band were scattered about the fields at Fontenay-aux-Roses.

When they returned home, very late at night, Colline, who during the day had discharged the duties of treasurer, stated that they had omitted to spend six francs, and placed this balance on the table.

"What shall we do with it?" asked Marcel.

"Suppose we invest it in Government stock," said Schaunard.

XVIII

Francine's Muff

A mong the true Bohemians of the real Bohemia I used to know one, named Jacques D. He was a sculptor, and gave promise of great talent. But poverty did not give him time to fulfill this promise. He died of debility in March, 184-, at the Saint Louis Hospital, on bed No. 14 in the Sainte Victoria ward.

I made the acquaintance of Jacques at the hospital, when I was detained there myself by a long illness. Jacques had, as I have said, the makings of a great talent, and yet he was quite unassuming about it. During the two months I spent in his company, and during which he felt himself cradled in the arms of Death, I never once heard him complain or give himself up to those lamentations which render the unappreciated artist so ridiculous. He died without attitudinizing. His death brings to my mind, too, one of the most horrible scenes I ever saw in that caravanserai of human sufferings. His father, informed of the event, came to reclaim the body, and for a long time haggled over giving the thirty-six francs demanded by the hospital authorities. He also haggled over the funeral service, and so persistently that they ended by knocking off six francs. At the moment of putting the corpse into the coffin, the male nurse took off the hospital sheet, and asked one of the deceased's friends who was there for money for a shroud. The poor devil, who had not a sou, went to Jacques' father, who got into a fearful rage, and asked when they would finish bothering him.

The sister of charity, who was present at this horrible discussion, cast a glance at the corpse, and uttered these simple and feeling words:

"Oh! sir, you cannot have him buried like that, poor fellow, it is so cold. Give him at least a shirt, that he may not arrive quite naked before his God."

The father gave five francs to the friend to get a shirt, but recommended him to go to a wardrobe shop in the Rue Grace-aux-Belles, where they sold second-hand linen.

"It will be cheaper there," said he.

This cruelty on the part of Jacques' father was explained to me later on. He was furious because his son had chosen an artistic career, and his anger remained unappeased even in the presence of a coffin.

But I am not very far from Mademoiselle Francine and her muff. I will return to them. Mademoiselle Francine was the first and only mistress of Jacques, who did not die very old, for he was scarcely three and twenty when his father would have had him laid naked in the earth. The story of his love was told me by Jacques himself when he was No. 14 and I was No. 16 in the Sainte Victoire ward—an ugly spot to die in.

Ah reader! Before I begin this story, which would be a touching one if I could tell it as it was told to me by my friend Jacques, let me take a pull or two at the old clay pipe he gave me on the day that the doctor forbade its use by him. Yet at night, when the male nurse was asleep, my friend Jacques would borrow his pipe with a little tobacco from me. It is so wearisome at night in those vast wards, when one suffers and cannot sleep.

"Only two or three whiffs," he would say, and I would let him have it; and Sister Sainte-Genevieve did not seem to notice the smoke when she made her round. Ah, good sister! How kind you were, and how beautiful you looked, too, when you came to sprinkle us with holy water. We could see you approaching, walking slowly along the gloomy aisles, draped in your white veil, which fell in such graceful folds, and which our friend Jacques admired so much. Ah kind sister! You were the Beatrice of that Inferno. So sweet were your consolations that we were always complaining in order to be consoled by you. If my friend Jacques had not died one snowy day he would have carved you a nice little Virgin Mary to put in your cell, good Sister Sainte-Genevieve.

Well, and the muff? I do not see anything of the muff.

ANOTHER READER: And Mademoiselle Francine, where about is she, then?
FIRST READER: This story is not very lively.
SECOND READER: We shall see further on.

I really beg your pardon, gentlemen, it is my friend Jacques' pipe that has led me away into these digressions. But, besides, I am not pledged to make you laugh. Times are not always gay in Bohemia.

Jacques and Francine had met in a house in the Rue de la Tour-d'Auvergne, into which they had both moved at the same time at the April quarter.

The artist and the young girl were a week without entering on those neighborly relations which are almost always forced on one when dwelling on the same floor. However, without having exchanged a word, they were already acquainted with one another. Francine knew that her neighbor was a poor devil of an artist, and Jacques had learned that his was a little seamstress who had quitted her family to escape the ill-usage of a stepmother. She accomplished miracles of economy to make both ends meet, and, as she had never known pleasure, had no longing for it. This is how the pair came under the common law of partition walls. One evening in April, Jacques came home worn out with fatigue, fasting since morning, and profoundly sad with one of those vague sadnesses which have no precise cause, and which seize on you anywhere and at all times; a kind of apoplexy of the heart to which poor wretches living alone are especially subject. Jacques, who felt stifling in his narrow room, opened the window to breathe a little. The evening was a fine one, and the setting sun displayed its melancholy splendors above the hills of Montmartre. Jacques remained pensively at his window listening to the winged chorus of spring harmony which added to his sadness. Seeing a raven fly by uttering a croak, he thought of the days when ravens brought food to Elijah, the pious recluse, and reflected that these birds were no longer so charitable. Then, not being able to stand it any longer, he closed his window, drew the curtain, and, as he had not the wherewithal to buy oil for his lamp, lit a resin taper that he had brought back from a trip to the Grande-Chartreuse. Sadder than ever he filled his pipe.

"Luckily, I still have enough tobacco to hide the pistol," murmured he, and he began to smoke.

My friend Jacques must have been very sad that evening to think about hiding the pistol. It was his supreme resource on great crises, and was usually pretty successful. The plan was as follows. Jacques smoked tobacco on which he used to sprinkle a few drops of laudanum, and he would smoke until the cloud of smoke from his pipe became thick enough to veil from him all the objects in his little room, and, above all, a pistol hanging on the wall. It was a matter of half a score pipes. By the time the pistol was wholly invisible it almost always happened that the smoke and the laudanum combined would send Jacques off to sleep, and it also often happened that his sadness left him at the commencement of his dreams.

HENRI MURGER

But on this particular evening he had used up all his tobacco; the pistol was completely hidden, and yet Jacques was still bitterly sad. That evening, on the contrary Mademoiselle Francine was extremely light-hearted when she came home, and like Jacques' sadness, her light-heartedness was without cause. It was one of those joys that come from heaven, and that God scatters amongst good hearts. So Mademoiselle Francine was in a good temper, and sang to herself as she came upstairs. But as she was going to open her door a puff of wind, coming through the open staircase window, suddenly blew out her candle.

"Oh, what a nuisance!" exclaimed the girl, "six flights of stairs to go down and up again."

But, noticing the light coming from under Jacques' door, the instinct of idleness grafted on a feeling of curiosity, advised her to go and ask the artist for a light. "It is a service daily rendered among neighbors," thought she, "and there is nothing compromising about it."

She tapped twice, therefore, at the door, and Jacques opened it, somewhat surprised at this late visit. But scarcely had she taken a step into the room than the smoke that filled it suddenly choked her, and, before she was able to speak a word, she sank fainting into a chair, dropping her candle and her room door key onto the ground. It was midnight, and everyone in the house was asleep. Jacques thought it better not to call for help. He was afraid, in the first place, of compromising his neighbor. He contented himself, therefore, with opening the window to let in a little fresh air, and, after having sprinkled a few drops of water on the girl's face, saw her open her eyes and by degrees come to herself. When, at the end of five minutes' time, she had wholly recovered consciousness, Francine explained the motive that had brought her into the artist's room, and made many excuses for what had happened.

"Now, then, I am recovered," said she. "I can go into my own room."

He had already opened the door, when she perceived that she was not only forgetting to light her candle, but that she had not the key of her room.

"Silly thing that I am," said she, putting her candle to the flame of the resin taper, "I came in here to get a light, and I was going away without one."

But at the same moment the draft caused by the door and window, both of which had remained open, suddenly blew out the taper, and the two young folk were left in darkness.

"One would think that it was done on purpose," said Francine. "Forgive me sir, for all the trouble I am giving you, and be good enough to strike a light so that I may find my key."

"Certainly mademoiselle," answered Jacques, feeling for the matches.

He had soon found them. But a singular idea flashed across his mind, and he put the matches in his pocket saying, "Dear me, mademoiselle, here is another trouble. I have not a single match here. I used the last when I came in."

"Oh!" said Francine, "after all I can very well find my way without a light, my room is not big enough for me to lose myself in it. But I must have my key. Will you be good enough, sir, to help me to look for it? It must have fallen to the ground."

"Let us look for it, mademoiselle," said Jacques.

And both of them began to seek the lost article in the dark, but as though guided by a common instinct, it happened during this search, that their hands, groping in the same spot, met ten times a minute. And, as they were both equally awkward, they did not find the key.

"The moon, which is hidden just now by the clouds, shines right into the room," said Jacques. "Let us wait a bit; by-and-by it will light up the room and may help us."

And, pending the appearance of the moon, they began to talk. A conversation in the dark, in a little room, on a spring night; a conversation which, at the outset trifling and unimportant, gradually enters on the chapter of personal confidences. You know what that leads to. Language by degrees grows confused, full of reticences; voices are lowered; words alternate with sighs. Hands meeting complete the thought which from the heart ascends to the lips, and—. Seek the conclusion in your recollection, young couples. Do you remember, young man. Do you remember, young lady, you who now walk hand-in-hand, and who, up to two days back, had never seen one another?

At length the moon broke through the clouds, and her bright light flooded the room. Mademoiselle Francine awoke from her reverie uttering a faint cry.

"What is the matter?" asked Jacques, putting his arm around her waist.

"Nothing," murmured Francine. "I thought I heard someone knock."

And, without Jacques noticing it, she pushed the key that she had just noticed under some of the furniture.

She did not want to find it now.

First Reader: I certainly will not let my daughter read this story.

Second Reader: Up till now I have not caught a glimpse of a single hair of Mademoiselle Francine's muff; and, as to the young woman herself, I do not know any better what she is like, whether she is fair or dark.

Patience, readers, patience. I have promised you a muff, and I will give you one later on, as my friend Jacques did to his poor love Francine, who had become his mistress, as I have explained in the line left blank above.

She was fair was Francine, fair and lovely, which is not usual. She had remained ignorant of love until she was twenty, but a vague presentiment of her approaching end counselled her not to delay if she would become acquainted with it.

She met Jacques and loved him. Their connection lasted six months. They had taken one another in the spring; they were parted in the autumn. Francine was consumptive. She knew it and her lover Jacques knew it too; a fortnight after he had taken up with her he had learned it from one of his friends, who was a doctor.

"She will go with the autumn leaves," said the latter.

Francine heard this confidence, and perceived the grief it caused her lover.

"What matters the autumn leaves?" said she, putting the whole of her love into a smile. "What matters the autumn; it is summer, and the leaves are green; let us profit by that, love. When you see me ready to depart from this life, you shall take me in your arms and kiss me, and forbid me to go. I am obedient you know, and I will stay."

And for five months this charming creature passed through the miseries of Bohemian life, a smile and a song on her lips. As to Jacques, he let himself be deluded. His friend often said to him, "Francine is worse, she must be attended to." Then Jacques went all over Paris to obtain the wherewithal for the doctor's prescription, but Francine would not hear of it, and threw the medicine out of the window. At night, when she was seized with a fit of coughing, she would leave the room and go out on the landing, so that Jacques might not hear her.

One day, when they had both gone into the country, Jacques saw a tree the foliage of which was turning to yellow. He gazed sadly at Francine, who was walking slowly and somewhat dreamily.

Francine saw Jacques turn pale and guessed the reason of his pallor.

"You are foolish," said she, kissing him, "we are only in July, it is three months to October, loving one another day and night as we do, we shall double the time we have to spend together. And then, besides, if I feel worse when the leaves turn yellow, we will go and live in a pine forest, the leaves are always green there."

In October Francine was obliged to keep her bed. Jacques' friend attended her. The little room in which they lived was situated at the top of the house and looked into a court, in which there was a tree, which day by day grew barer of foliage. Jacques had put a curtain to the window to hide this tree from the invalid, but Francine insisted on its being drawn back.

"Oh my darling!" said she to Jacques. "I will give you a hundred times more kisses than there are leaves." And she added, "Besides I am much better now. I shall soon be able to go out, but as it will be cold and I do not want to have red hands, you must buy me a muff."

During the whole of her illness this muff was her only dream.

The day before All Saints', seeing Jacques more grief stricken than ever, she wished to give him courage, and to prove to him that she was better she got up.

The doctor arrived at that moment and forced her to go to bed again.

"Jacques," whispered he in the artist's ear, "you must summon up your courage. All is over; Francine is dying."

Jacques burst into tears.

"You may give her whatever she asks for now," continued the doctor, "there is no hope."

Francine heard with her eyes what the doctor had said to her lover.

"Do not listen to him," she exclaimed, holding out her arm to Jacques, "do not listen to him; he is not speaking the truth. We will go out tomorrow—it is All Saints' Day. It will be cold—go buy me a muff, I beg of you. I am afraid of chilblains this winter."

Jacques was going out with his friend, but Francine detained the doctor.

"Go and get my muff," said she to Jacques. "Get a nice one, so that it may last a good while."

When she was alone she said to the doctor.

"Oh sir! I am going to die, and I know it. But before I pass away give me something to give me strength for a night, I beg of you. Make me well for one more night, and let me die afterwards, since God does not wish me to live longer."

As the doctor was doing his best to console her, the wind carried into the room and cast upon the sick girl's bed a yellow leaf, torn from the tree in the little courtyard.

Francine opened the curtain, and saw the tree entirely bare.

"It is the last," said she, putting the leaf under her pillow.

"You will not die until tomorrow," said the doctor. "You have a night before you."

"Ah, what happiness!" exclaimed the poor girl. "A winter's night—it will be a long one."

Jacques came back. He brought a muff with him.

"It is very pretty," said Francine. "I will wear it when I go out."

So passed the night with Jacques.

The next day—All Saints'—about the middle of the day, the death agony seized on her, and her whole body began to quiver.

"My hands are cold," she murmured. "Give me my muff."

And she buried her poor hands in the fur.

"It is the end," said the doctor to Jacques. "Kiss her for the last time."

Jacques pressed his lips to those of his love. At the last moment they wanted to take away her muff, but she clutched it with her hands.

"No, no," she said, "leave it me; it is winter, it is cold. Oh my poor Jacques! My poor Jacques! What will become of you? Oh heavens!"

And the next day Jacques was alone.

FIRST READER: I told you that this was not a very lively story.

What would you have, reader? We cannot always laugh.

It was the morning of All Saints. Francine was dead.

Two men were watching at the bedside. One of them standing up was the doctor. The other, kneeling beside the bed, was pressing his lips to the dead girl's hands, and seemed to rivet them there in a despairing kiss. It was Jacques, her lover. For more than six hours he had been plunged in a state of heart broken insensibility. An organ playing under the windows had just roused him from it.

This organ was playing a tune that Francine was in the habit of singing of a morning.

One of those mad hopes that are only born out of deep despair flashed across Jacques' mind. He went back a month in the past—to the period when Francine was only sick unto death; he forgot the present, and imagined for a moment that the dead girl was but sleeping, and that she would wake up directly, her mouth full of her morning song.

But the sounds of the organ had not yet died away before Jacques had already come back to the reality. Francine's mouth was eternally closed to all songs, and the smile that her last thought had brought to her lips was fading away from them beneath death's fingers.

"Take courage, Jacques," said the doctor, who was the sculptor's friend.

Jacques rose, and said, looking fixedly at him, "it is over, is it not—there is no longer any hope?"

Without replying to this wild inquiry, Jacques' friend went and drew the curtains of the bed, and then, returning to the sculptor, held out his hand.

"Francine is dead," said he. "We were bound to expect it, though heaven knows that we have done what we could to save her. She was a good girl, Jacques, who loved you very dearly—dearer and better than you loved her yourself, for hers was love alone, while yours held an alloy. Francine is dead, but all is not over yet. We must now think about the steps necessary for her burial. We must set about that together, and we will ask one of the neighbors to keep watch here while we are away."

Jacques allowed himself to be led away by his friend. They passed the day between the registrar of deaths, the undertaker, and the cemetery. As Jacques had no money, the doctor pawned his watch, a ring, and some clothes, to cover the cost of the funeral, that was fixed for the next day.

They both got in late at night. The neighbor who had been watching tried to make Jacques eat a little.

"Yes," said he. "I will. I am very cold and I shall need a little strength for my work tonight."

The neighbor and the doctor did not understand him.

Jacques sat down at the table and ate a few mouthfuls so hurriedly that he was almost choked. Then he asked for drink. But on lifting his glass to his lips he let it fall. The glass, which broke on the floor, had awakened in the artist's mind a recollection which itself revived his momentary dulled pain. The day on which Francine had called on him for the first time she had felt ill, and he had given her to drink out of this glass. Later, when they were living together, they had regarded it as a love token.

During his rare moments of wealth the artist would buy for his love one or two bottles of the strengthening wine prescribed for her, and it was from this glass that Francine used to sip the liquid whence her love drew a charming gaiety.

Jacques remained for more than half an hour staring without uttering a word at the scattered fragments of this frail and cherished token. It seemed to him that his heart was also broken, and that he could feel the fragments tearing his breast. When he had recovered himself, he picked up the pieces of glass and placed them in a drawer. Then he asked the neighbor to fetch him two candles, and to send up a bucket of water by the porter.

"Do not go away," said he to the doctor, who had no intention of doing so. "I shall want you presently."

The water and the candles were brought and the two friends left alone.

"What do you want to do?" asked the doctor, watching Jacques, who after filling a wooden bowl with water was sprinkling powdered plaster of Paris into it.

"What do I mean to do?" asked the artist, "cannot you guess? I am going to model Francine's head, and as my courage would fail me if I were left alone, you must stay with me."

Jacques then went and drew the curtains of the bed and turned down the sheet that had been pulled up over the dead girl's face. His hand began to tremble and a stifled sob broke from his lips.

"Bring the candles," he cried to his friend, "and come and hold the bowl for me."

One of the candles was placed at the head of the bed so as to shed its light on Francine's face, the other candle was placed at the foot. With a brush dipped in olive oil the artist coated the eye-brows, the eye-lashes and the hair, which he arranged as Francine usually wore it.

"By doing this she will not suffer when we remove the mold," murmured Jacques to himself.

These precautions taken and after arranging the dead girl's head in a favorable position, Jacques began to lay on the plaster in successive coats until the mold had attained the necessary thickness. In a quarter of an hour the operation was over and had been thoroughly successful.

By some strange peculiarity a change had taken place in Francine's face. The blood, which had not had time to become wholly congealed, warmed no doubt by the warmth of the plaster, had flowed to the upper part of the corpse and a rosy tinge gradually showed itself on the dead whiteness of the cheeks and forehead. The eyelids, which had lifted when the mold was removed, revealed the tranquil blue eyes in which a vague intelligence seemed to lurk; from out the lips, parted by the beginning of a smile, there seemed to issue that last word, forgotten during the last farewell, that is only heard by the heart.

Who can affirm that intelligence absolutely ends where insensibility begins? Who can say that the passions fade away and die exactly at the last beat of the heart which they have agitated? Cannot the soul sometimes remain a voluntary captive within the corpse already dressed for the coffin, and note for a moment from the recesses of its fleshly prison house, regrets and tears? Those who depart have so many reasons to mistrust those who remain behind.

At the moment when Jacques sought to preserve her features by the aid of art who knows but that a thought of after life had perhaps returned to awaken Francine in her first slumber of the sleep that knows no end. Perhaps she had remembered the he whom she had just left was an artist at the same time as a lover, that he was both because he could not be one without the other, that for him love was the soul of heart and that if he had loved her so, it was because she had been for him a mistress and a woman, a sentiment in form. And then, perhaps, Francine, wishing to leave Jacques the human form that had become for him an incarnate ideal, had been able though dead and cold already to once more clothe her face with all the radiance of love and with all the graces of youth, to resuscitate the art treasure.

And perhaps too, the poor girl had thought rightly, for there exist among true artists singular Pygmalions who, contrary to the original one, would like to turn their living Galateas to marble.

In presence of the serenity of this face on which the death pangs had no longer left any trace, no one would have believed in the prolonged sufferings that had served as a preface to death. Francine seemed to be continuing a dream of love, and seeing her thus one would have said that she had died of beauty.

The doctor, worn out with fatigue, was asleep in a corner.

As to Jacques, he was again plunged in doubt. His mind beset with hallucinations, persisted in believing that she whom he had loved so well was on the point of awakening, and as faint nervous contractions, due to the recent action of the plaster, broke at intervals the immobility of the corpse, this semblance of life served to maintain Jacques in his blissful illusion, which lasted until morning, when a police official called to verify the death and authorize internment.

Besides, if it needed all the folly of despair to doubt of her death on beholding this beautiful creature, it also needed all the infallibility of science to believe it.

While the neighbor was putting Francine into her shroud, Jacques was led away into the next room, where he found some of his friends who had come to follow the funeral. The Bohemians desisted as regards Jacques, whom, however, they loved in brotherly fashion, from all those consolations which only serve to irritate grief. Without uttering one of those remarks so hard to frame and so painful to listen to, they silently shook their friend by the hand in turn.

"Her death is a great misfortune for Jacques," said one of them.

"Yes," replied the painter Lazare, a strange spirit who had been able at the very outset to conquer all the rebellious impulses of youth by the inflexibility of one set purpose, and in whom the artist had ended by stifling the man, "yes, but it is a misfortune that he incurred voluntarily. Since he knew Francine, Jacques has greatly altered."

"She made him happy," said another.

"Happy," replied Lazare, "what do you call happy? How can you call a passion, which brings a man to the condition in which Jacques is at this moment, happiness? Show him a masterpiece and he would not even turn his eyes to look at it; on a Titian or a Raphael. My mistress is immortal and will never deceive me. She dwells in the Louvre, and her name is Joconde."

While Lazare was about to continue his theories on art and sentiment, it was announced that it was time to start for the church.

After a few prayers the funeral procession moved on to the cemetery. As it was All Souls' Day an immense crowd filled it. Many people turned to look at Jacques walking bareheaded in rear of the hearse.

"Poor fellow," said one, "it is his mother, no doubt."

"It is his father," said another.

"It is his sister," was elsewhere remarked.

A poet, who had come there to study the varying expressions of regret at this festival of recollections celebrated once a year amidst November fogs, alone guessed on seeing him pass that he was following the funeral of his mistress.

When they came to the grave the Bohemians ranged themselves about it bareheaded, Jacques stood close to the edge, his friend the doctor holding him by the arm.

The grave diggers were in a hurry and wanted to get things over quickly.

"There is to be no speechifying," said one of them. "Well, so much the better. Heave, mate, that's it."

The coffin taken out of the hearse was lowered into the grave. One man withdrew the ropes and then with one of his mates took a shovel and began to cast in the earth. The grave was soon filled up. A little wooden cross was planted over it.

In the midst of his sobs the doctor heard Jacques utter this cry of egoism—

"Oh my youth! It is you they are burying."

Jacques belonged to a club styled the Water Drinkers, which seemed to have been founded in imitation of the famous one of the Rue des Quatre-Vents, which is treated of in that fine story *"Un Grand Homme de Province."* Only there was a great difference between the heroes of the latter circle and the Water Drinkers who, like all imitators, had exaggerated the system they sought to put into practice. This difference will be understood by the fact that in Balzac's book the members of the club end by attaining the object they proposed to themselves, while after several years' existence the club of the Water Drinkers was naturally dissolved by the death of all its members, without the name of anyone of them remaining attached to a work attesting their existence.

During his union with Francine, Jacques' intercourse with the Water Drinkers had become more broken. The necessities of life had obliged the artist to violate certain conditions solemnly signed and sworn by the Water Drinkers the day the club was founded.

Perpetually perched on the stilts of an absurd pride, these young fellows had laid down as a sovereign principle in their association, that they must never abandon the lofty heights of art; that is to say, that despite their mortal poverty, not one of them would make any concession to necessity. Thus the poet Melchior would never have consented to abandon what he called his lyre, to write a commercial prospectus or an electoral address. That was all very well for the poet Rodolphe, a good-for-nothing who was ready to turn his hand to anything, and who never let a five franc piece flit past him without trying to capture it, no matter how. The painter Lazare, a proud wearer of rags, would never have soiled his brushes by painting the portrait of a tailor holding a parrot on his forefinger, as our friend the painter Marcel had once done in exchange for the famous dress coat nicknamed

Methuselah, which the hands of each of his sweethearts had starred over with darns. All the while he had been living in communion of thought with the Water Drinkers, the sculptor Jacques had submitted to the tyranny of the club rules; but when he made the acquaintance of Francine, he would not make the poor girl, already ill, share of the regimen he had accepted during his solitude. Jacques' was above all an upright and loyal nature. He went to the president of the club, the exclusive Lazare, and informed him that for the future he would accept any work that would bring him in anything.

"My dear fellow, your declaration of love is your artistic renunciation. We will remain your friends if you like, but we shall no longer be your partners. Work as you please, for me you are no longer a sculptor, but a plasterer. It is true that you may drink wine, but we who continue to drink our water, and eat our dry bread, will remain artists."

Whatever Lazare might say about it, Jacques remained an artist. But to keep Francine with him he undertook, when he had a chance, any paying work. It is thus that he worked for a long time in the workshop of the ornament maker Romagnesi. Clever in execution and ingenious in invention, Jacques, without relinquishing high art, might have achieved a high reputation in those figure groups that have become one of the chief elements in this commerce. But Jacques was lazy, like all true artists, and a lover after the fashion of poets. Youth in him had awakened tardily but ardent, and, with a presentiment of his approaching end, he had sought to exhaust it in Francine's arms. Thus it happened that good chances of work knocked at his door without Jacques answering, because he would have had to disturb himself, and he found it more comfortable to dream by the light of his beloved's eyes.

When Francine was dead the sculptor went to see his old friends the Water Drinkers again. But Lazare's spirit predominated in this club, in which each of the members lived petrified in the egoism of art. Jacques did not find what he came there in search of. They scarcely understood his despair, which they strove to appease by argument, and seeing this small degree of sympathy, Jacques preferred to isolate his grief rather than see it laid bare by discussion. He broke off, therefore, completely with the Water Drinkers and went away to live alone.

Five or six days after Francine's funeral, Jacques went to a monumental mason of the Montparnasse cemetery and offered to conclude the following bargain with him. The mason was to furnish Francine's grave with a border, which Jacques reserved the right of designing, and in addition to supply the sculptor with a block of white marble. In return for this Jacques would place himself for three months at his disposition, either as a journeyman stone-cutter or sculptor. The monumental mason then had several important orders on hand. He visited Jacques' studio, and in presence of several works begun there, had proof that the chance which gave him the sculptor's services was a lucky one for him. A week later, Francine's grave had a border, in the midst of which the wooden cross had been replaced by a stone one with her name graven on it.

Jacques had luckily to do with an honest fellow who understood that a couple of hundredweight of cast iron, and three square feet of Pyrenean marble were no payment for three months' work by Jacques, whose talent had brought him in several thousand francs. He offered to give the artist a share in the business, but Jacques would not consent. The lack of variety in the subjects for treatment was repugnant to his inventive disposition, besides he had what he wanted, a large block of marble, from the recesses of which he wished to evolve a masterpiece destined for Francine's grave.

At the beginning of spring Jacques' position improved. His friend the doctor put him in relation with a great foreign nobleman who had come to settle in Paris, and who was having a magnificent mansion built in one of the most fashionable districts. Several celebrated artists had been called in to contribute to the luxury of this little palace. A chimney piece was commissioned from Jacques. I can still see his design, it was charming; the whole poetry of winter was expressed in the marble that was to serve as a frame to the flames. Jacques' studio was too small, he asked for and obtained a room in the mansion, as yet uninhabited, to execute his task in. A fairly large sum was even advanced him on the price agreed on for his work. Jacques began by repaying his friend the doctor the money the latter had lent him at Francine's death, then he hurried to the cemetery to cover the earth, beneath which his mistress slept, with flowers.

But spring had been there before him, and on the girl's grave a thousand flowers were springing at hazard amongst the grass. The artist had not the courage to pull them up, for he thought that these flowers might perhaps hold something of his dead love. As the gardener asked him what was to be done with the roses and pansies he had brought with him, Jacques bade him plant them on a neighboring grave, newly dug, the poor grave of some poor creature, without any border and having no other memorial over it than a piece of wood stuck in the ground and surmounted by a crown of flowers in blackened paper, the scant offering of some pauper's grief. Jacques left the cemetery in quite a different frame of mind to what he had entered it. He looked with happy curiosity at the bright spring sunshine, the same that had so often gilded Francine's locks when she ran about the fields culling wildflowers with her white hands. Quite a swarm of pleasant thoughts hummed in his heart. Passing by a little tavern on the outer Boulevard he remembered that one day, being caught by a storm, he had taken shelter there with Francine, and that they had dined there. Jacques went in and had dinner served at the same table. His dessert was served on a plate with a pictorial pattern; he recognized it and remembered that Francine had spent half an hour in guessing the rebus painted on it, and recollected, too, a song sung by her when inspired by the violet hued wine which does not cost much and has more gaiety in it than grapes. But this flood of sweet remembrances recalled his love without reawakening his grief. Accessible to superstition, like all poetical and dreamy intellects, Jacques fancied that it was Francine, who, hearing his step beside her, had wafted him these pleasant remembrances from her grave, and he would not damp them with a tear. He quitted the tavern with firm step, erect head, bright eye, beating heart, and almost a smile on his lips, murmuring as he went along the refrain of Francine's song—

"Love hovers round my dwelling
My door must open be."

This refrain in Jacques' mouth was also a recollection, but then it was already a song, and perhaps without suspecting it he took that evening the first step along the road which leads from sorrow to melancholy, and thence onward to forgetfulness. Alas! Whatever one may wish and whatever one may do the eternal and just law of change wills it so.

Even as the flowers, sprung perhaps from Francine, had sprouted on her tomb the sap of youth stirred in the heart of Jacques, in which the remembrance of the old love awoke new aspirations for new ones. Besides Jacques belonged to the race of artists and poets who make passion an instrument of art and poetry, and whose mind only shows activity in proportion as it is set in motion by the motive powers of the heart. With Jacques invention was really the daughter of sentiment, and he put something of himself into the smallest things he did. He perceived that souvenirs no longer sufficed him, and that, like the millstone which wears itself away when corn runs short, his heart was wearing away for want of emotion. Work had no longer any charm for him, his power of invention, of yore feverish and spontaneous, now only awoke after much patient effort. Jacques was discontented, and almost envied the life of his old friends, the Water Drinkers.

He sought to divert himself, held out his hand to pleasure, and made fresh acquaintances. He associated with the poet Rodolphe, whom he had met at a cafe, and each felt a warm sympathy towards the other. Jacques explained his worries, and Rodolphe was not long in understanding their cause.

"My friend," said he, "I know what it is," and tapping him on the chest just over the heart he added, "Quick, you must rekindle the fire there, start a little love affair at once, and ideas will recur to you."

"Ah!" said Jacques. "I loved Francine too dearly."

"It will not hinder you from still always loving her. You will embrace her on another's lips."

"Oh!" said Jacques. "If I could only meet a girl who resembled her."

And he left Rodolphe deep in thought.

SIX WEEKS LATER JACQUES HAD recovered all his energy, rekindled by the tender glances of a young girl whose name was Marie, and whose somewhat sickly beauty recalled that of poor Francine. Nothing, indeed, could be prettier than this pretty Marie, who was within six weeks of being eighteen years of age, as she never failed to mention. Her love affair with Jacques had its birth by moonlight in the garden of an open air ball, to the strains of a shrill violin, a grunting double bass, and a clarinet that trilled like a blackbird. Jacques met her one evening when gravely walking around the space reserved for the dancers. Seeing him pass stiffly in his eternal black coat buttoned to the throat, the pretty and noisy frequenters of the place, who knew him by sight, used to say amongst themselves, "What is that undertaker doing here? Is there anyone who wants to be buried?"

And Jacques walked on always alone, his heart bleeding within him from the thorns of a remembrance which the orchestra rendered keener by playing a lively quadrille which sounded to his ears as mournful as a *De Profundis*. It was in the midst of this reverie that he noticed Marie, who was watching him from a corner, and laughing like a wild thing at his gloomy bearing. Jacques raised his eyes and saw this burst of laughter in a pink bonnet within three paces of him. He went up to her and made a few remarks, to which she replied. He offered her his arm for a stroll around the garden which she accepted. He told her that he thought her as beautiful as an angel, and she made him repeat it twice over. He stole some green apples hanging from the trees of the garden for her, and she devoured them eagerly to the accompaniment of that ringing laugh which seemed the burden of her constant mirth. Jacques thought of the Bible, and thought that we should never despair as regards any woman, and still less as regards those who love apples. He took another turn round the garden with the pink bonnet, and it is thus that arriving at the ball alone he did not return from it so.

However, Jacques had not forgotten Francine; bearing in mind Rodolphe's words he kissed her daily on Marie's lips, and wrought in secret at the figure he wished to place on the dead girl's grave.

One day when he received some money Jacques bought a dress for Marie—a black dress. The girl was pleased, only she thought that black was not very lively for summer wear. But Jacques told her that he was very fond of black, and that she would please him by wearing this dress every day. Marie obeyed.

One Saturday Jacques said to her:

"Come early tomorrow, we will go into the country."

"How nice!" said Marie. "I am preparing a surprise for you. You shall see. It will be sunshiny tomorrow."

Marie spent the night at home finishing a new dress that she had bought out of her savings—a pretty pink dress. And on Sunday she arrived clad in her smart purchase at Jacques' studio.

The artist received her coldly, almost brutally.

"I thought I should please you by making this bright toilette," said Marie, who could not understand his coolness.

"We cannot go into the country today," replied he. "You had better be off. I have some work today."

Marie went home with a full heart. On the way she met a young man who was acquainted with Jacques' story, and who had also paid court to herself.

"Ah! Mademoiselle Marie, so you are no longer in mourning?" said he.

"Mourning?" asked Marie. "For whom?"

"What, did you not know? It is pretty generally known, though, the black dress that Jacques gave you—"

"Well, what of it?" asked Marie.

"It was mourning. Jacques made you wear mourning for Francine."

From that day Jacques saw no more of Marie.

This rupture was unlucky for him. Evil days returned; he had no more work, and fell into such a fearful state of wretchedness that, no longer knowing what would become of him, he begged his friend the doctor to obtain him admission to a hospital. The doctor saw at first glance that this admission would not be difficult to obtain. Jacques, who did not suspect his condition, was on the way to rejoin Francine.

As he could still move about, Jacques begged the superintendent of the hospital to let him have a little unused room, and he had a stand, some tools, and some modelling clay brought there. During the first fortnight he worked at the figure he intended for Francine's grave. It was an angel with outspread wings. This figure, which was Francine's portrait, was never quite finished, for Jacques could soon no longer mount the stairs, and in short time could not leave his bed.

One day the order book fell into his hands, and seeing the things prescribed for himself, he understood that he was lost. He wrote to his family, and sent for Sister Sainte-Genevieve, who looked after him with charitable care.

"Sister," said Jacques, "there is upstairs in the room that was lent me, a little plaster cast. This statuette, which represents an angel, was intended for a tomb, but I had not time to execute it in marble. Yes, I had a fine block—white marble with pink veins. Well, sister, I give you my little statuette for your chapel."

Jacques died a few days later. As the funeral took place on the very day of the opening of the annual exhibition of pictures, the Water Drinkers were not present. "Art before all," said Lazare.

Jacques' family was not a rich one, and he did not have a grave of his own.

He is buried somewhere.

XIX

MUSETTE'S FANCIES

It may be, perhaps, remembered how the painter Marcel sold the Jew Medici his famous picture of "The Passage of the Red Sea," which was destined to serve as the sign of a provision dealer's. On the morrow of this sale, which had been followed by a luxurious dinner stood by the Jew to the Bohemians as a clincher to the bargain, Marcel, Schaunard, Colline, and Rodolphe woke up very late. Still bewildered by the fumes of their intoxication of the day before, at first they no longer remembered what had taken place, and as noon rung out from a neighboring steeple, they all looked at one another with a melancholy smile.

"There goes the bell that piously summons humanity to refresh itself," said Marcel.

"In point of fact," replied Rodolphe, "it is the solemn hour when honest folk enter their dining-room."

"We must try and become honest folk," murmured Colline, whose patron saint was Saint Appetite.

"Ah, milk jug of my nursery!—ah! Four square meals of my childhood, what has become of you?" said Schaunard. "What has become of you?" he repeated, to a soft and melancholy tune.

"To think that at this hour there are in Paris more than a hundred thousand chops on the gridiron," said Marcel.

"And as many steaks," added Rodolphe.

By an ironical contrast, while the four friends were putting to one another the terrible daily problem of how to get their breakfast, the waiters of a restaurant on the lower floor of the house kept shouting out the customers' orders.

"Will those scoundrels never be quiet?" said Marcel. "Every word is like the stroke of a pick, hollowing out my stomach."

"The wind is in the north," said Colline, gravely, pointing to a weathercock on a neighboring roof. "We shall not breakfast today, the elements are opposed to it."

"How so?" inquired Marcel.

"It is an atmospheric phenomenon I have noted," said the philosopher. "A wind from the north almost always means abstinence, as one from the south usually means pleasure and good cheer. It is what philosophy calls a warning from above."

Gustave Colline's fasting jokes were savage ones.

At that moment Schaunard, who had plunged one of his hands into the abyss that served him as a pocket, withdrew it with a yell of pain.

"Help, there is something in my coat!" he cried, trying to free his hand, nipped fast in the claws of a live lobster.

To the cry he had uttered, another one replied. It came from Marcel, who, mechanically putting his hand into his pocket, had there discovered a silver mine that he had forgotten—that is to say, the hundred and fifty francs which Medici had given him the day before in payment for "The Passage of the Red Sea."

Memory returned at the same moment to the Bohemians.

"Bow down, gentlemen," said Marcel, spreading out on the table a pile of five-franc pieces, amongst which glittered some new louis.

"One would think they were alive," said Colline.

"Sweet sounds!" said Schaunard, chinking the gold pieces together.

"How pretty these medals are!" said Rodolphe. "One would take them for fragments of sunshine. If I were a king I would have no other small change, and would have them stamped with my mistress's portrait."

"To think that there is a country where there are mere pebbles," said Schaunard. "The Americans used to give four of them for two sous. I had an ancestor who went to America. He was interred by the savages in their stomachs. It was a misfortune for the family."

"Ah, but where does this animal come from?" inquired Marcel, looking at the lobster which had began to crawl about the room.

"I remember," said Schaunard, "that yesterday I took a turn in Medicis' kitchen, I suppose the reptile accidentally fell into my pocket; these creatures are very short-sighted. Since I have got it," added he, "I should like to keep it. I will tame it and paint it red, it will look livelier. I am sad since Phemie's departure; it will be a companion to me."

"Gentlemen," exclaimed Colline, "notice, I beg of you, that the weathercock has gone round to the south, we shall breakfast."

"I should think so," said Marcel, taking up a gold piece, "here is something we will cook with plenty of sauce."

They proceeded to a long and serious discussion on the bill of fare. Each dish was the subject of an argument and a vote. Omelette soufflé, proposed by Schaunard, was anxiously rejected, as were white wines, against which Marcel delivered an oration that brought out his oenophilistic knowledge.

"The first duty of wine is to be red," exclaimed he, "don't talk to me about your white wines."

"But," said Schaunard, "Champagne—"

"Bah! A fashionable cider! An epileptic licorice-water. I would give all the cellars of Epernay and Ai for a single Burgundian cask. Besides, we have neither grisettes to seduce, nor a vaudeville to write. I vote against Champagne."

The program once agreed upon, Schaunard and Colline went to the neighboring restaurant to order the repast.

"Suppose we have some fire," said Marcel.

"As a matter of fact," said Rodolphe, "we should not be doing wrong, the thermometer has been inviting us to it for some time past. Let us have some fire and astonish the fireplace."

He ran out on the landing and called to Colline to have some wood sent in. A few minutes later Schaunard and Colline came up again, followed by a charcoal dealer bearing a heavy bundle of firewood.

As Marcel was looking in a drawer for some spare paper to light the fire, he came by chance across a letter, the handwriting of which made him start, and which he began to read unseen by his friends.

It was a letter in pencil, written by Musette when she was living with Marcel and dated day for day a year ago. It only contained these words:—

My dear love,

Do not be uneasy about me, I shall be in shortly. I have gone out to warm myself a bit by walking, it is freezing indoors and the wood seller has cut off credit. I broke up the last two rungs of the chair, but they did not burn long enough to cook an egg by. Besides, the wind comes in through the window as if it were at home, and whispers a great deal of bad advice which it would vex you if I were to listen to. I prefer to go out a bit; I shall take a look at the shops. They say that there is some velvet at ten francs a yard. It is incredible, I must see it. I shall be back for dinner.

Musette

"Poor girl," said Marcel, putting the letter in his pocket. And he remained for a short time pensive, his head resting on his hands.

At this period the Bohemians had been for some time in a state of widowhood, with the exception of Colline, whose sweetheart, however, had still remained invisible and anonymous.

Phemie herself, Schaunard's amiable companion, had met with a simple soul who had offered her his heart, a suite of mahogany furniture, and a ring with his hair—red hair—in it. However, a fortnight after these gifts, Phemie's lover wanted to take back his heart and his furniture, because he noticed on looking at his mistress's hands that she wore a ring set with hair, but black hair this time, and dared to suspect her of infidelity.

Yet Phemie had not ceased to be virtuous, only as her friends had chaffed her several times about her ring with red hair, she had had it dyed black. The gentleman was so pleased that he bought Phemie a silk dress; it was the first she had ever had. The day she put it on for the first time the poor girl exclaimed:

"Now I can die happy."

As to Musette, she had once more become almost an official personage, and Marcel had not met her for three or four months. As to Mimi, Rodolphe had not heard her even mentioned, save by himself when alone.

"Hallo!" suddenly exclaimed Rodolphe, seeing Marcel squatting dreamily beside the hearth. "Won't the fire light?"

"There you are," said the painter, setting light to the wood, which began to crackle and flame.

While his friends were sharpening their appetites by getting ready the feast, Marcel had again isolated himself in a corner and was putting the letter he had just found by chance away with some souvenirs that Musette had left him. All at once he remembered the address of a woman who was the intimate friend of his old love.

"Ah!" he exclaimed, loud enough to be overheard. "I know where to find her."

"Find what?" asked Rodolphe. "What are you up to?" he added, seeing the artist getting ready to write.

"Nothing, only an urgent letter I had forgotten," replied Marcel, and he wrote:—

My dear girl,
    I have wealth in my desk, an apoplectic stroke of fortune.
We have a big feed simmering, generous wines, and have lit

fires like respectable citizens. You should only just see it, as you used to say. Come and pass an hour with us. You will find Rodolphe, Colline and Schaunard. You shall sing to us at dessert, for dessert will not be wanting. While we are there we shall probably remain at table for a week. So do not be afraid of being too late. It is so long since I heard you laugh. Rodolphe will compose madrigals to you, and we will drink all manner of things to our dead and gone loves, with liberty to resuscitate them. Between people like ourselves—the last kiss is never the last. Ah! If it had not been so cold last year you might not have left me. You jilted me for a faggot and because you were afraid of having red hands; you were right. I am no more vexed with you over it this time than over the others, but come and warm yourself while there is a fire. With as many kisses as you like,

Marcel

This letter finished, Marcel wrote another to Madame Sidonie, Musette's friend, begging her to forward the one enclosed in it. Then he went downstairs to the porter to get him to take the letters. As he was paying him beforehand, the porter noticed a gold coin in the painter's hand, and before starting on his errand went up to inform the landlord, with whom Marcel was behind with his rent.

"Sir," said he, quite out of breath, "the artist on the sixth floor has money. You know the tall fellow who laughs in my face when I take him his bill?"

"Yes," said the landlord, "the one who had the imprudence to borrow money of me to pay me something on account with. He is under notice to quit."

"Yes sir. But he is rolling in gold today. I caught sight of it just now. He is giving a party. It is a good time—"

"You are right," said the landlord. "I will go up and see for myself by-and-by."

Madame Sidonie, who was at home when Marcel's letter was brought, sent on her maid at once with the one intended for Musette.

The latter was then residing in a charming suite of rooms in the Chaussee d'Antin. At the moment Marcel's letter was handed to her, she had company, and, indeed, was going to give a grand dinner party that evening.

"Here is a miracle," she exclaimed, laughing like a mad thing.

"What is it?" asked a handsome young fellow, as stiff as a statuette.

"It is an invitation to dinner," replied the girl. "How well it falls out."

"How badly," said the young man.

"Why so?" asked Musette.

"What, do you think of going?"

"I should think so. Arrange things as you please."

"But, my dear, it is not becoming. You can go another time."

"Ah, that is very good, another time. It is an old acquaintance, Marcel, who invites me to dinner, and that is sufficiently extraordinary for me to go and have a look at it. Another time! But real dinners in that house are as rare as eclipses."

"What, you would break your pledge to us to go and see this individual," said the young man, "and you tell me so—"

"Whom do you want me to tell it to, then? To the Grand Turk? It does not concern him."

"This is strange frankness."

"You know very well that I do nothing like other people."

"But what would you think of me if I let you go, knowing where you are going to? Think a bit, Musette, it is very unbecoming both to you and myself; you must ask this young fellow to excuse you—"

"My dear Monsieur Maurice," said Mademoiselle Musette, in very firm tones, "you knew me before you took up with me, you knew that I was full of whims and fancies, and that no living soul can boast of ever having made me give one up."

"Ask of me whatever you like," said Maurice, "but this! There are fancies and fancies."

"Maurice, I shall go and see Marcel. I am going," she added, putting on her bonnet. "You may leave me if you like, but it is stronger than I am; he is the best fellow in the world, and the only one I have ever loved. If his head had been gold he would have melted it down to give me rings. Poor fellow," said she, showing the letter, "see, as soon as he has a little fire, he invites me to come and warm myself. Ah, if he had not been so idle, and if there had not been so much velvet and silk in the shops! I was very happy with him, he had the gift of making me feel; and it is he who gave me the name of Musette on account of my songs. At any rate, going to see him you may be sure that I shall return to you. . . unless you shut your door in my face."

"You could not more frankly acknowledge that you do not love me," said the young man.

"Come, my dear Maurice, you are too sensible a man for us to begin a serious argument on that point," rejoined Musette. "You keep me like a fine horse in your stable—and I like you because I love luxury, noise, glitter, and festivity, and that sort of thing; do not let us go in for sentiment, it would be useless and ridiculous."

"At least let me come with you."

"But you would not enjoy yourself at all," said Musette, "and would hinder us from enjoying ourselves. Remember that he will necessarily kiss me."

"Musette," said Maurice. "Have you often found such accommodating people as myself?"

"Viscount," replied Musette, "one day when I was driving in the Champs Elysees with Lord _____, I met Marcel and his friend Rodolphe, both on foot, both ill dressed, muddy as water-dogs, and smoking pipes. I had not seen Marcel for three months, and it seemed to me as if my heart was going to jump out of the carriage window. I stopped the carriage, and for half an hour I chatted with Marcel before the whole of Paris, filing past in its carriages. Marcel offered me a sou bunch of violets that I fastened in my waistband. When he took leave of me, Lord _____ wanted to call him back to invite him to dinner with us. I kissed him for that. That is my way, my dear Monsieur Maurice, if it does not suit you you should say so at once, and I will take my slippers and my nightcap."

"It is sometimes a good thing to be poor then," said Vicomte Maurice, with a look of envious sadness.

"No, not at all," said Musette. "If Marcel had been rich I should never have left him."

"Go, then," said the young fellow, shaking her by the hand. "You have put your new dress on," he added, "it becomes you splendidly."

"That is so," said Musette. "It is a kind of presentiment I had this morning. Marcel will have the first fruits of it. Goodbye, I am off to taste a little of the bread of gaiety."

Musette was that day wearing a charming toilette. Never had the poem of her youth and beauty been set off by a more seductive binding. Besides, Musette had the instinctive genius of taste. On coming into the world, the first thing she had looked about for had been a looking glass to settle herself in her swaddling clothes by, and before being christened she had already been guilty of the sin of coquetry. At the time when her position was of the humblest, when she was reduced to cotton print frocks, little white caps and kid shoes, she wore in charming style this poor and simple uniform of the grisettes, those pretty girls, half bees, half grasshoppers, who sang at their work all week, only asked God for a little sunshine on Sunday, loved with all their heart, and sometimes threw themselves out of a window.

A breed that is now lost, thanks to the present generation of young fellows, a corrupted and at the same time corrupting race, but, above everything, vain, foolish and brutal. For the sake of uttering spiteful paradoxes, they chaffed these poor girls about their hands, disfigured by the sacred scars of toil, and as a consequence these soon no longer earned even enough to buy almond paste. By degrees they succeeded in inoculating them with their own foolishness and vanity, and then the grisette disappeared. It was then that the lorette sprung up. A hybrid breed of impertinent creatures of mediocre beauty, half flesh, half paint, whose boudoir is a shop in which they sell bits of their heart like slices of roast beef. The majority of these girls who dishonor pleasure, and are the shame of modern gallantry, are not always equal in intelligence to the very birds whose feathers they wear in their bonnets. If by chance they happen to feel, not love nor even a caprice, but a common place desire, it is for some counter jumping mountebank, whom the crowd surrounds and applauds at public balls, and whom the papers, courtiers of all that is ridiculous, render celebrated by their puffs. Although she was obliged to live in this circle Musette had neither its manners nor its ways, she had not the servile cupidity of those creatures who can only read Cocker and only write in figures. She was an intelligent and witty girl, and some drops of the blood of Mansu in her veins and, rebellious to all yokes, she had never been able to help yielding to a fancy, whatever might be the consequences.

Marcel was really the only man she had ever loved. He was at any rate the only one for whose sake she had really suffered, and it had needed all the stubbornness of the instincts that attracted her to all that glittered and jingled to make her leave him. She was twenty, and for her luxury was almost a matter of existence. She might do without it for a time, but she could not give it up completely. Knowing her inconstancy, she had never consented to padlock her heart with an oath of fidelity. She had been ardently loved by many young fellows for whom she had herself felt a strong fancy, and she had always acted towards them with far-sighted probity; the engagements into which she entered were simple, frank and rustic as the love-making of Moliere's peasants. "You want me and I should like you too, shake hands on it and let us enjoy ourselves." A dozen times if she had liked Musette could have secured a good position, which is termed a future, but she did not believe in the future and professed the scepticism of Figaro respecting it.

"Tomorrow," she sometimes remarked, "is an absurdity of the almanac, it is a daily pretext that men have invented in order to put off their business today. Tomorrow may be an earthquake. Today, at any rate, we are on solid ground."

One day a gentleman with whom she had stayed nearly six months, and who had become wildly in love with her, seriously proposed marriage. Musette burst out laughing in his face at this offer.

"I imprison my liberty in the bonds of matrimony? Never," said she.

"But I pass my time in trembling with fear of losing you."

"It would be worse if I were your wife. Do not let us speak about that any more. Besides, I am not free," she added, thinking no doubt of Marcel.

Thus she passed her youth, her mind caught by every straw blown by the breeze of fancy, causing the happiness of a great many and almost happy herself. Vicomte Maurice, under whose protection she then was, had a great deal of difficulty in accustoming himself to her untamable disposition, intoxicated with freedom, and it was with jealous impatience that he awaited the return of Musette after having seen her start off to Marcel's.

"Will she stay there?" he kept asking himself all the evening.

"Poor Maurice," said Musette to herself on her side. "He thinks it rather hard. Bah! Young men must go through their training."

Then her mind turning suddenly to other things, she began to think of Marcel to whom she was going, and while running over the recollections reawakened by the name of her erst adorer, asked herself by what miracle the table had been spread at his dwelling. She re-read, as she went along, the letter that the artist had written to her, and could not help feeling somewhat saddened by it. But this only lasted a moment. Musette thought aright, that it was less than ever an occasion for grieving, and at that moment a strong wind spring up she exclaimed:

"It is funny, even if I did not want to go to Marcel's, this wind would blow me there."

And she went on hurriedly, happy as a bird returning to its first nest.

All at once snow began to fall heavy. Musette looked for a cab. She could not see one. As she happened to be in the very street in which dwelt her friend Madame Sidonie, the same who had sent on Marcel's letter to her, Musette decided to run in for a few minutes until the weather cleared up sufficiently to enable her to continue her journey.

When Musette entered Madame Sidonie's rooms she found a gathering there. They were going on with a game of lansquenet that had lasted three days.

"Do not disturb yourselves," said Musette. "I have only just popped in for a moment."

"You got Marcel's letter all right?" whispered Madame Sidonie to her.

"Yes, thanks," replied Musette. "I am going to his place, he has asked me to dinner. Will you come with me? You would enjoy yourself."

"No, I can't," said Madame Sidonie, pointing to the card table. "Think of my rent."

"There are six louis," said the banker.

"I'll go two of them," exclaimed Madame Sidonie.

"I am not proud, I'll start at two," replied the banker, who had already dealt several times. "King and ace. I am done for," he continued, dealing the cards. "I am done for, all the kings are out."

"No politics," said a journalist.

"And the ace is the foe of my family," continued the banker, who then turned up another king. "Long live the king! My dear Sidonie, hand me over two louis."

"Put them down," said Sidonie, vexed at her loss.

"That makes four hundred francs you owe me, little one," said the banker. "You would run it up to a thousand. I pass the deal."

Sidonie and Musette were chatting together in a low tone. The game went on.

At about the same time the Bohemians were sitting down to table. During the whole of the repast Marcel seemed uneasy. Everytime a step sounded on the stairs he started.

"What is the matter?" asked Rodolphe of him. "One would think you were expecting someone. Are we not all here?"

But at a look from the artist the poet understood his friend's preoccupation.

"True," he thought, "we are not all here."

Marcel's look meant Musette, Rodolphe's answering glance, Mimi.

"We lack ladies," said Schaunard, all at once.

"Confound it," yelled Colline, "will you hold your tongue with your libertine reflections. It was agreed that we should not speak of love, it turns the sauces."

And the friends continued to drink fuller bumpers, whilst without the snow still fell, and on the hearth the logs flamed brightly, scattering sparks like fireworks.

Just as Rodolphe was thundering out a song which he had found at the bottom of his glass, there came several knocks at the door. Marcel, torpid from incipient drunkenness, leaped up from his chair, and ran to open it. Musette was not there.

A gentleman appeared on the threshold; he was not only bad looking, but his dressing gown was wretchedly made. In his hand he held a slip of paper.

"I am glad to see you so comfortable," he said, looking at the table on which were the remains of a magnificent leg of mutton.

"The landlord!" cried Rodolphe. "Let us receive him with the honors due to his position!" and he commenced beating on his plate with his knife and fork.

Colline handed him a chair, and Marcel cried:

"Come, Schaunard! Pass us a clean glass. You are just in time," he continued to the landlord, "we were going to drink to your health. My friend there, Monsieur Colline, was saying some touching things about you. As you are present, he will begin over again, out of compliment to you. Do begin again, Colline."

"Excuse me, gentlemen," said the landlord, "I don't wish to trouble you, but—" and he unfolded the paper which he had in his hand.

"What's the document?" asked Marcel.

The landlord, who had cast an inquisitive glance around the room, perceived some gold on the chimney piece.

"It is your receipt," he said hastily, "which I had the honor of sending you once already."

"My faithful memory recalls the circumstance," replied the artist. "It was on Friday, the eighth of the month, at a quarter past twelve."

"It is signed, you see, in due form," said the landlord, "and if it is agreeable to you—"

"I was intending to call upon you," interrupted Marcel. "I have a great deal to talk to you about."

"At your service."

"Oblige me by taking something," continued the painter, forcing a glass of wine on the landlord. "Now, sir," he continued, "you sent me lately a little paper, with a picture of a lady and a pair of scales on it. It was signed Godard."

"The lawyer's name."

"He writes a very bad hand; I had to get my friend here, who understands all sorts of hieroglyphics and foreign languages,"—and he pointed to Colline—"to translate it for me."

"It was a notice to quit; a precautionary measure, according to the rule in such cases."

"Exactly. Now I wanted to have a talk with you about this very notice, for which I should like to substitute a lease. This house suits me. The staircase is clean, the street gay, and some of my friends live near; in short, a thousand reasons attach me to these premises."

"But," and the landlord unfolded his receipt again, "there is that last quarter's rent to pay."

"We shall pay it, sir. Such is our fixed intention."

Nevertheless, the landlord kept his eye glued to the money on the mantelpiece and such was the steady pertinacity of his gaze that the coins seemed to move towards him of themselves.

"I am happy to have come at a time when, without inconveniencing yourself, you can settle this little affair," he said, again producing his receipt to Marcel, who, not being able to parry the assault, again avoided it.

"You have some property in the provinces, I think," he said.

"Very little, very little. A small house and farm in Burgundy; very trifling returns; the tenants pay so badly, and therefore," he added, pushing forward his receipt again, "this small sum comes just in time. Sixty francs, you know."

"Yes," said Marcel, going to the mantelpiece and taking up three pieces of gold. "Sixty, sixty it is," and he placed the money on the table just out of the landlord's reach.

"At last," thought the latter. His countenance lighted up, and he too laid down his receipt on the table.

Schaunard, Colline, and Rodolphe looked anxiously on.

"Well, sir," quoth Marcel, "since you are a Burgundian, you will not be sorry to see a countryman of yours." He opened a bottle of old Macon, and poured out a bumper.

"Ah, perfect!" said the landlord. "Really, I never tasted better."

"An uncle of mine who lives there, sends me a hamper or two occasionally."

The landlord rose, and was stretching out his hand towards the money, when Marcel stopped him again.

"You will not refuse another glass?" said he, pouring one out.

The landlord did not refuse. He drank the second glass, and was once more attempting to possess himself of the money, when Marcel called out:

"Stop! I have an idea. I am rather rich just now, for me. My uncle in Burgundy has sent me something over my usual allowance. Now I may spend this money too fast. Youth has so many temptations, you know. Therefore, if it is all the same to you, I will pay a quarter in advance." He took sixty francs in silver and added them to the three louis which were on the table.

"Then I will give you a receipt for the present quarter," said the landlord. "I have some blank ones in my pocketbook. I will fill it up and date it ahead. After all," thought he, devouring the hundred and twenty francs with his eyes, "this tenant is not so bad."

Meanwhile, the other three Bohemians, not understanding Marcel's diplomacy, remained utterly stupefied.

"But this chimney smokes, which is very disagreeable."

"Why didn't you tell me before? I will send the workmen in tomorrow," answered the landlord, not wishing to be behindhand in this contest of good offices. He filled up the second receipt, pushed the two over to Marcel, and stretched out his hand once more towards the heap of money. "You don't know how timely this sum comes in," he continued, "I have to pay some bills for repairs, and was really quite short of cash."

"Very sorry to have made you wait."

"Oh, it's no matter now! Permit me."—and out went his hand again.

"Permit me," said Marcel. "We haven't finished with this yet. You know the old saying, 'when the wine is drawn—'" and he filled the landlord's glass a third time.

"One must drink it," remarked the other, and he did so.

"Exactly," said the artist, with a wink at his friends, who now understood what he was after.

The landlord's eyes began to twinkle strangely. He wriggled on his chair, began to talk loosely, in all senses of the word, and promised Marcel fabulous repairs and embellishments.

"Bring up the big guns," said the artist aside to the poet. Rodolphe passed along a bottle of rum.

After the first glass the landlord sang a ditty, which absolutely made Schaunard blush.

After the second, he lamented his conjugal infelicity. His wife's name being Helen, he compared himself to Menelaus.

After the third, he had an attack of philosophy, and threw up such aphorisms as these:

"Life is a river."

"Happiness depends not on wealth."

"Man is a transitory creature."

"Love is a pleasant feeling."

Finally, he made Schaunard his confidant, and related to him how he had "Put into mahogany" a damsel named Euphemia. Of this young person and her loving simplicity he drew so detailed a portrait, that Schaunard began to be assailed by a fearful suspicion, which suspicion was reduced to a certainty when the landlord showed him a letter.

"Cruel woman!" cried the musician, as he beheld the signature. "It is like a dagger in my heart."

"What is the matter!" exclaimed the Bohemians, astonished at this language.

"See," said Schaunard, "this letter is from Phemie. See the blot that serves her for a signature."

And he handed round the letter of his ex-mistress, which began with the words, "My dear old pet."

"I am her dear old pet," said the landlord, vainly trying to rise from his chair.

"Good," said Marcel, who was watching him. "He has cast anchor."

"Phemie, cruel Phemie," murmured Schaunard. "You have wounded me deeply."

"I furnished a little apartment for her at 12, Rue Coquenard," said the landlord. "Pretty, very pretty. It cost me lots of money. But such love is beyond price and I have twenty thousand francs a year. She asks me for money in her letter. Poor little dear, she shall have this," and he stretched out his hand for the money—"hallo! Where is it?" he added in astonishment feeling on the table. The money had disappeared.

"It is impossible for a moral man to become an accomplice in such wickedness," said Marcel. "My conscience forbids me to pay money to this old profligate. I shall not pay my rent, but my conscience will at any rate be clear. What morals, and in a bald headed man too."

By this time the landlord was completely gone, and talked at random to the bottles. He had been there nearly two hours, when his wife, alarmed at his prolonged absence, sent the maid after him. On seeing her master in such a state, she set up a shriek, and asked, "what are they doing to him?"

"Nothing," answered Marcel. "He came a few minutes ago to ask for the rent. As we had no money we begged for time."

"But he's been and got drunk," said the servant.

"Very likely," replied Rodolphe. "Most of that was done before he came here. He told us that he had been arranging his cellar."

"And he had so completely lost his head," added Colline, "that he wanted to leave the receipt without the money."

"Give these to his wife," said Marcel, handing over the receipts. "We are honest folk, and do not wish to take advantage of his condition."

"Good heavens! What will madame say?" exclaimed the maid, leading, or rather dragging off her master, who had a very imperfect idea of the use of his legs.

"So much for him!" exclaimed Marcel.

"He has smelt money," said Rodolphe. "He will come again tomorrow."

"When he does, I will threaten to tell his wife about Phemie and he will give us time enough."

When the landlord had been got outside, the four friends went on smoking and drinking. Marcel alone retained a glimmer of lucidity in his intoxication. From time to time, at the slightest sound on the staircase, he ran and opened the door. But those who were coming up always halted at one of the lower landings, and then the artist would slowly return to his place by the fireside. Midnight struck, and Musette had not come.

"After all," thought Marcel, "perhaps she was not in when my letter arrived. She will find it when she gets home tonight, and she will come tomorrow. We shall still have a fire. It is impossible for her not to come. Tomorrow."

And he fell asleep by the fire.

At the very moment that Marcel fell asleep dreaming of her, Mademoiselle Musette was leaving the residence of her friend Madame Sidonie, where she had been staying up till then. Musette was not alone, a young man accompanied her. A carriage was waiting at the door. They got into it and went off at full speed.

The game at lansquenet was still going on in Madame Sidonie's room.

"Where is Musette?" said someone all at once.

"Where is young Seraphin?" said another.

Madame Sidonie began to laugh.

"They had just gone off together," said she. "It is a funny story. What a strange being Musette is. Just fancy. . ." And she informed the company how Musette, after almost quarreling with Vicomte Maurice and starting off to find Marcel, had stepped in there by chance and met with young Seraphin.

"I suspected something was up," she continued. "I had an eye on them all the evening. He is very sharp, that youngster. In short, they have gone off on the quiet, and it would take a sharp one to catch them up. All the same, it is very funny when one thinks how fond Musette is of her Marcel."

"If she is so fond of him, what is the use of Seraphin, almost a lad, and who had never had a mistress?" said a young fellow.

"She wants to teach him to read, perhaps," said the journalist, who was very stupid when he had been losing.

"All the same," said Sidonie, "what does she want with Seraphin when she is in love with Marcel? That is what gets over me."

FOR FIVE DAYS THE BOHEMIANS went on leading the happiest life in the world without stirring out. They remained at table from morning till night. An admired disorder reigned in the room which was filled with a Pantagruelic atmosphere. On a regular bed of oyster shells reposed an army of empty bottles of every size and shape. The table was laden with fragments of every description, and a forest of wood blazed in the fireplace.

On the sixth day Colline, who was director of ceremonies, drew up, as was his wont every morning, the bill of fare for breakfast, lunch, dinner, and supper, and submitted it to the approval of his friends, who each initialed it in token of approbation.

But when Colline opened the drawer that served as a cashbox, in order to take the money necessary for the day's consumption, he started back and became as pale as Banquo's ghost.

"What is the matter?" inquired the others, carelessly.

"The matter is that there are only thirty sous left," replied the philosopher.

"The deuce. That will cause some modification in our bill of fare. Well, thirty sous carefully laid out. All the same it will be difficult to run to truffles," said the others.

A few minutes later the table was spread. There were three dishes most symmetrically arranged—a dish of herrings, a dish of potatoes, and a dish of cheese.

On the hearth smoldered two little brands as big as one's fist.

Snow was still falling without.

The four Bohemians sat down to table and gravely unfolded their napkins.

"It is strange," said Marcel, "this herring has a flavor of pheasant."

"That is due to the way in which I cooked it," replied Colline. "The herring has never been properly appreciated."

At that moment a joyous song rose on the staircase, and a knock came at the door. Marcel, who had not been able to help shuddering, ran to open it.

Musette threw her arms round his neck and held him in an embrace for five minutes. Marcel felt her tremble in his arms.

"What is the matter?" he asked.

"I am cold," said Musette, mechanically drawing near the fireplace.

"Ah!" said Marcel. "And we had such a rattling good fire."

"Yes," said Musette, glancing at the remains of the five days' festivity, "I have come too late."

"Why?" said Marcel.

"Why?" said Musette, blushing slightly.

She sat down on Marcel's knee. She was still shivering, and her hands were blue.

"You were not free, then," whispered Marcel.

"I, not free!" exclaimed the girl. "Ah Marcel! If I were seated amongst the stars in Paradise and you made me a sign to come down to you I should do so. I, not free!"

She began to shiver again.

"There are five chairs here," said Rodolphe, "which is an odd number, without reckoning that the fifth is of a ridiculous shape."

And breaking the chair against the wall, he threw the fragments into the fireplace. The fire suddenly burst forth again in a bright and merry flame, then making a sign to Colline and Schaunard, the poet took them off with him.

"Where are you going?" asked Marcel.

"To buy some tobacco," they replied.

"At Havana," added Schaunard, with a sign of intelligence to Marcel, who thanked him with a look.

"Why did you not come sooner?" he asked Musette when they were alone together.

"It is true, I am rather behindhand."

"Five days to cross the Pont Neuf. You must have gone round by the Pyrenees?"

Musette bowed her head and was silent.

"Ah, naughty girl," said the artist, sadly tapping his hand lightly on his mistress' breast, "what have you got inside here?"

"You know very well," she retorted quickly.

"But what have you been doing since I wrote to you?"

"Do not question me," said Musette, kissing him several times. "Do not ask me anything, but let me warm myself beside you. You see I put on my best dress to come. Poor Maurice, he could not understand it when I set off to come here, but it was stronger than myself, so I started. The fire is nice," she added, holding out her little hand to the flames, "I will stay with you till tomorrow if you like."

"It will be very cold here," said Marcel, "and we have nothing for dinner. You have come too late," he repeated.

"Ah, bah!" said Musette. "It will be all the more like old times."

RODOLPHE, COLLINE, AND SCHAUNARD, TOOK twenty-four hours to get their tobacco. When they returned to the house Marcel was alone.

After an absence of six days Vicomte Maurice saw Musette return.

He did not in any way reproach her, and only asked her why she seemed sad.

"I quarreled with Marcel," said she. "We parted badly."

"And yet, who knows," said Maurice. "But you will again return to him."

"What would you?" asked Musette. "I need to breathe the air of that life from time to time. My life is like a song, each of my loves is a verse, but Marcel is the refrain."

XX

Mimi in Fine Feather

No, no, no, you are no longer Lisette! No, no, no, you are no
longer Mimi. You are today, my lady the viscomtess, the day after
tomorrow you may, perhaps, be your grace the duchess; the doorway
of your dreams has at length been thrown wide open before you, and
you have passed through it victorious and triumphant. I felt certain you
would end up by doing so, some night or other. It was bound to be;
besides, your white hands were made for idleness, and for a long time
past have called for the ring of some aristocratic alliance. At length you
have a coat of arms. But, we still prefer the one which youth gave to
your beauty, when your blue eyes and your pale face seemed to quarter
azure on a lily field. Noble or serf, you are ever charming, and I readily
recognized you when you passed by in the street the other evening, with
rapid and well-shod foot, aiding the wind with your gloved hand in
lifting the skirts of your new dress, partly in order not to let it be soiled,
but a great deal more in order to show your embroidered petticoats
and open-worked stockings. You had on a wonderful bonnet, and even
seemed plunged in deep perplexity on the subject of the veil of costly
lace which floated over this bonnet. A very serious trouble indeed, for
it was a question of deciding which was best and most advantageous to
your coquetry, to wear this veil up or down. By wearing it down, you
risked not being recognized by those of your friends whom you might
meet, and who certainly would have passed by you ten times without
suspecting that this costly envelope hid Mademoiselle Mimi. On the
other hand, by wearing this veil up, it was it that risked escaping notice,
and in that case, what was the good of having it? You had cleverly
solved the difficulty by alternately raising and lowering at every tenth
step; this wonderful tissue, woven no doubt, in that country of spiders,
called Flanders, and which of itself cost more than the whole of your
former wardrobe."

"Ah, Mimi! Forgive me—I should say, ah, vicomtess! I was quite
right, you see, when I said to you: 'Patience, do not despair, the future
is big with cashmere shawls, glittering jewels, supper parties, and the
like.' You would not believe me, incredulous one. Well, my predictions

are, however, realized, and I am worth as much, I hope, as your 'Ladies' Oracle,' a little octavo sorcerer you bought for five sous at a bookstall on the Pont Neuf, and which you wearied with external questions. Again, I ask, was I not right in my prophecies; and would you believe me now, if I tell you that you will not stop at this? If I told you that listening, I can hear faintly in the depths of your future, the tramp and neighing of the horses harnessed to blue brougham, driven by a powdered coachmen, who lets down the steps, saying, 'Where to madam?' Would you believe me if I told you, too, that later on—ah, as late as possible, I trust— attaining the object of a long cherished ambition, you will have a table d'hote at Belleville Batignolles, and will be courted by the old soldiers and bygone dandies who will come there to play lansquenet or baccarat on the sly? But, before arriving at this period, when the sun of your youth shall have already declined, believe me, my dear child, you will wear out many yards of silk and velvet, many inheritances, no doubt, will be melted down in the crucibles of your fancies, many flowers will fade about your head, many beneath your feet, and you will change your coat of arms many times. On your head will glitter in turn the coronets of baroness, countess, and marchioness, you will take for your motto, 'Inconstancy,' and you will, according to caprice or to necessity, satisfy each in turn, or even all at once, all the numerous adorers who will range themselves in the ante-chamber of your heart as people do at the door of a theater at which a popular piece is being played. Go on then, go straight onward, your mind lightened of recollections which have been replaced by ambition; go, the road is broad, and we hope it will long be smooth to your feet, but we hope, above all, that all these sumptuosities, these fine toilettes, may not too soon become the shroud in which your liveliness will be buried."

Thus spoke the painter Marcel to Mademoiselle Mimi, whom he had met three or four days after her second divorce from the poet Rodolphe. Although he was obliged to veil the raillery with which he besprinkled her horoscope, Mademoiselle Mimi was not the dupe of Marcel's fine words, and understood perfectly well that with little respect for her new title, he was chaffing her to bits.

"You are cruel towards me, Marcel," said Mademoiselle Mimi, "it is wrong. I was always very friendly with you when I was Rodolphe's mistress, and if I have left him, it was, after all, his fault. It was he who packed me off in a hurry, and, besides, how did he behave to me during the last few days I spent with him. I was very unhappy, I can tell you. You do not know what a man Rodolphe was; a mixture of anger and jealousy, who killed me by bits. He loved me, I know, but his love was as dangerous as a loaded gun. What a life I led for six months. Ah, Marcel! I do not want to make myself out better than I am, but I suffered a great deal with Rodolphe; you know it too, very well. It is not poverty that made me leave him, no I assure you I had grown accustomed to it, and I repeat it was he who sent me away. He trampled on my self-esteem; he told me that he no longer loved me; that I must get another lover. He even went so far as to indicate a young man who was courting me, and by his taunts, he served to bring me and this young man together. I went with him as much out of spite as from necessity, for I did not love him. You know very well yourself that I do not care for such very young fellows. They are as wearisome and sentimental as harmonicas. Well, what is done is done. I do not regret it, and I would do the same over again. Now that he no longer has me with him, and knows me to be happy with another, Rodolphe is furious and very unhappy. I know someone who met him the other day; his eyes were quite red. That does not astonish me. I felt quite sure it would come to this, and that he would run after me, but you can tell him that he will only lose his time, and that this time it is quite in earnest and for good. Is it long since you saw him, Marcel and is it true that he is much altered?" inquired Mimi in quite another tone.

"He is greatly altered indeed," replied Marcel.

"He is grieving, that is certain, but what am I to do? So much the worse for him, he would have it so. It had to come to an end somehow. Try to console him."

"Oh!" answered Marcel quickly. "The worst of the job is over. Do not disturb yourself about it, Mimi."

"You are not telling the truth, my dear fellow," said Mimi, with an ironical little pout. "Rodolphe will not be so quickly consoled as all that. If you knew what a state he was in the night before I left. It was a Friday, I would not stay that night at my new lover's because I am superstitious, and Friday is an unlucky day."

"You are wrong, Mimi, in love affairs Friday is a lucky day; the ancients called it Dies Veneris."

"I do not know Latin," said Mademoiselle Mimi, continuing her narration. "I was coming back then from Paul's and found Rodolphe waiting for me in the street. It was late, past midnight, and I was hungry for I had had no dinner. I asked Rodolphe to go and get something for supper. He came back half an hour later, he had run about a great deal to get nothing worth speaking of, some bread, wine, sardines, cheese, and an apple tart. I had gone to bed during his absence, and he laid the table beside the bed. I pretended not to notice him, but I could see him plainly, he was pale as death. He shuddered and walked about the room like a man who does not know what he wants to do. He noticed several packages of clothes on the floor in one corner. The sight of them seemed to annoy him, and he placed the screen in front of them in order not to see them. When all was ready we began to sup, he tried to make me drink, but I was no longer hungry or thirsty, and my heart was quite full. He was cold, for we had nothing to make a fire of, and one could hear the wind whistling in the chimney. It was very sad. Rodolphe looked at me, his eyes were fixed; he put his hand in mine and I felt it tremble, it was burning and icy all at once. 'This is the funeral supper of our loves,' he said to me in a low tone. I did not answer, but I had not the courage to withdraw my hand from his. 'I am sleepy,' said I at last, 'it is late, let us go to sleep.' Rodolphe looked at me. I had tied one of his handkerchiefs about my head on account of the cold. He took it off without saying a word. 'Why do you want to take that off?' said I. 'I am cold.' 'Oh, Mimi!' said he. 'I beg of you, it will not matter to you, to put on your little striped cap for tonight.' It was a nightcap of striped cotton, white and brown. Rodolphe was very fond of seeing me in this cap, it reminded him of several nights of happiness, for that was how we counted our happy days. When I thought it was the last time that I should sleep beside him I dared not refuse to satisfy this fancy of his. I got up and hunted out my striped cap that was at the bottom of one of my packages."

"Out of forgetfulness I forgot to replace the screen. Rodolphe noticed it and hid the packages just as he had already done before. 'Good night,' said he. 'Good night,' I answered. I thought that he was going to kiss me and I should not have hindered him, but he only took my hand, which he carried to his lips. You know, Marcel, how fond he was of kissing my hands. I heard his teeth chatter and I felt his body as cold as marble. He still held my hand and he laid his head on my shoulder, which was soon quite wet. Rodolphe was in a fearful state. He bit the sheets to avoid crying out, but I could plainly hear his stifled sobs and I still felt his tears flowing on my shoulder, which was first scalded and then chilled. At that moment I needed all my courage and I did need it, I can tell you. I had only to say a word, I had only to turn my head, and my lips would have met those of Rodolphe, and we should have made it up once more. Ah! For a moment I really thought that he was going to die in my arms, or that, at least, he would go mad, as he almost did once before, you remember? I felt I was going to yield, I was going to recant first, I was going to clasp him in my arms, for really one must have been utterly heartless to remain insensible to such grief. But I recollected the words he had said to me the day before, 'You have no spirit if you stay with me, for I no longer love you,' Ah! As I recalled those bitter words I would have seen Rodolphe ready to die, and if it had only needed a kiss from me to save him, I would have turned away my lips and let him perish."

"At last, overcome by fatigue, I sank into a half-sleep. I could still hear Rodolphe sobbing, and I can swear to you, Marcel, that this sobbing went on all night long, and that when day broke and I saw in the bed, in which I had slept for the last time, the lover whom I was going to leave for another's arms, I was terribly frightened to see the havoc wrought by this grief on Rodolphe's face. He got up, like myself, without saying a word, and almost fell flat at the first steps he took, he was so weak and downcast. However, he dressed himself very quickly, and only asked me how matters stood and when I was going to leave. I told him that I did not know. He went off without bidding goodbye or shaking hands. That is how we separated. What a blow it must have been to his heart no longer to find me there on coming home, eh?"

"I was there when Rodolphe came in," said Marcel to Mimi, who was out of breath from speaking so long. "As he was taking his key from the landlady, she said, 'The little one has left.' 'Ah!' replied Rodolphe. 'I am not astonished, I expected it.' And he went up to his room, whither I followed him, fearing some crisis, but nothing occurred. 'As it is too late to go and hire another room this evening we will do so tomorrow morning,' said he, 'we will go together. Now let us see after some dinner.' I thought that he wanted to get drunk, but I was wrong. We dined very quietly at a restaurant where you have sometimes been with him. I had ordered some Beaune to stupefy Rodolphe a bit. 'This was Mimi's favorite wine,' said he, 'we have often drunk it together at this very table.' I remember one day she said to me, holding out her glass, which she had already emptied several times, 'Fill up again, it is good for one's bones.' A poor pun, eh? Worthy, at the most, of the mistress of a farce writer. Ah! She could drink pretty fairly."

"Seeing that he was inclined to stray along the path of recollection I spoke to him about something else, and then it was no longer a question of you. He spent the whole evening with me and seemed as calm as the Mediterranean. But what astonished me most was, that this calmness was not at all affected. It was genuine indifference. At midnight we went home. 'You seem surprised at my coolness in the position in which I find myself,' said he to me, 'well, let me point out a comparison to you, my dear fellow, it if is commonplace it has, at least, the merit of being accurate. My heart is like a cistern the tap of which has been turned on all night, in the morning not a drop of water is left. My heart is really the same, last night I wept away all the tears that were left me. It is strange, but I thought myself richer in grief, and yet by a single night of suffering I am ruined, cleaned out. On my word of honor it is as I say. Now, in the very bed in which I all but died last night beside a woman who was no more moved than a stone, I shall sleep like a deck laborer after a hard day's work, while she rests her head on the pillow of another.' 'Hambug,' I thought to myself. 'I shall no sooner have left him than he will be dashing his head against the wall.' However, I left Rodolphe alone and went to my own room, but I did not go to bed. At three in the morning I thought I heard a noise in Rodolphe's room and I went down in a hurry, thinking to find him in a desperate fever."

"Well?" said Mimi.

"Well my dear, Rodolphe was sleeping, the bed clothes were quite in order and everything proved that he had soon fallen asleep, and that his slumbers had been calm."

"It is possible," said Mimi, "he was so worn out by the night before, but the next day?"

"The next day Rodolphe came and roused me up early and we went and took rooms in another house, into which we moved the same evening."

"And," asked Mimi, "what did he do on leaving the room we had occupied, what did he say on abandoning the room in which he had loved me so?"

"He packed up his things quietly," replied Marcel, "and as he found in a drawer a pair of thread gloves you had forgotten, as well as two or three of your letters—"

"I know," said Mimi in a tone which seemed to imply, "I forgot them on purpose so that he might have some souvenir of me left! What did he do with them?" she added.

"If I remember rightly," said Marcel, "he threw the letters into the fireplace and the gloves out of the window, but without any theatrical effort, and quite naturally, as one does when one wants to get rid of something useless."

"My dear Monsieur Marcel, I assure you that from the bottom of my heart I hope that this indifference may last. But, once more in all sincerity, I do not believe in such a speedy cure and, in spite of all you tell me, I am convinced that my poet's heart is broken."

"That may be," replied Marcel, taking leave of Mimi, "but unless I may be very much mistaken, the pieces are still good for something."

During this colloquy in a public thoroughfare, Vicomte Paul was awaiting his new mistress, who was behindhand in her appointment, and decidedly disagreeable towards him. He seated himself at her feet and warbled his favorite strain, namely, that she was charming, fair as a lily, gentle as a lamb, but that he loved her above all on account of the beauties of her soul.

"Ah!" thought Mimi, loosening the waves of her dark hair over her snowy shoulders, "my lover Rodolphe, was not so exclusive."

As Marcel had stated, Rodolphe seemed to be radically cured of his love for Mademoiselle Mimi, and three or four days after his separation, the poet reappeared completely metamorphosed. He was attired with an elegance that must have rendered him unrecognizable by his very looking glass. Nothing, indeed, about him seemed to justify the fear that he intended to commit suicide, as Mademoiselle Mimi had started the rumor, with all kinds of hypocritical condolences. Rodolphe was, in fact, quite calm. He listened with unmoved countenance to all the stories told him about the new and sumptuous existence led by his mistress—who took pleasure in keeping him informed on these points—by a young girl who had remained her confidant, and who had occasion to see Rodolphe almost every evening.

"Mimi is very happy with Vicomte Paul," the poet was told. "She seems thoroughly smitten with him, only one thing causes her any uneasiness, she is afraid least you should disturb her tranquillity by coming after her, which by the way, would be dangerous for you, for the vicomte worships his mistress and is a good fencer."

"Oh," said Rodolphe. "She can sleep in peace, I have no wish to go and cast vinegar over the sweetness of her honeymoon. As to her young lover, he can leave his dagger at home like Gastibelza. I have no wish to attempt the life of a young gentleman who has still the happiness of being nursed by illusions."

As they did not fail to carry back to Mimi the way in which her ex-lover received all these details, she on her part did not forget to reply, shrugging her shoulders:

"That is all very well, you will see what will come of it in a day or two."

However, Rodolphe was himself, and more than any one else, astonished at this sudden indifference which, without passing through the usual transitions of sadness and melancholy, had followed the stormy feelings by which he had been stirred only a few days before. Forgetfulness, so slow to come—above all for the virtues of love—that forgetfulness which they summon so loudly and repulse with equal loudness when they feel it approaching, that pitiless consoler that had all at once, and without his being able to defend himself from it, invaded Rodolphe's heart, and the name of the woman he so dearly loved could now be heard without awakening any echo in it. Strange fact; Rodolphe, whose memory was strong enough to recall to mind things that had occurred in the farthest days of his past and beings who had figured in or influenced his most remote existence—Rodolphe could not, whatever efforts he might make, recall with clearness after four days' separation, the features of that mistress who had nearly broken his life between her slender fingers. He could no longer recall the softness of the eyes by the light of which he had so often fallen asleep. He could no longer remember the notes of that voice whose anger and whose caressing utterances had alternately maddened him. A poet, who was a friend of his, and who had not seen him since his absence, met him one evening. Rodolphe seemed busy and preoccupied, he was walking rapidly along the street, twirling his cane.

"Hallo," said the poet, holding out his hand, "so here you are," and he looked curiously at Rodolphe. Seeing that the latter looked somewhat downcast he thought it right to adopt a consoling tone.

"Come, courage, my dear fellow. I know that it is hard, but then it must always have come to this. Better now than later on; in three months you will be quite cured."

"What are you driving at?" said Rodolphe. "I am not ill, my dear fellow."

"Come," said the other, "do not play the braggart. I know the whole story and if I did not, I could read it in your face."

"Take care, you are making a mistake," said Rodolphe, "I am very much annoyed this evening, it is true, but you have not exactly hit on the cause of my annoyance."

"Good, but why defend yourself? It is quite natural. A connection that has lasted a couple of years cannot be broken off so readily."

"Everyone tells me the same thing," said Rodolphe, getting impatient. "Well, upon my honor, you make a mistake, you and the others. I am very vexed, and I look like it, that is possible, but this is the reason why; I was expecting my tailor with a new dress coat today, and he had not come. That is what I am annoyed about."

"Bad, bad," said the other laughing.

"Not at all bad, but good on the contrary, very good, excellent in fact. Follow my argument and you shall see."

"Come," said the poet, "I will listen to you. Just prove to me how any one can in reason look so wretched because a tailor has failed to keep his word. Come, come, I am waiting."

"Well," said Rodolphe, "you know very well that the greatest effects spring from the most trifling causes. I ought this evening to pay a very important visit, and I cannot do so for want of a dress coat. Now do you see it?"

"Not at all. There is up to this no sufficient reason shown for a state of desolation. You are in despair because—. You are very silly to try to deceive. That is my opinion."

"My friend," said Rodolphe, "you are very opinionated. It is always enough to vex us when we miss happiness, and at any rate pleasure, because it is almost always so much lost for ever, and we are wrong in saying, 'I will make up for it another time.' I will resume; I had an appointment this evening with a lady. I was to meet her at a friend's house, whence I should, perhaps taken her home to mine, if it were nearer than her own, and even if it were not. At this house there was a party. At parties one must wear a dress coat. I have no dress coat. My tailor was to bring me one; he does not do so. I do not go to the party. I do not meet the lady who is, perhaps, met by someone else. I do not see her home either to my place or hers, and she is, perhaps, seen home by another. So as I told you, I have lost an opportunity of happiness and pleasure; hence I am vexed; hence I look so, and quite naturally."

"Very good," said his friend, "with one foot just out of one hell, you want to put the other foot in another; but, my dear fellow, when I met you, you seemed to be waiting for some one."

"So I was."

"But," continued the other, "we are in the neighborhood in which your ex-mistress is living. What is there to prove that you were not waiting for her?"

"Although separated from her, special reasons oblige me to live in this neighborhood. But, although neighbors, we are as distant as if she were at one pole and I at the other. Besides, at this particular moment, my ex-mistress is seated at her fireside taking lessons in French grammar from Vicomte Paul, who wishes to bring her back to the paths of virtue by the road of orthography. Good heavens, how he will spoil her! However, that regards himself, now that he is editor-in-chief of her happiness. You see, therefore, that your reflections are absurd, and that, instead of following up the half-effaced traces of my old love, I am on the track of my new one, who is already to some extent my neighbor, and will become yet more so: for I am willing to take all the necessary steps, and if she will take the rest, we shall not be long in coming to an understanding."

"Really," said the poet, "are you in love again already?"

"This is what it is," replied Rodolphe, "my heart resembles those lodgings that are advertised to let as soon as a tenant leaves them. As soon as one love leaves my heart, I put up a bill for another. The locality besides is habitable and in perfect repair."

"And who is this new idol? Where and when did you make her acquaintance?"

"Come," said Rodolphe, "let us go through things in order. When Mimi went away I thought that I should never be in love again in my life, and imagined that my heart was dead of fatigue, exhaustion, whatever you like. It had been beating so long and so fast, too fast, that the thing was probable. In short I believed it dead, quite dead, and thought of burying it like Marlborough. In honor of the occasion I gave a little funeral dinner, to which I invited some of my friends. The guests were to assume a melancholy air, and the bottles had crape around their necks."

"You did not invite me."

"Excuse me, but I did not know your address in that part of cloudland which you inhabit. One of the guests had brought a young lady, a young woman also abandoned a short time before by her lover. She was told my story. It was one of my friends who plays very nicely upon the violoncello of sentiment who did this. He spoke to the young widow of the qualities of my heart, the poor defunct whom we were about to inter, and invited her to drink to its eternal repose. 'Come now,' said she, raising her glass, 'I drink, on the contrary, to its very good health,' and she gave me a look, enough, as they say, to awake the dead. It was indeed the occasion to say so, for she had scarcely finished her toast than I heard my heart singing the *O Filii* of the Resurrection. What would you have done in my place?"

"A pretty question—what is her name?"

"I do not know yet, I shall only ask her at the moment we sign our lease. I know very well that in the opinion of some people I have overstepped the legal delays, but you see I plead in my own court, and I have granted a dispensation. What I do know is that she brings me as a dowry cheerfulness, which is the health of the soul, and health which is the cheerfulness of the body."

"Is she pretty?"

"Very pretty, especially as regards her complexion; one would say that she made up every morning with Watteau's palate, 'She is fair, and her conquering glances kindle love in every heart.' As witness mine."

"A blonde? You astonish me."

"Yes. I have had enough of ivory and ebony; I am going in for a blonde," and Rodolphe began to skip about as he sang:

> *"Praises sing unto my sweet,*
> *She is fair,*
> *Yellow as the ripening wheat*
> *Is her hair."*

"Poor Mimi," said his friend, "so soon forgotten."

This name cast into Rodolphe's mirthsomeness, suddenly gave another turn to the conversation. Rodolphe took his friend by the arm, and related to him at length the causes of his rupture with Mademoiselle Mimi, the terrors that had awaited him when she had left; how he was in despair because he thought that she had carried off with her all that remained to him of youth and passion, and how two days later he had recognized his mistake on feeling the gunpowder in his heart, though swamped with so many sobs and tears, dry, kindle, and explode at the first look of love cast at him by the first woman he met. He narrated the sudden and imperious invasion of forgetfulness, without his even having summoned it in aid of his grief, and how this grief was dead and buried in the said forgetfulness.

"Is it not a miracle?" said he to the poet, who, knowing by heart and from experience all the painful chapters of shattered loves, replied:

"No, no, my friend, there is no more of a miracle for you than for the rest of us. What has happened to you has happened to myself. The women we love, when they become our mistresses, cease to be for us what they really are. We do not see them only with a lover's eyes, but with a poet's. As a painter throws on the shoulders of a lay figure the imperial purple or the star-spangled robe of a Holy Virgin, so we have always whole stores of glittering mantles and robes of pure white linen which we cast over the shoulders of dull, sulky, or spiteful creatures, and when they have thus assumed the garb in which our ideal loves float before us in our waking dreams, we let ourselves be taken in by this disguise, we incarnate our dream in the first corner, and address her in our language, which she does not understand. However, let this creature at whose feet we live prostrate, tear away herself the dense envelope beneath which we have hidden her, and reveal to us her evil nature and her base instincts; let her place our hands on the spot where her heart should be, but where nothing beats any longer, and has perhaps never beaten; let her open her veil, and show us her faded eyes, pale lips, and haggard features; we replace that veil and exclaim, 'It is not true! It is not true! I love you, and you, too, love me! This white bosom holds a heart that has all its youthfulness; I love you, and you love me! You are beautiful, you are young. At the bottom of all your vices there is love. I love you, and you love me!' Then in the end, always quite in the end, when, after having all very well put triple bandages over our eyes, we see ourselves the dupes of our mistakes, we drive away the wretch who was our idol of yesterday; we take back from her the golden veils of poesy, which, on the morrow, we again cast on the shoulders of some other unknown, who becomes at once an aureola-surrounded idol. That is what we all are—monstrous egoists—who love love for love's sake—you understand me? We sip the divine liquor from the first cup that comes to hand. 'What matter the bottle, so long as we draw intoxication from it?'"

"What you say is as true as that two and two make four," said Rodolphe to the poet.

"Yes," replied the latter, "it is true, and as sad as three quarters of the things that are true. Good night."

Two days later Mademoiselle Mimi learned that Rodolphe had a new mistress. She only asked one thing—whether he kissed her hands as often as he used to kiss her own?

"Quite as often," replied Marcel. "In addition, he is kissing the hairs of her head one after the other, and they are to remain with one another until he has finished."

"Ah!" replied Mimi, passing her hand through her own tresses. "It was lucky he did not think of doing the same with me, or we should have remained together all our lives. Do you think it is really true that he no longer loves me at all?"

"Humph—and you, do you still love him?"

"I! I never loved him in my life."

"Yes, Mimi, yes. You loved him at those moments when a woman's heart changes place. You loved him; do nothing to deny it; it is your justification."

"Bah!" said Mimi, "he loves another now."

"True," said Marcel, "but no matter. Later on the remembrance of you will be to him like the flowers that we place fresh and full of perfume between the leaves of a book, and which long afterwards we find dead, discolored, and faded, but still always preserving a vague perfume of their first freshness."

ONE EVENING, WHEN SHE WAS humming in a low tone to herself, Vicomte Paul said to Mimi, "What are you singing, dear?"

"The funeral chant of our loves, that my lover Rodolphe has lately composed."

And she began to sing:—

> *"I have not a sou now, my dear, and the rule*
> *In such a case surely is soon to forget,*
> *So tearless, for she who would weep is a fool,*
> *You'll blot out all mem'ry of me, eh, my pet?*
>
> *Well, still all the same we have spent as you know*
> *Some days that were happy—and each with its night,*
> *They did not last long, but, alas, here below,*
> *The shortest are ever those we deem most bright."*

XXI

Romeo and Juliet

A ttired like a fashion plate out of his paper, the "Scarf of Iris," with new gloves, polished boots, freshly shaven face, curled hair, waxed moustache, stick in hand, glass in eye, smiling, youthful, altogether nice looking, in such guise our friend, the poet Rodolphe, might have been seen one November evening on the boulevard waiting for a cab to take him home.

Rodolphe waiting for a cab? What cataclysm had then taken place in his existence?

At the very hour that the transformed poet was twirling his moustache, chewing the end of an enormous regalia, and charming the fair sex, one of his friends was also passing down the boulevard. It was the philosopher, Gustave Colline. Rodolphe saw him coming, and at once recognized him; as indeed, who would not who had once seen him? Colline as usual was laden with a dozen volumes. Clad in that immortal hazel overcoat, the durability of which makes one believe that it must have been built by the Romans, and with his head covered by his famous broad brimmed hat, a dome of beaver, beneath which buzzed a swarm of hyperphysical dreams, and which was nicknamed Mambrino's Helmet of Modern Philosophy, Gustave Colline was walking slowly along, chewing the cud of the preface of a book that had already been in the press for the last three months—in his imagination. As he advanced towards the spot where Rodolphe was standing, Colline thought for a moment that he recognized him, but the supreme elegance displayed by the poet threw the philosopher into a state of doubt and uncertainty.

"Rodolphe with gloves and a walking stick. Chimera! Utopia! Mental aberration! Rodolphe curled and oiled; he who has not so much as Father Time. What could I be thinking of? Besides, at this present moment my unfortunate friend is engaged in lamentations, and is composing melancholy verses upon the departure of Mademoiselle Mimi, who, I hear, has thrown him over. Well, for my part, I too, regret the loss of that young woman. She was a dab hand at making coffee, which is the beverage of serious minds. But I trust that Rodolphe will console himself, and soon get another Kettle-holder."

Colline was so delighted with his wretched joke, that he would willingly have applauded it, had not the stern voice of philosophy woke up within him, and put an energetic stop to this perversion of wit.

However, as he halted close to Rodolphe, Colline was forced to yield to evidence. It was certainly Rodolphe, curled, gloved, and with a cane. It was impossible, but it was true.

"Eh! Eh! By Jove!" said Colline. "I am not mistaken. It is you, I am certain."

"So am I," replied Rodolphe.

Colline began to look at his friend, imparting to his countenance the expression pictorially made use of by M. Lebrun, the king's painter in ordinary, to express surprise. But all at once he noted two strange articles with which Rodolphe was laden—firstly, a rope ladder, and secondly, a cage, in which some kind of a bird was fluttering. At this sight, Gustave Colline's physiognomy expressed a sentiment which Monsieur Lebrun, the king's painter in ordinary, forgot to depict in his picture of "The Passions."

"Come," said Rodolphe to his friend, "I see very plainly the curiosity of your mind peeping out through the window of your eyes; and I am going to satisfy it, only, let us quit the public thoroughfare. It is cold enough here to freeze your questions and my answers."

And they both went into a cafe.

Colline's eyes remained riveted on the rope ladder as well as the cage, in which the bird, thawed by the atmosphere of the cafe, began to sing in a language unknown to Colline, who was, however, a polyglottist.

"Well then," said the philosopher pointing to the rope ladder, "what is that?"

"A connecting link between my love and me," replied Rodolphe, in lute like accents.

"And that?" asked Colline, pointing to the bird.

"That," said the poet, whose voice grew soft as the summer breeze, "is a clock."

"Tell me without parables—in vile prose, but truly."

"Very well. Have you read Shakespeare?"

"Have I read him? 'To be or not to be?' He was a great philosopher. Yes, I have read him."

"Do your remember *Romeo and Juliet*?"

"Do I remember?" said Colline, and he began to recite:

> *"Wilt thou begone? It is not yet day,*
> *It was the nightingale, and not the lark."*

"I should rather think I remember. But what then?"

"What!" said Rodolphe, pointing to the ladder and the bird. "You do not understand! This is the story: I am in love, my dear fellow, in love with a girl named Juliet."

"Well, what then?" said Colline impatiently.

"This. My new idol being named Juliet, I have hit on a plan. It is to go through Shakespeare's play with her. In the first place, my name is no longer Rodolphe, but Romeo Montague, and you will oblige me by not calling me otherwise. Besides, in order that everyone may know it, I have had some new visiting cards engraved. But that is not all. I shall profit by the fact that we are not in Carnival time to wear a velvet doublet and a sword."

"To kill Tybalt with?" said Colline.

"Exactly," continued Rodolphe. "Finally, this ladder that you see is to enable me to visit my mistress, who, as it happens, has a balcony."

"But the bird, the bird?" said the obstinate Colline.

"Why, this bird, which is a pigeon, is to play the part of the nightingale, and indicate every morning the precise moment when, as I am about to leave her loved arms, my mistress will throw them about my neck and repeat to me in her sweet tones the balcony scene, 'It is not yet near day,' that is to say, 'It is not yet eleven, the streets are muddy, do not go yet, we are comfortable here.' In order to perfect the imitation, I will try to get a nurse, and place her under the orders of my beloved and I hope that the almanac will be kind enough to grant me a little moonlight now and then, when I scale my Juliet's balcony. What do you say to my project, philosopher?"

"It is very fine," said Colline, "but could you also explain to me the mysteries of this splendid outer covering that rendered you unrecognizable? You have become rich, then?"

Rodolphe did not reply, but made a sign to one of the waiters, and carelessly threw down a louis, saying:

"Take for what we have had."

Then he tapped his waistcoat pocket, which gave forth a jingling sound.

"Have you got a bell in your pocket, for it to jingle as loud as that?"

"Only a few louis."

"Louis! In gold?" said Colline, in a voice choked with wonderment. "Let me see what they are like."

After which the two friends parted, Colline to go and relate the opulent ways and new loves of Rodolphe, and the latter to return home.

This took place during the week that had followed the second rupture between Rodolphe and Mademoiselle Mimi. The poet, when he had broken off with his mistress, felt a need of change of air and surroundings, and accompanied by his friend Marcel, he left the gloomy lodging house, the landlord of which saw both him and Marcel depart without overmuch regret. Both, as we have said, sought quarters elsewhere, and hired two rooms in the same house and on the same floor. The room chosen by Rodolphe was incomparably more comfortable than any he had inhabited up till then. There were articles of furniture almost imposing, above all a sofa covered with red stuff, that was intended to imitate velvet, and did not.

There were also on the mantelpiece two china vases, painted with flowers, between an elaborate clock, with fearful ornamentation. Rodolphe put the vases in a cupboard, and when the landlord came to wind up the clock, begged him to do nothing of the kind.

"I am willing to leave the clock on the mantel shelf," said he, "but only as an object of art. It points to midnight—a good hour; let it stick to it. The day it marks five minutes past I will move. A clock," continued Rodolphe, who had never been able to submit to the imperious tyranny of the dial, "is a domestic foe who implacably reckons up to your existence hour by hour and minute by minute, and says to you every moment, 'Here is a fraction of your life gone.' I could not sleep in peace in a room in which there was one of these instruments of torture, in the vicinity of which carelessness and reverie are impossible. A clock, the hands of which stretch to your bed and prick yours whilst you are still plunged in the soft delights of your first awakening. A clock, whose voice cries to you, 'Ting, ting, ting; it is the hour for business. Leave your charming dream, escape from the caresses of your visions, and sometimes of realities. Put on your hat and boots. It is cold, it rains, but go about your business. It is time—ting, ting.' It is quite enough already to have an almanac. Let my clock remain paralyzed, or—."

Whilst delivering this monologue he was examining his new dwelling, and felt himself moved by the secret uneasiness which one almost always feels when going into a fresh lodging.

"I have noticed," he reflected, "that the places we inhabit exercise a mysterious influence upon our thoughts, and consequently upon our actions. This room is cold and silent as a tomb. If ever mirth reigns here it will be brought in from without, and even then it will not be for long, for laughter will die away without echoes under this low ceiling, cold and white as a snowy sky. Alas! What will my life be like within these four walls?"

However, a few days later this room, erst so sad, was full of light, and rang with joyous sounds, it was the house warming, and numerous bottles explained the lively humor of the guests. Rodolphe allowed himself to be won upon by the contagious good humor of his guests. Isolated in a corner with a young woman who had come there by chance, and whom he had taken possession of, the poet was sonnetteering with her with tongue and hands. Towards the close of the festivities he had obtained a rendezvous for the next day.

"Well!" said he to himself when he was alone, "the evening hasn't been such a bad one. My stay here hasn't begun amiss."

The next day Mademoiselle Juliet called at the appointed hour. The evening was spent only in explanations. Juliet had learned the recent rupture of Rodolphe with the blue eyed girl whom he had so dearly loved; she knew that after having already left her once before Rodolphe had taken her back, and she was afraid of being the victim of a similar reawakening of love.

"You see," said she, with a pretty little pout, "I don't at all care about playing a ridiculous part. I warn you that I am very forward, and once *mistress* here," and she underlined by a look the meaning she gave to the word, "I remain, and do not give up my place."

Rodolphe summoned all his eloquence to the rescue to convince her that her fears were without foundation, and the girl, having on her side a willingness to be convinced, they ended by coming to an understanding. Only they were no longer at an understanding when midnight struck, for Rodolphe wanted Juliet to stay, and she insisted on going.

"No," she said to him as he persisted in trying to persuade her. "Why be in such a hurry? We shall always arrive in time at what we want to, provided you do not halt on the way. I will return tomorrow."

And she returned thus every evening for a week, to go away in the same way when midnight struck.

This delay did not annoy Rodolphe very much. In matters of love, and even of mere fancy, he was one of that school of travelers who prolong their journey and render it picturesque. The little sentimental preface had for its result to lead on Rodolphe at the outset further than he meant to go. And it was no doubt to lead him to that point at which fancy, ripened by the resistance opposed to it, begins to resemble love, that Mademoiselle Juliet had made use of this stratagem.

At each fresh visit that she paid to Rodolphe, Juliet remarked a more pronounced tone of sincerity in what he said. He felt when she was a little behindhand in keeping her appointment an impatience that delighted her, and he even wrote her letters the language of which was enough to give her hopes that she would speedily become his legitimate mistress.

When Marcel, who was his confidant, once caught sight of one of Rodolphe's epistles, he said to him:

"Is it an exercise of style, or do you really think what you have said here?"

"Yes, I really think it," replied Rodolphe, "and I am even a bit astonished at it: but it is so. I was a week back in a very sad state of mind. The solitude and silence that had so abruptly succeeded the storms and tempests of my old household alarmed me terribly, but Juliet arrived almost at the moment. I heard the sounds of twenty year old laughter ring in my ears. I had before me a rosy face, eyes beaming with smiles, a mouth overflowing with kisses, and I have quietly allowed myself to glide down the hill of fancy that might perhaps lead me on to love. I love to love."

However, Rodolphe was not long in perceiving that it only depended upon himself to bring this little romance to a crisis, and it was than that he had the notion of copying from Shakespeare the scene of the love of *Romeo and Juliet*. His future mistress had deemed the notion amusing, and agreed to share in the jest.

It was the very evening that the rendezvous was appointed for that Rodolphe met the philosopher Colline, just as he had bought the rope ladder that was to aid him to scale Juliet's balcony. The birdseller to whom he had applied not having a nightingale, Rodolphe replaced it by a pigeon, which he was assured sang every morning at daybreak.

Returned home, the poet reflected that to ascend a rope ladder was not an easy matter, and that it would be a good thing to rehearse the balcony scene, if he would not in addition to the chances of a fall, run the risk of appearing awkward and ridiculous in the eyes of her who was awaiting him. Having fastened his ladder to two nails firmly driven into the ceiling, Rodolphe employed the two hours remaining to him in practicing gymnastics, and after an infinite number of attempts, succeeded in managing after a fashion to get up half a score of rungs.

"Come, that is all right," he said to himself, "I am now sure of my affair and besides, if I stuck half way, 'love would lend me his wings.'"

And laden with his ladder and his pigeon cage, he set out for the abode of Juliet, who lived near. Her room looked into a little garden, and had indeed a balcony. But the room was on the ground floor, and the balcony could be stepped over as easily as possible.

Hence Rodolphe was completely crushed when he perceived this local arrangement, which put to naught his poetical project of an escalade.

"All the same," said he to Juliet, "we can go through the episode of the balcony. Here is a bird that will arouse us tomorrow with his melodious notes, and warn us of the exact moment when we are to part from one another in despair."

And Rodolphe hung up the cage beside the fireplace.

The next day at five in the morning the pigeon was exact to time, and filled the room with a prolonged cooing that would have awakened the two lovers—if they had gone to sleep.

"Well," said Juliet, "this is the moment to go into the balcony and bid one another despairing farewells—what do you think of it?"

"The pigeon is too fast," said Rodolphe. "It is November, and the sun does not rise till noon."

"All the same," said Juliet, "I am going to get up."

"Why?"

"I feel quite empty, and I will not hide from you the fact that I could very well eat a mouthfull."

"The agreement that prevails in our sympathies is astonishing. I am awfully hungry too," said Rodolphe, also rising and hurriedly slipping on his clothes.

Juliet had already lit a fire, and was looking in her sideboard to see whether she could find anything. Rodolphe helped her in this search.

"Hullo," said he, "onions."

"And some bacon," said Juliet.

"Some butter."

"Bread."

Alas! That was all.

During the search the pigeon, a careless optimist, was singing on its perch.

Romeo looked at Juliet, Juliet looked at Romeo, and both looked at the pigeon.

They did not say anything, but the fate of the pigeon-clock was settled. Even if he had appealed it would have been useless, hunger is such a cruel counsellor.

Rodolphe had lit some charcoal, and was turning bacon in the spluttering butter with a solemn air.

Juliet was peeling onions in a melancholy attitude.

The pigeon was still singing, it was the song of the swan.

To these lamentations was joined the spluttering of the butter in the stew pan.

Five minutes later the butter was still spluttering, but the pigeon sang no longer.

Romeo and Juliet grilled their clock.

"He had a nice voice," said Juliet sitting down to table.

"He is very tender," said Rodolphe, carving his alarum, nicely browned.

The two lovers looked at one another, and each surprised a tear in the other's eye.

Hypocrites, it was the onions that made them weep.

XXII

Epilogue To The Loves Of Rodolphe
And Mademoiselle Mimi

Shortly after his final rupture with Mademoiselle Mimi, who had left him, as may be remembered, to ride in the carriage of Vicomte Paul, the poet Rodolphe had sought to divert his thoughts by taking a new mistress.

She was the same blonde for whom we have seen him masquerading as Romeo. But this union, which was on the one part only a matter of spite, and on the other one of fancy, could not last long. The girl was after all only a light of love, warbling to perfection the gamut of trickery, witty enough to note the wit of others and to make use of it on occasion, and with only enough heart to feel heartburn when she had eaten too much. Add to this unbridled self-esteem and a ferocious coquetry, which would have impelled her to prefer a broken leg for her lover rather than a flounce the less to her dress, or a faded ribbon to her bonnet. A commonplace creature of doubtful beauty, endowed by nature with every evil instinct, and yet seductive from certain points of view and at certain times. She was not long in perceiving that Rodolphe had only taken her to help him forget the absent, whom she made him on the contrary regret, for his old love had never been so noisy and so lively in his heart.

One day Juliet, Rodolphe's new mistress, was talking about her lover, the poet, with a medical student who was courting her. The student replied,—

"My dear child, that fellow only makes use of you as they use nitrate to cauterize wounds. He wants to cauterize his heart and nerve. You are very wrong to bother yourself about being faithful to him."

"Ah, ah!" cried the girl, breaking into a laugh. "Do you really think that I put myself out about him?"

And that very evening she gave the student a proof to the contrary.

Thanks to the indiscretion of one of those officious friends who are unable to retain unpublished news capable of vexing you, Rodolphe soon got wind of the matter, and made it a pretext for breaking off with his temporary mistress.

He then shut himself up in positive solitude, in which all the flitter-mice of *ennui* soon came and nested, and he called work to his aid but in vain. Every evening, after wasting as much perspiration over the job as he did in ink, he produced a score of lines in which some old idea, as worn out as the Wandering Jew, and vilely clad in rags cribbed from the literary dust heap, danced clumsily on the tight rope of paradox. On reading through these lines Rodolphe was as bewildered as a man who sees nettles spring up in a bed in which he thought he had planted roses. He would then tear up the paper, on which he had just scattered this chaplet of absurdities, and trample it under foot in a rage.

"Come," said he, striking himself on the chest just above the heart, "the cord is broken, there is nothing but to resign ourselves to it."

And as for some time past a like failure followed all his attempts at work, he was seized with one of those fits of depression which shake the most stubborn pride and cloud the most lucid intellects. Nothing is indeed more terrible than these hidden struggles that sometimes take place between the self-willed artist and his rebellious art. Nothing is more moving than these fits of rage alternating with invocation, in turn supplicating or imperative, addressed to a disdainful or fugitive muse.

The most violent human anguish, the deepest wounds to the quick of the heart, do not cause suffering approaching that which one feels in these hours of doubt and impatience, so frequent for those who give themselves up to the dangerous calling of imagination.

To these violent crises succeeded painful fits of depression. Rodolphe would then remain for whole hours as though petrified in a state of stupefied immobility. His elbows upon the table, his eyes fixed upon the luminous patch made by the rays of the lamp falling upon the sheet of paper,—the battlefield on which his mind was vanquished daily, and on which his pen had become foundered in its attempts to pursue the unattainable idea—he saw slowly defile before him, like the figures of dissolving views with which the children are amused, fantastic pictures which unfolded before him the panorama of his past. It was at first the laborious days in which each hour marked the accomplishment of some task, the studious nights spent in *tete-a-tete* with the muse who came to adorn with her fairy visions his solitary and patient poverty. And he remembered then with envy the pride of skill that intoxicated him of yore when he had completed the task imposed on him by his will.

"Oh, nothing is equal to you!" he exclaimed. "Voluptuous fatigues of labor which render the mattresses of idleness so sweet. Not the satisfaction of self-esteem nor the feverish slumbers stifled beneath the heavy drapery of mysterious alcoves equals that calm and honest joy, that legitimate self satisfaction which work bestows on the laborer as a first salary."

And with eyes still fixed on these visions which continued to retrace for him the scenes of bygone days, he once more ascended the six flights of stairs of all the garrets in which his adventurous existence had been spent, in which the Muse, his only love in those days, a faithful and persevering sweetheart had always followed him, living happily with poverty and never breaking off her song of hope. But, lo, in the midst of this regular and tranquil life there suddenly appears a woman's face, and seeing her enter the dwelling where she had been until then sole queen and mistress, the poet's Muse rose sadly and gave place to the new-comer in whom she had divined a rival. Rodolphe hesitated a moment between the Muse to whom his look seemed to say, "Stay," whilst a gesture addressed to the stranger said, "Come."

And how could he repulse her, this charming creature who came to him armed with all the seductions of a beauty at its dawn? Tiny mouth and rosy lips, speaking in bold and simple language, full of coaxing promises. How refuse his hand to this little white one, delicately veined with blue, that was held out to him full of caresses? How say, "Get you gone," to these eighteen years, the presence of which already filled the home with a perfume of youth and gaiety? And then with her sweet voice, tenderly thrilling, she sang the cavatina of temptation so well. With her bright and sparkling eyes she said so clearly, "I am love," with her lips, where kisses nestled, "I am pleasure," with her whole being, in short, "I am happiness," that Rodolphe let himself be caught by them. And, besides, was not this young girl after all real and living poetry, had he not owed her his freshest inspirations, had she not often initiated him into enthusiasms which bore him so far afield in the ether of reverie that he lost sight of all things of earth? If he had suffered deeply on account of her, was not this suffering the expiation of the immense joys she had bestowed upon him? Was it not the ordinary vengeance of human fate which forbids absolute happiness as an impiety? If the law of Christianity forgives those who have much loved, it is because they have also much suffered, and terrestrial love never became a divine passion save on condition of being purified by tears. As one grows intoxicated by breathing the odor of faded roses, Rodolphe again became so by reviving in recollection that past life in which every day brought about a fresh elegy, a terrible drama, or a grotesque comedy. He went through all the phases of his strange love from their honeymoon to the domestic storms that had brought about their last rupture, he recalled all the tricks of his ex-mistress, repeated all her witty sayings. He saw her going to and fro about their little household, humming her favorite song, and facing with the same careless gaiety good or evil days.

And in the end he arrived at the conclusion that common sense was always wrong in love affairs. What, indeed, had he gained by their rupture? At the time when he was living with Mimi she deceived him, it was true, but if he was aware of this it was his fault after all that he was so, and because he gave himself infinite pains to become aware of it, because he passed his time on the alert for proofs, and himself sharpened the daggers which he plunged into his heart. Besides, was not Mimi clever enough to prove to him at need that he was mistaken? And then for whose sake was she false to him? It was generally a shawl or a bonnet—for the sake of things and not men. That calm, that tranquillity which he had hoped for on separating from his mistress, had he found them again after her departure? Alas, no! There was only herself the less in the house. Of old his grief could find vent, he could break into abuse, or representations—he could show all he suffered and excite the pity of her who caused his sufferings. But now his grief was solitary, his jealousy had become madness, for formerly he could at any rate, when he suspected anything, hinder Mimi from going out, keep her beside him in his possession, and now he might meet her in the street on the arm of her new lover, and must turn aside to let her pass, happy no doubt, and bent upon pleasure.

This wretched life lasted three or four months. By degrees he recovered his calmness. Marcel, who had undertaken a long journey to drive Musette out of his mind, returned to Paris, and again came to live with Rodolphe. They consoled one another.

One Sunday, crossing the Luxembourg Gardens, Rodolphe met Mimi resplendently dressed. She was going to a public ball. She nodded to him, to which he responded by a bow. This meeting gave him a great shock, but his emotion was less painful than usual. He walked about for a little while in the gardens, and then returned home. When Marcel came in that evening he found him at work.

"What!" said Marcel, leaning over his shoulder. "You are working—verses?"

"Yes," replied Rodolphe cheerfully, "I believe that the machine will still work. During the last four hours I have once more found the go of bygone time, I have seen Mimi."

"Ah!" said Marcel uneasily. "On what terms are you?"

"Do not be afraid," said Rodolphe, "we only bowed to one another. It went no further than that."

"Really and truly?" asked Marcel.

"Really and truly. It is all over between us, I feel it; but if I can get to work again I forgive her."

"If it is so completely finished," said Marcel, who had read through Rodolphe's verses, "why do you write verses about her?"

"Alas!" replied the poet, "I take my poetry where I can find it."

For a week he worked at this little poem. When he had finished it he read it to Marcel, who expressed himself satisfied with it, and who encouraged Rodolphe to utilize in other ways the poetical vein that had come back to him.

"For," remarked he, "it was not worth while leaving Mimi if you are always to live under her shadow. After all, though," he continued, smiling, "instead of lecturing others, I should do well to lecture myself, for my heart is still full of Musette. Well, after all, perhaps we shall not always be young fellows in love with such imps."

"Alas!" said Rodolphe, "there is no need to say in one's youth, 'Be off with you.'"

"That is true," observed Marcel, "but there are days on which I feel I should like to be a respectable old fellow, a member of the Institute, decorated with several orders, and, having done with the Musettes of this circle of society; the devil fly away with me if I would return to it. And you," he continued, laughing, "would you like to be sixty?"

"Today," replied Rodolphe, "I would rather have sixty francs."

A few days later, Mademoiselle Mimi having gone into a cafe with young Vicomte Paul, opened a magazine, in which the verses Rodolphe had written on her were printed.

"Good," said she, laughing at first, "here is my friend Rodolphe saying nasty things of me in the papers."

But when she finished the verses she remained intent and thoughtful. Vicomte Paul guessing that she was thinking of Rodolphe, sought to divert her attention.

"I will buy you a pair of earrings," said he.

"Ah!" said Mimi, "you have money, you have."

"And a Leghorn straw hat," continued the viscount.

"No," said Mimi. "If you want to please me, buy me this."

And she showed him the magazine in which she had just been reading Rodolphe's poetry.

"Oh! As to that, no," said the viscount, vexed.

"Very well," said Mimi coldly. "I will buy it myself with money I will earn. In point of fact, I would rather that it was not with yours."

And for two days Mimi went back to her old flower maker's workrooms, where she earned enough to buy this number. She learned Rodolphe's poetry by heart, and, to annoy Vicomte Paul, repeated it all day long to her friends. The verses were as follows:

> *When I was seeking where to pledge my truth*
> *Chance brought me face to face with you one day;*
> *once I offered you my heart, my youth,*
> *"Do with them what you will," I dared to say.*
>
> *But "what you would," was cruel, dear; alas!*
> *The youth I trusted with you is no more:*
> *The heart is shattered like a fallen glass,*
> *And the wind sings a funeral mass*
> *On the deserted chamber floor,*
> *Where he who loved you ne'er may pass.*
>
> *Between us now, my dear, 'tis all Up,*
> *I am a spectre and a phantom you,*
> *Our love is dead and buried; if you agree,*
> *We'll sing around its tombstone dirges due.*
>
> *But let us take an air in a low key,*
> *Lest we should strain our voices, more or less;*
> *Some solemn minor, free from flourishes;*
> *I'll take the bass, sing you the melody.*
>
> *Mi, re, mi, do, re, la,—ah! not that song!*
> *Hearing the song that once you used to sing*
> *My heart would palpitate—though dead so long—*
> *And, at the De Profundis, upward spring.*

Do, mi, fa, sol, mi, do,—this other brings
Back to the mind a valse of long ago,
The fife's shrill laughter mocked the sounding strings
That wept their notes of crystal to the bow.

Sol, do, do, si, si, la,—ah! stay your hand!
This is the air we sang last year in chorus,
With Germans shouting for their fatherland
In Meudon woods, while summer's moon stood o'er us.

Well, well, we will not sing nor speculate,
But—since we know they never more may be—
On our lost loves, without a grudge or hate,
Drop, while we smile, a final memory.

What times we had up there; do you remember?
When on your window panes the rain would stream,
And, seated by the fire, in dark December,
I felt your eyes inspire me many a dream.

The live coal crackled, kindling with the heat,
The kettle sang, melodious and sedate,
A music for the visionary feet
Of salamanders leaping in the grate:

Languid and lazy, with an unread book,
You scarcely tried to keep your lids apart,
While to my youthful love new growth I took,
Kissing your hands and yielding you my heart.

In merely entering one night believe,
One felt a scent of love and gaiety,
Which filled our little room from morn to eve,
For fortune loved our hospitality.

And winter went: then, through the open sash,
Spring flew, to say the year's long night was done;
We heard the call, and ran with impulse rash
In the green country side to meet the sun.

It was the Friday of the Holy Week,
The weather, for a wonder, mild and fair;
From hill to valley, and from plain to peak,
We wandered long, delighting in the air.

At length, exhausted by the pilgrimage,
We found a sort of natural divan,
Whence we could view the landscape, or engage
Our eyes in rapture on the heaven's wide span.

Hand clasped in hand, shoulder on shoulder laid,
With sense of something ventured, something missed,
Our two lips parted, each; no word was said,
And silently we kissed.

Around us blue-bell and shy violet
Their simple incense seemed to wave on high;
Surely we saw, with glances heavenward set,
God smiling from his azure balcony.

"Love on!" he seemed to say, "I make more sweet
The road of life you are to wander by,
Spreading the velvet moss beneath your feet;
Kiss, if you will; I shall not play the spy."

Love on, love on! In murmurs of the breeze,
In limpid stream, and in the woodland screen
That burgeons fresh in the renovated green,
In stars, in flowers, and music of the trees,

Love on, love on! But if my golden sun,
My spring, that comes once more to gladden earth,
If these should move your breasts to grateful mirth,
I ask no thanksgiving, your kiss is one.

A month passed by; and, when the roses bloomed
In beds that we had planted in the spring,
When least of all I thought my love was doomed,
You cast it from you like a noisome thing.

Not that your scorn was all reserved for me,
It flies about the world by fits and starts;
Your changeful fancy fits impartially
From knave of diamonds to knave of hearts.

And now you are happy, with a brilliant suite
Of bowing slaves and insincere gallants;
Go where you will, you see them at your feet;
A bed of perfumed posies round you flaunts:

The Ball's your garden: an admiring globe
Of lovers rolls about the lit saloon,
And, at the rustling of your silken robe,
The pack, in chorus, bay you like the moon.

Shod in the softness of a supple boot
Which Cinderella would have found too small,
One scarcely sees your little pointed foot
Flash in the flashing circle of the Ball.

Shod in the softness of a supple boot
Which Cinderella would have found too small,
One scarcely sees your little pointed foot
Flash in the flashing circle of the Ball.

In the soft baths that indolence has brought
Your once brown hands have got the ivory white,
The pallor of the lily which has caught
The silver moonbeam of a summer night:

On your white arm half clouded, and half clear,
Pearls shine in bracelets made of chiselled gold;
On your trim waist a shawl of true Cashmere
Aesthetically falls in waving fold:

Honiton point and costly Mechlin lace,
With gothic guipure of a creamy white—
The matchless cobwebs of long vanished days—
Combine to make your presence rich and bright.

But I preferred a simpler guise than that,
Your frock of muslin or plain calico,
Simple adornments, with a veilless hat,
Boots, black or grey, a collar white and low.

The splendor your admirers now adore
Will never bring me back my ancient heats;
And you are dead and buried, all the more
For the silk shroud where heart no longer beats.

So when I worked at this funereal dirge,
Where grief for a lost lifetime stands confessed,
I wore a clerk's costume of sable serge,
Though not gold eye glasses or pleated vest.

My penholder was wrapped in mournful crape,
The paper with black lines was bordered round
On which I labored to provide escape
For love's last memory hidden in the ground.

And now, when all the heart that I can save
Is used to furnish forth its epitaph.
Gay as a sexton digging his own grave
I burst into a wild and frantic laugh;

A laugh engendered by a mocking vein;
The pen I grasped was trembling as I wrote;
And even while I laughed, a scalding rain
Of tears turned all the writing to a blot.

It was the 24th of December, and that evening the Latin Quarter bore a special aspect. Since four o'clock in the afternoon the pawnbroking establishments and the shops of the second hand clothes dealers and booksellers had been encumbered by a noisy crowd, who, later in the evening, took the ham and beef shops, cook shops, and grocers by assault. The shopmen, even if they had had a hundred arms, like Briareus, would not have sufficed to serve the customers who struggled with one another for provisions. At the baker's they formed a string as in times of dearth. The wine shop keepers got rid of the produce of three vintages, and a clever statistician would have found it difficult to reckon up the number of knuckles of ham and of sausages which were sold at the famous shop of Borel, in the Rue Dauphine. In this one evening Daddy Cretaine, nicknamed Petit-Pain, exhausted eighteen editions of his cakes. All night long sounds of rejoicing broke out from the lodging houses, the windows of which were brilliantly lit up, and an atmosphere of revelry filled the district.

The old festival of Christmas Eve was being celebrated.

That evening, towards ten o'clock, Marcel and Rodolphe were proceeding homeward somewhat sadly. Passing up the Rue Dauphine they noticed a great crowd in the shop of a provision dealer, and halted a moment before the window. Tantalized by the sight of the toothsome gastronomic products, the two Bohemians resembled, during this contemplation, that person in a Spanish romance who caused hams to shrink only by looking at them.

"That is called a truffled turkey," said Marcel, pointing to a splendid bird, showing through its rosy and transparent skin the Perigordian tubercles with which it was stuffed. "I have seen impious folk eat it without first going down on their knees before it," added the painter, casting upon the turkey looks capable of roasting it.

"And what do you think of that modest leg of salt marsh mutton?" asked Rodolphe. "What fine coloring! One might think it was just unhooked from that butcher's shop in one of Jordaen's pictures. Such a leg of mutton is the favorite dish of the gods, and of my godmother Madame Chandelier."

"Look at those fish!" resumed Marcel, pointing to some trout. "They are the most expert swimmers of the aquatic race. Those little creatures, without any appearance of pretension, could, however, make a fortune by the exhibition of their skill; fancy, they can swim up a perpendicular waterfall as easily as we should accept an invitation to supper. I have almost had a chance of tasting them."

"And down there—those large golden fruit, the foliage of which resembles a trophy of savage sabre blades! They are called pineapples, and are the pippins of the tropics."

"That is a matter of indifference to me," said Marcel. "So far as fruits are concerned, I prefer that piece of beef, that ham, or that simple gammon of bacon, cuirassed with jelly as transparent as amber."

"You are right," replied Rodolphe. "Ham is the friend of man, when he has one. However, I would not repulse that pheasant."

"I should think not; it is the dish of crowned heads."

And as, continuing on their way, they met joyful processions proceeding homewards, to do honor to Momus, Bacchus, Comus, and all the other divinities with names ending in "us," they asked themselves who was the Gamacho whose wedding was being celebrated with such a profusion of victuals.

Marcel was the first who recollected the date and its festival.

"It is Christmas Eve," said he.

"Do you remember last year's?" inquired Rodolphe.

"Yes," replied Marcel. "At Momus's. It was Barbemuche who stood treat. I should never have thought that a delicate girl like Phemie could have held so much sausage."

"What a pity that Momus has cut off our credit," said Rodolphe.

"Alas," said Marcel, "calendars succeed but do not resemble one another."

"Would not you like to keep Christmas Eve?" asked Rodolphe.

"With whom and with what?" inquired the painter.

"With me."

"And the coin?"

"Wait a moment," said Rodolphe, "I will go into the cafe, where I know some people who play high. I will borrow a few sesterces from some favorite of fortune, and I will get something to wash down a sardine or a pig's trotter."

"Go," said Marcel. "I am as hungry as a dog. I will wait for you here," Rodolphe went into the cafe where he knew several people. A gentleman who had just won three hundred francs at cards made a regular treat of lending the poet a forty sous piece, which he handed over with that ill humor caused by the fever of play. At another time and elsewhere than at a card-table, he would very likely have been good for forty francs.

"Well?" inquired Marcel, on seeing Rodolphe return.

"Here are the takings," said the poet, showing the money.

"A bite and a sup," said Marcel.

With this small sum they were however able to obtain bread, wine, cold meat, tobacco, fire and light.

They returned home to the lodging-house in which each had a separate room. Marcel's, which also served him as a studio, being the larger, was chosen as the banquetting hall, and the two friends set about the preparations for their feast there.

But to the little table at which they were seated, beside a fireplace in which the damp logs burned away without flame or heat, came a melancholy guest, the phantom of the vanished past.

They remained for an hour at least, silent, and thoughtful, but no doubt preoccupied by the same idea and striving to hide it. It was Marcel who first broke silence.

"Come," said he to Rodolphe, "this is not what we promised ourselves."

"What do you mean?" asked Rodolphe.

"Oh!" replied Marcel. "Do not try to pretend with me now. You are thinking of that which should be forgotten and I too, by Jove, I do not deny it."

"Well?"

"Well, it must be for the last time. To the devil with recollections that make wine taste sour and render us miserable when everybody else are amusing themselves," exclaimed Marcel, alluding to the joyful shouts coming from the rooms adjoining theirs. "Come, let us think of something else, and let this be the last time."

"That is what we always say and yet—," said Rodolphe, falling anew into the reverie.

"And yet we are continually going back to it," resumed Marcel. "That is because instead of frankly seeking to forget, we make the most trivial things a pretext to recall remembrances, which is due above all to the fact that we persist in living amidst the same surroundings in which the beings who have so long been our torment lived. We are less the slaves of passion than of habit. It is this captivity that must be escaped from, or we shall wear ourselves out in a ridiculous and shameful slavery. Well, the past is past, we must break the ties that still bind us to it. The hour has come to go forward without looking backward; we have had our share of youth, carelessness, and paradox. All these are very fine—a very pretty novel could be written on them; but this comedy of amourous follies, this loss of time, of days wasted with the prodigality of people who believe they have an eternity to spend—all this must have an end. It is no longer possible for us to continue to live much longer on the outskirts of society—on the outskirts of life almost—under the penalty of justifying the contempt felt for us, and of despising ourselves. For, after all, is it a life we lead? And are not the independence, the freedom of mannerism of which we boast so loudly, very mediocre advantages? True liberty consists of being able to dispense with the aid of others, and to exist by oneself, and have we got to that? No, the first scoundrel, whose name we would not bear for five minutes, avenges himself for our jests, and becomes our lord and master the day on which we borrow from him five francs, which he lends us after having made us dispense the worth of a hundred and fifty in ruses or in humiliations. For my part, I have had enough of it. Poetry does not alone exist in disorderly living, touch-and-go happiness, loves that last as long as a bedroom candle, more or less eccentric revolts against those prejudices which will eternally rule the world, for it is easier to upset a dynasty than a custom, however ridiculous it may be. It is not enough to wear a summer coat in December to have talent; one can be a real poet or artist whilst going about well shod and eating three meals a day. Whatever one may say, and whatever one may do, if one wants to attain anything one must always take the commonplace way. This speech may astonish you, friend Rodolphe; you may say that I am breaking my idols, you will call me corrupted; and yet what I tell you is the expression of my sincere wishes. Despite myself, a slow and salutary metamorphosis has taken place within me; reason has entered my mind—burglariously, if you like, and perhaps against my will, but it has got in at last—and has proved to me that I was on a wrong track, and that it would be at once ridiculous and dangerous to persevere in it. Indeed, what will happen if we continue this monotonous and idle vagabondage? We shall get to thirty, unknown, isolated, disgusted with all things and with ourselves, full of envy towards all those whom we see reach their goal, whatever it may be, and obliged, in order to live, to have recourse to shameful parasitism. Do not imagine that this is a fancy picture I have conjured up especially to frighten you. The future does not systematically appear to be all black, but neither does it all rose colored; I see it clearly as it is. Up till now the life we have led has been forced upon us—we had the excuse of necessity. Now we are no longer to be excused, and if we do not re-enter the world, it will be voluntarily, for the obstacles against which we have had to struggle no longer exist."

"I say," said Rodolphe, "what are you driving at? Why and wherefore this lecture?"

"You thoroughly understand me," replied Marcel, in the same serious tones. "Just now I saw you, like myself, assailed by recollections that made you regret the past. You were thinking of Mimi and I was thinking of Musette. Like me, you would have liked to have had your mistress beside you. Well, I tell you that we ought neither of us to think of these creatures; that we were not created and sent into the world solely to sacrifice our existence to these commonplace Manon Lescaut's, and that the Chevalier Desgrieux, who is so fine, so true, and so poetical, is only saved from being ridiculous by his youth and the illusions he cherishes. At twenty he can follow his mistress to America without ceasing to be interesting, but at twenty-five he would have shown Manon the door, and would have been right. It is all very well to talk; we are old, my dear fellow; we have lived too fast, our hearts are cracked, and no longer ring truly; one cannot be in love with a Musette or a Mimi for three years with impunity. For me it is all over, and I wish to be thoroughly divorced from her remembrance. I am now going to commit to the flames some trifles that she has left me during her various stays, and which oblige me to think of her when I come across them."

And Marcel, who had risen, went and took from a drawer a little cardboard box in which were the souvenirs of Musette—a faded bouquet, a sash, a bit of ribbon, and some letters.

"Come," said he to the poet, "follow my example, Rodolphe."

"Very well, then," said the latter, making an effort, "you are right. I too will make an end of it with that girl with the white hands."

And, rising suddenly, he went and fetched a small packet containing souvenirs of Mimi of much the same kind as those of which Marcel was silently making an inventory.

"This comes in handy," murmured the painter. "This trumpery will help us to rekindle the fire which is going out."

"Indeed," said Rodolphe, "it is cold enough here to hatch polar bears."

"Come," said Marcel, "let us burn in a duet. There goes Musette's prose; it blazes like punch. She was very fond of punch. Come Rodolphe, attention!"

And for some minutes they alternately emptied into the fire, which blazed clear and noisily, the reliquaries of their past love.

"Poor Musette!" murmured Marcel to himself, looking at the last object remaining in his hands.

It was a little faded bouquet of wildflowers.

"Poor Musette, she was very pretty though, and she loved me dearly, is it not so, little bouquet? Her heart told you so the day she wore you at her waist. Poor little bouquet, you seem to be pleading for mercy; well, yes; but on one condition; it is that you will never speak to me of her any more, never, never!"

And profiting by a moment when he thought himself unnoticed by Rodolphe, he slipped the bouquet into his breast pocket.

"So much the worse, it is stronger than I am. I am cheating," thought the painter.

And as he cast a furtive glance towards Rodolphe, he saw the poet, who had come to the end of his auto-da-fe, putting quietly into his own pocket, after having tenderly kissed it, a little night cap that had belonged to Mimi.

"Come," muttered Marcel, "he is as great a coward as I am."

At the very moment that Rodolphe was about to return to his room to go to bed, there were two little taps at Marcel's door.

"Who the deuce can it be at this time of night?" said the painter, going to open it.

A cry of astonishment burst from him when he had done so.

It was Mimi.

As the room was very dark Rodolphe did not at first recognize his mistress, and only distinguishing a woman, he thought that it was some passing conquest of his friend's, and out of discretion prepared to withdraw.

"I am disturbing you," said Mimi, who had remained on the threshold.

At her voice Rodolphe dropped on his chair as though thunderstruck.

"Good evening," said Mimi, coming up to him and shaking him by the hand which he allowed her to take mechanically.

"What the deuce brings you here and at this time of night?" asked Marcel.

"I was very cold," said Mimi shivering. "I saw a light in your room as I was passing along the street, and although it was very late I came up."

She was still shivering, her voice had a cristalline sonority that pierced Rodolphe's heart like a funeral knell, and filled it with a mournful alarm. He looked at her more attentively. It was no longer Mimi, but her ghost.

Marcel made her sit down beside the fire.

Mimi smiled at the sight of the flame dancing merrily on the hearth.

"It is very nice," said she, holding out her poor hands blue with cold. "By the way, Monsieur Marcel, you do not know why I have called on you?"

"No, indeed."

"Well," said Mimi, "I simply came to ask you whether you could get them to let me a room here. I have just been turned out of my lodgings because I owe a month's rent and I do not know where to go to."

"The deuce!" said Marcel, shaking his head, "we are not in very good odor with our landlord and our recommendation would be a most unfortunate one, my poor girl."

"What is to be done then?" said Mimi. "The fact is I have nowhere to go."

"Ah!" said Marcel. "You are no longer a viscountess, then?"

"Good heavens, no! Not at all."

"But since when?"

"Two months ago, already."

"Have you been playing tricks on the viscount, then?"

"No," said she, glancing at Rodolphe, who had taken his place in the darkest corner of the room, "the viscount kicked up a row with me on account of some verses that were written about me. We quarrelled, and I sent him about his business. He is a nice skin flint, I can tell you."

"But," said Marcel, "he had rigged you out very finely, judging by what I saw the day I met you."

"Well," said Mimi, "would you believe it, that he took everything away from me when I left him, and I have since heard that he raffled all my clothes at a wretched table d'hote where he used to take me to dine. He is wealthy enough, though, and yet with all his fortune he is as miserly as a clay fireball and as stupid as an owl. He would not allow me to drink wine without water, and made me fast on Fridays. Would you believe it, he wanted me to wear black stockings, because they did not want washing as often as white ones. You have no idea of it, he worried me nicely I can tell you. I can well say that I did my share of purgatory with him."

"And does he know your present situation?" asked Marcel.

"I have not seen him since and I do not want to," replied Mimi. "It makes me sick when I think of him. I would rather die of hunger than ask him for a sou."

"But," said Marcel, "since you left him you have not been living alone."

"Yes, I assure you, Monsieur Marcel," exclaimed Mimi quickly. "I have been working to earn my living, only as artificial flower making was not a very flourishing business I took up another. I sit to painters. If you have any jobs to give me," she added gaily.

And having noticed a movement on the part of Rodolphe, whom she did not take her eyes off whilst talking to his friend, Mimi went on:

"Ah, but I only sit for head and hands. I have plenty to do, and I am owed money by two or three, I shall have some in a couple of days, it is only for that interval that I want to find a lodging. When I get the money I shall go back to my own. Ah!" said she, looking at the table, which was still laden with the preparation for the modest feast which the two friends had scarcely touched, "you were going to have supper?"

"No," said Marcel, "we are not hungry."

"You are very lucky," said Mimi simply.

At this remark Rodolphe felt a horrible pang in his heart, he made a sign to Marcel, which the latter understood.

"By the way," said the artist, "since you are here Mimi, you must take pot luck with us. We were going to keep Christmas Eve, and then— why—we began to think of other things."

"Then I have come at the right moment," said Mimi, casting an almost famished glance at the food on the table. "I have had no dinner," she whispered to the artist, so as not to be heard by Rodolphe, who was gnawing his handkerchief to keep him from bursting into sobs.

"Draw up, Rodolphe," said Marcel to his friend, "we will all three have supper together."

"No," said the poet remaining in his corner.

"Are you angry, Rodolphe, that I have come here?" asked Mimi gently. "Where could I go to?"

"No, Mimi," replied Rodolphe, "only I am grieved to see you like this."

"It is my own fault, Rodolphe, I do not complain, what is done is done, so think no more about it than I do. Cannot you still be my friend, because you have been something else? You can, can you not? Well then, do not frown on me, and come and sit down at the table with us."

She rose to take him by the hand, but was so weak, that she could not take a step, and sank back into her chair.

"The heat has dazed me," she said, "I cannot stand."

"Come," said Marcel to Rodolphe, "come and join us."

The poet drew up to the table, and began to eat with them. Mimi was very lively.

"My dear girl, it is impossible for us to get you a room in the house."

"I must go away then," said she, trying to rise.

"No, no," said Marcel. "I have another way of arranging things, you can stay in my room, and I will go and sleep with Rodolphe."

"It will put you out very much, I am afraid," said Mimi, "but it will not be for long, only a couple of days."

"It will not put us out at all in that case," replied Marcel, "so it is understood, you are at home here, and we are going to Rodolphe's room. Good night, Mimi, sleep well."

"Thanks," said she, holding out her hand to Marcel and Rodolphe, who moved away together.

"Do you want to lock yourself in?" asked Marcel as he got to the door.

"Why?" said Mimi, looking at Rodolphe, "I am not afraid."

When the two friends were alone in Rodolphe's room, which was on the same floor, Marcel abruptly said to his friend, "Well, what are you going to do now?"

"I do not know," stammered Rodolphe.

"Come, do not shilly-shally, go and join Mimi! If you do, I prophecy that tomorrow you will be living together again."

"If it were Musette who had returned, what would you do?" inquired Rodolphe of his friend.

"If it were Musette that was in the next room," replied Marcel, "well, frankly, I believe that I should not have been in this one for a quarter of an hour past."

"Well," said Rodolphe, "I will be more courageous than you, I shall stay here."

"We shall see that," said Marcel, who had already got into bed. "Are you coming to bed?"

"Certainly," replied Rodolphe.

But in the middle of the night, Marcel waking up, perceived that Rodolphe had left him.

In the morning, he went and tapped discreetly at the door of the room in which Mimi was.

"Come in," said she, and on seeing him, she made a sign to him to speak low in order not to wake Rodolphe who was asleep. He was seated in an arm chair, which he had drawn up to the side of the bed, his head resting on a pillow beside that of Mimi.

"It is like that that you passed the night?" said Marcel in great astonishment.

"Yes," replied the girl.

Rodolphe woke up all at once, and after kissing Mimi, held out his hand to Marcel, who seemed greatly puzzled.

"I am going to find some money for breakfast," said he to the painter. "You will keep Mimi company."

"Well," asked Marcel of the girl when they were alone together, "what took place last night?"

"Very sad things," said Mimi. "Rodolphe still loves me."

"I know that very well."

"Yes, you wanted to separate him from me. I am not angry about it, Marcel, you were quite right, I have done no good to the poor fellow."

"And you," asked Marcel, "do you still love him?"

"Do I love him?" said she, clasping her hands. "It is that that tortures me. I am greatly changed, my friend, and it needed but little time for that."

"Well, now he loves you, you love him and you cannot do without one another, come together again and try and remain."

"It is impossible," said Mimi.

"Why?" inquired Marcel. "Certainly it would be more sensible for you to separate, but as for your not meeting again, you would have to be a thousand leagues from one another."

"In a little while I shall be further off than that."

"What do you mean?"

"Do not speak of it to Rodolphe, it would cause him too much pain, but I am going away forever."

"But whither?"

"Look here, Marcel," said Mimi sobbing, "look."

And lifting up the sheet of the bed a little she showed the artist her shoulders, neck and arms.

"Good heavens!" exclaimed Marcel mournfully, "poor girl."

"Is it not true, my friend, that I do not deceive myself and that I am soon going to die."

"But how did you get into such a state in so short a time?"

"Ah!" replied Mimi, "with the life I have been leading for the past two months it is not astonishing; nights spent in tears, days passed in posing in studios without any fire, poor living, grief, and then you do not know all, I tried to poison myself with Eau de Javelle. I was saved but not for long as you see. Besides I have never been very strong, in short it is my fault, if I had remained quietly with Rodolphe I should not be like this. Poor fellow, here I am again upon his hands, but it will not be for long, the last dress he will give me will be all white, Marcel, and I shall be buried in it. Ah! If you knew how I suffer because I am going to die. Rodolphe knows that I am ill, he remained for over an hour without speaking last night when he saw my arms and shoulders so thin. He no longer recognized his Mimi. Alas! My very looking glass does not know me. Ah! All the same I was pretty and he did love me. Oh, God!" she exclaimed, burying her face in Marcel's hands. "I am going to leave you and Rodolphe too, oh God!" and sobs choked her voice.

"Come, Mimi," said Marcel, "never despair, you will get well, you only want care and rest."

"Ah, no!" said Mimi. "It is all over, I feel it. I have no longer any strength, and when I came here last night it took me over an hour to get up the stairs. If I found a woman here I should have gone down by way of the window. However, he was free since we were no longer together, but you see, Marcel, I was sure he loved me still. It was on account of that," she said, bursting into tears, "it is on account of that that I do not want to die at once, but it is all over with me. He must be very good, poor fellow, to take me back after all the pain I have given him. Ah! God is not just, since he does not leave me only the time to make Rodolphe forget the grief I caused him. He does not know the state in which I am. I would not have him lie beside me, for I feel as if the earthworms were already devouring my body. We passed the night in weeping and talking of old times. Ah! How sad it is, my friend, to see behind one the happiness one has formerly passed by without noticing it. I feel as if I had fire in my chest, and when I move my limbs it seems as if they were going to snap. Hand me my dress, I want to cut the cards to see whether Rodolphe will bring in any money. I should like to have a good breakfast with you, like we used to; that would not hurt me. God cannot make me worse than I am. See," she added, showing Marcel the pack of cards she had cut, "Spades—it is the color of death. Clubs," she added more gaily, "yes we shall have some money."

Marcel did not know what to say in presence of the lucid delirium of this poor creature, who already felt, as she said, the worms of the grave.

In an hour's time Rodolphe was back. He was accompanied by Schaunard and Gustave Colline. The musician wore a summer jacket. He had sold his winter suit to lend money to Rodolphe on learning that Mimi was ill. Colline on his side had gone and sold some books. If he could have got anyone to buy one of his arms or legs he would have agreed to the bargain rather than part with his cherished volumes. But Schaunard had pointed out to him that nothing could be done with his arms or his legs.

Mimi strove to recover her gaiety to greet her old friends.

"I am no longer naughty," said she to them, "and Rodolphe has forgiven me. If he will keep me with him I will wear wooden shoes and a mob-cap, it is all the same to me. Silk is certainly not good for my health," she added with a frightful smile.

At Marcel's suggestion, Rodolphe had sent for one of his friends who had just passed as a doctor. It was the same who had formerly attended Francine. When he came they left him alone with Mimi.

Rodolphe, informed by Marcel, was already aware of the danger run by his mistress. When the doctor had spoken to Mimi, he said to Rodolphe: "You cannot keep her here. Save for a miracle she is doomed. You must send her to the hospital. I will give you a letter for La Pitie. I know one of the house surgeons there; she will be well looked after. If she lasts till the spring we may perhaps pull her through, but if she stays here she will be dead in a week."

"I shall never dare propose it to her," said Rodolphe.

"I spoke to her about it," replied the doctor, "and she agreed. Tomorrow I will send you the order of admission to La Pitie."

"My dear," said Mimi to Rodolphe, "the doctor is right; you cannot nurse me here. At the hospital they may perhaps cure me, you must send me there. Ah! You see I do so long to live now, that I would be willing to end my days with one hand in a raging fire and the other in yours. Besides, you will come and see me. You must not grieve, I shall be well taken care of: the doctor told me so. You get chicken at the hospital and they have fires there. Whilst I am taking care of myself there, you will work to earn money, and when I am cured I will come back and live with you. I have plenty of hope now. I shall come back as pretty as I used to be. I was very ill in the days before I knew you, and I was cured. Yet I was not happy in those days, I might just as well have died. Now that I have found you again and that we can be happy, they will cure me again, for I shall fight hard against my illness. I will drink all the nasty things they give me, and if death seizes on me it will be by force. Give me the looking glass: it seems to me that I have little color in my cheeks. Yes," said she, looking at herself in the glass, "my color is coming back, and my hands, see, they are still pretty; kiss me once more, it will not be the last time, my poor darling," she added, clasping Rodolphe round the neck, and burying his face in her loosened tresses.

Before leaving for the hospital, she wanted her friends the Bohemians to stay and pass the evening with her.

"Make me laugh," said she, "cheerfulness is health to me. It is that wet blanket of a viscount made me ill. Fancy, he wanted to make me learn orthography; what the deuce should I have done with it? And his friends, what a set! A regular poultry yard, of which the viscount was the peacock. He marked his linen himself. If he ever marries I am sure that it will be he who will suckle the children."

Nothing could be more heart breaking than the almost posthumous gaiety of poor Mimi. All the Bohemians made painful efforts to hide their tears and continue the conversation in the jesting tone started by the unfortunate girl, for whom fate was so swiftly spinning the linen of her last garment.

The next morning Rodolphe received the order of admission to the hospital. Mimi could not walk, she had to be carried down to the cab. During the journey she suffered horribly from the jolts of the vehicle. Admist all her sufferings the last thing that dies in woman, coquetry, still survived; two or three times she had the cab stopped before the drapers' shops to look at the display in the windows.

On entering the ward indicated in the letter of admission Mimi felt a terrible pang at her heart, something within her told her that it was between these bare and leprous walls that her life was to end. She exerted the whole of the will left her to hide the mournful impression that had chilled her.

When she was put to bed she gave Rodolphe a final kiss and bid him goodbye, bidding him come and see her the next Sunday which was a visitors' day.

"It does not smell very nice here," said she to him, "bring me some flowers, some violets, there are still some about."

"Yes," said Rodolphe, "goodbye till Sunday."

And he drew together the curtains of her bed. On hearing the departing steps of her lover, Mimi was suddenly seized with an almost delirious attack of fever. She suddenly opened the curtains, and leaning half out of bed, cried in a voice broken with tears:

"Rodolphe, take me home, I want to go away."

The sister of charity hastened to her and tried to calm her.

"Oh!" said Mimi, "I am going to die here."

On Sunday morning, the day he was to go and see Mimi, Rodolphe remembered that he had promised her some violets. With poetic and loving superstition he went on foot in horrible weather to look for the flowers his sweetheart had asked him for, in the woods of Aulnay and Fontenay, where he had so often been with her. The country, so lively and joyful in the sunshine of the bright days of June and July, he found chill and dreary. For two hours he beat the snow covered thickets, lifting the bushes with a stick, and ended by finding a few tiny blossoms, and as it happened, in a part of the wood bordering the Le Plessis pool, which had been their favorite spot when they came into the country.

Passing through the village of Chatillon to get back to Paris, Rodolphe met in the square before the church a baptismal procession, in which he recognized one of his friends who was the godfather, with a singer from the opera.

"What the deuce are you doing here?" asked the friend, very much surprised to see Rodolphe in those parts.

The poet told him what had happened.

The young fellow, who had known Mimi, was greatly saddened at this story, and feeling in his pocket took out a bag of christening sweetmeats and handed it to Rodolphe.

"Poor Mimi, give her this from me and tell her I will come and see her."

"Come quickly, then, if you would come in time," said Rodolphe, as he left him.

When Rodolphe got to the hospital, Mimi, who could not move, threw her arms about him in a look.

"Ah, there are my flowers!" said she, with the smile of satisfied desire.

Rodolphe related his pilgrimage into that part of the country that had been the paradise of their loves.

"Dear flowers," said the poor girl, kissing the violets. The sweetmeats greatly pleased her too. "I am not quite forgotten, then. The young fellows are good. Ah! I love all your friends," said she to Rodolphe.

This interview was almost merry. Schaunard and Colline had rejoined Rodolphe. The nurses had almost to turn them out, for they had overstayed visiting time.

"Goodbye," said Mimi. "Thursday without fail, and come early."

The following day on coming home at night, Rodolphe received a letter from a medical student, a dresser at the hospital, to whose care he had recommended the invalid. The letter only contained these words:—

"My dear friend, I have very bad news for you. No. 8 is dead. This morning on going through the ward I found her bed vacant."

Rodolphe dropped on to a chair and did not shed a tear. When Marcel came in later he found his friend in the same stupefied attitude. With a gesture the poet showed him the latter.

"Poor girl!" said Marcel.

"It is strange," said Rodolphe, putting his hand to his heart; "I feel nothing here. Was my love killed on learning that Mimi was to die?"

"Who knows?" murmured the painter.

Mimi's death caused great mourning amongst the Bohemians.

A week later Rodolphe met in the street the dresser who had informed him of his mistress's death.

"Ah, my dear Rodolphe!" said he, hastening up to the poet. "Forgive me the pain I caused you by my heedlessness."

"What do you mean?" asked Rodolphe in astonishment.

"What," replied the dresser, "you do not know? You have not seen her again?"

"Seen whom?" exclaimed Rodolphe.

"Her, Mimi."

"What?" said the poet, turning deadly pale.

"I made a mistake. When I wrote you that terrible news I was the victim of an error. This is how it was. I had been away from the hospital for a couple of days. When I returned, on going the rounds with the surgeons, I found Mimi's bed empty. I asked the sister of charity what had become of the patient, and she told me that she had died during the night. This is what had happened. During my absence Mimi had been moved to another ward. In No. 8 bed, which she left, they put another woman who died the same day. That will explain the mistake into which I fell. The day after that on which I wrote to you, I found Mimi in the next ward. Your absence had put her in a terrible state; she gave me a letter for you and I took it on to your place at once."

"Good God!" said Rodolphe. "Since I thought Mimi dead I have not dared to go home. I have been sleeping here and there at friends' places. Mimi alive! Good heavens! What must she think of my absence? Poor girl, poor girl! How is she? When did you see her last?"

"The day before yesterday. She was neither better nor worse, but very uneasy; she fancies you must be ill."

"Let us go to La Pitie at once," said Rodolphe, "that I may see her."

"Stop here for a moment," said the dresser, when they reached the entrance to the hospital, "I will go and ask the house surgeon for permission for you to enter."

Rodolphe waited in the hall for a quarter of an hour. When the dresser returned he took him by the hand and said these words:

"My friend, suppose that the letter I wrote to you a week ago was true?"

"What!" exclaimed Rodolphe, leaning against a pillar, "Mimi—"

"This morning at four o'clock."

"Take me to the amphitheatre," said Rodolphe, "that I may see her."

"She is no longer there," said the dresser. And pointing out to the poet a large van which was in the courtyard drawn up before a building above which was inscribed, "Amphiteatre," he added, "she is there."

It was indeed the vehicle in which the corpses that are unclaimed are taken to their pauper's grave.

"Goodbye," said Rodolphe to the dresser.

"Would you like me to come with you a bit?" suggested the latter.

"No," said Rodolphe, turning away, "I need to be alone."

XXIII

Youth Is Fleeting

A year after Mimi's death Rodolphe and Marcel, who had not quitted one another, celebrated by a festival their entrance into the official world. Marcel, who had at length secured admission to the annual exhibition of pictures, had had two paintings hung, one of which had been bought by a rich Englishman, formerly Musette's protector. With the product of this sale, and also of a Government order, Marcel had partly paid off his past debts. He had furnished decent rooms, and had a real studio. Almost at the same time Schaunard and Rodolphe came before the public who bestow fame and fortune—the one with an album of airs that were sung at all the concerts, and which gave him the commencement of a reputation; the other with a book that occupied the critics for a month. As to Barbemuche he had long since given up Bohemianism. Gustave Colline had inherited money and made a good marriage. He gave evening parties with music and light refreshments.

One evening Rodolphe, seated in his own armchair with his feet on his own rug, saw Marcel come in quite flurried.

"You do not know what has just happened to me," said he.

"No," replied the poet. "I know that I have been to your place, that you were at home, and that you would not answer the door."

"Yes, I heard you. But guess who was with me."

"How do I know?"

"Musette, who burst upon me last evening like a bombshell, got up as a *debardeur*."

"Musette! You have once more found Musette!" said Rodolphe, in a tone of regret.

"Do not be alarmed. Hostilities were not resumed. Musette came to pass with me her last night of Bohemianism."

"What?"

"She is going to be married."

"Bah!" said Rodolphe. "Who is the victim?"

"A postmaster who was her last lover's guardian; a queer sort of fellow, it would seem. Musette said to him, 'My dear sir, before definitely giving you my hand and going to the registrar's I want to drink my last glass of Champagne, dance my last quadrille, and embrace for the last time my lover, Marcel, who is now a gentleman, like everybody else is seems.' And for a week the dear creature has been looking for me. Hence it was that she burst upon me last evening, just at the moment I was thinking of her. Ah, my friend! Altogether we had a sad night of it. It was not at all the same thing it used to be, not at all. We were like some wretched copy of a masterpiece? I have even written on the subject of this last separation a little ballad which I will whine out to you if you will allow me," and Marcel began to chant the following verses:—

I saw a swallow yesterday,
He brought Spring's promise to the air;
"Remember her," he seemed to say,
"Who loved you when she'd time to spare;"
And all the day I sate before
The almanac of yonder year,
When I did nothing but adore,
And you were pleased to hold me dear.

But do not think my love is dead,
Or to forget you I begin.

If you sought entry to my shed
My heart would leap to let you in:
Since at your name it trembles still—
Muse of oblivious fantasy!—
Return and share, if share you will,
Joy's consecrated bread with me.

The decorations of the nest
Which saw our mutual ardor burn,
Already seem to wear their best
At the mere hope of return.
Come, see if you can recognize
Things your departure reft of glee,
The bed, the glass of extra size,
In which you often drank for me.

You shall resume the plain white gown
You used to look so nice in, then;
On Sunday we can still run down
To wander in the woods again.
Beneath the bower, at evening,
Again we'll drink the liquid bright
In which your song would dip its wing
Before in air it took to flight.

Musette, who has at last confessed
The carnival of life was gone,
Came back, one morning, to the nest
Whence, like a wild bird, she had flown:
But, while I kissed the fugitive,
My heart no more emotion knew,
For, she had ceased, for me, to live,
And "You," she said, "no more are you."

"Heart of my heart!" I answered, "Go!
We cannot call the dead love back;
Best let it lie, interred, below
The tombstone of the almanac
Perhaps a spirit that remembers
The happy time it notes for me
May find some day among its embers
Of a lost Paradise the key."

"Well," said Marcel, when he had finished, "you may feel reassured now, my love for Musette is dead and buried here," he added ironically, indicating the manuscript of the poem.

"Poor lad," said Rodolphe, "your wit is fighting a duel with your heart, take care it does not kill it."

"That is already lifeless," replied the painter, "we are done for, old fellow, we are dead and buried. Youth is fleeting! Where are you going to dine this evening?"

"If you like," said Rodolphe, "we will go and dine for twelve sous at our old restaurant in the Rue du Four, where they have plates of huge crockery, and where we used to feel so hungry when we had done dinner."

"No," replied Marcel, "I am quite willing to look back at that past, but it must be through the medium of a bottle of good wine and sitting in a comfortable armchair. What would you, I am corrupted. I only care for what is good!"

A Note About the Author

Henri Murger (1822–1861) was a French novelist and poet. Born in Paris to a working-class family, Murger left school at 15 to find work in a lawyer's office, writing poems and essays on the side. Discovered by prominent dramatist Étienne de Jouy, Murger gained a reputation as a leading young voice in French literature. Encouraged by Realist critic Champfleury to focus on fiction, Murger found success with *Scenes of Bohemian Life* (1851), an experimental novel based on his experience as an impoverished Parisian artist. He continued to publish his writing until his death at 38, brought on by recurring health problems exacerbated by a life in poverty. *Scenes of Bohemian Life* would inspire Puccini's beloved opera *La bohème* (1896), itself source material for countless films, songs, and musicals.

A Note from the Publisher

Spanning many genres, from non-fiction essays to literature classics to children's books and lyric poetry, Mint Edition books showcase the master works of our time in a modern new package. The text is freshly typeset, is clean and easy to read, and features a new note about the author in each volume. Many books also include exclusive new introductory material. Every book boasts a striking new cover, which makes it as appropriate for collecting as it is for gift giving. Mint Edition books are only printed when a reader orders them, so natural resources are not wasted. We're proud that our books are never manufactured in excess and exist only in the exact quantity they need to be read and enjoyed.

bookfinity™

Discover more of your favorite classics with Bookfinity™.

- Track your reading with custom book lists.
- Get great book recommendations for your personalized Reader Type.
- Add reviews for your favorite books.
- AND MUCH MORE!

Visit **bookfinity.com** and take the fun Reader Type quiz to get started.

Enjoy our classic and modern companion pairings!

Printed in the USA
CPSIA information can be obtained
at www.ICGtesting.com
JSHW022216140824
68134JS00018B/1090

9 781513 292311